"GOOD LORD, NOT AGAIN!"

Judith recoiled in horror. She might not be the Old Inncreeper, but Judith knew a corpse when she saw one.

Or did she? Was this some kind of publicity stunt? Judith decided to check for a pulse. But before she could move, all hell broke loose. Led by a man with a video camera and a plump, red-headed young woman, two, three, at least half a dozen more people pushed and shoved their way into the room, some of them throwing an occasional punch. They wielded microphones, cameras, and equipment Judith didn't recognize as she was shunted aside, feeling as if she'd been on the wrong end of a cattle stampede.

The redheaded woman faced her, nose to nose. "What the hell's going on here?" she demanded.

"I just got here," Judith said. "I haven't any idea, except that woman on the bed may be dead. Or not."

"She's dead, all right," the redhead declared. "Is this our lucky day or what?"

MARY DAHEIM

A STREETCAR NAMED EXPIRE

A BED-AND-BREAKFAST MYSTERY

AVON BOOKS

An Imprint of HarperCollins*Publishers*

AVON BOOKS
An Imprint of HarperCollins*Publishers*
10 East 53rd Street
New York, New York 10022-5299

First Avon Books paperback printing: January 2001

10 9 8 7 6 5 4 3 2 1

A
STREETCAR
NAMED
EXPIRE

SECOND FLOOR

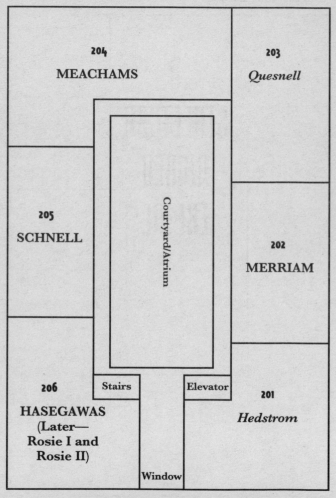

204
MEACHAMS

203
Quesnell

205
SCHNELL

Courtyard/Atrium

202
MERRIAM

206
**HASEGAWAS
(Later—
Rosie I and
Rosie II)**

Stairs

Elevator

201
Hedstrom

Window

Tenants from 1930 on in boldface

THIRD FLOOR

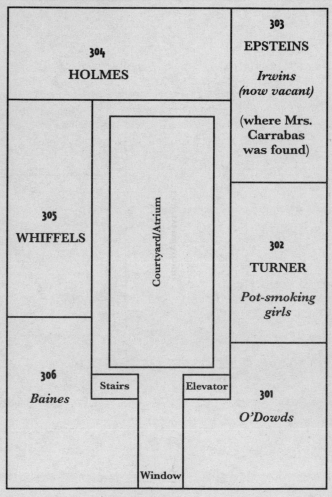

More recent tenants in *italics*

ONE

JUDITH MCMONIGLE FLYNN juggled the box of old
linens, tripped over the cat, and flew headlong
down the stairs. The box bounced, sending napkins,
doilies, and tablecloths flying everywhere. The cat
raced past Judith and disappeared into the entry
hall. Linens floated like small ghosts over the hand-
carved banister, the carpeted stairs, the guest regis-
tration desk by the front door. Yelling, crying, and
swearing at the same time, Judith found herself in a
heap on the first landing with one foot stuck behind
the dieffenbachia planter.

"Sweetums!" she screamed, moving only enough
to see if any bones were broken. "You filthy little
beast! Where are you?"

There was no response. The linens were scattered
all over the floor, the box was upside down next to
the elephant-foot umbrella stand. Determining that
she'd suffered no serious damage, Judith managed
to extricate her leg from behind the potted plant.
Then she sat up. Sweetums appeared from somewhere near the door to the downstairs bathroom.
He had one of Grandma Grover's embroidered
table napkins draped like a shawl over his tubby little orange-and-white body.

1

"You horrible cat," Judith said, sitting down on the second step and yanking the napkin off Sweetums. The cat kept going, his plumelike tail swishing in disdain.

"Where are you?" called a voice from the kitchen. "It's me."

"Me" was Judith's cousin Renie, more formally known as Serena Grover Jones.

"I'm in the entryway," Judith called, rubbing her knee. For once, she wasn't happy to see Renie. The visit boded ill, as Judith knew from her cousin's phone call an hour earlier. Some wag had said that there was no such thing as an accident; maybe Judith had tripped on purpose, hoping to break a leg and put herself out of Renie's reach.

"Hi," Renie said with forced cheer and a look of surprise. "What are you doing with a doily on your head?"

"Shut up," Judith snapped. "Here, give me a hand."

Renie lifted Judith to her feet; Judith removed the doily and tossed it aside in disgust. "Sweetums tripped me," she said, rubbing at her back.

"Rotten cat," Renie murmured, looking around the entry hall and into the living room. "Where'd he go?"

"Who knows?" Judith retorted, limping in the direction of the kitchen. "Who cares? Outside to eat some birds, I suppose. I wish we had buzzards in this neighborhood. Maybe they'd eat him."

"Your mother saw an ostrich this morning," Renie said, following Judith through the dining room.

"Right," Judith said. "Yesterday it was a saber-toothed tiger."

"They've been extinct for quite a while," Renie noted.

"Sometimes I think Mother's brain has been extinct for quite a while," Judith replied, cautiously lowering herself into a chair at the kitchen table. "She's becoming delusional."

"Do you really think so, coz?" Renie asked as she helped herself to a mug of coffee, then gestured at Judith with the pot. "Want a refill?"

"Why not?" Judith sighed. "And while you're at it, grab me a couple of aspirin from the windowsill and a glass of water."

"Still hurting, huh?" Renie said with sympathy. "Are you sure you didn't break or sprain anything?"

"I don't think so," Judith said, then swallowed the aspirin in one gulp. "It's these damned hips. Maybe Dr. Alfonso is right."

"It was that stupid pogo stick when we were kids," Renie said, sitting across the table from Judith. "I was never foolish enough to try it."

"You were too chicken," Judith responded.

"Maybe," Renie allowed. "In some ways, you've always been more daring than I am."

"But less outspoken," Judith said with a smirk.

Renie shrugged. "We each have our strengths and our weaknesses. Maybe that's why we get along most of the time."

"Maybe so." Judith stretched her legs out under the table. The cousins had both been only children two years apart, but they'd grown up as close as sisters, maybe closer. At the end of a play day, their mothers could send one of them home. Neither Gertrude Grover nor Aunt Deb hesitated to lay down the law when the cousins started bickering. Unfortunately, the two sisters-in-law didn't apply the same rules to themselves, but had continued arguing into their dotage.

"I have to admit," Judith said, "that Mother likes to tease. She's definitely more forgetful, but the delusions are new."

"My mother isn't as dotty as yours," Renie said, "but her martyr's crown gets heavier each day. She acts so pitiful that I should wear one of those signs that says, 'I'm Okay—You're *Really* Okay.' Reassuring her is an unending chore."

"Old age is very sad," Judith lamented. "And we're working our way there, coz. That's why I hate to go

back to Dr. Alfonso. I'm afraid he's going to tell me I
need a hip replacement."

"So what?" Renie countered. "Lots of people get
them. Look at my mother."

Judith grimaced. "I have looked. She's practically
confined to that wheelchair."

"Well . . ." Renie looked askance. "That's because she
doesn't try hard enough. Mom babies herself. And she
wouldn't keep up with the therapy. It's much better if I
wait on her instead."

"I suppose we'll be just as bad when we get to be their
age," Judith said. "*If* we ever get to be their age."

"They may outlive us," Renie said with a little shake
of her head. "To tell the truth, they're remarkable old
girls."

"Mmm," Judith murmured.

"Bill's actually looking forward to being put in a
nursing home," Renie said. "He swears he has one
picked out where the nurses wear long black stockings
with seams and garter belts, just like in the porno
flicks."

"Bill is crazier than his neurotic patients," Judith
declared. "Maybe he should give up his part-time
shrink practice. What's he doing, limiting it to nympho-
maniacs?"

"Gosh, no," Renie replied. "He's got several perverts,
too. But that's not why I'm here," she went on, suddenly
offering Judith her most engaging smile. "Tomorrow's
the tour. What time shall I pick you up?"

Judith's black eyes narrowed at Renie. "How about
never? Did I say I'd go with you?"

"You didn't say you wouldn't," Renie replied, looking affronted.

"That's because I try to be nice," Judith said, "which
gets me in trouble, even with you. Look, Hillside Manor
is full through the end of August and the first ten days
of September. I can't take time off. Didn't you say it was

a two-hour tour? That means three, between getting there and back. Ask one of your old pals like Madge Navarre or Melissa Bargroom."

"They're working," Renie said.

"So am I," Judith answered, scowling. She waved a hand around the old-fashioned, high-ceilinged kitchen. "Do you think this place runs by itself?"

"Jeez, coz," Renie said, making a face, "I work at home, too. Surely you're not like my mother and think that I have small mice doing the artwork for my graphic design business?"

"Sometimes it looks that way," Judith snapped, then saw a fire light in Renie's eyes. "Okay, okay, I don't always understand your design concepts. It's not my forte. But Joe and Bill won't get back from their Alaska fishing trip until the day after tomorrow. I hate to ask Arlene Rankers to fill in, because I don't want to do anything that'll further encourage her and Carl to move. They've been threatening, you know."

"I do," Renie said, her temper fading. "I talked to Arlene after Mass Sunday. She's sick of keeping up that big yard."

Judith half-stood up to look out the window toward the Rankerses' property. "It's that blasted hedge. It's had bees in it all summer."

"We're not talking about an overnight," Renie argued. "Two or three hours, that's all. Won't your idiot cleaning woman be here tomorrow?"

"Well, yes," Judith admitted. Phyliss Rackley had taken the day off so that she could undergo a brain scan, which, in Judith's opinion, was to determine if Phyliss actually had a brain. Between the cleaning woman's hypochondria and her religious mania, Judith was never sure if Phyliss's head was merely muddled or actually empty.

"Well then?" Renie prodded.

"Frankly," Judith said, "I have absolutely no interest

in anything as gruesome as a murder tour. I don't understand how the parish school could have allowed it to be an auction item."

"Because we take what we can get," Renie responded. "Our Lady, Star of the Sea Parochial School does not operate on air pudding. This year, we stand to clear over eighty grand from the live and silent auctions. Would you rather have to pony up a big wad for the Sunday collection or peddle a couple of questionable items for the auction?"

"Like birth control pills?" Judith shot back.

"We didn't do that," Renie replied, indignant. "That item was a free ob-gyn consultation with Dr. Bile, who happens to be a SOTs."

"I know he's one of our SOTs," Judith said, also using the nickname for Star of the Sea parishioners. "But Norma Paine and some of the other women felt it was iffy."

"Don't be a drip," Renie said. "Norma's always carping. I had to put up with a bunch of crap from her on the auction committee. Come on, say you'll go."

Judith shook her head. "I'll be too banged up by tomorrow. Stiff. Miserable."

"Coz . . ."

"You know damned well you don't want to go on this tour, either."

Renie winced. "Okay, so I didn't mean to bid. I was trying to get the waiter to bring me some more chicken. The piece I got looked like it came off a pigeon. But I raised my card to get his attention and the next thing I knew, I'd blown three hundred bucks on this stupid thing. Bill wanted to kill me. Having done it and being on the auction committee, I feel I have to take the blasted tour. Jeremy Lamar is the nephew or godson or something-or-other of the Butlers, who, as you know, have been SOTs for four generations and practically paid for the last big church renovation by themselves.

Father Hoyle would beat me to a pulp if I offended them by not helping Jeremy out on his maiden voyage."

Judith frowned. "Maiden voyage?"

"Yes," Renie said with a nod. "Jeremy's just starting this Toujours La Tour business. He's had organizational problems, which is why the first tour isn't starting until tomorrow."

As a B&B hostess, Judith was well-attuned to the tourist season. "That's too bad. It's the end of August. How's he going to survive through the winter?"

"Jeremy has several different tours scheduled," Renie replied, opening the sheep-shaped cookie jar and taking out three thumbprint cookies. "He's got an Indian summer tour which will become 'Autumn in the Northwest' later on, a Halloween tour which will include the murder mystery tour, and then all sorts of holiday and ski tours starting in November."

Judith vaguely knew the Butlers, pillars of the parish who lived in one of Heraldsgate Hill's most prestigious areas not far from Hillside Manor. If she had to be honest, she thought the Butlers were a bunch of stuffed shirts.

"So?" Renie inquired, her chin sprinkled with cookie crumbs.

"Don't look at me with those cocker spaniel eyes," Judith warned, wishing the aspirin would start to give her some relief. "I really don't want to go."

"Please?"

"No."

"I'll owe you."

"I don't care."

"I'll never speak to you again."

"Good."

Renie, her round face somehow looking very long, rose from the chair. "Then it's good-bye," she said solemnly.

"Afraid so."

Shoulders bowed and head down, Renie walked slowly toward the back door. As she pushed open the screen, she turned around. "I'll pick you up at eleven-thirty. The tour starts at noon from the bottom of the hill by the opera house."

Judith sighed. "Okay."

Renie left. Judith closed her eyes and shook her head. She could never say no to her cousin. Indeed, Judith had always had problems saying no to anyone. She was too softhearted. Often it seemed more like a flaw than a virtue.

Renie flew in through the back door. "Coz!" she cried. "There *is* an ostrich in your yard! He's eating your rosebush!"

Limping through the passageway between the kitchen and the back porch, Judith figured Renie was teasing her. But looming by the flowerbed beyond the patio was an enormous bird that certainly looked like an ostrich.

"Good grief!" Judith gasped. "That sucker must be eight feet tall! I can't shoo it away with a broom."

"How about an AK-47?" Renie asked, seeking safety next to Judith on the porch.

The ostrich was ignoring the cousins, its long neck bent down to chomp off not only Queen Elizabeth's pink buds and blooms, but the leaves as well.

"I'll call the humane society," Judith said. "Maybe this guy escaped from the zoo."

"He's not the only one," a raspy voice called out from the toolshed door. "You two look like the dogcatcher ought to be chasing you."

Gertrude Grover was leaning on her walker, chortling at her own remarks. At the moment, she seemed neither deaf nor ditzy.

"Very funny, Mother," Judith shot back. "You'd better get back inside your apartment. That bird must weigh three hundred pounds."

"Goodness me," Gertrude said, her voice suddenly very high and girlish, "he's almost as fat as you are."

"Mother!" Judith was furious. Always sensitive about her weight even though she could carry some extra pounds on her statuesque frame, Judith had never become immune to Gertrude's cutting comments.

"You're not fat," Renie murmured, going into the house. "I'll call the humane society. You argue with your mother."

Two heads appeared above the laurel hedge that divided the Flynn property from the Rankerses'. "Yoo-hoo," Arlene called, "is that your birdie?"

"I'm giving her the birdie," Gertrude put in before Judith could answer. "Phluphtt!"

"Have you ever seen this thing before?" Judith asked of Arlene and Carl.

"Not unless it's one of Arlene's relatives," Carl replied in his dry manner.

The ostrich had moved on to the Sterling Silver bush. "Damn!" Judith cried. "He's ruining my pet rosebushes. How can I discourage him?"

"How about making one of your casseroles for him?" Gertrude said. "That'd discourage anybody."

"I wouldn't mess with him," Carl advised. "They can run about forty miles an hour. You wouldn't have time to get back in the house."

Renie had returned, but she stayed behind the screen door. "The humane society will be here in half an hour," she said. "They don't know if an ostrich is missing from the zoo, but they said some people keep them as pets."

Having demolished Sterling Silver, the ostrich began devastating Peace. "Go inside, Mother. Please," Judith urged.

"What?" Gertrude shot back. "And miss all the fun? I haven't had this much excitement since I put my girdle on backwards."

Judith's eyes were glued to the ostrich. "Oh, no, not

my dahlias! Look at that thing! He's destroying the garden."

"Hey!" Gertrude slammed her walker on the concrete. "Take a hike! Go on with you!" She waved a gnarled hand. "Beat it, or I'll take out my dentures!"

To the amazement of the onlookers—except Gertrude—the ostrich lifted its head, turned beady eyes on the old lady, and ran out of the yard.

"That wasn't quite forty miles an hour," Carl remarked, glancing at his watch, "but it was pretty darned fast."

The humane society truck showed up twenty minutes later while Judith was trying to repair the damage the ostrich had done to her plantings. She informed the rescue workers that the bird had escaped—on foot. They told her that ostriches didn't fly. Judith said she didn't care, she never wanted to see the damned thing again. The rescue crew shrugged and drove away.

After the Thursday night guests had departed the next morning, Phyliss was cleaning the guest rooms and Judith was preparing her mother's lunch when Renie showed up.

"You're early," Judith declared, cutting a chicken salad sandwich into quarters. Gertrude might eat all of it; she might eat half of it; she might feed it to Sweetums. As she grew older, Judith's mother tended to eat less, at least of the wholesome foods that her daughter prepared for her.

"It's eleven twenty-five," Renie said, looking up at the old schoolhouse clock. "Anyway, I was ready. With Bill gone to Alaska and the three kids traveling in Europe on their own passports but on our money, I don't have all that much to do in the mornings."

"You don't get up until ten," Judith pointed out.

Renie nodded. "Just enough time to get over here early."

"I hope Joe and Bill are having good luck up at Shamrock Pass," Judith said, adding sweet pickles and potato chips to the plate. "Fresh salmon would be a wonderful treat. We could smoke and kipper some for the guests' appetizers. You know," she continued, "I need to do some updating before next season's visitors start making reservations. These days, B&Bs are offering their guests some pretty fancy amenities."

"You need a Web site," Renie asserted. "I've been telling you that for months."

"I'm on the Web," Judith responded.

"Only on lists with other B&Bs," Renie said, "which means in some cases, you're right there with your competition. You need your own page. I told you I'd design it for you."

Judith, who hated change as much as she loathed decisions, winced. "I suppose . . . But it seems so . . . pushy."

"Sheesh." Renie shook her head. "Move into the modern world, coz. Look, as soon as I finish my project for Drug Opprobrium, I'll start putting something together. You can feel free to add, subtract, multiply, or divide. Okay?"

"Well . . . okay." Judith sounded dubious, even though she knew Renie was right. Leaving her cousin in the kitchen, Judith delivered Gertrude's lunch, got into an argument, left with apologies to her mother, went upstairs to give Phyliss last-minute instructions, became entangled in a religious debate, agreed to disagree, and finally rejoined Renie.

"It's eleven forty-two," Renie said, tapping her foot and pointing to the schoolhouse clock. "We're going to be late."

"Oh, dear." Judith gasped, snatching up her purse. "I'm sorry. You've no idea how involved I can get between Mother and Phyliss."

"Oh, yes, I do," Renie replied, following Judith out the back door. "I spent almost an hour on the phone with my mother this morning. She's been worried sick the past few days because I've been home alone. She can't believe I like it that way once in a while. Plus, she's sure that I'll be assaulted by burglars, rapists, homicidal maniacs, and, her old favorite, the white slavers."

Judith couldn't help but laugh. "Has your mother ever seen any of those alleged villains? Even a burglar?"

Renie slipped behind the wheel of the Joneses' Toyota Camry. "A burglar, yes. You're too young to remember it, but when I was about four, Auntie Vance and Aunt Ellen chased a burglar out of our basement. There'd been a rash of robberies in the neighborhood. Dad was on one of his two-week sea voyages, and Mom was too scared to roust the intruder by herself. Instead of calling the cops, she phoned Grandma and Grandpa Grover. You know my mother, she didn't want to be a burden to the tax-supported police force. Anyway, Grandpa and Grandma sent Auntie Vance and Aunt Ellen over to rescue Mom and me. I don't know what our dear aunts did to that guy, but I can still hear him running down the alley, screaming his head off."

"Auntie Vance and Aunt Ellen can be very formidable," Judith noted as Renie reversed down the driveway and roared out of the cul-de-sac. "Hey, you don't need to go so fast."

"If I don't, we'll miss the tour's start," Renie replied.

"I'd like to arrive alive," Judith said as Renie screeched to a halt at the arterial, paused imperceptibly, and swung out in front of a transit bus.

"Coz!" Judith shouted as they flew down Heraldsgate Hill's long, steep south slope, "slow down! You've got a red light at the intersection."

"Not for long," Renie said as they shot by condos and apartment houses that were only a blur. "It's going to change in four seconds. One-one-thousand, two-one-thousand, three-one-thousand, four . . . See, it's green."

Somehow, the cars ahead of her managed to get out of the way, if barely. The bus had been left in the dust.

Two minutes later, they were parked near the opera

house in the lot reserved for tour participants. It was exactly eleven fifty-five.

Toujours La Tour featured a converted trolley painted black, gold, and red. The vehicle's exterior sported diabolical images: a dagger dripped blood; a bottle, presumably of poison, spilled onto what looked like somebody's last will and testament; the chalk outline of a corpse covered the front end. For being gruesome, it was tastefully done, at least according to Renie. By the time the cousins reached the conveyance, the guide was about to get in.

"Aha!" he called with a big toothy grin on his boyish face, "latecomers, huh? You don't want to miss this, ladies. We're off for a spot of murder and mayhem."

"Great," Judith muttered. "Haven't I had enough of that already in my life?"

"At least you don't have to listen to Joe's homicide reports anymore since he retired from the force," Renie reminded Judith.

"True," Judith allowed as they clambered onto the trolley and found the last two vacant seats at the rear. "I'll admit, though," she said as they seated themselves, "that some of his cases were more interesting than the insurance scams and missing poodle jobs he gets as a private investigator."

"They help pay the bills," Renie pointed out.

The grinning guide was introducing himself. "I'm Jeremy Lamar, owner and operator of Toujours La Tour," he said over a mike from the front of the trolley. "This is our inaugural trip, and we're going to do our darnedest to give you a killer of a treat. First, I'd like you to meet Nan Leech, my assistant." Jeremy paused as a blond middle-aged woman offered the tourists a tight little smile and a rigid little bow. "Nan will be doing part of the spiel while I drive, and she's ready to help anyone who might need it—we don't know yet if the tour's going to be too much for some folks—ha-ha! She'll also be available afterward if you want to sign on for some of our other offerings. How many of you are from out-of-town?"

Almost half the people in the forty-seat bus raised their hands.

"So we've got some locals," Jeremy said, still with his toothsome grin. "Then you know that this city isn't famous for big-time crime, but over the years we've certainly had our share of strange and lethal doings . . ."

"Is he going to talk us to death?" Renie hissed.

Judith was trying to get comfortable in the old-fashioned leather bucket seat. "I'm glad I took some aspirin before I left. Maybe I can nod off."

"Still hurting, huh?" Renie asked in a commiserating tone.

"It was hard to sleep last night," Judith replied. "It's my back more than—"

The two older people in front of the cousins turned around and told them to shush. Judith gave them a sheepish smile; Renie curled her lip.

"So off we go," Jeremy announced as he swung into the driver's seat. "First stop, 'Welcome, Corpses.' "

"What the heck is that?" Renie whispered.

Judith shrugged. "That old transient hotel downtown where some of the homeless people have been stabbed? The warehouse in the international district where those Asian gangsters massacred a dozen people?"

The couple in front of the cousins shot them another warning look. Judith apologized; Renie sneered.

Nan Leech was offering some background on the city itself, starting with the early pioneers. The cousins tuned her out. The trolley had moved into traffic, which was rather heavy for midday. Overhead, the morning clouds had broken, and the sun was shining in all its late summer splendor. Still, there were reminders everywhere that fall was coming: A September primary election had sprouted all sorts of campaign placards bearing candidates' names and platform slogans.

"I wish it'd rain," Renie said in an undertone. "We've had hot, dry weather for over a month."

"I know," Judith replied. "I'm sick of watering the garden. Not that I have much left out back, after that ostrich ate it."

"Will you please shut up?" the older man in front of them demanded.

"Sorry," Judith said again. "It's just that we live here, and we know all the—"

"Well, maybe some of us don't know everything like you do," the woman snapped. "And what have you got against sun, anyway?"

Judith shrank back into her seat; Renie glared at the couple, then stuck her tongue out when they turned to face the front. The trolley headed up the steep hill that the cousins had just descended. Nan had reached the mid-century, promising bloodcurdling labor union tales later in the tour.

Renie, meanwhile, had taken a notebook out of her purse and drawn a hangman's scaffold, a vat of oil, and five short horizontal lines. "Guess," she whispered to Judith.

"A?" Judith mouthed.

Renie shook her head, then sketched a head attached to the noose. Nan kept talking.

"E?" Judith hazarded.

Renie nodded, writing in an "E" in the second space.

"I?"

Renie drew a neck on the head.

"S?"

Renie put an "S" in the third and fifth blank spaces.

Judith studied the word. Renie nodded in the direction of the couple in front of them.

"T?" Judith offered, seeing the light.

Renie nodded again, putting the "T" between the "S's."

"P," Judith said aloud.

"Oh, good heavens," the woman cried, turning to face Judith. "You should have done that before you left!"

"But . . ." Judith began as Renie filled in the final letter of "PESTS."

"And here we are," Nan announced in triumph, "at one of the deadliest hostelries in North America. Don't be fooled by its charming décor of chintz bedcoverings and oak plate rails and old-fashioned gas range and stone fireplaces. At least three guests have died violent deaths while staying in this seemingly delightful establishment. Poison, shootings, strangulation—this old Edwardian house has seen it all. We like to refer to the owner as the Old Inncreeper. Ladies and gentlemen, welcome to Hillside Manor B&B!"

TWO

LEAPING OUT OF her seat, Judith felt sharp, wrenching pains stab at her back. A cry of anguish prevented her from making a protest. She went white and crumpled into her place.

Alarmed, Renie grabbed her hand. "Are you going to pass out? Shall I have them send for a doctor?"

"I . . . feel . . . sick," Judith gasped.

"Good," snapped the woman in front of them. "Now shut your yap so we can hear all about this awful death trap."

Judith couldn't do much else. Mortified and queasy, she listened as Jeremy Lamar took up the terrible tale of Corpses R Us or whatever ghastly name he had applied to her beloved B&B.

"A fortune-teller was the first tragic victim, poisoned at the dining room table before she could reveal the shameful secrets she saw in her crystal ball," Jeremy intoned, the grin gone and his voice lowered to a deep rumble.

"I can't move," Judith moaned.

"A world-famous tenor," Jeremy continued, "seeking a tasty snack from the B&B's death vault of a refrigerator . . ."

"Here," Renie urged, "let me help you sit up straight."

"A New York mobster, his bullet-riddled body found in the backyard . . ."

"It's spasms," Judith whispered shakily, but allowed Renie to help her change positions.

"A bloodcurdling shoot-out on this very street . . ."

"Let me massage your lower back," Renie offered.

"A helpless old woman cut up like a chicken by a hatchet-wielding fiend . . ."

"That's better," Judith said as the spasms eased under Renie's ministrations. "Let's see if I can stretch my legs a bit." Judith stretched, her long legs bumping the woman in front of her. "Oops!" Judith exclaimed, covering her mouth with her hands.

"That's it!" the woman cried. "I'm going to have you thrown off the bus!"

The bus, however, was pulling out of the cul-de-sac. But Jeremy wasn't finished:

"Aha!" he shouted, one arm extended in the direction of Hillside Manor. "Look to your right, at the front porch. Even now, the hideous old gargoyle who runs this nest of eternal rest is waving her broom at us!"

"It's Phyliss!" Judith shuddered as the cleaning woman, with sausage curls a-flying, diligently swept the steps.

Jeremy started the trolley again. "That's a special moment, completely unscheduled," he said into his microphone. "Nan will take over while we head for 'The Body in the Wall' at the Alhambra Arms."

A middle-aged man with black hair and mustache to match had risen from his seat across from the cousins. "Excuse me," he said with a little bow. "I'm Alfred Ashe, a licensed chiropractor. May I help you?"

"I think I'm beyond help," Judith said with a feeble attempt at a smile.

"I don't think so," Alfred Ashe replied with a smile. He was a short man with broad shoulders, a dimple in each cheek, large hands, and the longest eyelashes this side of Elizabeth Taylor. Or Mike Piazza. Judith was in too much pain to tell the difference. "If you lean forward and relax," Dr. Ashe suggested, "I'll see what I can do. Let me say that there's some risk, since I've never treated you before, but I can almost promise immediate relief."

The man in front of Judith and Renie was leaning across the woman who was presumably his wife. "Could you relieve this tour of her entirely? She's been nothing but a nuisance since we started."

"Now, now," Dr. Ashe said gently, "the poor lady's in pain. Please bear with us."

Judith did as the chiropractor had requested. Manipulating her neck and shoulders, he made three quick, jerky motions. Snap, crackle, and pop. Mouth agape and short of breath, Judith endured the brief treatment, then realized that the worst of the pain was gone.

"Oh, my." She sighed, with a grateful look for Dr. Ashe. "You're right. That's much better. How can I thank you?"

"Just promise not to sue me," Dr. Ashe smiled, sitting back down in his seat and showing off his delightful dimples.

At the front of the bus, Nan Leech had chosen to ignore the disruption. As Jeremy steered the trolley back down the hill and then maneuvered through the winding streets near the bottom, his assistant had been giving the history of a local landmark apartment house. Judith knew the building, but not much of its background. She gave Renie a puzzled look.

"Later," Renie mouthed.

"You know all about it?" Judith whispered back.

Renie nodded just as the trolley pulled to a stop. Nan exited, presumably to clear the way for the group's arrival, and Jeremy resumed his role as narrator.

"So after almost a hundred years, the Alhambra Arms has yielded up its deadliest secret. The elegance before

the First World War, the halcyon days of the Flapper
Era, the sadly faded years of the Great Depression. Yet,
by the end of World War Two, the Alhambra had come
full circle. Returning veterans desperately needed housing. Suddenly, this fifty-year-old palace, which had
grown as dowdy as an émigré duchess, was being
revamped, the tiaras polished, the furs taken out of storage, the satin gowns cleaned and pressed." Jeremy
paused for breath, allowing his tourists to admire the
structure's Moorish façade.

"I'm having it out with him," Judith said under her
breath. "Isn't this one of the places where we get out to
look around?"

"I think so," Renie murmured. "Face it, Jeremy had
no idea you were on this tour. The reservations were in
my name. Wait until the tour's finished. You need time
to put your thoughts in order, not to mention reassem-
ble your various body parts."

"I can't wait," Judith declared, grimly regarding the
vestiges of grandeur that could still be seen on the Alhambra's exterior. Elaborate grillwork covered the arched
windows, which included four stories of balconies ris-
ing above the main entrance. Movement behind the
third-floor balcony door caught Judith's eye.

"Look, coz," she whispered with a nudge for Renie.
"Somebody's watching us."

"So?" Renie shrugged.

"They're gone," Judith said softly. "As in evaporated."
Renie said nothing.

"As you can see from the scaffolding," Jeremy went
on after describing the original materials and careful
attention to detail, "a renaissance is underway. The
Alhambra is being converted by Guthrie Properties into
condominiums, a renovation that will not only hearken
back to the early part of century, but improve upon it
with the most modern amenities. We are very fortunate
that George Guthrie has given us permission to tour his
most recent project. You see," he added, dropping his

voice an octave or so, "it is because of this current undertaking—no pun intended—that a fifty-year-old mystery has been recently solved."

Jeremy raised a hand, beckoning to his rapt listeners. "So come along and enter into another era with a window on the future and a body in the—" He stopped for dramatic effect. "But wait. Nan will take up the tale once we get into the courtyard. She's gone on ahead to make sure we're not getting in the way of the construction crew. I'll check upstairs and meet you there. Meanwhile, I might point out that the fountain area you'll see was once a swimming pool. During the Depression, it became too expensive to maintain and had to be drained."

A large white van with big green letters reading GUTHRIE PROPERTIES was parked a few yards down the street. Judith and Renie were the last to exit the trolley.

"Don't you think I could sue Jeremy Lamar?" Judith asked in a whisper. "He not only smeared the B&B, he didn't even have his facts straight."

"You could probably get some kind of injunction to stop him from putting Hillside Manor on the tour," Renie said as they fell a few feet behind the rest of the group. Luckily, the couple who had been sitting in front of them had sprinted to the head of the pack, no doubt trying to avoid the cousins. "Lawsuits are expensive, even if you win."

"I know." Judith sighed. "But I've never been so outraged. If I hadn't thrown out my back, I might have killed him."

"Another first for Toujours La Tour." Renie grinned. "How fitting."

Stopping suddenly, Judith grabbed Renie by the arm. "Say—you didn't know about this all along, did you? Are you and Jeremy in cahoots just to drive me nuts?"

Renie's brown eyes widened. "That's crazy. I'd never do such a thing and you know it. Apologize. Here. Now."

Judith was embarrassed. "Okay. I apologize. But you can't blame me for being suspicious."

"Yes, I can," Renie retorted as they walked under the arched entrance. "You're paranoid."

Feeling foolish, Judith barely noticed the workers who were busily resurfacing a tiled pool in the middle of a handsome courtyard that was surrounded by a four-story loggia with arches in the curving Moorish style. Judith was reminded of her visit to the original Alhambra in Spain some thirty-odd years earlier.

Nan Leech was standing next to a big, burly man in an orange hard hat who waved to the group. He seemed to be in charge, and Judith vaguely wondered if he was Mr. Guthrie.

Nan had begun her spiel. "Before World War Two, a young couple named Harry and Dorothy Meacham moved into the Alhambra Arms. They had recently married, and this was their first home. In 1942, after war had broken out, two important events occurred in the Meachams' lives. Harry joined the army in February of that year, and three months later, their first child, a daughter named Anne-Marie, was born. The war years were typical for the Meachams, separated by ten thousand miles and haunted by the fear that Harry might never come back. Finally, when peace came, Harry returned from Europe to be reunited with his little family."

Nan paused. Judith turned to Renie. "I'm going to look for Jeremy right now. I can't just stand here and stew about his effrontery."

"Hold on," Renie cautioned. "Don't you want to hear about the Meachams?"

"Not particularly," Judith said as Nan led them into the entry hall, where candleflame lights sat in wrought-iron sconces. A staircase with a matching wrought-iron banister wound up to the next floor. Just as one of the workers turned on a jackhammer, Nan signaled for her little herd to follow her upstairs. Moving along the balcony, they finally reached the rear of the building, where Nan took up her tale.

"On a dark and rainy day in the autumn of 1946, Dorothy Meacham went downtown to buy a billfold for Harry's birthday present. Harry, who was going to the university to study engineering on the GI bill and working part-time at a clock company, got home around six. He was surprised to find that neither his wife nor his daughter was at the apartment. Dorothy had left a note saying that she would return by four and pick up Anne-Marie, who was visiting a friend. He called the friend's mother, who said that Anne-Marie was still there, but Dorothy hadn't shown up yet. Apparently, Harry was terribly worried and didn't want to pass his fears on to his daughter. He asked the neighbor to keep Anne-Marie until Dorothy showed up. She never did, and he finally called the police shortly before eleven."

Near Judith and Renie, Alfred Ashe was waving a hand. "Yes?" Nan said, though she didn't look pleased by the interruption.

"Exactly what did the note say?" Alfred inquired.

Nan scowled at the chiropractor. "I don't know. There's no copy extant." She waited a moment, but Alfred remained silent. "After forty-eight hours," Nan went on, her face again assuming its polite mask, "Dorothy was listed as a missing person. She had last been seen around two o'clock in the men's leather goods department at the Belle Epoch. Despite every effort made by the police, Dorothy Meacham was never seen again. Until last month."

Another pause. Nan slowly opened the door to the unit directly behind her.

"Where do you suppose that twerp Jeremy has gone?" Judith asked Renie. "I don't see him anywhere up here or out on the balconies."

"If you can't wait until the tour's over, at least hold off and nail him when we get back to the bus," Renie

said, following the rest of the group into what had probably been the living room of the Meacham apartment.

"When the renovations began on the Alhambra," Nan
said in her clear, precise voice, "many of the walls had
to be removed because the condos will actually be
larger units than the apartments. The Meacham unit is
one of those which will be expanded on both sides."

Everyone, including the cousins, gazed around the
partially gutted room. "When this wall was ripped out,"
Nan said, pointing to a large opening that revealed
I-beams, mortar, plaster, and a great deal of dust, "the
construction workers found a skeleton. The remains
were identified by dental charts as those of Dorothy
Meacham. She had not died of natural causes." Pause.
"Her skull had been smashed." Pause. "She had been
murdered."

Little gasps went up from the group. Nan waited, her
mouth set in a tight, almost smug line.

"Maybe that jerk of a Jeremy is hiding inside the
wall," Judith whispered. "If he jumps out to scare us,
I'm going to tackle him."

"You'll really cripple yourself if you do," Renie
warned.

"Harry Meacham had moved away a few months
after his wife disappeared," Nan was now saying. "He
remarried and moved to California. No further trace
was heard of him until the body was discovered. Naturally, in the case of a spouse's murder, the other spouse
is the usual suspect. There is no statute of limitations on
homicide, as you may know. The police went searching
for Harry Meacham. They never found him."

"A real let-down," Judith muttered, then waited for
her cousin to refocus her attention on Nan. What Renie
didn't know—or see—couldn't hurt either of them.

"We may never be sure if Harry Meacham killed his
wife," Nan was saying, "and then walled her body up
in the . . ."

Renie appeared riveted by the macabre recital. Judith

slipped out of the room and down the corridor that overlooked the courtyard. She saw Jeremy Lamar talking to the man in the orange hard hat. Although she still limped, Judith's aches and pains had lessened. Hurrying down the staircase, she reached the courtyard just as Jeremy disappeared into an elevator.

Judith pressed the button for the car, but it had already started its ascent. The elevator had an old-fashioned dial to indicate the floors; she saw it stop on three. Impatiently, she waited for its return, got in, and rose to the third floor.

Jeremy wasn't in sight. Judith stopped at the first door, but it was locked and bolted. She tried the second door, which swung open at a touch. While the rooms were in chaos, no one was there. Judith moved on to the third door, which was ajar.

"Jeremy?" she called.

Apparently the third unit hadn't yet yielded to the wrecking crew. A few pieces of furniture remained, though the carpets were rolled up in one corner. Judith wandered into the kitchen, where she couldn't help but smile. The fixtures were straight out of the middle part of the century, reminding Judith of how the kitchen at Hillside Manor had looked before she'd made her own renovations. A sense of nostalgia overcame her as she peeked into the bedroom.

Nostalgia was swiftly replaced by surprise. A woman was lying on the bed. Judith started to apologize, then noticed the ugly red blotch on her chest. Surprise gave way to alarm as Judith approached the woman.

"Good Lord, not again!" Judith whispered, recoiling in horror.

She might not be the Old Inncreeper, but Judith knew a corpse when she saw one.

Or did she? Was this some kind of stunt created by the tour group? Judith decided to check for a pulse, maybe even pinch the woman on the bed. But before she could move, all hell broke out. A bearded young man with a huge video camera charged into the room, followed by an even younger man carrying coils of cable. A plump redheaded woman directly behind them took one look at the body on the bed and let out a little yip. Two, three, at least a half-dozen more people pushed and shoved their way into the room, some of them throwing an occasional punch. They wielded microphones, cameras, and equipment Judith didn't recognize. She was shunted aside, feeling as if she'd been on the wrong end of a cattle stampede.

The cameraman who had led the onslaught was already taping. "Keep it rolling," the redhead cried in a strained voice. "What the hell is going on here?"

The question seemed to be aimed at Judith, who was clinging to an old walnut bureau. Cameras clicked and whirled, microphones waved like saplings in the wind.

"Stop!" Judith screamed, holding up both hands.

Though the cameras rolled on, the clamor of voices faded away. Judith tried to regain her composure as the redheaded woman faced her, nose-to-nose.

"I just got here," Judith finally said. "I haven't any idea what's going on, either, except"—she gestured at the motionless figure on the bed—"that woman on the bed may be dead. Or not. She might have been stabbed or shot, but I don't see a weapon. Still, somebody should call the police."

Cell phones were whipped out as the crowd edged closer to the bed. Gasps, squeals, and the hum of voices filled the room. Judith fanned herself with her hands. The afternoon had grown warm, and she felt suffocated by the dozen or more people who were jammed into the bedroom.

"She's dead, all right," the redhead declared. "Is this our lucky day or what?"

Aghast, Judith tried to find an opening in the crowd. She wanted air, she wanted quiet, she wanted out. Surely the redhead was mistaken. What did she know? She was only a journalist. But now armed with a microphone, the redhead accosted Judith before she could escape.

"Liz Ogilvy, KINE-TV," she announced in a polished voice. "And you're . . ."

"Ah . . ." Judith stammered. "An innocent by-stander?"

Liz shut off the mike. "Listen, this looks like a big story. Don't clown around. You won't be any more than a couple of sound bytes on the five o'clock news any-way."

Grimacing, Judith reluctantly gave her name. "I'm on the Toujours La Tour tour," she said, feeling stupid. "I came in here by mistake."

Liz gave a curt nod. "Okay, let's take it from the top." She turned the mike back on as several lenses focused on Judith's pained expression.

"This is Liz Ogilvy, reporting live from the Alhambra Arms where the body of a woman has just been discovered in a vacant unit. Police have been summoned, and we're here with Judith Flynn, who claims to have discovered the corpse just minutes ago. If only our KINE-TV cameras had been here earlier, we could have shown our viewers the actual murder in progress. Ms. Flynn, what was your reaction to finding a murdered woman in a vacant apartment?"

To Judith, the mike thrust into her face looked like the body of a fat, black spider. "Um . . . that she was dead?"

Liz made a menacing face. "Let's do that again. From 'your reaction.' "

Judith's knees felt weak; perspiration dripped down her aching back. It was pointless to resist. "I was shocked," she said. "And saddened."

"Thank you, Ms. Flynn." Liz turned to face the cam-era. "The irony is that this is the second time the media has been called to the Alhambra. Skeletal remains were found here just weeks ago during the ongoing renova-tion by Guthrie Properties. Today, another shock greeted workers when they began removing carpets and flooring only to find a veritable treasure trove. And now we seem to have an unidentified corpse in KINE-TV's broadcast from the Alhambra Arms."

The man in the orange hard hat stood in the doorway. Everyone, including Liz, turned to stare.

"You should have waited for me," he said in a voice that failed to conceal his anger. "First of all, you're in the wrong room."

"No, we're not," Liz declared as the rest of the media parted like the Red Sea. "Take a look, Mr. Guthrie."

Mr. Guthrie, who had silver curls poking out from under his hard hat, moved aggressively toward the bed. "What the hell?" he cried. "Is this some kind of prank? Where's that idiot Lamar?"

Liz Ogilvy held a hand up in front of George Guthrie. It occurred to Judith that Liz must be a local media queen, since the others seemed to defer to her. She recalled seeing Liz on the eleven o'clock news, spreading gloom and doom in a no-nonsense manner.

"This isn't a joke," Liz said grimly. "Ms. Flynn over here says she found the body just before we arrived to cover the treasure story."

Mr. Guthrie gave Judith an indifferent glance, then removed his hard hat and mopped his brow with his forearm. "Hey!" he exclaimed, pointing at the body, "that's Mrs. Carrabas!"

"You know her?" Liz asked, thrusting the microphone in front of Mr. Guthrie. In the distance, sirens could be heard.

"You bet." He nodded, sweat trickling down his high forehead. "She's my exorcist."

Liz's surprise was apparent only in the flicker of her eyelashes. She turned the mike on and faced the camera. "I'm with George Guthrie of Guthrie Properties who has just identified the body of a woman he says is his exorcist. Mr. Guthrie, what is the victim's full name and how do you know her in a professional capacity?"

Guthrie had taken a blue-and-white bandana handkerchief from his pocket and was wiping his face. "Her name's Mrs. Carrabas—I forget her first name—and she came here to exorcise this place. It was . . ." He paused, glancing at the body. "This is really terrible. I think."

Judith heard the sirens wind down as they pulled up outside the Alhambra. Her earlier desire to get out of the crowded bedroom was temporarily put aside. She had to admit that she was curious. None of these people were medical professionals. How could they be so sure that this Mrs. Carrabas was dead? She was an exorcist. Maybe the blood and the motionless state were part of her ritual.

"Let me say this." Guthrie was leaning into the mike, speaking very fast, apparently aware that he was about to be interrupted by the police. "Mrs. Carrabas is a well-known exorcist from California. I hired her to exorcise the ghosts from this building before its grand opening as Guthrie Gardens Condominiums with prices starting as low as two hundred and seventy-five thousand dollars. I invited her here today so that she could perform the exorcism after the press had an opportunity to look at the fabulous jewelry we found stashed between the second and third floors where our Swedish craftsmen were restoring the rich hardwoods that have been an integral part of the building since it was built in 1908. The original stucco walls will be . . ."

Still feeling stifled and noticing that some of the TV crew members had shifted positions to get a better angle on Guthrie, Judith decided to disappear. Edging around a trio of busy cameramen, she reached the hallway and peered into the living room. Sure enough, she noticed a gaping hole in the floor near the old-fashioned radiator. But before she could get closer, footsteps pounded in her direction.

No police for me, she thought, dashing to a door that she hoped led into another bedroom.

It didn't. Judith found herself in the dark. Apparently, she had gone into a coat closet.

But she wasn't alone. Heavy breathing met her ears. She stiffened, fumbling for the doorknob.

A hand reached out, gripping her by the upper arm. Judith sucked in her breath, then tried to pull away.

The grip was firm. The voice that echoed inside the empty closet wasn't.

"C-c-coz?"

"Coz?" Judith felt the hand fall away from her arm. "What are you doing in here?"

"Hiding from the cops," Renie replied, panting a bit. "I saw them coming up the stairs when I was looking for you from the balcony. You didn't kill Jeremy Lamar, did you?"

"Of course not. Someone else got killed instead," Judith replied, then paused to listen. She could hear more footsteps—medics, perhaps, or firefighters.

"Killed?" Renie sounded aghast. "Who?"

"An exorcist named Carrabas, from California," Judith said, still listening intently. "It could be a hoax."

"What do you mean?" Renie demanded.

"I don't know," Judith said in a bemused voice. "It's almost as if I expected to find a dead body. What's wrong with me?"

"You're numb," Renie replied.

"What if I'm callous?" Judith said in a weak voice.

"No. Not you." Renie also sounded weary. "Maybe you're right, it's a put-up job for publicity. And if it's real, it hasn't sunk in. I went looking for you and heard voices. How did the media get here so fast?"

"They came for something else," Judith answered. "Some kind of treasure the workmen found." She hauled herself into a standing position. "We've got to get out of here. It's hot and airless. I feel faint."

"Can you hear anybody in the living room?" Renie asked.

Judith listened. "No. We'd better make a run for it before they start coming out of the bedroom. I don't want any more microphones stuck in my face."

Pushing the door open wide, the cousins fled. Judith led the way, heading straight for the stairs. They clambered down the three flights, careful to avoid the occasional tool. Moments later, they were in the courtyard. Work had stopped, as the construction crew milled about, talking, smoking, and, it appeared, speculating on what had brought all the emergency vehicles to the Alhambra.

Judith hesitated only a few seconds, then hurried outside as fast as her aching body parts would permit.

"We're leaving?" Renie asked in surprise.

"You bet," Judith said. "I've had it. I find it utterly unbelievable that I could be slandered and come upon a corpse in less than an hour. I'm almost certain it's a prank, a stunt to promote the tour. Mrs. Carrabas isn't dead, she just knows how to hold her breath for a long time. So no more bodies, no more insults, no more overbearing reporters for this kid. I'll deal with Jeremy Lamar later. For now, I'm going home."

Renie looked flummoxed. "How?"

"See these?" Judith pointed to her feet. "Crippled I may be, but it's only about six blocks to the B&B."

"But my car's down by the opera house," Renie protested.

"I'll drive you down there to get it," Judith said, already heading across the street.

"But those six blocks are uphill," Renie pointed out in a voice that was growing desperate.

"If I can make it, you can. Anyway," she added, "it's only four blocks straight up. The last two are on the flat."

Renie made muttering noises, but traipsed behind Judith. After the noisy, crowded, stuffy bedroom with its gruesome remains, the walk uphill was more restorative than demanding. The mountain ash, maple, and chestnut trees were still in full leaf, providing welcome shade. Judith took deep breaths, savoring the blooms of a climbing rose on the wall of a big brick apartment

house in the next block. The farther she walked, the
more familiar the neighborhood became. The condos
and apartments on the south slope of Heraldsgate Hill
gave way to duplexes, family homes, and a small park.
By the time the cousins reached level ground, they were
among old, spacious homes with magnificent views of
downtown, the bay, and the mountains to the west.

"Are you okay?" Judith asked a trailing Renie.

"No," Renie replied, huffing and puffing. "I'm dead."

"Don't say that," Judith shot back. "No more dead,
remember?"

"If that woman really is dead, the police will want to
talk to you," Renie reminded her cousin.

Judith sighed. "I know. But I just couldn't face it. Not
after the cameras and the mikes and all those journal-
ists." Waiting for Renie to catch up, Judith brightened.
"Maybe they won't be able to find me. I had to give my
name to that TV woman, but I'm not on the tour list."

"They'll find you," Renie said dryly. "But at least
you'll be able to meet them on your own turf."

It was after one o'clock when the cousins arrived at
Hillside Manor. Instead of using the usual family
entrance at the back, they sneaked through the front,
hoping to avoid Gertrude.

"I need a few minutes to collect myself," Judith said,
collapsing into one of the kitchen chairs. "I also need a
drink."

"I'll do the honors while you fill me in on everything—body, treasure, media circus." Renie was standing on tiptoes, reaching for the bourbon and Scotch.

"Spirits!" cried Phyliss Rackley, who dropped a bun-
dle of cleaning rags and threw up her hands. "The Devil
is at work!"

"So are you," Renie retorted, deliberately pouring
more than just a shot into each glass. "What's up, Phyl?"

"Satan," Phyliss replied, glaring at Renie. "I've
always suspected you have cloven hooves and a tail.

You're an evil influence, Mrs. Jones. Haven't I always said that?"

"Pretty often," Renie said, getting ice out of the fridge. "Care for a drink?" She waved the Scotch bottle at the cleaning woman.

"Ayiee!" Phyliss recoiled, hands in front of her face. "You're doomed, Mrs. Jones, and you're taking poor Mrs. Flynn with you!"

"Let's hope it's a big handcart if we're going to hell in it," Renie said, handing Judith her drink and sitting down at the kitchen table.

Phyliss ripped off her apron and glowered at Judith. "I quit. I can't work in a house where Beelzebub reigns. Good-bye, Mrs. Flynn."

"Good-bye, Phyliss," Judith said. "See you Monday."

Renie watched Phyliss flounce out through the back door. "How come she's leaving early?"

"She has a two o'clock eye appointment," Judith said. "The tests she had done yesterday didn't reveal anything wrong with her brain—medically speaking, of course—so now she thinks she's going blind."

"Why couldn't she have become a Christian Scientist?" Renie said with a little sigh. "Then you would've been spared the hypochondria."

"I'd have been spared all of it," Judith said. "Christian Scientists don't run around trying to save people all the time. As it is, I'm not spared, and I may not be saved, either."

Sipping her bourbon, Renie smiled. "She's a good worker, though. Except for dumping dirty rags on the floor. I'll pick them up. You don't need another fall."

Just as Renie got up from the chair, the front doorbell rang. "Shall I?" Renie asked, gathering up the rags.

"Okay," Judith sighed. "Let's hope it's not guests. Check-in time isn't until four."

Taking another gulp from her Scotch, Judith also stood up and went over to the aspirin bottle on the windowsill. She had just swallowed two tablets when Renie appeared in the swinging door that separated the kitchen from the dining room.

"You've got visitors," Renie said, her face devoid of expression. "It's the cops."

THREE

ONLY THEN DID it dawn on Judith that she might have fled a crime scene. So unreal was the discovery of Mrs. Carrabas's body, so highly suspect, so utterly incredible, that Judith refused to believe any of it was real. Picking up her glass, she swigged down Scotch and tried to collect herself.

"Was that woman really dead?" she whispered as Renie waited between the swinging doors.

Renie shrugged. "Nobody's talking. About that, I mean," she added cryptically.

Curious, as well as upset, Judith followed Renie into the entry hall, where two uniformed officers stood outside the near door to the front parlor. That, she realized, was not a good sign. The primaries— the plainclothes detectives—would be waiting inside. Then again, maybe it was the bunco squad, investigating a hoax. Judith squared her wide shoulders and went into the parlor, which suddenly seemed more ominous than cozy.

When she saw the black man with the walrus mustache, she almost fainted in relief. "Woody!" she cried, and threw her arms around his neck.

Woodrow Wilson Price had been Joe's partner for years. He was one of Judith's favorite people, and

had been at Hillside Manor with his family last month
for a Fourth of July barbecue. But Judith greeted him as
if he'd been away for ten years.

Her euphoria ebbed when she saw his new partner,
Sancha Rael. Detective Rael was young, beautiful, and
not inclined to defer to anyone, including the wife of a
retired detective.

"Hello, Mrs. Flynn," she said, her dark eyes snapping. "I haven't seen you since my last promotion. In
fact, I've moved up two notches since you found the
other body over at the house on the cul-de-sac."

The comment—and what it implied—referred to a
hatchet murder that had occurred a few years earlier
during the holiday season. "Other body?" Judith said
bleakly as she let go of Woody.

Sancha frowned at Judith. "Are you kidding? With all
your experience, I would have thought you'd know a
corpse when you saw one. Mrs. Carrabas was shot twice
in the chest."

"Oh, dear!" Judith half-fell into one of the matching
club chairs. "I'm sorry, I was clinging to the hope that it
was some kind of publicity stunt for the murder tour."

Woody, whose serious demeanor was always in evidence during an investigation, shook his head. "I don't
blame you for wanting to believe that. But the fact is,
Mrs. Carrabas hadn't been dead for more than a few
minutes before you found her." He paused and cleared
his throat. "Naturally, we wondered why you left the
scene so hurriedly. It didn't seem like you. If you know
what I mean." He sounded apologetic.

"I . . ." Judith wished she'd brought her drink with
her. Renie must have guessed what she was thinking.

"Hey," Renie put in, "I'll make some coffee for you
folks. We were just having an adult beverage to restore
ourselves. It's been an awful day, as I'm sure Judith will
be able to tell you. I'll be right back."

Trying to unscramble her brain, Judith dredged up
her usual logical train of thought and began at the

beginning. "So naturally, I was upset," she said after relating how she and Renie came to be on a sightseeing tour that had kicked off with the dreadful stop at Hillside Manor. "I was upset. I wanted to see Jeremy Lamar so I could tell him to lay off my B&B before I took him to court. I tracked him down, but I didn't make it in time to the elevator. I saw that he got out on the third floor, so I did, too. The door to the unit where I found Mrs. Carrabas was open. I went in to see if Jeremy was there, but he wasn't. Instead . . . I found another damned body." Judith hung her head. Reality was setting in, and she didn't much like what she felt. Sick. Stupid. Still incredulous.

"What did you do then?" Woody asked in his soft, mellifluous voice.

"Nothing." Judith gulped. "There wasn't even time to see if I could find a pulse before all those reporters and cameramen rushed in. The next thing I knew, I was on TV, acting inane. Honestly, I thought it was a hoax."

Woody nodded slowly. "Unfortunately, it wasn't. I gather you'd never seen Mrs. Carrabas before?"

"Heavens, no," Judith replied. "I'd never heard of her, either."

Sancha leaned forward in the other club chair. "Are you sure? I heard that you've been known to hang out with fortune tellers and such."

Judith looked askance. "A guest invited a fortune teller to Hillside Manor. I'd never seen her before in my life. What are you implying?"

Sancha shrugged, the blue-black hair rippling over her shoulders. "It seems strange, that's all. Fortune tellers, exorcists, mediums—you do meet some odd people."

"I've never met a medium," Judith said staunchly. "Besides, as an innkeeper I meet all sorts of people. I suppose it's why I get mixed up in so many unfortunate situations."

Sancha smirked, but said nothing more. Woody

leaped in to fill the uncomfortable void. "How much did you know about this mystery tour and the Alhambra Arms before today?"

"She's ignorant," Renie declared as she entered the parlor carrying the cousins' cocktails. "This was all my doing. In fact, I forced her to go with me." Pausing, she handed Judith her Scotch. "Coffee will be along shortly. Let me explain about the SOTS auction."

"The what?" Sancha asked, wrinkling her nose.

"It's their church," Woody said in an aside to his partner.

"I don't doubt it," Sancha said with another smirk.

"Anyway," Renie continued, ignoring the female detective, "we held our annual auction last May, and I sort of got carried away and—"

"I'll check on the coffee," Judith interrupted, going out through the parlor door. In the hallway, she stopped as the arrival of a white van in the cul-de-sac caught her eye. It parked just down the street, in front of the Porters' house. No one got out, so Judith continued on into the kitchen.

By the time she returned to the parlor with a tray containing a carafe, mugs, sugar, and cream, Renie had finished the part about the Meacham murder.

"It was while the guide was finishing her spiel that I noticed Judith was missing," Renie said. "I was afraid she was in a knock-down-drag-out fight with Jeremy Lamar, so I went looking for her."

"Why did you end up in the bedroom?" Sancha inquired, turning to Judith.

"I was curious," Judith said, growing defensive. "The apartment hadn't yet been torn up, so I thought I'd see what the units had been like. The Alhambra is only six blocks from Hillside Manor, but it's off the beaten path, and I've never paid much attention to it."

"I have," Renie put in. "Several years ago, I put together a design package for the Heraldsgate Hill Historical Society. I went all through it then, along with some of the other landmark buildings in the neighborhood. I remembered quite a bit about the place, including the fact that the fountain in the courtyard was once a swimming pool. In its heyday, the Alhambra was a very exclusive apartment complex."

"Fascinating," Sancha declared in a bored voice.

Woody gave his partner a look of mild reproach. "It is, actually. I heard somewhere that a famous opera singer lived there in retirement. I can't recall the name offhand, but she was something of a recluse." He looked at Renie for help. They shared an interest in opera that had created a bond between them over the years.

"Luisa Della Robbia," Renie said promptly. "Coloratura, retired young due to vocal troubles. Before the turn of the century, she was heralded as one of the greatest Lucias of the era."

Woody snapped his fingers and grinned. "That's right. Unfortunately, her career was almost over when the phonograph came along. She made only a few recordings. Della Robbia was nicknamed 'The Diamond Necklace' because her voice had such sparkle."

"Fascinating," Sancha repeated, still bored. "What did you two know about this so-called treasure?"

"Nothing," Judith responded. "I didn't even know about the Meacham murder." She turned to Renie. "Did you, coz?"

Renie shook her head. "No. It was never mentioned. But that was because I did the design project before they started the renovation. At the time, Dorothy Meacham would still have been a missing person."

"Is there really a treasure?" Judith asked as unusual noises emanated from outside.

"Gold and silver jewelry, mostly," Woody said. "It was under the floor near the exterior wall in the living room. Given that Mrs. Carrabas was killed in that same unit, we've bundled it up as possible evidence. Mr. Guthrie wasn't very happy about it, though. He thinks the stuff is very old and very valuable."

"Who's been living in that apartment?" Judith asked as the noise grew louder.

"No one," Woody replied after quickly consulting his notes. "It's been vacant for several months. A man named Rufus Holmes lived next door until everybody had to leave. It seems that Guthrie has offered the previous rental tenants the opportunity to buy their refurbished units as condos. At a rather high price, of course. Most of the renters have decided to move on, but a few, such as Mr. Holmes and a retired school teacher, Helen Schnell, are staying. Meanwhile, though, they've had to move out until the renovation is completed."

Judith was on her feet. "Excuse me, there seems to be some commotion out front. Let's hope the tour bus didn't come back."

The Toujours La Tour trolley wasn't in evidence, but two more vans were parked in the cul-de-sac, and at least a half-dozen people were swarming across Judith's lawn.

"Oh, no!" Judith cried aloud. "It's the press. Again."

Cable cords crawled over the grass like so many snakes. Some of the faces behind the cameras already looked familiar. In fact, the woman who was marching toward the porch came from out of the past: The fine features, the smart blond coiffure, the aura of complete self-confidence might have been reassuring in any other context, but given the circumstances, KINE-TV's anchorwoman, Mavis Lean-Brodie, appeared like the Angel of Death.

"M-M-Mavis!" Judith stammered. "How . . . nice."

Mavis's smile, like the rest of her, was slightly brittle. "I haven't seen you since the fortune teller got killed here while we were having a not-so-jolly family overnight. I see you're up to your old tricks."

"W-w-well . . ." Judith was still stammering. "N-n-not exactly. I mean, what's going on with all these people?"

Mavis waved a hand over her shoulder. "When Liz Ogilvy came back to the station and mentioned your name, I was sure you must be the same person who had hosted our gruesome little gathering several years ago. It occurred to me that you had popped up in connection with some other murders. Judith McMonigle then, Judith Flynn now, right?" Mavis didn't wait for a response. "So here we are, ready to do an exclusive KINE-TV feature on Heraldsgate Hill's answer to Nancy Drew."

"Oh, no!" Judith protested in horror as the TV crew finished setting up. "Please, Mavis, I'm no sleuth. I just . . . sort of . . . you know . . . fall into things."

"Right." Mavis winked. "Could that be an unmarked police car in your driveway?"

Judith winced. "Yes, but that's only because—"

"Tell you what," Mavis interrupted in her chummiest manner, "let's show you coming to the door as if you're greeting guests." She turned to one of the cameramen. "Get a close-up of that Hillside Manor sign next to the sidewalk. Very tasteful, very discreet," she added in approval.

"Cousin Renie did it," Judith gulped.

"Oh, yes—Renie." Mavis rolled her eyes. "Now—go inside, shut the door, and come out again. Smiling. Got it?"

As usual, Judith couldn't say no. With a heavy sigh, she did as she was told. She was certain that the smile she presented for the camera probably looked like a death mask.

"Now what?" she inquired in a flat tone.

Mavis was consulting a ringed binder. "Let me think—we'll need to sit down and talk about some of your other cases. As I recall, your living room is large and very photogenic."

This time, Judith held firm. "I have the police inside, remember? We'll have to do this another time."

"The police!" Mavis beamed, then beckoned to her crew. "We're doing an indoor shoot. Let's hit it."

Before Judith could voice her objections, Mavis led the charge through the front door and into the parlor. Renie, Woody, and Sancha all looked up in surprise.

"Mavis?" Renie said.

Mavis gave Renie a quick nod. "Detective Price," the anchorwoman said, wringing Woody's hand. "We've met on several occasions. And you, Ms. . . . Sorry, I forget."

"Rael," Sancha replied coldly. "Sancha Rael. That's R-A-E . . ."

Mavis waved a hand. "Never mind, we don't spell on television. Okay, let's get a two-shot, Ms. Flynn and Detective Price." She jerked a thumb at Renie and Sancha. "You two move it. Make sure you're well out of camera range. Come on, let's—"

Renie hunkered down in the chair. "I can't move. I'm having a spell."

"Too bad the exorcist got killed," Mavis snapped. "Maybe she could have broken it. As it is," she went on with a menacing expression and the shaking of her fist, "I'm going to—"

"I'm Detective Price's partner," Sancha declared, not budging an inch. "We work as a team. If he gets on TV, so do I."

"I don't want to be on TV," Renie said. "I just want to cause trouble."

Apparently acknowledging that she was outnumbered, Mavis's face softened. "Of course. Stay put, Ms. Jones. Detective Rael, I'll do a close-up of you after I finish with Detective Price and Ms. Flynn. Now," she continued, gesturing at her technical support, "let's take up where you left off, Detective Price. I assume you were asking Ms. Flynn what ideas she has about who killed Mrs. Carrabas."

"Not exactly," Woody murmured. "At this point, our inquiries are strictly routine."

"We can't tip our hand at this stage of the investigation," Sancha asserted, thrusting her face next to Woody's.

Making another gesture at her cameraman, Mavis seemed undaunted. "Pretend, then, Detective Price."

Before Woody could respond, Renie swung her legs over the arm of the chair, hit the coffee carafe with her feet, and sent it crashing to the floor.

"Oops!" She jumped up to grab the carafe before it could spill onto the rug. "Sorry, folks. It's a good thing the carafe's stainless steel and not ceramic. See?" she said, holding it up in front of the camera. "The stopper doesn't open in these babies until you do this." Renie twisted the top; several drops of coffee splattered on Mavis's suede pumps. "Oops!" Renie said again.

Mavis was gritting her teeth as she grabbed a napkin from the tray and dabbed at her shoes. "I'd forgotten what a clumsy person you are," she said, eyes like daggers aimed at Renie. "Now let me see . . ." Mavis consulted her binder again. "Aimee Carrabas, of Studio City, California, age fifty-two. Owner and operator of Exes and Hexes, Inc. What do you think, Ms. Flynn? Better yet, you ask her that question, Detective Price."

"I can do it," Sancha put in. "Only let me rephrase so it sounds more—"

"Butt out!" Mavis commanded, then offered Woody a bogus smile. "Go ahead, Detective Price."

Woody scowled at Mavis. "As a matter of fact, Detective Rael and I were just about finished here. This isn't a media circus, Ms. Lean-Brodie, this is a homicide investigation. We're not playing parts for your—"

"Cut!" yelled Mavis. "Perfect, right up to 'We're not blah-blah.' Okay, let's follow Ms. Flynn and the detectives out the front door. Come on, guys, move it."

"Woody," Judith began as she got to her feet, "I'm so sorry about this. I had no idea."

"I know." Woody smiled, though otherwise he looked pained. "We'll be in touch. Meanwhile, don't worry. You're not a suspect. Have Joe call me when he gets back from Alaska."

"I will," Judith promised, then kissed Woody's cheek. "Give my love to Sondra and the kids."

"Me, too," Renie shouted, jumping up and down so that she could be seen behind the much taller TV personnel. "Bye, Woody."

"Great," Mavis enthused. "That kiss was perfect. Okay, Judith, let's do our interview. How about starting with the fortune teller? We'll just leave my name out of that one."

"I don't see how," Judith snapped. "You were a suspect."

"Hardly," Mavis said with scorn. "Okay, we'll skip it. How about the Easter Bunny?"

"No." Judith had finally found the courage to resist. "Mavis, I like you, I think you're an outstanding newswoman, but I'm not going to capitalize on what's been plain dumb luck, most of it bad. Please. I appreciate your interest, but I'm not really a sleuth."

"Okay." The sparkle in Mavis's eyes wasn't completely lost on Judith. "We'll wrap it up. Thanks, Judith. Got to run. Deadlines and all that."

Mavis and her minions departed. Judith leaned against the door-frame, shaking her head. "Drat. What a dumb idea for a TV feature. I'm no Nancy Drew."

"You're not eternally eighteen," Renie said, watching the KINE-TV crew load the vans. "Nancy never grew up. If she had, she'd probably be dead by now."

"Or at least as old as our mothers," Judith remarked, going back inside and firmly closing the door. "Why don't you stay for dinner?"

"Well . . ." Renie mulled. "Okay, but I'll need to check my messages from here. Then maybe I can start playing around with some ideas for your Web site. But first we have to collect my car."

When the cousins reached the bottom of the hill in Judith's Subaru, they saw the tour trolley, sitting empty. Briefly, Judith considered seeking out Jeremy Lamar. But there wasn't time. The B&B guests would be arriving any minute.

After letting Renie out to claim the Camry, Judith turned around to head back into traffic. The commute had already begun, with vehicles streaming toward the freeway entrance less than a mile away. Drumming her nails on the steering wheel, she gave a start when someone tapped on her window.

"Ma'am?" mouthed Alfred Ashe. "How are you?"

Quickly, Judith rolled the window down. "Dr. Ashe," she said in surprise. "I'm better, thanks to you."

"It was nothing," Alfred said modestly. "Is it true you found that dead woman?"

Judith nodded grimly. "I'm afraid so. Were you able to finish the tour?"

"No." Alfred looked miffed, his long eyelashes swooping downward. "The police had to question each of us, and then some of the other tourists had appointments elsewhere, so we had to get rainchecks. We only arrived back here a few minutes ago. I'm waiting for a cab."

Glancing in the rearview mirror, Judith saw Renie behind her, waving impatiently. "Can you take the tour again?" Judith asked as she eased up on the brake.

"I don't know," Alfred replied, his heavy black brows coming together in a frown. "I'm only in town for a few days. Tell me, do you know what kind of treasure they found at the Alhambra?"

"Some jewelry, I think," Judith replied, feeling Renie nudge the Subaru with the Camry's bumper. "I didn't see it. Excuse me, I really must go."

"Of course." Alfred stepped back as Renie let loose with a half-dozen honks of the horn.

Luckily, there was an opening in the parade of cars. The street was one-way, which meant Judith had to

cross three lanes to get over to the left so she could turn
back up the hill. It took her four blocks to squeeze into
the proper lane. Five minutes later, she was at Hillside
Manor. Renie was already there, leaning on the Camry's
roof. Judith didn't want to know what maniacal maneu-
vers her cousin had used to get back so fast.

"What kept you?" Renie asked in a vexed tone.

Judith was angry; her voice dripped with sarcasm.
"Don't ever bump my car again. I thought Cammy was
too precious to use as a battering ram."

"She is," Renie replied, giving her car an affectionate
pat. "But she's also very strong."

"Bunk," Judith said, going around to the back door.
"Couldn't you see I was talking to Dr. Ashe?"

"Dr. Ashe?" Renie frowned. "Is that who that was? I
thought it was some boob asking for directions."

"You're terrible when it comes to recognizing people," Judith declared, unlocking the door. "You can
identify antiques, architecture, paintings, even graffiti,
but faces mean nothing to you. I don't get it."

"Hey—knuckleheads!" Gertrude was stomping out
to the patio on her walker. "Where's my candy?"

Judith opened the door but stepped back. "What
candy?"

"Didn't you go to Gut Busters?" Gertrude demanded.
"You always get me that ten-pound bag of chocolate-
covered peanuts."

Judith stepped down to the walkway. "We didn't go
to Gut Busters. Renie and I took a mystery tour."

Gertrude's small, wrinkled face twisted like a
corkscrew. "You *what*?"

"Never mind." Judith waved a hand in dismissal. "I'll
go to Gut Busters on Monday."

Gertrude banged the walker so hard that the statue of
St. Francis on the small patio shook on its pedestal. "*Go
now*. I may be dead by Monday."

"No, you won't," Judith countered. "You've got boxes

of candy in your dresser drawer. Why don't you open one of them?"

"I did," Gertrude replied. "But it's half-gone. That redheaded woman ate most of it."

"What redheaded woman?" Judith rubbed at her temples. Gertrude's delusions were very upsetting.

"The one from TV," Gertrude replied. "Big woman. She shouldn't eat so much candy."

Aghast, Judith marched up to her mother. "Are you talking about Liz Ogilvy?" Sometimes the delusions were preferable to reality.

"Right," Gertrude responded, suddenly looking sly. "I'm going to be on the news. What do you think of that, toots?"

Judith felt as if all the color had drained out of her face. "What did you tell them?"

"Wouldn't you like to know," Gertrude snickered.

"Oh, good grief!" Judith held her head.

"Hey," Renie called from the porch, "how do you get into your B&B program on the computer?" She waved both hands over her head. "Hi, Aunt Gertrude."

"Hi, dopey," Gertrude shot back. "You got any candy?"

"Sorry, I'm fresh out," Renie replied, then swerved around. "Hey, there's somebody at the front door. Should I let them in?"

Rattled, Judith turned this way and that. "I'll do it," she finally said, half-stumbling back to the house. "It's probably guests."

"Hey," Gertrude shouted. *"Where's my candy?"*

"Look under your bloomers," Renie said. "Second drawer, to the right." She, too, went back inside.

By five o'clock, all the guests had arrived, filling Hillside Manor's six rooms. They were a far-flung bunch, from Suffolk, San Mateo, St. Louis, Saskatchewan, Singapore, and South Dakota. In between arrivals, Judith prepared the appetizers for the six o'clock social hour while Renie plied the computer and swore a lot.

"Think big," she said to Judith. "What's your theme?"

Judith frowned. "Comfort? Coziness? Congeniality?"

Renie shook her head. "No good. Think bigger."

"I can't, not now," Judith replied, sounding grumpy. "I'm too frazzled." She placed a tray of deviled eggs topped with crab and shrimp in the fridge, then looked up at the clock. "It's five-oh-five. Dare we?"

"The news?" Renie wrinkled her pug nose, then clicked the mouse several times. "I never watch the news. Almost never, anyway."

Judith grimaced. "I think I'd better. I'm going upstairs."

Renie heaved a big sigh. "Okay, I'll come with you," she said shutting down the B&B program. "You realize that if another big story has broken, you may not be on."

"That's what I'm hoping," Judith said as she started up the back stairs. "Either that, or we've missed it."

Joe had recently bought a large-screen TV for the sitting room in the third floor family quarters. Judith flopped down on the loveseat and clicked the remote. Mavis Lean-Brodie and a handsome young Asian man were seated behind a desk with the KINE-TV logo prominently displayed.

"... In the polluted waters of Lake ..." Mavis was saying as the picture on the screen switched to a brackish pool.

"That's not me," Judith said with relief. "I should have made drinks."

"I'm good," Renie said. "I stole a Pepsi while I was fiddling with your stuff on the computer."

An overhead shot of the Pentagon appeared next. "That's not me," Judith repeated. "Air strikes," "overt aggression," and "unspeakable atrocities" were the phrases that floated from a grim-visaged man in a dark suit and muted tie. A commercial break followed. Judith hit the mute button.

"You know," she said, "that was an odd question Dr. Ashe asked this afternoon. He stopped me while I was trying to pull out into traffic, and I forgot about it until now because you got me so riled."

"I did?" Renie's brown eyes were all innocence. "What did he say?"

"He asked what kind of treasure they found at the Alhambra," Judith replied.

"What's odd about that?"

"He didn't really ask about Mrs. Carrabas," Judith said. "Wouldn't that have been the natural thing to do?"

"Maybe he'd already been told about her," Renie said.

"Well . . . maybe." She remained silent for a moment as the news resumed, this time with a financial expert spouting stock quotes. "The rest of the tour group was questioned by the police. I suppose they filled them in on what had happened." Again, Judith grew quiet. The weatherman appeared, pointing to a map of the state's western half. "Except they don't. I mean, in a homicide investigation, witnesses aren't told anything."

Renie gave a little shrug. "They must have told them that Mrs. Carrabas had been murdered. What else would he need to know?"

"That's my point," Judith said. "You'd think Dr. Ashe would want to know more. Instead, he inquired after the treasure."

"You're being weird," Renie said, though without reproach. "Oh—sports. Turn the sound back on. Let's see how our team is faring on its road trip back east."

The local baseball team had lost the first end of a doubleheader. Renie groaned. "It's that damned bullpen," she lamented. "They couldn't stop our mothers."

"Neither can we," Judith said dryly as the sports reporter moved on to the local football team's upcoming season opener.

The phone rang on the side table next to the loveseat. Judith picked it up and, coincidentally, heard Aunt Deb's voice at the other end.

"Do you know where Renie is?" she asked in a frantic voice. "She should have been back hours ago from that crazy tour you two went on. I'm sure something's happened. With Bill and the grandchildren gone, and her all alone, I know she must have had some kind of accident or she would have called me by now. You never can tell these days with so many bad drivers out there, and Mrs. Parker was telling me this afternoon that her grandson was in a wreck last night only two blocks from his—"

"Aunt Deb!" Judith said sharply, having already tried to break into the nonstop monologue in gentler ways. "Renie's right here. We're having dinner together. Do you want to talk to her?"

"Of course I do!" Aunt Deb said in a strangled voice. "Thank goodness!"

Ignoring Renie's protests, Judith handed her cousin the phone just as the station switched to another commercial break. Once again, Judith hit the mute button, and wished she could do the same with Renie.

"I'm sorry," Renie was saying, her expression harassed. "I should have called from here . . . Well, it wasn't such a good tour after all . . . No, nobody got fresh with us . . . Yes, I kept warm. How could I not? It's over eighty . . . No, we didn't get off the bus without a chaperone . . . Yes, I wore sensible shoes, though you must remember, Mom, I haven't worn those high-top oxfords for several years now . . . No, I'd forgotten that your old boss, Mr. Whiffel, had lived with his sister in the Alhambra Arms . . . Yes, it was . . . um . . . an interesting place . . ."

Liz Ogilvy was in a close-up; Judith turned the sound back on.

"In KINE-TV's top story," Liz was saying, "we promised an insider's look at a woman who was on the murder scene today. Judith Flynn is a local B&B hostess who . . ."

Judith made wild gestures at Renie. The screen now showed a bug-eyed Judith in the bedroom at the Alhambra. Renie told her mother she had to ring off. Aunt Deb kept talking. Renie banged all the buttons with her fist, then shouted that the phone was broken and hung up.

". . . Not only discovered the body just before KINE-TV arrived at the scene," Liz was saying, "but has a reputation for actually solving several other homicides in the past ten years."

Judith saw herself still in the bedroom, sweat dripping down her high forehead, short salt-and-pepper hair plastered against her pale cheeks. "She might have been stabbed or shot, but I don't see a weapon."

Judith grimaced. As far as she could recall, she had said that. The scene shifted slightly. Judith now looked rubber-legged and half-crocked as she tried to balance herself on the walnut bureau. "I was shocked. And saddened."

"But," a brisk-voiced Mavis was now saying from the lawn in front of Hillside Manor, "it takes more than murder to put our heroine out of action. An hour or so later, she was back on the job—the *real* job—at Hillside Manor."

Judith, with a forced smile that looked ghoulish enough to be mistaken for the work of a drunken undertaker, opened the door to the B&B. Mavis did the voiceover. "Bodies or no bodies, Judith Flynn makes her guests feel like *somebody*. Even as she welcomes the latest visitors to Hillside Manor, detectives await her advice on today's brutal slaying."

Woody, slightly out of focus, scowled at the camera. His face took up most of the screen, with only a stray strand of Sancha's hair visible near his shoulder. "This is a homicide investigation," he asserted. "We're not playing."

"Hey," Judith cried as Sweetums wandered into the room. "They cut off the rest of what Woody said."

"I figured they would," Renie responded, eyes glued on the set which showed Judith kissing Woody good-bye.

"Obviously," Mavis purred, "there's great respect and affection between our city's detectives and Mrs. Flynn. How does she solve cases that defy even the experts? Maybe it's an inherited quality. KINE-TV's Liz Ogilvy spent some time this afternoon visiting with Judith's mother, Gertrude Grover, in her cozy apartment behind the B&B."

Gertrude was seated at her cluttered card table, proffering candy. The screen cut to a close-up; Gertrude mugged for the camera. "Sure, my girl's always had a way with her when it comes to trouble. You should have seen her first . . . murder. The second one was almost as gruesome. I swore I couldn't live . . . without her."

Judith gripped Renie's arm. "Mother's talking about my *husbands*, not homicides. They've chopped up the quotes. I'll bet she said she wanted to murder Dan and that she couldn't live under the same roof as Joe."

Renie merely nodded as Mavis resumed speaking. "Like mother like daughter, and both media-friendly. Indeed, our dauntless sleuth understands how the media, especially KINE-TV, can help."

On screen, Judith stood in the doorway. "I think you're an outstanding newswoman," she said with an earnest expression.

Mavis, still in the front yard with Hillside Manor behind her, beamed into the camera. "Thanks for those kind words, Judith Flynn. We know you'll be on top of this investigation, and KINE-TV will keep its viewers informed with every step our supersleuth takes."

Judith clicked off the TV, then put her head down and started to cry. "I can't stand it!" she wept.

"Hey," Renie said, putting an arm around Judith's

shoulder, "it's not that bad, really. You come off as a heroic figure."

"Heroic?" With tearstained cheeks, Judith looked up at Renie. "That's not quite what I meant. I can't stand up. It's these damned hips. What am I going to do?"

FOUR

RENIE SERVED THE guests their beverages and appetizers while Judith lay on the loveseat with a Scotch at her right hand and a heating pad on her right hip. It was seven o'clock before her cousin returned, bearing a tray with two green salads and two plates smothered in what looked suspiciously like Renie's infamous shrimp dump. Of a yellow, lumpy, glue-like consistency, a serving had once been used by the Jones's elder son, Tom, as ski wax. He'd told his mother it had worked quite well, but when it came to food, he'd prefer eating his skis. The rest of the Joneses, including Bill, sided with Tom.

Judith winced as she examined the glop on her plate. "Did you make this for Mother, too?"

Renie nodded.

"What did she say?"

"Nothing."

"You mean she ate it?"

"I didn't say that."

Judith winced some more. "What happened?"

"She gave it to Sweetums. He loved it. I went back into the house and fixed your mother a Hungry Hunk roast beef TV dinner."

Judith relaxed a bit. "Good."

54

"How do you feel?" Renie inquired, stuffing her face with shrimp dump.

"Stiff," Judith replied. "Sore. Upset. I'll call Dr. Alfonso first thing Monday for an appointment."

"Promise?"

"Yes."

"You'd better," Renie said in a warning voice. "You keep putting it off in your procrastinating way."

"Not this time," Judith said grimly. "It's gotten to the point where my hips hurt almost all the time."

"I'll spend the night," Renie volunteered.

"You don't have to."

"Of course I don't have to," Renie replied with a spark in her eyes. "But you know I will."

"How did it go with the guests?" Judith inquired, reluctantly tasting the shrimp dump. Somewhere underneath were two pastry puffs. Amazingly, the concoction was actually palatable.

"I got along fine with the current batch of visitors," Renie said. "I kept my mouth shut."

"That's a relief," Judith said. "Say, this isn't half-bad."

"Of course it's not," Renie said indignantly. "It's like what my father used to say about the singed cat. It tastes better than it looks."

"I've thought about singeing Sweetums," Judith said. "Say, did you bring in tonight's newspaper?"

"Yes." Renie gobbled salad.

"Where is it?"

"I'm not sure."

Unease crept over Judith. "What do you mean?"

Renie avoided Judith's gaze. "I was in a hurry, I had so much to do. Maybe I lost it."

"You did not. What's in it?" Judith demanded.

Renie made a face. "A picture? Some copy? The funny papers?"

"Coz . . ."

Renie threw up her hands, sending salad dressing in

several directions. "Okay, okay. I'll go get it. But you're not going to be happy."

"I'm not happy now." Judith sighed.

Renie was gone so long that Judith began to wonder if her cousin really had mislaid the newspaper. When she finally came back, Woody Price was with her.

"Woody!" Judith exclaimed. "I didn't expect to see you again so soon. Have a seat. Have you eaten?"

Woody cringed slightly as he looked at the remains of the shrimp dump on Judith's plate. "Er . . . no, but Sondra's making manicotti. Or something like that. Thanks anyway."

"Have a seat," Renie offered, pulling out the side chair that matched the loveseat.

Woody sat down, but he didn't look very comfortable. "I'm on my way home. In fact," he said, "I waited for the autopsy report on Mrs. Carrabas. She was shot twice at close range with a 9 mm handgun."

"Have you any leads?" Judith asked.

"Not yet," Woody admitted. "That apartment house was full of people, between the tour, the construction workers, and some of the residents who were still collecting their belongings from their old units."

Judith nodded. "That complicates matters. But certainly most of those people wouldn't know Mrs. Carrabas, let alone have a motive for killing her."

"Exactly." Woody shifted in the chair. "Which is sort of why I stopped by. Gosh, I'm sorry your hips are giving you trouble. Renie says you may need surgery."

"Possibly," Judith said. "I'm calling the surgeon next week."

"That's smart," Woody said. "The last time I saw Joe, he mentioned that you'd been having some problems."

"They've been coming on for quite a while," Judith began, then narrowed her eyes at Woody. "You're stalling. What's going on?"

Woody folded his hands in his lap and looked unhappy. For the first time, Judith noticed that there were flecks of gray in his dark hair and fine lines around his eyes and mouth. A decade ago, when she'd first met Woodrow Price, he'd been young, in his early thirties, with a new wife and a new partner, Joe Flynn. Now he was reaching middle age. Woody had the same wife, a different partner, and three children. Somehow, since Judith had been reunited with Joe after her unfortunate marriage to Dan, the ensuing years had flown by, like petals on a soft summer wind. She couldn't stop the bittersweet smile that formed on her lips.

Woody cleared his throat. "Maybe you've heard or read about some of the criticism lately regarding the force."

Judith had. Joe found much of the negative media reportage aggravating and unfounded. Still, he'd admitted, there were always chinks in the armor, bad apples in the barrel, and all those other cliché exceptions. What was worse, sometimes good cops got bum raps.

"Well," Woody continued, "there's all this talk about a citizens' advisory board of some kind. More involvement from the public. It seems," he said, and his expression was now pained, "that the chief caught that story about you on KINE-TV this evening. He called me in just as I was getting ready to go home. He felt it might be good publicity to get you involved."

"Woody . . ." Judith began.

He held up a hand. "Wait. Please. I know this is a terrible thing to ask. I know Joe won't like it, either. But the chief thinks that since you're the wife of a retired detective and the media are already on to you, it wouldn't hurt to have you serve in a consulting capacity. A citizens' advisory board is being set up. The chief would like you to serve on it. Naturally, you wouldn't have to do any real investigating, just give us some ideas and suggestions." Woody's dark eyes were pleading.

"Oh, Woody." Judith slowly shook her head.

"Hold it," Renie broke in. "Think this through. This afternoon you were practically foaming at the mouth because Jeremy Lamar painted Hillside Manor as Hotel Homicide. You can put a positive spin on that sorry little episode by taking the ball that Liz and Mavis tossed to you and running all the way to the end zone."

Judith glowered at Renie. "You've been watching too much preseason football."

Renie waved a hand in an impatient gesture. "You know what I mean. This is a golden opportunity. You're the Mystery Maven, the Queen of Crime, the Duchess of Death. Use it."

"That's absolutely awful," Judith said.

"Well, maybe it is a bit strong," Renie allowed, "but if you're worried about any bad publicity the tour may have generated, here's a way to turn it around in your favor."

Judith shook her head. "I don't like it. Not at all."

Woody was nodding. "I can understand that." With apparent effort, he rose from the chair. "I'll go back to the chief and tell him you refused."

Noting Woody's slumped shoulders, Judith grimaced. "Wait. I don't want to get you in trouble. You know I'd never do anything to hurt you." She paused, biting her lip. "Okay—but just in an advisory capacity. And only temporarily. I don't have much spare time to attend meetings."

Woody's face lit up. "Judith, you're wonderful." He hurried over to the loveseat and kissed her cheek.

"No soft soap," she warned. "It's because we're friends, and you know it. But if Joe disapproves, the deal's off the table."

Woody nodded eagerly. "Of course. But for now, I'll tell the chief you're considering it."

"Do I get paid?" Judith asked as an afterthought.

Halfway to the door, Woody stopped. "I don't know," he confessed.

"Check it out," Judith said with a straight face. "The Monarch of Mayhem doesn't come cheap."

Woody grinned and left the room.

* * *

The only solace Judith could find in the evening newspaper was that she didn't appear on page one. The story of Aimee Carrabas's murder did, however, though the account kept to the bare facts:

"The body of Aimee Carrabas, a self-styled exorcist, was found shot to death this afternoon at the Alhambra Arms on lower Heraldsgate Hill. The fifty-two-year old Carrabas of Studio City, California, had been shot twice in the chest. Police are investigating."

The article continued, mostly about the Alhambra condo project and George Guthrie's attempt to exorcise the ghost of a woman who had been murdered a half-century ago. A brief reference was made to the discovery of "a stash of jewels under the floorboards, the value of which has not yet been determined." The story jumped to a page toward the rear of the section where Judith gaped at a grainy two-column photograph of herself cowering next to the walnut bureau.

"I look hysterical, deranged," she wailed. "All I need is one of those black bandanas and a ragged shawl. I'd be mistaken for the mother of an earthquake victim or the widow of a slain refugee. Have you ever seen me so demented?"

Considering the question, Renie gazed at the photo for longer than Judith thought was necessary. "Well . . . Not since your mother dropped her dentures in the blender."

"Don't be such a smart-ass," Judith snapped. "I mean it—how could I look so crazed?"

"It's a bad angle," Renie replied, flicking at the photo with her finger. "Inadequate lighting, too. At least your pants aren't falling down."

"Thanks." Judith crumpled the newspaper and tossed it on the floor next to the loveseat. "First I get quoted out of context on TV, then I show up in the paper looking like I should be carted off to the booby hatch."

"I believe," Renie said with irksome calm, "it's called

a mental hospital these days. You sound like your mother."

"I *feel* like my mother," Judith grumbled. "All stiff and sore and about a hundred years old."

"I know," Renie soothed. "But at least the newspaper story kept your part brief."

That much was true. Judith had been relegated to the last paragraph:

"The body was found by Judith Flynn, a member of the Toujours La Tour group that was visiting the Alhambra as part of its inaugural excursion to various crime-related sites around the city."

The caption under the photograph had been only slightly less restrained: "Judith Flynn, a Heraldsgate Hill innkeeper, reacts with horror and dismay after finding the murdered body of Aimee Carrabas at the historic Alhambra Arms."

"See?" said Renie. "It could be worse."

She was right. Joe Flynn exploded when he spotted a similar, if less hideous, photo of his wife in the Saturday morning paper while en route from Alaska. Bill Jones confided to Renie that if Joe hadn't been wearing his seatbelt during a bout of turbulence, he might have hit his head on the DC-10's ceiling.

"How could you do this?" Joe raged at Judith after Renie had brought the returning fishermen from the airport.

"Three thirty-pound Kings," Bill said, smiling at Renie, "all in one morning. We couldn't believe it."

"I can't believe you could get yourself into a mess like this," Joe declared. "A tour? Why would you take a tour in your own hometown?"

"We took a side tour to see the humpback whales," Bill said, removing Joe's heavy-duty raingear from the Camry's trunk. "They're huge, magnificent. We saw a cow with her calf, both sending up water spouts. It was a truly remarkable sight."

"You look like a sight," Joe asserted, slapping at the picture of Judith on the front page of the local section. "Couldn't you have ducked away from the camera?"

"We saw ducks and geese and waterfowl I didn't even recognize," Bill said in an awestruck tone. "There were bear and deer, and the other morning we saw a moose wading in . . ."

Judith stomped into the house and slammed the door.

"What the hell's the matter with her?" Joe asked, suddenly looking puzzled.

Renie let go of Bill's arm and faced Joe. "She just realized that there was a jackass in the driveway. I think that's enough wildlife for Judith."

Joe passed a hand over his forehead. "Hey, I didn't mean to be so rough on her. But my God, I can't leave my wife alone for a few days without her getting into a big mess. What's worse, this time she landed in the newspaper."

"It's my fault," Renie insisted. "She had to be coaxed. Now go be nice to her. She's had a bad fall and her hips are killing her."

Joe scowled at Renie, but finally headed inside. Renie and Bill began unloading Joe's belongings, including his catch, from the Camry's trunk.

Judith was nowhere in sight, so Joe assumed she'd gone up to the family quarters. As he started for the back stairs, however, he heard voices coming from the front of the house.

Hearing her husband approach, Judith stiffened. She didn't know which was worse—Joe's angry outburst or Jeremy Lamar's attempt at an apology. Gertrude was right. Men were skunks.

"Please," Jeremy Lamar was saying, "if you'd let me in, I could explain everything. Please?"

"You defamed me," Judith asserted. "I should sue the socks off you. And you weren't even accurate."

Joe put an arm around Judith. "What's all this?" he asked, scowling at the newcomer in the doorway.

Judith jerked away from Joe. "It's a long story. Butt out."

"Please," Jeremy begged, "could I come in so we can sort this out?"

"What's the point?" Judith shot back. "Your intentions in stopping at Hillside Manor seemed pretty damned obvious. Not to mention that you got me into a situation where I found a dead body and I ended up on TV and all over the newspapers." She whirled on Joe. "Which is the reason my husband here is acting like a big jerk."

"Now wait a minute—" Joe began.

"Butt out, I said," Judith snapped, turning back to Jeremy Lamar. "Okay, I'll give you two minutes."

Judith led Jeremy into the front parlor. Joe lingered in the entry hall. "Now," Judith said, gingerly seating herself in one of the armchairs, "make it quick and to the point."

Jeremy had also sat down but he leaned way over in his chair, gazing at the door. "If that's your husband, then it must be Joe Flynn."

"Brilliant," Judith said sarcastically. "You've got one minute and forty seconds left."

"He's a private detective, isn't he?" Jeremy said. "I want to hire him."

Judith was taken aback. "You do? Why?"

"Because I've heard he's good," Jeremy replied, his boyish face earnest. Indeed, up close and no longer doing his tour guide shtick, he looked much older, perhaps close to forty. "Don't get me wrong, I respect the police, but I think this case is going to be difficult to solve. I mean, I've talked it over with George Guthrie, and we're both willing to pay Mr. Flynn more than the going rate."

Judith glanced into the entry hall. She couldn't see Joe, but she knew he was there. "You'd have to," she said. "He's very busy right now." That much was true, though Judith knew that the insurance scams, the divorce dirt digging, and the dognappings were wearing thin.

Jeremy nodded gravely. "I understand. But George and I will pay him enough to make up for any inconvenience. See, we figure an official investigation will go on forever, maybe even fall between the cracks if a bigger case comes along. But speed is of the essence. George can't sell condos with an unsolved murder on his hands."

"And you?" Judith inquired with a slight smile.

Jeremy's ruddy skin grew darker. "It'd be a feather in my cap to beat the police to the punch. I mean, here I am, running a murder mystery tour. If I could be in on the investigation—I mean, without interfering—that would be good publicity. As it is, it's sort of . . . bad."

"What about the bad publicity you've given me?" Judith countered.

"I don't see it that way," Jeremy said, still earnest. "Oh, sure, maybe I sort of overstated some of the facts, but look at the exposure you've gotten for your business. I mean, that can't be all bad, can it?"

Judith just stared at Jeremy.

"Anyway," he went on, "I'd hope that you'd sort of team up with Mr. Flynn. You know, like Nick and Nora Charles or Mr. and Mrs. North."

"Joe likes to work alone," Judith stated.

"He always worked with a partner when he was on the force," Jeremy pointed out.

"That was different," Judith said dryly. "Joe and Woody weren't married."

Jeremy's sky-blue eyes were pleading again. "Will you at least mention this to him?"

Judith sighed. "I'll see. Joe just got back from out of town. He has a lot of catching up to do. We'll get back to you in a few days." *When I'm speaking to Joe again*, Judith thought.

Jeremy grimaced. "I don't mean to rush you, but like I said, time is of the essence."

"Hmm," Judith murmured, drumming her finger-nails on the arm of the chair.

"I mean," Jeremy continued, "George Guthrie and I are talking about a thousand dollars a day, plus expenses."

Judith tried not to gape.

Joe's head popped into the open doorway. "I'll take it," he said. Then, seeing Judith's look of astonishment, he added, "I mean, *we'll* take it."

FIVE

ALL WASN'T COMPLETELY forgiven, but at least Judith had gotten over her desire to crack Joe's skull with the fireplace shovel. She also figured that his repentant mood was a propitious time to reveal Woody Price's request.

"Woody says the chief wants you on the citizens' advisory board?" Joe asked, incredulous.

The Flynns were sitting in the living room, where soft golden shafts of August sun slanted through the bay window. Renie and Bill had gone home, though they'd planned a detour to a fish cannery across the canal. The size and number of fish Joe and Bill had caught dictated that several salmon should be kippered, smoked, or otherwise canned for future use. The delicacies could be savored for months, even years, and in Judith's case, she'd made sure that the Joneses had put in an order for several cans of paté. Guests who'd never tasted good salmon before were always amazed by the wonderful flavor.

"It's the chief's program for citizen involvement," Judith replied, growing more civil with each swallow of Scotch.

Joe nodded. "The mayor put that bug up the

chief's behind. It's all eyewash, just to take the heat off the department."

"I told Woody I'd do it, at least for a while," Judith said, avoiding Joe's green-eyed gaze. "For Woody's sake. He seemed to be on the spot."

Joe made a face. "After ten years, I'd think you, of all people, would know when Woody's pulling his poor-me-I-came-out-of-the-ghetto-and-need-all-the-help-I-can-get routine. You know damned well that Woody was raised as solid middle-class as we were. He uses that act with perps, especially black ones. You're as gullible as they are."

"It's his eyes," Judith said. "They're so soulful."

"Sometimes he puts glycerin drops in them so it looks like he's tearing up," Joe said. "He didn't pull that one, did he?"

"N-n-no," Judith said uncertainly.

Joe set his drink down on the glass-topped coffee table and held his hands palms up. "So you committed yourself."

"I didn't want to," Judith said truthfully, "but I also didn't want Woody to get in trouble with the chief."

"Okay." Joe sighed. "By the time this advisory board is set up, you may change your mind. Since it's a city project, the bureaucracy will hem and haw for at least six months. For now, I need some background on this case. Let's start by going over your misadventures on the murder mystery tour."

By the time Judith had finished, including every detail and nuance she could recall, the guests had started returning to Hillside Manor. They were all holdovers from Friday who had been out sightseeing and shopping. While Judith prepared the hors d'oeuvres, Joe sat at the kitchen table, studying the notes he'd made.

"Except for being an exorcist from California, we don't know squat about the victim," he declared just as Judith was about to take the appetizer tray into the living room. "I'll have to check with Woody on that. And Guthrie, since he hired her. Say, you never said what she looked like."

Judith juggled the tray and winced as she recalled the blood-stained corpse. "Ordinary. Probably above average height. Middle-aged, short dark hair, maybe touched up, rather heavyset. A bit too much makeup. She was wearing a blue pantsuit, off-the-rack." She paused, trying to recall more details. "Sensible shoes. No jewelry."

"Not even a wedding ring?" Joe inquired.

Slowly, Judith shook her head. "No, I'm almost sure she didn't have one on. I'd have noticed it."

"You're not a bad observer." Joe grinned, following his wife into the living room.

"Thanks," Judith said dryly. She placed the tray on the gate-legged table, then offered Joe an ironic smile. "Am I still an idiot, or does snagging you a thousand-dollar-a-day job allow me to remove my dunce cap?"

Joe took Judith's hand, leading over to one of the matching sofas. "I'm really sorry about that, Jude-girl," he said, looking sheepish as he placed a hand on her knee. "I was cranky when I got off the plane. I saw your picture in the morning paper and it sort of set me off. You have to realize that I worry about you. Getting involved in murder can be very dangerous."

"You made a career of it," Judith pointed out.

"That's different," Joe said, his hand straying further up Judith's leg. "I was trained to be a homicide detective. I worked with a partner. And I always carried a weapon."

Judith searched Joe's face. "Do you really worry about me?"

Joe sighed and gave a little shake of his head. "Of course I do." Leaning closer, he brushed her lips with his. "I didn't put up with Herself for twenty-five years just to lose you when we were finally both free."

He was right. That quarter-century of separation had

made their union even stronger. When Joe had fallen
into a drunken stupor after his first encounter with fatal
teenage overdoses, he had lost control. He had also lost
Judith, as he allowed himself to be commandeered onto
a plane to Las Vegas. He barely recalled the casino wedding chapel; waking up the next morning with the
wrong Mrs. Flynn was indelibly etched on his memory.
Seeking revenge and a father for her unborn child,
Judith had married Dan McMonigle on the rebound.

"Dan never worried about me," Judith murmured,
putting her arms around Joe. "Dan never worried,
period. He let me do all of it for him."

Joe kissed Judith long and hard, then eased her backwards on the sofa. "He gave you plenty to worry about.
Let's not worry, let's not talk."

Judith felt a twinge in her right hip. "Uh . . . Maybe
we should wait. This sofa doesn't have much support
for my worn-out joints."

"I'll be careful," Joe promised, nuzzling her neck.

Judith, however, continued to resist. "It's after five-
thirty. The guests may start coming down any minute."

Joe shook his head. "They know the social hour
doesn't start until six. We've got plenty of time."

Unbidden, the image of Mrs. Carrabas's body floated
across Judith's mind's eye. No doubt when Aimee
Carrabas entered the Alhambra Friday, she'd thought
she had plenty of time. But life was uncertain.

Having shifted her weight to a more comfortable
position, Judith smiled up at Joe. "Maybe we don't have
as much time as we think we do. But we have time
enough. Now." She hooked her fingers around his neck
and drew him closer.

The phone rang. Judith gave a start.

Joe pressed on her shoulders. "Let it ring. The
machine can pick it up."

"What if it's Mike? I can't ignore my only child."

"He can leave a message." Joe slid his hands under
Judith's cotton tee.

"What if it's Mother, calling from the toolshed?"

"She never does that."

The phone stopped ringing. The magic eyes and the magic fingers were wreaking havoc with Judith's senses.

"Oh, Joe . . ." Judith sighed.

The phone rang again. Judith froze in Joe's arms. "Somebody really wants to get us."

"They sure do," Joe said, swearing under his breath. "Okay, answer the damned thing before you have the wrong kind of fit."

Adjusting her clothes, Judith got off the sofa and hurried across the room as fast as her aching hips would permit. She grabbed the receiver from the cherrywood table just before it trunked over to the answering machine.

"It's for you," Judith said in a breathless voice.

Joe swore again. "Who is it?"

Putting a hand over the mouthpiece, Judith shrugged. "Some man. I don't recognize the voice."

Reluctantly, Joe got up from the sofa and took the phone from Judith. A puzzled expression crossed his face as he responded in monosyllables. After a minute or two, he stared at Judith.

"What do you know about an ostrich named Emil?"

Judith's hand flew to her mouth. "Oh! His name is Emil?"

Joe's eyes rolled toward the ceiling. "You *do* know Emil, then." He resumed speaking into the phone. "Yes, I guess Emil paid us a call, but I'm not able to take your case just now. I've got too many previous commitments. Sorry." He paused, apparently waiting for the person at the other end to talk. "I wish you luck all the same," Joe finally said and rang off.

He moved toward Judith with open arms. "Where were we?"

A noise from the entry hall made Judith retreat a step. "Hi, there," said the tall, rawboned man who was either from Saskatchewan or South Dakota. Judith couldn't remember which, but noticed that he himself looked a bit like an ostrich.

"Oh, my—so many goodies!" exclaimed his stout little wife. "How nice!"

Judith glanced at Joe. "Later," she whispered.

Again, Joe swore under his breath.

Late that night, with the moon shining through the branches of the Rankerses' cedar tree, the Flynns lay in each other's arms, spent and happy.

"Say, I forgot to ask you more about the ostrich," Joe said.

"Oh. He came into the yard the other day. Thursday, I think." She yawned and snuggled closer to Joe. "Mother saw him first. I thought she was having one of her delusions. Renie called the humane society, but the ostrich— Emil—ran off before they got here."

"He belongs to a family named Baines a couple of blocks over and down the hill," Joe replied. "Emil's been gone for four days. The last sighting was in Falstaff's parking lot early this morning. The poultry truck had just arrived for its delivery. It's a wonder they didn't grab Emil and try to sell him off in the butcher shop."

"Falstaff's occasionally has ostrich for sale." Judith laughed. "I've been too chicken—excuse the expression—to try it. So they wanted to hire you to find him?"

"Right." Joe was also chuckling. "I can't take on anything else now that I've got this Carrabas investigation. It's a good thing I wound up most of my other cases before I left for Alaska."

"You have to admit, an ostrich search would be different," Judith remarked, and yawned.

"True." Joe hugged Judith. "Say, what about the jewelry stash? Did you see it?"

"No," Judith answered, yawning some more. "It was

in the same unit where Mrs. Carrabas was killed, though. Renie might have glimpsed it when she was running to hide from the police. Are you figuring that the so-called treasure may be a motive for the murder?"

"Sure. Wouldn't you?"

"That's funny," Judith said in a perplexed tone. "I hadn't really thought about it. If anything, I guess I figured it might be part of a setup, too. You know—to get more publicity for Jeremy Lamar's tours."

"That's possible," Joe said. "If it's true, Jeremy better admit it quick. Even though tomorrow's Sunday, I'll meet with him and Guthrie. It doesn't pay to let much time elapse when you're investigating a homicide."

"So you've told me," Judith responded in a drowsy voice. "What about Woody?"

"He wasn't home this evening," Joe said. "I suppose he and Sondra and the kids went someplace. I'll touch base with him tomorrow, too."

"Good." Judith felt herself sinking into sleep.

"Love you," Joe whispered.

Judith didn't answer. She didn't need to. Joe knew, had always known, that she loved him without qualification. Which, she realized upon occasion, was why he could sometimes be a jackass and get away with it.

After Mass, Joe headed for Woody's home in the suburbs east of the lake. He would be back by one-thirty for his appointment with George Guthrie and Jeremy Lamar, which was scheduled for two o'clock at Hillside Manor.

Judith spent the rest of the morning playing cribbage with Gertrude, who was still yapping about her TV appearance.

"I looked pretty cute, didn't I?" she chortled. "But how come they mixed up what I said? About those gruesome men you married, I mean. Did I miss something?"

"No," Judith said. "They did the same with my interview. They cut out certain phrases and sentences, then splice the rest together so that it doesn't always come out exactly as we meant it."

"Hunh," Gertrude snorted, using her automatic card shuffler to deal a new hand. "That's dumb. Still, I got on TV, and Deb didn't. Boy, is she jealous. Your turn, kiddo."

Judith played a card. "She is? That doesn't sound like Aunt Deb."

"Oh, no? First off, she couldn't believe I was on TV. She doesn't watch the news like I do, she'd rather read the paper." Gertrude paused to consider her hand. "Then she tells me that she didn't know why they'd put me on the news just because you were at Alcatraz or some goofy place with Renie." Gertrude paused again as Judith discarded. "Now why did you and Renie go to Alcatraz? Is that a prison or a restaurant?"

"It used to be a prison," Judith said, "and we didn't go there. We went to the Alhambra Arms down at the bottom of the hill. You've been by there a million times. It's that big old Spanish-style place."

"Oh." Gertrude played again. "Lots of balconies and arches and metal grilles at the windows and doors. You sure it isn't a prison?"

"It's not," Judith assured her mother. "In fact, it's not an apartment house anymore, either. It's being turned into condos."

"Condos." Gertrude huffed. "I don't get it."

"They're like apartments, except you own them instead of renting," Judith said as she played her last card.

Gertrude frowned and gazed around her tiny dwelling space. "You mean like this? Why don't they call them *can*dos? This thing's about as big as a tin can."

"Most of them are somewhat bigger," Judith noted with a straight face as she began to count up the cards.

"Anyway," Gertrude continued, watching Judith like a hawk, "Deb said that her old boss, Mr. Whiffel, used to live there with his sister, so I know darned well she thought she should have been on TV instead of me."

"Oh," Judith said. "I get it." She didn't, but arguing with her mother was as futile as the Charge of the Light Brigade.

Gertrude took her turn to count, moving the pegs along the board with surprising alacrity. "Fifteen-two, fifteen-four, fifteen-six, a double run is eight, and His Nobs makes one more to put me out." She cackled in triumph. "I win again."

"You crazy old coot," Judith murmured, though her tone was not only affectionate, but admiring. It never ceased to amaze Judith that no matter how addled her mother might seem otherwise, her card-playing skills were still razor-sharp.

"So Deb wouldn't admit how envious she was," Gertrude said as Judith shuffled for a new game, "but I told her that I knew somebody who lived there, too."

Judith gazed at her mother with interest. "You do? Who?"

"I forget." Briefly, Gertrude looked confused, then perked up as she cut the cards and turned over the one on top of the deck's lower half. "An ace. My play."

The game continued for almost five minutes before Gertrude suddenly pounded her fist on the card table. "Helen Schnell. She taught with your father at the high school. English, I think. Old maid, kind of homely. I think she was sweet on your father."

The name was familiar to Judith. "Someone mentioned her," she said, searching her brain for the source. "Woody, maybe."

"She still alive?" Gertrude asked.

"Yes. In fact," Judith continued, "I recall now that she's going to buy one of the condos."

"Hunh." Gertrude made a face. "Sounds like her. She's the kind who'd like to live in Alcatraz."

Joe invited Judith to sit in on his meeting with Messrs. Guthrie and Lamar. Not that he had much choice. Judith had already threatened to hide under the coffee table in the living room and eavesdrop. Since the coffee table was made of glass, it wasn't a particularly viable idea.

The two men arrived together in the big white van that bore Guthrie's company logo. George didn't look overly pleased to see Judith standing next to her husband in the entry hall.

"You were there," he said accusingly. "You found the body." George turned to Jeremy. "Did you tell me about her?"

Jeremy nodded jerkily. "Yes, George, I sure did. That's why we decided to hire Mr. Flynn here."

"Okay." George brushed past Judith. "Where do you want us?"

"In a civil state," Joe said in his deceptively mild manner. "How about starting with the sofas in the living room?"

George and Jeremy shared one of the sofas; Judith and Joe took the other. A tray with coffee and mugs was already on the coffee table, along with a plate of chocolate madeleines that Judith had baked before going to church.

"Let's talk about Aimee Carrabas," Joe said after Judith had performed her hostess duties. "What motivated you to hire an exorcist in the first place?"

George lifted his shoulders. "It seemed like a good idea. I've heard of cases where it really worked." He turned to Jeremy. "You told me about one of them, some Indian woman over on the Peninsula."

Jeremy nodded with enthusiasm. "Somebody had murdered some chief about forty years ago. Whoever did it—it was a member of the tribe—ran away and was never caught. A few years later, he was killed in a car wreck up in British Columbia. But all that time, and even afterward, the villagers had nothing but bad luck, including being hit by a tsunami which almost destroyed the whole place. I mean, they were just about wiped out. So four or five years ago, the tribal elders tracked down a woman from a different tribe east of the mountains who could perform exorcisms. She came to the Peninsula and did her thing, and now they're building a casino."

Joe had cocked his head to one side. "Interesting." He turned to George. "So you believe in such things?"

"You bet," George said. "I had a great or great-great-grandmother who could do that. Or so I'm told. She was also a water witch. You know, she could take one of those sticks and find a spring or a well."

"Actually," Judith put in, "I had a great-aunt like that. I was very small, but I remember her going around our family cabin with one of those sticks. Sure enough, she found a spring out back right under the spot where my grandfather was going to build an outhouse."

Joe gave Judith a slightly withering glance before posing his next question to George. "So how did you get in touch with Aimee Carrabas?"

George, who was wearing a short-sleeved cotton shirt, rubbed at his forearms, where curly gray hair stood out against his deep tan. "I heard about her through somebody. I thought the idea of an exorcist was really good. You know, get rid of the past, especially the bad stuff."

"Couldn't you find somebody local?" Joe inquired.

"I didn't try," George replied, taking his second madeleine from the plate. "Whoever told me about Mrs. Carrabas swore she was the real deal." He turned to Jeremy. "Did I tell you who recommended her?"

Jeremy shook his head. "No. Why would you?"

George now scratched at his bald spot. "Guess I wouldn't. Maybe it was the O'Dowds."

"Who are they?" Joe asked.

"Former tenants," George said. "They lived at the Alhambra for several years after they sold the family home, but they didn't want to buy in. Nice folks, older, of course, but not a lot of capital, I guess. They found another apartment a couple of blocks away."

Joe made a note. "Did they say how they knew Mrs. Carrabas?"

"No, they just said she was the goods," George replied. "I think one of their kids lives in Garden Grove. Maybe that was where the recommendation came from originally. Anyway, the next thing I know, Mrs. Carrabas calls me about a month ago and we set the date for yesterday."

"She called you?" Judith asked.

George nodded. "That's right. The O'Dowds must have gotten in touch with her. Or maybe they told their kid. Anyway, I was real glad to hear from her. I wanted to get the thing over with, and it turned out that we could do it while Jeremy here was taking his tour through."

Jeremy leaned forward on the sofa. "See, we were supposed to go from the Meacham apartment to the unit where the jewelry had been stashed. Then Mrs. Carrabas was going to come out and do her exorcism while my group watched. I thought it'd be a real thrill. I mean, how many people ever get to see an exorcist do whatever exorcists do?"

"A real show," Joe remarked. "Was this jewelry for real or part of the performance?"

"Hell, no," George broke in, his face flushed. "We found that stuff a few days ago. I had a jewelry appraiser come in to look it over to make sure it wasn't just junk. Most of it was gold and silver, not many stones—chains, bracelets, pins, necklaces. The appraiser said the stuff was the real McCoy, topnotch quality. I locked it up in my safe at work, then brought it back this morning. See, I decided we might as well hold off telling anybody until we had Mrs. Carrabas on hand and the tour was coming through. That's why I called the TV and newspaper people. It would have made a great story on its own. We didn't need Mrs. Carrabas to get killed."

"She probably didn't need it, either," Joe said in that

same mild tone. "Let's get back to her. When did she arrive in the city?"

George shrugged. "Thursday, I suppose. She called me that afternoon. That's when we set the exact time. She agreed to show up around noon and was scheduled to do her thing at one, or whenever the tour group reached the unit where she was waiting."

"Tell me," Judith said, "what did she have to do to set up?"

George and Jeremy both looked puzzled. "What do you mean?" George asked.

"Candles?" Judith said. "Crosses? Incense? I understand exorcists often create some sort of atmosphere. Of course, in the Catholic Church it's strictly a religious ceremony."

George frowned and scratched his cheek. "Mrs. Carrabas did mention something about incantations and . . . what was the word? Milieu?"

Judith nodded. "I'm sure she did. She'd want to set the scene, as it were. But unless I missed something, I didn't see any sign of props."

"I get it," Jeremy said with his boyish grin. "Showbiz."

"Hell, no!" George growled. "This wasn't a circus act, it was serious stuff. I'm no showman like you are. I wanted to do something sincere."

"Sure you did," Joe soothed. "Let's get back to Mrs. Carrabas. Did you see her when she got to the Alhambra?"

"Yeah," George replied, calming down. "I was in the courtyard with some of my guys. She came through and I took her up to the vacant unit. We checked it out, and then I told her about the jewelry stash. Mrs. Carrabas was real intrigued, but I told her not to touch it. That was going to be the other newsworthy bit, for afterward. See, I figured we'd get her doing the exorcism, then I'd show everybody the treasure in the floor and say something about how the Alhambra's luck had already changed."

"And you said you aren't a showman," Jeremy sneered.

"Hey!" George shot back. "I'm not! I'm just a guy who's trying to make a living."

"Excuse me," Judith said gently. "Do you know a tenant named Helen Schnell?"

Jeremy looked blank but George turned a startled face on Judith. "Sure. Is she a friend of yours?"

"I know of her," Judith replied. "She taught at the same high school where my father did. She's retired, I think."

"Right," George said. "She's one of the ones who's buying a condo. Not her original unit—she wanted to be higher up—but the one just above it. Miss Schnell and her mother lived at the Alhambra forever. The old lady died a couple of years back, about the same time that Miss Schnell retired."

"She's not all that old then," Judith remarked.

"Nope," George answered. "Mid, late sixties. The old lady must have been almost ninety."

Judith gave a nod, then turned thoughtful as she deferred to Joe.

"What time did Mrs. Carrabas arrive?" he asked, his jaw tightening slightly.

"Umm . . ." George considered. "A few minutes after noon. Most of the crew had just started their lunch break."

Joe made another note. "When did you last see Mrs. Carrabas?"

"Umm . . ." Again, George reflected. "We must've been upstairs for about fifteen minutes. I waited around a bit while she sort of looked the place over."

"Excuse me," Judith put in. "I'm confused. Why did you take her to the vacant apartment when the Meacham murder had occurred on the floor below and one unit over?"

"Because," George explained, "that's where we'd stashed the jewelry. We couldn't ask the media folks to run from one unit to the other. They had all that gear. Several of the apartments are torn up, as you probably noticed. We wanted to show what the originals looked like, capture another era. Several of the tenants had left furniture behind because they didn't want it anymore or couldn't use it where they were moving. Besides, Mrs. Carrabas said it didn't matter what room she used as long as it was inside the building."

"I see," Judith said, though she wasn't quite sure that she did. She could understand the convenience of it, but not the logistics. It seemed to Judith that Mrs. Carrabas would have wanted to get as close as possible to the actual murder location.

"Did Mrs. Carrabas talk much while you were with her?" Joe asked, a trifle testy.

"No, she sort of clucked."

"Clucked?"

"Yeah. You know"—George clucked several times with his tongue—"like she was approving or maybe not approving certain things."

"Did she say anything of interest? That is," Joe clarified, "that might have any connection whatsoever with a sense of danger or a premonition?"

"I don't get you," George said, looking puzzled.

"Bad vibrations," Joe offered. "Fear, concern, anything at all that might indicate she was worried."

"Nope," George said. "She seemed pretty cheerful."

"Hey," Jeremy broke in, "a happy medium. I like that."

"She wasn't a medium, you moron," George snarled. "You know better, with your Indian tales. Mrs. Carrabas was an exorcist."

"Well," Jeremy said, looking chastened, "at least she was happy."

"Did she mention any names?" Joe queried.

"Of people?" George frowned. "No. Only the Meachams."

"Was she carrying—" Joe began.

"How did she mention them?" Judith broke in.

George stared at Judith, then rubbed at the back of his neck. "Like, 'poor Dorothy' and 'tragic Harry' and 'pitiful little Anne-Marie.' Or something like that."

Joe shot Judith a warning glance. "As I was saying, what did Mrs. Carrabas bring with her?"

"A suitcase," George replied. "Well, not exactly a suitcase. More like a briefcase. But a big one."

"What happened to it?" asked Joe.

"I don't know," George responded, looking mystified. "I never thought about it. Maybe the cops took it. They would, wouldn't they?"

"Yes," Joe replied, "they would if they'd found it. But they didn't." Again, he turned to Judith. "Did you see anything like that?"

"No," Judith said, sounding miffed. "But I didn't get a chance to look. Right after I found the body, the press came pouring in. I got pinned against a bureau."

Joe stared at Judith. He made another note.

Judith knew what Joe was thinking.

SIX

"YOU DIDN'T HAVE to get so snippy with me," Judith declared after George and Jeremy had left. "I was only trying to help."

"Sitting in on an interview doesn't mean taking over," Joe asserted. "I've been interrogating witnesses for years. There's a certain way I go about it, conforming to the type of person I'm interviewing, of course. Jumping in with side issues really cramps my style."

Judith started to pout, then thought better of it. Joe, after all, was right, at least as far his own style of inquiry was concerned. "I tend to seize the moment," she said. "I'm used to talking to people, not interviewing them. I don't take notes, I just chat. So I leap on things as they come out, in the natural flow of conversation."

"That's fine, you're not a professional," Joe pointed out as he started for the back door. "But I am. Try to remember that next time."

"Where're you going?" Judith asked.

"To the Alhambra," Joe replied, one hand on the screen door. "Woody's got a couple of uniforms on duty there for the next few days. In fact, he and Sancha Rael haven't finished their search. I'm going to do a little snooping of my own."

Judith took an eager step forward. "Can I come?"

Joe scowled at Judith. "No. You've already been there. I haven't."

"You're going to look in that bureau, aren't you?" she said in a pettish tone. "You think Mrs. Carrabas's brief-case may still be there."

"I doubt it," Joe replied impatiently. "But it's got to be somewhere. See you later."

Ordinarily, Judith would have begged to go along, but she knew she couldn't leave the house. It was after three-thirty, and the guests would start arriving at any minute. Resignedly, she went to the freezer section of the fridge, seeking inspiration for dinner. The afternoon had grown very warm, well over eighty degrees. Maybe they should barbecue. Judith pulled out a package of boneless sirloin just as the phone rang.

"Hi," Renie said. "Are you really going to Gut Busters tomorrow?"

"I can," Judith replied. "Are you?"

"Yes. I'm out of Pepsi."

Judith was well aware of her cousin's addiction. She couldn't get through a workday in her graphic design business without guzzling at least three or four cans, caffeine, calories, and all. Thus, Renie bought Pepsi by the case, saving on cost by going to the large discount store in the south end of town.

"Okay," Judith said. "Who's driving?"

"Me?" Renie responded. "How's eleven o'clock for you?"

The cousins agreed on the time. "I'm not sure I like this cooperative venture between Joe and me," Judith said. "He's making all the rules."

"So? Bill does that sometimes. Just break them."

"You don't always," Judith objected.

"No, I don't. But once in a while they don't make sense. Is Joe making sense?"

"Only from his point of view."

"That's what I mean."

Judith sighed. "I don't know why Bill hasn't strangled you. Sometimes I feel sorry for him."

"You know I'm kidding," Renie said. "Sort of. Is Joe being unreasonable?"

"No," Judith admitted, and then related the interview with George and Jeremy. "I'd like to call on Miss Schnell. Since she taught with Dad, I hope she'll be cooperative."

"Where is she living while the Alhambra is being restored?" Renie asked.

"I asked George that as he and Jeremy were leaving," Judith said. "She rented an inexpensive apartment at the bottom of the hill. Shall I arrange a meeting after we go to Gut Busters?"

"As long as I get back home by one o'clock," Renie said. "I've got a deadline on my art museum project."

"Hmm," Judith murmured. "That's cutting it close. It always takes us at least an hour to shop at Gut Busters."

"Then we'd better take separate cars," Renie said. "I'll meet you at Gut Busters, eleven-fifteen."

Joe returned home shortly after six.

"You can barbecue the shish kebabs," Judith said, still petulant. "The grill's ready to go. I just got the guests settled in for the social hour. What did you find out at the Alhambra? Or is it a deep, dark secret?"

Joe made a face at Judith. "I'm not keeping secrets from you, Jude-girl. But in point of fact, I didn't find much. The bureau was empty."

"Completely empty?" Judith pressed.

"That's right," Joe said, taking a beer out of the fridge. "Cleaned out. Vacant. Zero. Unless," he went on, opening the cupboard to the liquor cabinet and pointing to Judith's favorite Scotch, "you count the remnants of a long-ago sachet."

Judith looked up at the bottle on the top shelf. "Thanks, but no thanks," she said, feeling perverse. "I'd rather have a Bloody Mary. I'll fix it myself. You always forget I don't like olives. I prefer an asparagus spear, not celery."

"Okay." Resignedly, Joe put on his chef's apron, picked up his heat-proof mitts, and headed for the backyard. Ordinarily, Joe loved to cook, but upon this occasion, he seemed to move on feet of lead.

Sweetums came in as Joe went out. Judith rushed to the phone and dialed Renie's number. The cat wove in and out between Judith's ankles, mewing piteously. The call trunked over to the Joneses' voice messaging after the fourth ring.

"Damn!" Judith exclaimed under her breath. It was between six and seven. Bill and Renie had a law at their house, prohibiting phone calls during the dinner hour. Judith left a message, asking Renie to call her back ASAP. Sweetums collapsed on the floor, paws outstretched, eyes closed. He appeared to be dead.

"So Mother didn't feed you again," Judith said, stepping over the cat and going out to the pantry. "How about some of Martha Stewpot's Gourmet for Cats? It's all the rage."

Sweetums liked the new dish just fine. Judith watched him devour the entire can and wash it down with a few swigs of milk.

"There's more than one way to skin a cat," she murmured, and wished that Renie would call back soon.

"I have to run an errand with Renie," Judith said as she and Joe finished dinner on the patio.

"On a Sunday night?" Joe looked perplexed.

Judith nodded vigorously. "It has something to do with the brochure she's designing for the art museum's upcoming Native American exhibit. She didn't have time to explain, but she needs me to come along."

"Okay," Joe said. "Don't be late. There are a couple of good movies on TV tonight."

"Good movies" to Joe meant Clint Eastwood or John Wayne. "I won't be long," Judith assured him breezily as Gertrude appeared in the toolshed doorway.

"Hey, dummies," she called, waving a bamboo shish kebab skewer. "How do you expect me to eat this stick with my dentures?"

"You don't eat the stick, Mother," Judith said. "It's just for serving purposes."

"What purpose?" Gertrude demanded. "Stabbing the beef after it's already dead? It's too big to be a tooth-pick."

"It's not to be used after the meal is served." Judith sighed. "It's part of the presentation."

"Tommyrot," Gertrude snapped. "Why waste a good stick?" She flipped the skewer in the direction of the patio, backed into the toolshed, and slammed the door.

"Bill thinks you're nuts," Renie said after Judith had picked up her cousin fifteen minutes later.

"You told him what we're doing?" Judith asked in surprise.

"Sure," Renie said. "He won't tell Joe. You know how closemouthed Bill is. Besides, he tends to forget."

"Maybe I am nuts," Judith allowed as the cousins cruised through the commercial district on top of the hill. "But somehow I have this weird feeling that Joe missed something in that bureau."

"But he told you it was empty," Renie pointed out. "What could you possibly expect to find?"

"I don't know," Judith admitted. "Certainly Woody and his people searched the unit. Maybe it's just that I feel like I bonded with that damned bureau. I was stuck there long enough."

"Maybe," Renie said with a wry expression, "you just want another look inside the Alhambra."

Judith gave Renie a sheepish glance. "Maybe you're right."

* * *

The two uniformed officers, both young and looking bored, were skeptical at first. But Judith showed her ID and promised not to stay inside for more than ten minutes.

"Since Joe retired from the force," she explained, "he's gotten a trifle careless. He tends to drop things or just leave them lying around. To tell the truth"—she winced a bit, since she was lying through her teeth—"I can't imagine how he left his wallet here this afternoon."

The taller of the two officers shrugged. "Okay, but one of us will have to go with you. And no going beyond the third floor. That's been pretty well searched, but Detective Price hasn't finished with the top floors yet."

The shorter officer, whose name was Petrovich, dutifully led the way up the staircase. "If your husband left his wallet on one of the other floors, he's going to have to wait until tomorrow," Petrovich warned Judith. "Detective Price will get here early, though."

"That's fine," Judith replied as they reached the third floor and headed for the scene of the crime.

"In here," Petrovich said, opening the door.

"I know." Judith offered the young man her most winsome smile. "I found the body."

"You did?" Petrovich's dark eyes bulged. "Are you a suspect?"

"Hardly." Judith laughed. "I guess you didn't see me on TV."

"I only watch sports," Petrovich responded.

They were in the living room, where both cousins made a cursory effort at searching behind what furniture remained in place. Then they moved on to the bedroom.

"Joe mentioned looking in this bureau," Judith said, pulling out drawers one at a time. When she reached the fourth and bottom drawer, she asked Renie to help her. "My hips, you know. It's hard to bend."

Renie knew her cue. Apparently stumbling over the carpet, she fell against Petrovich. "Oof!" she cried, steadying herself with the young man's help. "Sorry. I'm kind of awkward."

"I got it open," Judith exclaimed in triumph. "Here's the wallet. Oh, I'm so relieved!"

Renie joined Judith, staring into the empty drawer. The wallet was in Judith's hand. Renie helped her cousin stand up. "You sure are lucky," she remarked.

Out on the sidewalk, Judith paused, staring up at the third floor. "Remember when I said someone was watching us from that middle balcony window? It was on the third floor. Now which unit would that have been?"

"It's not a unit, it's the open area," Renie replied. "See, the middle windows on each floor have balconets, not balconies. A balconet is just decor, with no floor jutting out. Anyway, let me congratulate you on your sleight of hand."

"I hope Joe doesn't look for his wallet before we get back," Judith said, as they reached the Subaru. "It wasn't easy to pick his pocket. I had to wait until he was bending over to load the dishwasher. He thought I was trying to give him a wedgie."

Renie grinned at Judith. "As I said, very adroit. But the drawers were definitely empty. Are you disappointed?"

"No," Judith replied smugly. "Not at all. What did you smell?"

Renie stared at Judith. "There were some bits of what looked like sachet in the bottom drawer."

"Sachet—or incense?" Judith queried, heading back to the main avenue.

Renie grinned again, this time more slowly. "Yes, it could have been incense. But the scent that predominated was something else. What was it?"

"Beeswax," Judith said. "As in candles." She braked at the four-way stop at the top of the hill. "As in what

Mrs. Carrabas might have had in her briefcase. Now why was it important to hide the briefcase and then make off with it before the police could search the room?"

Renie had no explanation. "What about the gun? Has Woody found it?"

"No," Judith said. "Or if he has, he didn't tell Joe. Or if Woody told Joe, Joe didn't tell me. Goodness, I hate all this second-and third-hand passing of information."

"I suppose nobody heard the shots because of all the construction noise," Renie mused as they drove past Falstaff's customary smug reader board, which currently proclaimed, "Peaches from Paradise" and "Corn from Mr. Elysian's Fields."

"Exactly," Judith agreed. "Say, I wonder if we should talk to Mr. and Mrs. O'Dowd."

"The ones who recommended Mrs. Carrabas?"

"Right. I'm going around the block to use the pay phone at Falstaff's so we can find out where they live and if they'll see us."

Renie balked. "I told Bill I wouldn't be gone more than half an hour. He'll worry."

"Call him," Judith suggested. "Tell him we've been detained."

"I can't call him," Renie replied. "I always turn the ringer off when I leave. You know how Bill hates the telephone, even more than your mother does."

Judith sighed. "Okay, I'll go alone. But if Joe calls to see where I am, don't answer it. You've got Caller ID, right?"

Renie did. Judith used the Joneses' phone to call directory assistance, then dialed the O'Dowds' number. Mr. O'Dowd seemed wary at first, then, after Judith had explained how she and Joe were involved in the murder investigation, he finally yielded.

"They're Billy and Midge O'Dowd," Judith told Renie in the Joneses' entry hall. "He sounded rather nice. I'm heading there now."

"So am I," said Renie, picking up her huge purse which looked very much like a feed bag for horses. She glanced into the living room where Bill was seated in his favorite chair, eyes glued to the TV set. "I can only take so much of Clint Eastwood making my day."

The apartment house where the O'Dowds lived was an older one-story building that took up half a block. Each unit in the half-timbered Tudor-style structure had its own garage, which meant that Judith had to find on-street parking. Given that it was a Sunday night and most of the neighborhood's residents were home, the cousins were forced to walk almost two blocks from where Judith finally found a space for the Subaru.

"We're only two or three blocks west of the Alhambra," Renie pointed out. "The O'Dowds didn't move very far."

"I'm sure they liked the neighborhood," Judith said. "Who wouldn't? It's so convenient, and this far down the hill they're virtually on the flat."

The grounds were beautifully landscaped, and each unit had its own entrance. Only the omnipresent electioneering signs marred the surroundings, with their garish colors and alarming slogans such as "End the Violence!" and "Keep Your Arms to Yourself!"

No such political messages were planted in the O'Dowds' front yard, however. They were in Number Five, near the far end of the building. Judith pressed the buzzer, and the door opened almost immediately.

"Good Lord!" the man on the threshold exclaimed. "It's you!"

Judith gaped and Renie let out a little squawk. Billy O'Dowd was the man who had sat in front of them on the tour trolley. His wife, Midge, stalked into the hallway, gaping incredulously.

"Are you here to apologize?" she demanded. "You better be. You just about ruined the tour for us."

"I thought the dead body might have done that," Renie said, firmly planting one foot inside the door.

Hoping to defuse the situation, Judith tried to edge Renie out of the way. "I am sorry," Judith said. "It was a terribly upsetting day for us from the start. If you'd be so kind as to let us in, I could explain everything."

"I thought," Billy O'Dowd said with suspicion in his dark blue eyes, "you called yourself a detective."

"My husband is a detective," Judith replied. "He's investigating the murder at the Alhambra. I'm helping him. As I mentioned on the phone, I found Mrs. Carrabas's body."

Midge O'Dowd stuck her broad, homely face out from around her husband's shoulder. "How do we know *you* didn't kill her?"

"I didn't," Judith said simply. "If I did, my husband would've had me arrested by now. He's a very good detective."

Apparently, this explanation made some sort of sense to Billy. "Okay." He sighed. "We agreed to see you, so we will. But make it quick."

"Hold it!" Midge burst out. "Did I say *I* agreed? Since when do you make all the rules?"

"Come off it, Midge," Billy said in a weary voice. "They're here, they look harmless."

"They weren't harmless on the bus," Midge declared with a bulldog expression. "They were a couple of nuisances." Although she stepped aside, her expression exuded distrust.

The O'Dowd living room was rather small, dark, and crowded. Still, the furnishings were tasteful, if modest, and despite the hostility of their hosts, the atmosphere seemed comfortable.

"This is nice," Judith said. "I've driven by these apartments many times. They always look cozy."

"They suit us just fine," Midge declared, indicating that the cousins should sit on the navy blue loveseat. "We don't have as much room as we had in the Alhambra, though. Then again, we sure didn't have the space there that we had in our family home up the hill."

Judith nodded in sympathy. "It's hard, isn't it? To move, especially when you have to get rid of beloved possessions. When I was widowed a few years ago, I had to give up our family home." She tried not to wince. The only home that she and Dan had ever owned had been repossessed. "It broke my heart to part with some of the things I couldn't take with me when I moved in with my mother." The seedy rental out in the city's south end had been crammed with junk, mostly Dan's so-called bargain appliances and gadgets that had long since broken or become obsolete. Judith had jubilantly flung them all into a Dumpster, wishing she could do the same with her unhappy memories. "It's hard work, too," she added on a final note of truth.

"You bet," Midge said, then looked at Renie. "You haven't apologized. What's wrong, you only talk when you're not supposed to?"

Judith watched Renie out of the corner of her eye, hoping her cousin would play along and at least feign repentance.

"I'm overcome," Renie said, and let it go at that.

Apparently, the O'Dowds interpreted the remark as an apology. "I suppose," Midge said, "you're wondering why we took that tour. We knew the Alhambra was part of it, and we wanted to see what that crook, George Guthrie, was doing to the place. You wouldn't believe the prices he's asking for those condos."

"Staggering," Judith agreed. "Or so I've heard."

Billy O'Dowd nodded, a shock of silver hair falling onto his forehead. "That's right. At our age, it didn't make sense. The wife and I are almost eighty. Why would we want to pay three, four hundred thousand dollars just to stay put?"

"We're not poor," Midge said with a scowl for her husband. "Don't make us out to be some kind of broken-down old coots. We're not foolish, that's all."

"I didn't say we were foolish," Billy shot back. "Did I say that? Did I?"

"You better not," Midge snapped, then folded her arms across her heavy bosom, sat back in the armchair, and dug her heels into the shag carpet.

"I gather that only a few of the former tenants have agreed to buy in," Judith commented.

The O'Dowds exchanged glances. "That's right," Billy said. "The schoolteacher and Rufus Holmes. Hell's bells, Miss Schnell never lived anyplace else and hardly ever spent a dime. No wonder she can afford to buy a condo. And Rufus—well, he's crazy."

"Crazy like a fox," Midge put in. "You just think he's crazy because he didn't always agree with you."

"Heck," Billy responded, "Rufus hardly ever talked to me. Or to anybody else, either."

"Who's Rufus?" Renie asked.

"Who I said he was," Billy responded. "Rufus Holmes. He's another one who never lived anywhere else. He never goes anywhere, never does anything. Never worked, either. I'll be darned if I know where he gets his money."

"Stocks," Midge put in. "I heard he has lots of stocks and such. Helen Schnell told me once that he had a knack for picking winners, just like my cousin Bernie has for handicapping horses."

"If your cousin Bernie is so smart, why is he always asking us for money?" Billy demanded. "Bernie's only handicap is his brain. It broke a long time ago, if you ask me."

"I didn't ask," Midge shot back.

"Is Rufus a recluse?" Judith asked, trying to steer the O'Dowds back on track.

Billy nodded. "I'd say so. I guess he got married once, but it didn't last long. He probably wouldn't take her anywhere."

"I wouldn't blame her," Midge said, then turned to Billy. "When was the last time we went anywhere? I haven't seen a movie since *The Sound of Music*."

"How long did you live at the Alhambra?" Renie

inquired, now settling into the spirit of things.

"Over ten years," Midge answered. "We sold the house a couple of years after Billy retired from the postal service. We should have waited because prices on the hill started going sky-high about then. But Billy knew it all, he was suddenly a real estate genius."

Billy glared at Midge. "We got a good price. It would've been silly to stay put. Heck, the kids were raised, with families of their own."

"Yes," Judith said with a smile, "I understand one of your children lives in California."

"Where'd you hear that?" Midge demanded.

"From George Guthrie, I think," Judith said. "He mentioned that one of them recommended Mrs. Carrabas."

The O'Dowds exchanged glances again, this time looking mystified. "No such thing," Midge asserted. "Why would Frankie or Danny do that? They don't know any exercisers."

"We haven't even talked to Guthrie since we moved out six months ago," Billy said. "Where'd he get such a damned fool notion?"

"It sounds like him," Midge huffed. "All hot air—and sly. Did you know that he couldn't raise the rent on the apartments? It's one of those historical landmarks, so he had to follow some kind of formula with only small increases allowed for inflation. But then he figured out a way to get around the building codes and such by turning the place into condominiums. All he had to do was keep the outside the same and not mess with the courtyard. That's why I think he's a big crook. I'll bet he bribed somebody down at city hall."

"How long has he owned the property?" Renie inquired.

"Not long," Billy replied. "A year or two, I think."

"Two years and seven months," Midge interjected. "Don't think, Billy. You'll wear out your brain."

"Like cousin Bernie?" Billy retorted.

Midge ignored the barb. "Guthrie bought the building from Mrs. Folger. She and her husband had owned and managed it for years. Then Mr. Folger died, so Mrs. Folger sold it to Guthrie. She passed on last winter. Pneumonia took her."

"It wasn't pneumonia," Billy countered. "It was emphysema."

Judith quickly jumped in before the O'Dowds could start another argument. "You didn't live at the Alhambra when the Meachams did, of course. But how many of the tenants who were renters back then are still around?"

"You mean who still lived in the building when Guthrie decided to renovate it?" Midge asked.

"Yes," Judith said. "You mentioned Miss Schnell and Mr. Holmes. Who else?"

"That's it," Midge responded. "Oh, several of the renters had lived at the Alhambra for years and years, but nobody else going back that far. The reason so many people stayed put is because of the low rent. Then Guthrie pulls this condo stunt, so just about everybody had to find another place. Like us."

"Rufus didn't leave right away," Billy noted. "They had to haul him out. It took three men to do it."

Midge shot her husband an incredulous look. "I never heard any such thing. Why would he do that?"

"Because," Billy retorted with his jaw thrust out, "he's crazy. Isn't that what I said a minute ago?"

"Where's Rufus now?" Judith asked.

"In some fleabag hotel downtown," Midge said. "He's cheap."

Billy glared at his wife. "How can he be cheap when he's shelling out four hundred grand for a condo?"

Midge didn't reply, but sat stonily in her chair. Billy again addressed the cousins. "What does all this have to do with that woman who got herself killed?"

"I don't know," Judith admitted. "I'm just trying to get some background on the building itself. Was there anything unusual about any of the other tenants?"

"The two girls next door smoked pot," Midge said. "Awful smell. What's wrong with young people these days? Why can't they get drunk like the rest of us?"

"The couple next to Mrs. Folger weren't married," Billy put in. "I don't think much of this free love stuff. Then again," he muttered with a dark glance at his wife, "the kind you pay for isn't always so good, either."

"Do you remember the Whiffels?" Judith asked. "A brother and sister, in 305."

Billy looked blank, but Midge nodded vigorously. "He was a lawyer with big buck teeth. I think she'd been a schoolteacher. They moved to a retirement home. I forget who came along next. Seems to me there were several different tenants. Newlyweds, a couple of them. The wife would get pregnant and they'd go looking for a bigger place with a yard."

Judith calculated that there was still a third floor unit that hadn't been accounted for. "Who lived in the apartment across the front hall from you?"

"Dave and Emily Baines," Midge replied.

The name sounded familiar. "Had they been there long?" Judith asked.

Billy shook his head. "Less than a year. They got evicted."

"How come?" queried Renie.

Midge looked disgusted. "No pets were allowed after Guthrie took over. When the Baineses moved in, they had a bird they didn't tell anybody about. One day it got loose and ran all over the place. Somebody finally cornered it by the courtyard fountain."

"The bird ran?" Renie asked, puzzled.

"A big bird," Billy said. "It was an ostrich named Emil."

"You didn't tell me that Joe had been asked to find Emil," Renie said as she and Judith made yet another trip across Heraldsgate Hill. "As for the Baineses, I don't agree that it can't be a coincidence. You always insist that things are linked together in some bizarre fashion, just so you can beat your brain trying to figure it all out."

"It just seems strange," Judith said. "But I suppose Emil couldn't have guessed that he'd end up in the yard of somebody who was about to find a dead body in the apartment house where he used to live."

"Illegally," Renie noted. "And I don't think ostriches are very bright."

"Maybe Joe should have agreed to find Emil," Judith said. "What if there's a connection?"

Renie was looking exasperated. "There isn't. I already said that. It's just a damned coincidence. Come on, coz, where's your famous logic?"

They had reached the steep street that led to Renie's neighborhood. "You're right," Judith conceded. "I got carried away. I'd better concentrate on Helen Schnell and Rufus Holmes."

"Why?" Renie asked as Judith pulled up in front of the Joneses' Dutch Colonial. "They weren't around when Mrs. Carrabas got killed."

"Not that we know of," Judith allowed.

"Give it a rest," Renie said, getting out of the car. "See you tomorrow at Gut Busters."

"Right." Judith smiled weakly. "G'night."

She waited until Renie got inside the house. Then she slowly drove back home, wondering about coincidences. No doubt Renie was right about the ostrich.

But there was another coincidence that bothered her more than Emil. Despite a fifty-year gap, the deaths of Dorothy Meacham and Aimee Carrabas struck Judith as odd.

Joe would say she had too much imagination. Renie would tell her she was making something out of nothing. Bill might diagnose her as nuts.

Still, Judith couldn't help but wonder.

SEVEN

DURING THE NOON hour on Monday, Judith and Renie returned to Gut Busters' parking lot to load their separate cars with cases of toilet paper, drums of bleach, wheels of cheese, bricks of butter, and heroic-sized hams.

"Are you sure you can't go with me to see Helen Schnell?" Judith asked, carefully wedging a carton of hundred-watt light bulbs between a case of Merlot and a box filled with forty-eight deodorant roll-ons.

"Really, I can't," Renie said, barely able to shut the Camry's trunk. "Sorry." She started toward the driver's side, then stopped and clapped her hands to her head. "Damn! I forgot the Pepsi! See you."

Envying her cousin's agile hips, Judith watched Renie race back to the Gut Busters' entrance. With a sigh, she got into the Subaru and headed out of the industrial warehouse area.

Helen Schnell had professed mild pleasure when Judith had called her that morning. Helen certainly remembered Mr. Grover, such a kind man and an exceptional mentor. But Helen was somewhat puzzled by Judith's interest in the Alhambra. Judith said she'd explain when they met in person.

It wasn't an apartment where Helen was temporarily lodged, but a two-story frame house that had been divided into a duplex. Helen lived on the second floor. There was a separate entrance, and it took some time for the retired teacher to answer Judith's ring.

"Judith Grover?" the tall, plain woman with short gray hair said as she opened the door.

"Judith Flynn, actually," Judith replied, catching her breath and putting out her hand. "I really appreciate your hospitality."

"I've made tea and there's some banana bread," Helen said, leading the way up the narrow wooden stairs. Her voice was very precise and her carriage ramrod straight. "You must excuse the sparse furnishings, but I put most of my things in storage until I can move into the condo."

Entering the living room, Judith saw what Helen meant. The only furniture was a sofa, two chairs, and an end table that held a tray with the tea items. The walls were bare, though an old but handsome Oriental carpet covered the living room floor. Judith sat down on the sofa.

"You must tell me about your interest in the Alhambra," Helen said, pouring tea into two mugs, one of which read "Teacher of the Century" and the other, "Money Can't Buy Brains Unless You're Going to Stanford."

Judith accepted the tea and a slice of banana bread, then related her adventure on the mystery tour.

"My word!" Helen cried when Judith got to the discovery of Mrs. Carrabas's body. "How horrible. Then it was your picture in Friday's evening paper."

Judith realized there was no television set in sight, which might indicate that Helen hadn't seen the dreadful feature on KINE-TV news. "I'm afraid so," Judith admitted. "I'd rather not have had them run it."

"I can see why," Helen said, exhibiting indignation

for Judith's sake. "Now tell me, please, how your husband fits into all this."

Judith did, including Joe's credentials as a long-time homicide detective. "Helping him with the background is something I can do, even though I'm certainly no sleuth." She tried not to wince; at least the newspaper accounts hadn't mentioned her previous brushes with murder. "I understand you've lived all your life at the Alhambra."

"That's true," Helen said with a solemn nod. "My parents moved there shortly after they were married. The Depression hit them quite hard. I was born a few years later. They liked the location very much, and the rent was always reasonable. Then the war came along, and my father was killed shortly before V-E Day. Mother had no reason to move, so there we remained. It's the only home I know, which is why I'm willing to buy a condo there. Perhaps it's foolish, but I can't imagine living anywhere other than at the Alhambra."

"That's understandable," Judith said. "Do you have any sisters or brothers?"

With a sad little smile, Helen shook her head. "I always assumed that my parents didn't have any more children because they couldn't afford to raise a larger family. Still, we got along very nicely. I was able to attend college, and then I got a teaching job. That was how I met your father. I had student-taught under him, and because he was so impressed with my ability—" Helen stopped, flushed, and put a hand to her mouth. "Goodness, that sounds so conceited. Anyway, your father recommended me for a permanent position at the same high school. Such a fine man. I was sorry to learn that he died rather young."

"His heart," Judith said. "He'd had rheumatic fever as a boy. It left him with an enlarged heart."

Both women were silent for a few moments, lost in their memories of Donald Grover. Judith agreed with

Helen Schnell's assessment. Her father had indeed been a kind man, intelligent, patient, and extremely indulgent when it came to his only child.

"Tell me," Judith said at last, "had you ever heard of this Mrs. Carrabas?"

"No," Helen replied. "I knew nothing about the exorcism, either, until I read it in the newspaper. Such a silly idea, in my opinion. I can't help but wonder if Mr. Guthrie was trying to call attention to the Alhambra merely to help make sales."

"It's a thought," Judith allowed. "He certainly was going to use that cache of jewelry as a promotional ploy."

"Yes." Helen got up to fetch the teapot. "Let me warm that up for you. I'm sorry about those rather hideous mugs, but I packed away all the good china."

Judith accepted the refill. "How many different renters lived in the apartment where the body was found?"

Helen reseated herself and appeared thoughtful. "A youngish couple had that unit until just about the time World War Two started. I don't recall their names. Then came the Epsteins, Jewish refugees from Germany. They died twenty years or so ago, within months of each other. After that, there were the Irwins. He became quite ill, so they moved into a retirement home that had nursing facilities. Unfortunately, he died not long afterward. The last I heard, Mrs. Irwin had Alzheimer's, poor woman."

"So that's why the apartment was vacant," Judith remarked.

"Yes, like the Folger unit upstairs." Helen carefully poured cream into her tea. "Since Mr. Guthrie was planning to renovate the Alhambra, it was pointless to bring in new tenants."

"But there was still furniture left in the Irwin unit," Judith pointed out.

"I know," Helen said. "Mrs. Irwin had very little space in the retirement home. She left many of her things for Mr. Guthrie to dispose of. To be honest," Helen added with a sad little smile, "I think Florence— Mrs. Irwin—was already in mental decline."

"Alzheimer's is a terrible curse," Judith noted. "Tell me—would either the Epsteins or the Irwins be the type to hide jewelry under the floor?"

"I wouldn't think so," Helen replied, "but you never know about people, do you? When I read about the so-called treasure, it crossed my mind that the Epsteins might have brought it with them when they fled Nazi Germany. But why they would keep it hidden baffles me. You also have to remember that there had been other tenants in that unit before the young couple I knew from my childhood."

Judith finally went to the heart of the matter. "How well did you know the Meachams?"

"Not very well," Helen replied. "They lived in the unit next door, but I saw them only in passing. In the elevator, on the stairs, that sort of thing. The daughter— Anne-Marie?—was a sweet little thing."

"Did you ever hear the Meachams quarrel?" Judith asked.

"Not that I recall," Helen said. "Harry Meacham was gone for almost four years, serving in Europe. You must also realize the Alhambra is soundly built. You couldn't hear footsteps overhead or furniture being moved or loud radios and televisions. I don't remember hearing voices from any of the surrounding apartments unless I was passing through the hallway."

"I can see why you want to stay," Judith said. "The fact that two women were murdered in the Alhambra obviously doesn't scare you."

Briefly, Helen's expression betrayed what might have passed for a little thrill, though her words were sober enough. "In a big city, people die violent deaths almost every day. I barely knew the Meachams, and I'd never heard of the Carrabas woman. I don't mean to sound callous, but the deaths didn't affect me. In any event, I didn't realize that Mrs. Meacham had been killed until recently. My mother was convinced that she—Mrs. Meacham—ran off with another man. So many marriages failed after the war. It seemed plausible."

The remark put an idea into Judith's head. "While Harry Meacham was serving in the army, do you know if Dorothy had male visitors?"

"Not that I ever heard of," Helen replied. "Mother would have noticed if she'd seen strange men in the building."

"Who else lived on that floor besides the Meachams and Mr. Holmes?"

"Let me think," Helen said, smoothing her short gray hair at the temple. "A woman named Turner who was an executive secretary downtown.

"No," she corrected herself, "Miss Turner was on three. Straight across the atrium there was a family named Merriam, with three grown children—they had one of the larger units. There were also the Hasegawas, but unfortunately, they were sent to one of those dreadful internment camps during the war. Two young women moved into their unit. I can't recall their names, but because they worked in the shipyards, my parents referred to them as Rosie the Riveter, One and Two." Helen put a hand to her lips, suppressing a smile. "My parents had quite a sense of humor."

Judith felt like asking for an example, but forced a small chuckle instead. "That's five units. How many condos will there be on each floor?"

"Three," Helen replied. "Mine will run all the way across the end of the building."

"Are the sales going well for Mr. Guthrie?" Judith inquired.

"I'm not sure," Helen said. "I don't believe he's gotten

that far into the marketing phase. It's not easy for most people to visualize the finished condos. He may want to hold off until the major renovations are completed."

Judith tried to think if there was anything else she could ask Helen Schnell. So far, the information had proved mundane. "How long did Harry stay after Dorothy turned up missing?"

"A few months, off and on. Then Mother heard he was getting remarried," Helen went on. "I suppose he had to get a divorce first, since Dorothy was believed to be missing rather than dead. Mother thought he acted too hastily."

"Did you ever see the second Mrs. Meacham?" Judith asked.

"Yes, once," Helen replied. "He and Anne-Marie were in the elevator with a rather handsome-looking blond. Mr. Meacham didn't introduce us. Mother felt that was very queer. But she assumed the woman was his bride-to-be. I do recall that when he spoke to her by name, it was Betty or Beth or something like that. I had an Aunt Elizabeth, so I suppose that's why I remember it."

"Did you mention any of this to the police?"

Helen shook her head. "They never asked. Detective Price and that young woman with the long black hair concentrated only on Mrs. Carrabas's murder. That and the jewelry. Naturally, I could be of no real help." Helen got up again. "More tea?"

"No, thank you," Judith said. "I should be going. I didn't mean to take up so much of your time."

"It's no bother," Helen insisted. "Now that I've retired, I sometimes get a trifle bored. All those plans and activities that seemed so enticing while I still taught no longer appeal to me. I'm considering tutoring children, especially the disadvantaged."

Judith had also gotten to her feet. "That's an admirable idea. You still have a lot to give young people."

The praise seemed to embarrass Helen Schnell. "Perhaps." She walked Judith to the top of the steep stairs. "By the way, is your mother still living?"

"Yes," Judith replied.

Helen's expression grew wistful. "You're very lucky. I still can't quite believe that my mother is gone. I'm sure you wake up every morning and thank the good Lord for letting your mother live so long."

"I do," Judith lied, and felt guilty of at least two sins. "Oh—one other thing," she said, urging her conscience to shut up, "do you have Rufus Holmes's current address?"

"No," Helen said. "Mr. Guthrie would have it, though."

"Of course," Judith said, firmly grasping the handrail. "Thanks again."

"You're more than—" Helen stopped. "Did I mention that Mr. Meacham's lady friend had an accent?"

Still gripping the rail, Judith turned her head. "No. What kind?"

"German or Scandinavian," Helen replied. "Or so Mother thought. The woman spoke only briefly in the elevator, which made it hard to tell."

Judith again murmured her thanks, then headed out into the golden August afternoon. Helen Schnell's duplex was located almost at the bottom of Heraldsgate Hill. Jeremy Lamar's tour office was just three blocks away. Traversing the long aisles of Gut Busters while pushing a heavy cart had taken its toll on Judith's hips. She had to drive, rather than walk, the short distance, but luckily found a parking space only a few yards from the Toujours La Tour headquarters.

The door of the one-story brick building was open, but the interior was completely dark. In the patch of light coming from outside, Judith could see another door to her left. She moved toward it on aching hips as the door behind her closed.

Before she could find the doorknob, a ghastly apparition materialized from a scant twenty feet down the hall. Judith let out a strangled cry. The figure was all fluid white motion, with black holes for eyes and a slack-jawed mouth with a lolling black tongue. It seemed to float, coming ever closer to Judith.

Frantic, she fumbled for the doorknob. Clawlike hands reached out to her. Judith screamed and tried to duck out of the way.

The door opened from the other side. Nan Leech stood on the threshold, looking annoyed. The apparition withdrew.

"Dennis, that's not funny," Nan said angrily. "Go practice somewhere else."

The apparition stopped moving, except for its head, which jutted forward. "Boo!"

Judith jumped. The claws tugged at the head, and the face of a freckled young man appeared. "Hi. Did I scare you?"

"You sure did," Judith gasped. "I almost had a heart attack."

Nan stepped forward. "This is Dennis Lamar, Jeremy's younger brother. He's practicing for the Halloween tour." She wagged a finger at Dennis. "Don't ever do that when there might be clients around. You'll scare off business. And turn those hall lights back on right now."

Tucking his spare head under his arm, Dennis trudged away. Nan turned to Judith, as if seeing her for the first time. "Oh. You're—?"

"Judith Flynn," Judith replied. "Otherwise known as the Doyenne of Death. Or, after this little episode, I should be known as dead, period."

"Come in," Nan said. "I apologize for Dennis behaving so thoughtlessly."

Gratefully, Judith collapsed into an upholstered chair in front of Nan's modular desk. Apparently, this was the reception area. A half-dozen other chairs lined one wall, and there were posters everywhere, promoting Tou-jours La Tour's various offerings.

"Let's not waste time," Nan said in her brisk manner. "Have you decided to sue us?"

"What?" Judith was still collecting what was left of her wits. "No. That is, Jeremy apologized and agreed to cut Hillside Manor from his tour."

Nan's cool blue eyes betrayed a touch of amusement. "Hiring your husband didn't hurt, either, did it?"

Judith stared at Nan. "Was that a bribe?"

"No," Nan replied. "It was George's idea. But I'm sure it played some part in persuading you to consider what happened Friday as an embarrassing mistake, rather than a smear tactic."

"Well . . . in a way," Judith admitted.

"So what can I do for you?" Nan inquired, hands folded on the desk, strong features alert and expectant. "A refund, perhaps?"

"No," Judith said, beginning to gather her compo-sure. "My cousin bought the tour at our church school's auction. Since Joe—my husband—is investigating the Carrabas murder, I'm collecting a little background on the case. Frankly, I'm confused. Who recommended Mrs. Carrabas to George Guthrie?"

Nan pushed her half-glasses up on her forehead and gazed at the ceiling. "Hmm. Let me think. Someone called the office and gave her name as an accomplished and successful exorcist. Now who was that? I thought it was one of the former tenants at the Alhambra."

"George said it was the O'Dowds, but they deny it," Judith said.

"Hunh." Nan looked puzzled. "I didn't take the call myself, I just passed it on to George. Now I wonder . . ." The sentence trailed away.

"Excuse me," Judith broke in. "I'm getting more con-fused than ever. The recommendation came through which office? I understood it was at Guthrie Properties."

"It was." Nan's wide mouth twisted in what passed for a smile. "I worked for George Guthrie for several years before I took this job. Jeremy's first secretary didn't pan out and he had to fire her before the tours actually started. He was desperate and I was looking for a change. Toujours La Tour sounded intriguing. I'd had enough of work orders and eviction notices and subcontractors and all the other drudgery that goes into a construction and property management business. I've been on the job here for two weeks as of today."

"That sounds like a good move on your part," Judith said. "You must have had to bone up pretty fast on the tour spiels, though."

Nan's expression was wry. "I moved up here from L.A. many years ago. I've always been a history buff. There is no history in L.A.—how can there be when the motto is 'What have you done for me lately, baby?' One of the first things I did after I moved here was to join the city's historical society."

"With a special emphasis on Heraldsgate Hill?" Judith asked.

"No, not particularly," Nan replied. "I live in one of the condos George built between the hill and downtown. I have no specialized geographical interest. I'm more intrigued by the period covering the Depression and World War Two. It was a time of enormous change around here. Now," Nan continued, still brisk, "what would you like to know regarding Mrs. Carrabas's murder? I can't tell you much, of course. If I could, George and Jeremy wouldn't have hired your husband."

Judith expelled a little sigh. "There has to be a connection between someone here—by that I mean someone with ties to the Alhambra—and Mrs. Carrabas. I expect that Joe will have some background information on her by this afternoon. But can you think of anyone— anyone at all—who might have known her in some other way?"

Nan looked blank. "I can't. I wish I knew who left

that phone message about her a few weeks ago. But it was on one of these"—Nan held up a pink phone memo pad—"with her name, the number to call, and something scribbled about her being a highly recommended exorcist. I thought the recommendation came from the O'Dowds, but I must have read it wrong."

"You don't know who wrote the note?" Judith asked.

Nan shook her head. "I think I'd gone to lunch at the time. All sorts of people went in and out of that office. Other employees, construction crew, real estate salespersons, you name it. If they were waiting around for George, sometimes they'd answer the phone if it kept ringing. We had trouble with our system, and the messaging service was all fouled up."

"I see." Judith grew thoughtful. "I'm interested in the past, too. Does it strike you as strange that Mrs. Carrabas should be murdered at the Alhambra just a short time after Mrs. Meacham's body was found?"

"I hadn't thought about it," Nan said.

"Who did the research on the Meacham murder for the tour presentation?"

"Jeremy, originally," Nan said, "but after I came to work for him, he turned it over to me." She pulled her chair away from the desk and opened a file drawer. "All the information is here. Would a copy of it be helpful?"

"Definitely," Judith said, feeling excitement well up inside. "Do you mind?"

"It won't take long." Nan took the file over to a copy machine in the corner of the reception area. "There's nothing private about this. We got it all from old newspaper accounts and public records."

"And no one knows what happened to Harry Meacham?"

Nan turned on the copy machine and began feeding it pages from the file. "Not as far as we could discover. He'd told the neighbors he was moving to California for a fresh start. Maybe he went someplace else instead. Everybody flocked to California in those days."

"Including your parents?" Judith inquired.

Nan was putting the copies in order. "No. They'd come out from Texas during the Depression. I suppose that's one reason the period intrigues me." She slipped the fresh pages into an envelope, then turned to Judith. "They never found their pot of gold. I used to wonder why they didn't go back."

Judith rose as Nan handed her the envelope. "Thanks so much. You've been very helpful."

"I doubt it," Nan said. "Frankly, I can't imagine how the two murders could be connected, except by location. Lightning can strike twice, you know."

Judith started to smile, then saw that Nan's cool blue gaze had turned downright frigid. As she left the offices of Toujours La Tour, Judith wondered if Nan's last comments were just an opinion—or a warning.

Joe arrived home shortly before five. As Judith had predicted, he'd gotten Aimee Carrabas's background from Woody.

"She was born Aimee Elise Ritter in Santa Monica," he said as he sat down at the computer in the kitchen. "She was married at least twice, to an Augustus Aure, whom she divorced, and to James Carrabas, who died six years ago. No children. She got into the exorcism business not long after Mr. Carrabas passed on. Woody tracked down a feature story on her in the Orange County paper. She got her start by visiting a medium who tried to put her in touch with her late husband. Apparently, the venture was a success, at least by Mrs. Carrabas's standards, and she became interested in all forms of spiritualism. According to the article, she's performed several successful exorcisms, including a fundamentalist church in Anaheim, a city park in Oceanside, and the bullpen at Dodger Stadium."

"You're joking," Judith said. "At least about that last one."

"No, I'm not. I've got a copy of the article right here."

He tapped the file folder on the counter. "A couple of years back, a middle-relief pitcher swore that his ERA was so high because his grandmother was haunting him. She'd wanted him to be a lawyer instead of a baseball player. So the guy hired Mrs. Carrabas to exorcise Granny's spirit."

"And it worked?" Judith asked in amazement.

"I don't know," Joe replied. "Two days later he got traded to the Mets."

Judith, who'd decided it was cool enough to turn on the oven, finished placing tiny pastry cups on a cookie sheet. "Is there any connection between Mrs. Carrabas and the Alhambra?"

"None that Woody or I could see," Joe admitted. "Homicide detectives down there are interviewing the neighbors and some of her clients. That'll take some time, but it should turn up something."

"Have you found out when she actually arrived in town?" Judith asked, putting the cookie sheet into the oven.

"She flew up Friday morning," Joe said, making more entries into the computer. "No help there. She had a round-trip ticket with a return to John Wayne Airport that evening. Obviously, she didn't plan to stick around and visit potential killers."

"Frankly," Judith said, "her résumé doesn't impress me."

"Read the article," Joe said, handing Judith the file folder.

The photo of Mrs. Carrabas struck Judith first. Seated in front of a bookcase and wearing a flowered blouse along with a friendly smile, she looked like a pleasant, ordinary woman who'd make a good neighbor. Judith recalled the contorted face of the bloodstained woman on the bed in the Alhambra and felt a sharp pang.

The article, bylined "Alexis Mayo, Staff Reporter," bordered on the tongue-in-cheek. It was clear, however, that Aimee Carrabas took her calling seriously:

"Evil exists in the world," Mrs. Carrabas was quoted as saying, "though many people scoff at the idea. But while the spirits who spread misfortune and tragedy are very real, they can be dispelled through belief in a Higher Power, which translates as Good in capital letters. Certain people possess the gift to rid the world of these negative forces. I believe I'm one of those who have been given that ability. Perhaps it's because I've encountered evil in my own life and have overcome it."

Judith scanned the rest of the background material that Woody had passed on to Joe. Mrs. Carrabas had lived in various places in and around Los Angeles. Apparently, she had moved away twice, once in the mid-sixties, and again in the early seventies. Her occupations had included hairdressing, retail sales, grocery store demonstrator, and running an art gallery in Pasadena. Financial assets uncovered so far included a house assessed at a hundred and eighty thousand dollars, a savings account of almost thirty thousand dollars, and an IRA worth twenty-five thousand dollars. She had no criminal record, not so much as a traffic ticket. Her life didn't seem to point toward a violent death.

"She sounds harmless," Judith remarked.

"So she does," Joe agreed, frowning at the computer screen. "How do I merge documents? Which goes into which? Does it matter? I hate these damned things. They drove me nuts at work."

Judith leaned over Joe's shoulder. "Here," she said, moving the mouse. "Do this . . . then this . . . then that. Voilà!"

"Sure," Joe grumbled, "it's easy when you know how."

An item in the newly merged documents caught Judith's eye. "What's that about a four-hundred-thousand dollar loan application? I didn't see that in the file."

"Oh—Woody hadn't had time to enter it," Joe said.

"A couple of weeks ago, Mrs. Carrabas applied for a real estate loan through one of the local banks. Approval hadn't come through yet."

"She was buying another house?" Judith inquired, straightening up and emitting a little groan.

"I guess." Joe turned around in the swivel chair. "What's wrong? The hips acting up? Did you call Dr. Alfonso?"

Judith's hands flew to her cheeks. "I forgot! I'll do it first thing tomorrow."

"You'd better," Joe said with concern. "How could you forget when you're in such pain?"

"We women play through pain," Judith replied, half-serious. She removed the pastry cups from the oven and put them on the counter. "I have a file of my own to show you. I hope you don't mind, but I did a little sleuthing, too. By accident," she added hastily. It was best to omit the previous night's visit to the O'Dowds or the afternoon conversation with Helen Schnell. Joe would be angry with her not only for getting in too deep, but for neglecting her health.

Turning off the computer, Joe regarded his wife with justifiable suspicion. "You were sleuthing by accident?"

"Yes," Judith said, avoiding Joe's gaze as she poured out two measures of Scotch. "On the way back from Gut Busters, I stopped by Jeremy Lamar's office to make sure that Hillside Manor wouldn't be on the mystery tour anymore."

"Jeremy agreed to that yesterday," Joe said, still suspicious.

"I know," Judith replied, adding ice before handing Joe his glass. "But with so much going on with Jeremy right now, I thought maybe he hadn't remembered to get the message through to his staff, especially Nan Leech, the other tour guide." In retrospect, the fib sounded quite plausible.

Joe must have thought so, too. "So you got it squared away?"

Judith nodded. "While I was there, I asked about the historical background that had gone into the Alhambra visit, especially regarding the Meacham murder." Judith picked up the envelope that Nan had given her. "Here. This is all the research. I haven't had time to go through it myself, so I thought we could study it together."

Joe gave Judith a perplexed look. "What for? That's from fifty-odd years ago. Are you trying to connect the two murders?"

"Well," Judith replied, "maybe."

Joe shook his head in disbelief. "Don't bother yourself. How in the world could you possibly go from the Meacham woman to Aimee Carrabas?"

"The jewelry, for one thing," Judith responded. "What if the jewelry stash tied in with Dorothy Meacham's death? Suddenly it's found, right after her body is discovered. Then Mrs. Carrabas shows up and gets killed. Can you honestly rule out a connection?"

Joe took a deep drink from his glass and sighed. "Maybe not. But it's an awfully big stretch, Jude-girl. I prefer to concentrate on the here and now."

"Okay," Judith said. "Let me work on the 'then.' "

"Go ahead," Joe replied, almost too agreeably. "That sounds like your kind of thing."

Judith shot a sharp glance at Joe. He was patronizing her, she was sure of it. Just as a biting remark formed in her brain, the front doorbell rang.

"I'll get it," she said, vexed at the interruption. While the B&B still had a vacancy on this Monday night, all the guests with reservations had already arrived. Judith trudged out to the entry hall and opened the door.

Dr. Alfred Ashe stood on the porch, his long-lashed black eyes darting in every direction.

"May I come in?" the chiropractor asked in a voice that trembled.

"Of course," Judith said, stepping aside. "What's wrong?"

Alfred practically dove into the house. "Can you lock that?" he asked as Judith closed the door.

"Yes, but . . ."

"Please." His skin had turned a sallow shade and the hands that held an attaché case shook as if palsied.

Dutifully, Judith shot the dead bolt and regarded the newcomer with concern. "Can you tell me what's upset you, Dr. Ashe?"

"May I stay here tonight?" he asked on a gulp. "I'm sorry to bother you, but I think someone's trying to kill me."

EIGHT

SCOTCH IN HAND, Joe had come into the entry hall. "What's going on?" he asked, sounding more like a cop than a husband.

Quickly, Judith explained how she'd met Dr. Ashe on the tour and how he had helped her with his chiropractic skills. "He's got a problem," Judith said. "He thinks he's in danger."

With a practiced eye, Joe studied the short, sturdy middle-aged man. "Let's go into the front parlor. You can tell us all about it. I'm a retired cop, by the way."

Surprise spread over Alfred's broad features, but he attempted a small smile. "Twice today someone tried to run me down," he said after being seated in one of the parlor's armchairs and given a glass of brandy. "The first time, around ten o'clock this morning, I thought it was just an accident. I was downtown, coming from my hotel. A car jumped the curb and almost hit me. Now, while I was walking from the bus stop on that steep avenue a block from here, it happened again, only this time I was crossing the street to get here."

"Did you see the driver?" Joe asked.

Alfred shook his head. "All I can tell you is that it

was a medium-sized sedan, a dark color, and probably a fairly late model. Cars all look alike to me these days."

"You were coming here?" Judith said. "Why?"

"I was leaving town this evening," Alfred replied, his hands finally steady. "I'd checked out of the hotel. But I wanted to talk to you one more time about that jewelry. My hobby is old gold and silver. I'm something of a collector."

"Why," Joe asked, "would anyone want to kill you?"

Alfred looked bewildered. "I've no idea. I really don't know anyone in town."

"Where do you live, Doctor?" Judith inquired, listening for the guests' arrival in the living room.

Alfred hesitated before answering. "San Francisco," he finally replied. "I came here last week for a chiropractic meeting, and decided to stay on for a few days to see the sights. This is my first visit."

Joe was still in his policeman's mode. "You're absolutely certain that the two incidents involved the same car?"

Alfred grimaced. "I think so. I have to admit, I don't drive. San Francisco has terrible traffic. So I'm afraid I just don't pay much attention to makes and models and such. This morning, everything happened so fast. I sensed, rather than saw, the car come over the curb. Naturally, I jumped out of the way. By the time I collected myself, the car was lost in traffic."

"And just now?" Joe prompted.

"I'd crossed the avenue, and when I got to the other side, I had to cross again because your place is on the north side of the street," Alfred explained. "There were cars parked along both sides. I checked to see if anyone was coming, but I saw nothing. I started out, and all of a sudden a car came as if from nowhere. It must have missed me by inches. I turned around to look at it, but it was already gone around the corner. I don't even know which direction it might have been headed."

Judith could hear the voices of guests on the staircase.

As she excused herself, she heard Joe ask if the car might not have been waiting near the intersection. Unfortunately, she couldn't catch Alfred's response, but was certain that Joe was probably right. The view was clear for the east-west street that led from the north-south avenue. Alfred would have been able to see an oncoming car from at least three blocks away.

By the time Judith had finished serving the guests and made conversation in an uncharacteristically detached manner, Joe was concluding his interview with Alfred.

"Dr. Ashe wants to spend the night here," Joe said as Judith reentered the parlor. "You've got a vacant room, right?"

"Yes," Judith replied. "Room Two. By chance, it's our only single accommodation."

Alfred nodded and stood up. "I'll cancel my flight. I'm very grateful for your hospitality." He made a formal little bow to Judith.

"It's no problem," she assured him, leading the way into the entry hall and up the stairs. "I shouldn't ask, but wouldn't you feel safer leaving town?"

Alfred shook his head. "If someone's trying to kill me, they may know my original plans. This way, I can put them off the scent. They'd never guess that I was coming here."

Judith supposed that Alfred's reasoning made sense, though she wondered if he was overreacting. After showing him the small but cozy room in the front of the house, she left him in the upstairs hall, using the phone to have his luggage sent from the hotel where he'd left it with the bell captain.

Joe was in the kitchen, preparing T-bone steaks for dinner. "Well?" he asked. "What do you make of Dr. Ashe?"

"Frightened," Judith said. "Unnerved."

Joe looked up from applying meat tenderizer to Gertrude's steak. "You think so?"

Judith stared at her husband. "Don't you?"

"I'm not sure," Joe answered slowly. "After you left to take care of the guests, he asked quite a few questions about that jewelry stash at the Alhambra."

"Really," Judith said, recalling how interested Alfred had been in the treasure when she'd run into him by the opera house Friday afternoon. "He mentioned that his hobby was old gold and silver. I suppose that's why."

"Maybe," Joe said. "I think I'll have Woody run him through the computer."

"You think he's a crook?" Judith asked in surprise.

"Not necessarily," Joe replied. "But it never hurts to check."

Judith felt obligated to defend Alfred Ashe. "He's a fine chiropractor," she declared. "I'd still be sitting in that damned trolley seat if it hadn't been for him."

The golden flecks in Joe's green eyes danced. "You mean he's well-adjusted?"

Judith ignored the remark.

After dinner, Judith used Renie as an excuse to get out of the house. "Renie needs some more help with that art exhibition project. I'm meeting her at Toot Suite's."

Joe looked up from loading the dishwasher. "I don't get it," he said, his manner bemused. "How can you be so much help to Renie all of a sudden?"

"I'm . . . a stand-in," Judith fibbed. "She's using me to frame photographs before she has the actual model available."

Joe's expression was quizzical. "Renie's doing graphic designs for a Native American art exhibit at Toot Suite's? How come? To see how many hot fudge sundaes it takes to inspire native artisans?"

"No, no," Judith said, heading for the back door. "We're just meeting there. See you."

The local ice cream parlor was only two blocks away, and ordinarily Judith would have walked the distance. But her hips were too painful, so she took the car. Luckily, most of the shops along the avenue were closed for the day, and she found a parking space across the street.

Renie was waiting for her, studying a menu with all the concentration of a banker staring at what might be a counterfeit hundred-dollar bill.

"As you know," Renie said as Judith sat down at the marble-topped table, "I'm not crazy about sweets until I actually see them before me."

"Yes," Judith agreed. "You prefer large roasts and several pounds of Dungeness crab, among other things."

"Don't be snide," Renie said, putting the menu aside. "You're just jealous because my busy little metabolism allows me to eat myself into a fit without getting fat."

"You're absolutely right," Judith said, "but I've lost weight this summer, so I can splurge. I don't have much of an appetite in warm weather."

The waitress, who was a member of a large family at Our Lady, Star of the Sea, took the cousins' orders. Out of the corner of her eye, Judith spotted Norma Paine, yet another parishioner, sidle into the ice cream parlor with the collar of her cotton jacket pulled up and a cloche hat pulled down to conceal her face.

"Norma," Judith hissed, "pretending she's not here indulging her sweet tooth."

Renie glanced over at the corner table where Norma had seated herself. "Norma, that big fat Paine," she murmured. "We're on to her."

"But she thinks we aren't," Judith said as she got out the file folder that Nan Leech had given her that afternoon.

"I had to sneak this into my purse," Judith said. "I also had to lie to Joe. He thinks that digging into the Meacham murder is silly."

"Did he believe you?" Renie asked.

"No, but he pretended." Judith opened the folder. "I haven't had time to look at this myself. I suspect it's pretty much what we heard Friday at the Alhambra.

The only problem is, I was so mad at Jeremy Lamar then that I didn't pay close attention."

"It was pretty cut and dried," Renie said. "Harry came home from work, Dorothy wasn't there, the little girl was at the neighbor's, Harry finally called the cops later that evening. Dorothy was never found until George Guthrie opened up a wall and out she came, somewhat skinnier than she used to be."

"Hold it," Judith said. "Why didn't anyone notice? I mean, wouldn't there have been a stench?"

"From inside a wall?" Renie frowned. "Eventually, I suppose. But if there was, only the occupants of that apartment would've noticed, right? And if Harry killed Dorothy, he might put up with it for a while. As I recall, he moved out a short time later."

"You're right," Judith agreed. "If the police came to see Harry that night or even the next day, they wouldn't have noticed any odd odors that soon. He'd have removed any trace of his handiwork with the wall, and at that point, I doubt that the cops would have been looking for a body in the apartment. After all, it was Harry who had reported his wife as missing. At that point, he wouldn't have been a suspect because it was undoubtedly assumed that Dorothy was alive and well, but either wandering in a daze or had run off with another man."

"Not an uncommon thing to happen with war-time marriages," Renie noted. "The GIs came home and discovered that their wives had fallen in love with someone else. Maybe Dorothy had, maybe that was the motive. It just took her a while to get up the nerve to tell Harry she was leaving him."

"It's possible," Judith allowed. "But would she leave without her daughter?"

"It happens," Renie said.

Judith looked at the file, most of which was old newspaper clippings, though there was a police report concerning the missing woman.

"Harry reported at eleven twenty-six that night that his wife should have been home by five o'clock, six at the latest," Judith recounted to Renie. "The neighbor who had taken care of Anne-Marie stated that Dorothy promised to be back by four-thirty. The neighbor was . . . Oh, my God!"

Renie leaned closer. "What? Who?"

"The neighbor was Mildred, Mrs. William, O'Dowd."

"I thought," Renie said after the shock had settled in, "the O'Dowds didn't live in the building at that time."

"They didn't," Judith said, noting that Norma Paine was hiding behind the menu. "Their address is given at a residence two blocks away. The children must have been friends. The O'Dowds mentioned having two children, Frankie and Danny. They must have been about Anne-Marie's age."

"We didn't ask if they knew the Meachams," Renie said suddenly. "They merely told us they didn't live in the Alhambra at the time of Dorothy's disappearance. We just assumed they weren't acquainted."

"You're right," Judith said with a wry expression. "Never assume anything. We know better. Now we'll have to go back and talk to them again."

"And have all that fun?" Renie remarked sarcastically. "Why not stab ourselves in the gums and bleed into a fruit bowl?"

"Hey, do you remember the old *Comet*?" Judith asked, ignoring her cousin's remark.

"Sure," Renie replied. "I was just a kid, but it went out of business not long after the war. They did a lot of human interest stuff, with real sob-sister reporters. You know, what they used to call there's-a-light-burning-in-the-window journalism."

"This article is from the *Comet* and suits that style perfectly," Judith said. "It was written a few days after Dorothy disappeared, and I quote, 'A bereaved Harry Meacham, whose wife, Dorothy, has been missing since

Tuesday, moved out of the apartment the couple shared on lower Heraldsgate Hill. He has sent his adorable yet bewildered four-year-old daughter, Anne-Marie, to live with kindly relatives while he continues the search for his beloved wife. A pale and haggard Meacham allowed that he might return to the apartment later, but for now, he is too grief-stricken to stay on. Still, Meacham isn't giving up hope, and expressed his belief that Dorothy may yet return to their once-happy home'."

"She had, actually, though legally dead," Renie said, and then frowned. "Relatives? What relatives?"

Judith's banana split and Renie's hot strawberry sundae arrived. "I never heard about any relatives," Judith said, giving her unwanted maraschino cherry to Renie. "Harry's relatives? Dorothy's relatives?"

"He came back to the apartment," Renie pointed out, swallowing the cherry in one gulp. "Isn't that what you said on the phone?"

Judith nodded. "Eventually, Helen Schnell saw them, along with the woman presumed to be the future second Mrs. Meacham. I gather that Helen's mother didn't miss much. It's too bad the old girl is dead."

"So Harry left until Old Stinky faded away?" Renie suggested, oblivious to the strawberry syrup she was dribbling down the front of her cream-colored tee.

"Probably," Judith said. "Maybe they went to live with the foreign blond. Damn. Why do you suppose no one was ever able to trace Harry after he moved away?"

"Did anyone try?" Renie asked, as more syrup dripped from her short chin.

"You have a point," Judith conceded, trying not to regard Renie with dismay. "There wouldn't have been that much paperwork for Harry to handle, since Dorothy couldn't be declared dead. It has to make you wonder, though, about those so-called relatives."

"Maybe they were Dorothy's," Renie offered. Her entire front was now covered with thick, red, strawberry syrup. "Maybe they didn't exist. Maybe we're crazy. Why are we doing this deep background?"

"I told you," Judith persisted, noting that Norma Paine had just been served the Toot Suite Hog Trough Special. "I have a feeling the two murders are connected."

"I don't," Renie said bluntly. "I'm with Joe. But I'll humor you."

"Thanks." Judith shot Renie a dirty look, which wasn't hard to do, given her cousin's disgusting appearance. "What about the jewelry? Why couldn't that be tied to Dorothy Meacham, and why couldn't Aimee Carrabas be connected with it, too?"

"Because Aimee had never been to the Alhambra before in her life? Because she lived in California? Because she probably didn't know it existed?"

"Yes, she did," Judith countered. "George Guthrie told her about it, because they were staging the exorcism in the same unit as the treasure."

"Well . . . maybe," Renie allowed, swerving around in her wire-back chair to look at Norma, who was shoveling in large spoonfuls of ice cream and various toppings. "But that doesn't mean Mrs. Carrabas had anything to do with the stash. Good grief," Renie said, lowering her voice, "how can anyone eat like such a pig?" Jumping up from the chair, Renie accidentally knocked her spoon onto the marble-topped table, causing a sharp report. "Hey, Norma!" she shouted. "Hi, there!"

The sound of the spoon had already caught Norma's attention. Her head had jerked up and her mouth flew open. "Oh, my God!" she cried. "She's been shot!" Jamming the hat further down on her head, and gathering her jacket around her, Norma fled Toot Suite's in a cloud of chopped pecans.

The other customers stared at the departing figure, then stared at Renie. Their horrified reaction finally caused her to look down at her chest. "Oh, shoot," she muttered, "I've soiled myself. Again." With a sigh, she sat down.

"It was pointless to warn you," Judith said. "This is about as messy as I've ever seen you. Can't you talk and eat at the same time?"

"I just did," Renie said, looking rather bleak. "The problem is, I talk, eat, and slop at the same time."

"Okay." Judith sighed, putting down her spoon and folding her hands on the small table. "Let's get back to business. Try looking at my situation from another point of view. Joe's been hired to help find out who killed Mrs. Carrabas. No matter what he says, he really doesn't want me interfering with his investigation. On the other hand, he isn't interested in the Meacham murder. I am. So I figure it's okay for me to work on the earlier case without rankling Joe. Who knows? I may actually turn up something helpful."

Renie tipped her head to one side. "Okay. I see your point. He's Mr. Present, you're Mrs. Past."

"Right." Judith nodded before taking another spoonful of ice cream. "Our next step is seeing the O'Dowds again."

"Not an easy step," Renie pointed out. "Will they let us in?"

"They didn't throw us out," Judith noted.

"True," Renie allowed. "Are we going there now?"

"We could," Judith said, but there was uncertainty in her voice. "I wonder if it might prove more beneficial to visit the Alhambra."

"What excuse do you use to get in this time?" Renie asked, finishing her sundae without spilling another drop. "You know the uniforms will still be there, and maybe a night watchman as well."

"I thought I'd tell the truth," Judith said. "I'm helping Joe."

"But you're not," Renie pointed out. "So it isn't the truth."

"Well," Judith hedged, "it is, indirectly."

The cousins paid their bill and made ready for departure, which included several extra minutes to mop up Renie, the chair, the table, and the floor. "It would have been nice if you'd brought along some drawing paper," Judith said as they took the Subaru down to the bottom of the hill. "I'd like to make a floor plan of the Alhambra."

"I can draw it on the file folder," Renie said, pulling on her tee to help dry it out. "Then I'll put it on the computer. No problem."

On the last day of August, the sun was already going down by eight o'clock. In the western sky over the bay and behind the mountains, soft shades of gold merged with lavender. A homeward-bound ferryboat caught the fading sun, and the portholes glittered like diamonds.

The sight reminded Judith of the treasure. "Say," she said, turning off the steep avenue and heading for the Alhambra, "I just thought of something. Why was the rug pulled up in the unit where Mrs. Carrabas was killed?"

"Because of the stash," Renie replied. "Guthrie had to—" She stopped, her jaw dropping. "Shoot. That unit hadn't been cleared out yet. They wouldn't pull up the carpets until the furniture was gone. I don't get it."

"They'd pull up the carpet to put the treasure there, not to find it," Judith said excitedly. "George never said where it was found, I just assumed . . . So is it a real treasure or a plant?"

"As in, publicity stunt?" Renie said. "Could be. We've suspected both Guthrie and Jeremy Lamar of doing that sort of thing."

"Dorothy Meacham's body was not a plant," Judith said, pulling up outside the Alhambra. "It doesn't make sense that it would be, it's too gruesome. But it gave George Guthrie the idea of hiring an exorcist to negate the evil vibes or whatever. Maybe he added the treasure as another plus."

"That makes sense," Renie said as the cousins got out of the car.

"Which means," Judith said, sounding disappointed, "that the jewelry is just a red herring. If it was put there by George, I don't see how it could tie in with Mrs. Carrabas's murder."

"So there is no connection between her death and Dorothy's?" Renie asked as they approached the apartment house entrance.

"Not that I could see," Judith admitted. "The link was the stash, tying it to Dorothy Meacham then and Aimee Carrabas now."

"Don't feel bad," Renie said, patting Judith on the back. "Maybe you'll get another idea."

Petrovich and his partner were again on duty as they had been the previous night. The taller officer, whose name tag identified him as "L. Swanson," eyed the cousins with suspicion.

"You're back," he said in a flat voice.

"We're doing a little scouting for Joe, my husband," Judith said. "He wants my cousin—she's an artist—to make a floor plan."

"Detective Price already did that," Petrovich put in. "Why can't Mr. Flynn use that one?"

"He forgot to get it copied," Judith fibbed. For all she knew, the floor plan was already tucked away in Joe's file. "It won't take us long."

"That's what you said before." Petrovich sighed. "Okay, okay. I suppose I shouldn't mess with Detective Flynn's wife."

"You shouldn't," Judith responded. "He may be retired, but he still has friends on the force. Like Woody Price, his former partner."

Petrovich turned pugnacious. "Is that a threat?"

"No, of course not," Judith said in mock horror. "I just meant that you wouldn't want any hurt feelings."

"That's true," Petrovich admitted. "Okay, Larry here can go in with you this time."

Once again, the cousins headed for the second floor, though Judith insisted on using the elevator to spare her aching hips. The open hallway was alight, but Apartment 204 lay in darkness. Petrovich hit the switch.

In 204, the Meacham apartment, the cousins revisited the site of the grisly discovery in the wall. The floor plan was similar to that of 303, where Mrs. Carrabas had been found, except that the former Meacham unit had two bedrooms. The living room wall on the left where Dorothy's body had been found was only partially destroyed. Recalling the position of the coat closet in 303, Judith turned to Renie:

"I'll bet Harry sealed Dorothy up in the closet, removed the door, and put in a new wall. It wouldn't be that hard. Harry was training to be an engineer. Maybe he'd had some kind of carpentry experience in the army."

"While Anne-Marie stayed with the O'Dowds?" Renie suggested.

"We'll ask them that," Judith said as they moved on to the next unit.

Swanson trailed after the cousins as they proceeded to Apartment 205. "I don't know who lived in some of these other units, but this one," Judith said, relieved to find that the door swung open at a touch, "belonged to the Schnells."

"So they were right next to the Meachams," Renie said.

"That's right. But they never heard anything, like quarrels or throwing each other across the room," Judith said as Swanson turned on the lights.

The former Schnell unit had been stripped, which figured, since Helen had moved out all of her belongings. One of the walls had been removed between the living room and the kitchen, and a new window was being framed over what apparently had been the sink. There were no fixtures or appliances; plaster dust floated on the air like spring pollen.

The rugs were gone, too. So was at least half the kitchen floor. Judith stared down into a dark hole about the size of a big bathtub.

"I wonder . . ." she murmured.

Renie eyed her curiously. "What?"

"Never mind," Judith said under her breath. "Later."

The remaining unit on the second floor was empty. "The Hasegawas, way back when," Judith murmured with a sad shake of her head.

The cousins and Officer Swanson had come back to where they started, by the elevator.

As if on cue, Renie glanced at Judith. "We may as well check out the other units, just so I can get an idea of how to identify them on the floor plan."

"I'd like a look at the third floor myself," Judith said to Swanson. "Do you mind?"

"Nope," Swanson replied. "It gives me something to do besides stand around like a statue."

"No problems? No intruders?" Judith asked casually as they got into the elevator.

"Not really," Swanson replied. "Just some kids trying to sneak in to look at the courtyard last night. I guess the day shift caught some guy poking around today before we came on at six."

"Oh?" Judith said as they exited the elevator. "What did he want?"

"He wanted in," Swanson replied as they stood in front of Apartment 301. "Some of the construction guys were here. They're allowed to work in certain areas the police have either searched or figure don't count, like the courtyard. Anyway, one of them found this man lurking around and told him to take a hike."

"Was he homeless?" Renie inquired as they stepped into another empty unit.

"No," Swanson said. "I heard he was a well-dressed middle-aged guy carrying an attaché case."

Judith and Renie exchanged quick glances. "Did he say why he was snooping?" Judith asked.

Swanson shrugged. "I think he said something about being interested in buying one of the condos. He seemed harmless, so the uniforms on duty let him go."

"When was that?" Judith asked.

"Umm . . ." Swanson's high forehead furrowed under his regulation hat. "Not long before we came aboard. Five o'clock, maybe? I think it was just before the construction crew knocked off, which is about then."

"Alfred Ashe," Judith whispered to Renie as they peeked into Apartment 302. "By the way, the O'Dowds lived in 301."

"Got it," Renie said. "What about this one?"

Apartment 302 was also empty, but untouched by the wrecking ball. "Ah . . . I forget," Judith said. "Oh—a woman named Turner, somebody's executive secretary. That was in the forties. The O'Dowds said the pot-smoking girls were in here before the big move."

Nothing in 303 seemed to have been moved since the cousins' previous visit. With Renie trailing, Judith poked her head into each room, then returned to the living room. After glancing into the closet where she'd found Renie hiding, Judith went across the room to where the treasure had supposedly been found. The carpet was rolled back no more than two feet, with a gaping hole half that size where the floorboards had been.

"This is the only part of the floor in this apartment that's been torn up," Judith whispered to Renie. "Joe and Woody both must realize this was a put-up job. The jewelry probably belongs to George's mother."

Rufus Holmes had lived in 304. Perhaps it was Judith's imagination, but the empty unit seemed cold and lonely. She wondered if the atmosphere reflected the man himself. Recluse or not, Judith determined to see him the next day.

They went on to the last two units on the floor, where they found only a minimum of destruction. Apartment 305 had belonged to the Whiffels. Judith half-expected to see old lady Whiffel's ghost, smashing whiskey barrels and melting down poker chips. The former Baines apartment, 306, showed no signs of Emil's occupancy. If the ostrich had tried to bury his head in the carpet, repairs had been made.

"Is that it?" Swanson asked, making an effort to conceal his boredom.

"Yes," Judith said as they crossed over to the elevator. "Thanks very much." Waiting for the car, she turned to Renie. "This is fascinating, a microcosm of life in the past fifty years. Twice that long, if we knew more about it. Take that last apartment on two," she went on as the elevator doors opened. "That's a sad story in itself."

Swanson let out a wide, deep yawn. Judith made a face behind his back, but took the hint. "Later," she said to Renie.

It was only about three minutes later that the cousins got into the Subaru and Judith was able to relate the tragic account of the Hasegawa family.

"They were shipped off to one of those horrible internment camps," she said, starting the car. "Doesn't that just make you wild?"

"It's one of the sorriest episodes in American history," Renie declared, "not to mention just plain stupid. Did you know that while all the West Coast Japanese were being rounded up, they never did anything about the ones who lived in Hawaii? Not that they should have, but the islands were much closer to Japan. The whole thing defies common sense."

"I was a baby when it happened," Judith said, "but my dad raved about it all during the war."

"Idiocy," Renie asserted. "Dumb as a bag of dirt. So what happened to the poor Hasegawas?"

"I don't know," Judith said as they headed back up the steep hill.

"You don't know? That's the story? Sheesh." Renie shook her head.

"Okay, okay," Judith said, "let's move on."

"You have no choice," Renie said dryly. "Your short story was really short."

"So why is Alfred Ashe being chased by somebody with deadly intentions, why is he holed up at Hillside Manor, and why was he found lurking around the Alhambra this afternoon?"

Renie sighed. "I can't answer the first question. Come to think of it, I can't answer the second or the third, either. Can you?"

"He's interested in that jewelry," Judith said. "He admits that much. He's a collector. But the jewelry isn't at the Alhambra, the police took it. Maybe somebody else is after the jewelry, too. They want Alfred out of the way. He's hiding at the B&B because he doesn't want to leave town yet. Is any of this making sense?"

Judith had pulled into the parking lot of the local convenience store, just a few steps away from where Renie had parked her car. "It makes *some* sense," Renie said. "But Alfred isn't from around here. Didn't you mention that this is his first visit to the city?"

"That's what he said," Judith responded. "It may not be true. But he's such a cute little guy with those dimples and long eyelashes. I have to admit, I find him rather endearing."

"I'm sure he knows that," Renie said. "Men always do. Confront him, tell him you're on to him. With all that cute stuff going on, at least he doesn't look dangerous."

"That doesn't mean anything," Judith said. "Haven't we met a few so-called harmless types before and then they turned out to be homicidal maniacs?"

"One or two, maybe," Renie admitted. "Hey, got to run. Bill will begin to think I don't love him anymore."

Judith held up a hand. "Wait. One other thing. That hole in the Schnell kitchen—it gave me an idea."

"Okay, let's hear it," Renie said, one hand on the door lever.

"If," Judith said, "and it's a big if—that jewelry

wasn't found in the unit where Mrs. Carrabas was killed, it might—a big might—have been found somewhere else in the building. Why not in the floor of Helen Schnell's former apartment?"

Renie scratched her head. "It might have been. It might also have come from Grandma Guthrie's jewel case or a pawnshop downtown or at the bottom of the ocean on a sunken Spanish galleon. Next question."

"Scoff if you will," Judith said, her jaw set in a hard line. "But tomorrow, I'm going to get the truth out of George Guthrie, even if it kills me."

Renie opened the car door and swung her legs out. But before she got out, she gave Judith one last look. "Given your past history, coz, that's exactly what might happen."

NINE

JUDITH WAS AS good as her word. After Joe left to pursue his investigations and Phyliss Rackley showed up to start cleaning the house, Judith headed out to the industrial part of town to call on George Guthrie. Since Guthrie Properties was located only a short way from Gut Busters, she planned to use the discount warehouse as her excuse for being in the neighborhood.

The company headquarters was located in a nondescript two-story building. Chain-link fences protected the heavy equipment and vehicles out back. Once inside, the open office area looked modern and well-designed. Judith had called ahead, making sure that George would be in. She hadn't given her name.

A young man with a clean-shaven head and a single silver earring looked up from what appeared to be the receptionist's desk. "May I help you?" he asked.

"Yes," Judith said with a smile. "I'd like to see George for a minute, if he's free."

The young man smiled back. "May I give your name?"

"Tell him it's Mrs. Flynn," Judith replied. "My

husband is working for him on the Alhambra homicide."

Briefly, the young man looked disturbed. "Terrible," he murmured, pressing a button somewhere on his desk. "Mrs. Flynn to see you, Mr. Guthrie."

Judith couldn't hear George's response, but the young man was frowning. "No, I realize she doesn't have an—Yes, Mr. Guthrie . . . Of course."

With a raised hand, Judith forestalled the receptionist. "Tell George it's okay if he doesn't want to see me. But ask him why he moved the treasure from the Schnell apartment to the one where I found the corpse."

The young man paled. "You . . . found . . . the . . . ?"

Judith nodded. "Just ask him, please."

Somewhat timorously, the receptionist passed the question on to his employer. A moment later, George Guthrie jerked open a door at the far end of the long, partitioned room.

"Come in," he said in an angry voice.

"Good morning," Judith said, walking between the cubicles where employees worked at computers and talked on telephones. "I was on my way to Gut Busters, and I—"

"Wanted to upset me," George grumbled, closing the door behind them. "Sit down, but it'll have to be quick. How did you know we moved the gold and silver stuff?"

Judith's eyes roamed around the large, well-appointed office with its mahogany desk and mounted sailfish trophy. "You should have torn up more of the floor in 303," she said lightly. "That was a dead giveaway. I'm surprised the media didn't catch on."

"They did," George said with a scowl. "At least Liz Ogilvy figured it out. But she's keeping her mouth shut. A treasure's a treasure, and anyway, the murder sort of buried the treasure. So to speak."

"You still haven't answered my question," Judith said calmly. "Or did you already tell Woody and Joe?"

"No," George sighed. "I didn't see any point. In fact, I sort of forgot. A dead body tends to put the small stuff out of your mind." He paused and picked up a coffee mug bearing the Guthrie Properties logo. "The old Schnell unit was already torn up pretty bad. It wasn't a proper setting for an exorcism, just like the Meacham apartment wouldn't have worked as well. I had to pick a unit where we hadn't done much damage yet. We couldn't use any of the first floor because my guys were working there. The third floor was best because 303 was in decent shape. That's all there is to it."

The explanation's logic made sense to Judith. "So you really did find the gold and silver in the old Schnell unit?"

Guthrie nodded. "It was in the kitchen. I hear the cops are still waiting to get more information from the experts. If they can date that stuff, then we'll have some idea of when it was put there."

"The Schnells have lived in 205 since around 1930," Judith pointed out. "Have you asked Helen about it?"

"Hell, no," George retorted. "What if it's not hers? What if it goes back to when the place was first built over ninety years ago? She might try to claim it anyway. That wouldn't be right. If possible, the stuff should be returned to the rightful owner. Or at least the owner's heirs. That's another reason the old Irwin unit in 303 was a better site. They're long-gone." George scowled at Judith. "You weren't going to mention any of this to Helen Schnell, were you?"

"No," Judith responded, "though Helen strikes me as an honest woman."

George laughed without humor. "Mrs. Flynn, if you'd been in the property management and construction business as long as I have, you'd know there is no such thing as an honest woman—or an honest man. Everybody's out to get something for nothing. A bigger bathtub here, a higher grade of glass there, a couple of more light fixtures in the ceiling—all for the original quote.

Hell, most people would chisel you out of a handful of nails if they thought they could get them for free."

Judith didn't doubt the lessons of George's experience. "So Helen doesn't know," she murmured.

"And won't, as far as I'm concerned," George declared. "Just keep your mouth shut about it, okay? If that stuff's hers, wouldn't she have had it removed before she left the apartment house?"

Judith conceded that George had a point. "One other thing," she said. "Could you give me Rufus Holmes's temporary address?"

George looked suspicious. "What for?"

Judith shrugged. "Joe asked me to get it," she lied.

"Okay," George said. "Rory has it someplace."

"Rory?"

"My secretary-receptionist, the one you were talking to. He replaced Nan Leech," George explained.

Judith rose from the chair. "I understand Nan worked for you a long time."

"Over twenty years," George said. "I'd just taken over the business from my dad. He got his start during the postwar building boom. Nan had been selling real estate, and she was sick of it, so I hired her. I guess she got burned out here, too. But a quarter of a century is a long time to stick with one job."

"Yes," Judith said, "almost a quarter of a century can seem like an eon." It was how long she'd been apart from Joe. It might as well have been a lifetime. "Thanks, George," Judith said, heading for the door. "I appreciate your candor."

"Sure," George said with a wave of his hand. "Oh— by the way—one curious thing which might help date that treasure."

"Yes?" Judith said, turning in the doorway.

"I noticed something weird about a pair of silver earrings in that chest," George said. "They had swastikas on them."

* * *

Rory provided Judith with Rufus Holmes's current address, which was in an old hotel in the historic lower part of downtown. Having visions of a four-story walk-up, she also got Rufus's number and called him from a pay phone on the street by the parking lot.

A gruff voice answered on the third ring. It turned out not to be Rufus, but the desk clerk.

"He don't have no phone in his room," the voice growled. "Wanna leave a message?"

Judith hesitated. "Yes," she finally said. "Tell him I'll meet him at the Commercial Café in twenty minutes. Breakfast is on me."

"Does he know who 'me' is?" the desk clerk inquired.

"I'm his ex-wife," Judith said, and wondered what on earth had prompted her to say such an outrageous thing.

"Okay," the desk clerk said. "But you oughtta know Rufus don't get out much. I ain't guaranteein' he'll show."

Judith decided to take the chance. Traffic was heavy as she drove into downtown. It was after ten, which meant that Rufus had probably eaten breakfast. If he ate breakfast. She couldn't be certain that he'd fall for the ruse. The O'Dowds had mentioned a brief marriage, but they'd been vague and could be mistaken. She supposed that if Rufus didn't come to the café, she could somehow manage to see him in the hotel. But she preferred not to: The building was on the fringe of respectability, and she'd rather stay in a safer area.

The Commercial Café was a venerable landmark, dating back to the turn of the century. Like much of the surrounding neighborhood, it had been refurbished in the past two decades. What was once a seedy, run-down district had become fashionable and gentrified. The red and brown and cream-colored brick buildings had been restored to their former glory, and now housed shops, offices and condominiums.

Like the Alhambra, the café retained its original

period features. A massive oak bar, supposedly brought 'round the Horn from Boston, covered one entire wall. The wooden tables and booths looked as if they'd been there forever, though they were highly polished and well-sanded.

Midway between breakfast and lunch, the restaurant was virtually empty this time of day. Judith sat down in one of the booths with her eyes on the entrance. After telling the waiter that she was meeting a Mr. Holmes who wouldn't recognize her, she ordered coffee and waited.

And waited. Twenty minutes later, she was about to give up and make the sacrifice of walking the four blocks to the old hotel. But just as she was trying to get her server's attention, a tall, gaunt man of sixty came through the door. He stopped to speak to the waiter just as Judith accidentally knocked her purse on the floor. She was bending down to retrieve it when she heard a terrible moan.

Judith looked up just in time to see the man in the doorway collapse in a dead faint.

The waiter, who was young and apparently inexperienced in the ways of the world, called out into the back room for the manager. Instead, the cook, a chubby black woman, came racing out from the kitchen.

"Don't just stand there, Greg, call 911," she ordered.

Judith had gotten out of the booth and was standing by the fallen man. "Do you know him?" she asked of the cook and the waiter.

Greg looked vague; the cook gave a slight nod. "Occasionally, at least in the past couple of months." She waved a dimpled hand at Greg. "Call 911! Move it!"

The man was coming around, however, one thin hand suddenly flung over his face. He groaned. Greg went off to the phone.

"You know this guy?" the cook asked.

"Not exactly," Judith replied, feeling awkward.

The man moved his hand away from his face. His gray eyes were open and so was his mouth. "My love . . ." he moaned, then blinked up at Judith, and passed out again.

"You sure you don't know him?" the cook persisted, her dark eyes suspicious.

"I think I know who he is," Judith said. "His name is Rufus Holmes."

"Well," the cook said, folding her arms across her big bosom, "he sure took one look at you and passed right out. If you don't know each other, how come? You don't have a face that would stop any clock I've ever seen."

"Thanks," Judith murmured. "Honestly, I don't know why he fainted."

Greg had returned from the phone. "The medics are on their way, Alva," he said to the cook. "Where's Phil?"

"Phil went out for a smoke," Alva replied, then glanced at Judith. "Phil's the manager. He won't like all this commotion one bit."

"It's not my fault," Judith insisted. "For all I know, this man isn't the person I was supposed to . . ."

Even as Judith spoke, the man began to revive again. He strained his eyes at Judith, gave a little shake of his head, and, with Greg's help, struggled to sit up.

Alva brought him a glass of water. "Here, sir," she said, at her most polite, "take a sip."

The man started to refuse, then apparently thought better of it, and duly swallowed a small amount from the glass. "Who the hell are you?" he demanded, glaring at Judith.

"I'm Judith Flynn," she replied in what she hoped was a soothing tone. "Are you Rufus Holmes?"

"Hell, no," the man shouted, scrambling to his feet. "Never heard of him." With that, he raced out of the café.

Judith rummaged in her purse, found her wallet, and shoved a twenty-dollar bill into Alva's hand. "Thanks," she said. "Bye."

She ran as fast as she could out onto the sidewalk. The gaunt man was also running, faster than Judith. At the corner, he just managed to get across the street before the light changed and a medic's van came tearing around the corner. When the van had passed on toward the café, the man had disappeared. Judith went limp, her hips hurting, her head suddenly aching.

"They should have come for me," she said under her breath, and leaned against a storefront.

The hotel where Rufus lived was three blocks east and one block south. Judith didn't know if she could walk that far. Maybe the man who had come into the Commercial Café wasn't Rufus Holmes. Maybe Rufus was still holed up in his hotel room. There probably wouldn't be any parking nearby. Surrendering to pain, Judith walked the block and a half to the public garage where she'd left the Subaru.

Renie was just about to go down into the basement to start her workday when Judith showed up at the Jones residence.

"You look like bird poop," Renie said. "What's wrong?"

"Can you make tea?" Judith begged. "Please? I've had too much coffee for one morning."

"Sure, come in, sit down in the dinette, tell your loving cousin everything," Renie said, leading the way into the kitchen.

"Where's Bill?" Judith asked, collapsing into one of the oak chairs at the butcher-block kitchen table.

"One of his old patients had some kind of spell," Renie answered as she turned the water on under the cow-shaped tea kettle. "Mr. Burpee thinks he's been captured by Amazons."

"He's complaining?" Judith asked.

"No, but Mrs. Burpee is," Renie said, sitting down at the table across from Judith. "Bill went over there to calm them both down."

Judith began her account of the morning's adventures, pausing when the tea kettle sang and Renie got up. "I like your deck a lot," Judith remarked. "I don't see any way we could have one at our house."

"You've got a patio," Renie replied. "Besides, your backyard is on the level. Ours drops down not only from the house but further out in the yard."

"I know," Judith said, admiring the lush late summer growth of the evergreens and fruit trees. "You have a much larger yard, all the way back to the next street."

"You bet," Renie said, gloating a little as she handed Judith her tea. "A second legal lot. We're sitting on a gold mine."

"Speaking of which," Judith said, "I was about to get to the part about the swastikas on the earrings."

Renie stared. "Huh?"

Judith recounted what George Guthrie had told her. "What I was wondering," she went on, "is if all that jewelry could be treasure stolen from the Nazis?"

Renie drew back in her chair. "Huh?" she repeated.

"Think about it," Judith said. "We don't know about all the people who lived in the Alhambra before and during and after the war, but we do know that Harry Meacham served in Europe, the Epsteins were Jewish refugees, and apparently Mr. Schnell was killed in the war. We also know that the second Mrs. Meacham was probably a woman from northern Europe, maybe even Germany."

"You're off somewhere with Mr. Burpee and the Amazons," Renie remarked, adding a large amount of sugar to her tea.

Judith looked askance. "No, I'm not. There are all sorts of tales about the looting of Nazi treasures after Germany was defeated. Who else but Nazis would have swastikas on their jewelry?"

Renie started to open her mouth to reply when a large shadow seemed to hover outside on the deck. She leaned toward the window as footsteps could be heard close by. Suddenly, a form appeared on the deck outside the window. "Yikes!" Renie cried. "It's Emil!"

The ostrich flapped its wings and thrust its beak at the glass. Both cousins leaped out of their chairs and backpedaled away from the table. Emil seemed very angry.

"Where's the damned phone?" Renie exclaimed, her head turning every which way. "Ah! There it is, on the counter." She grabbed the receiver and began punching in numbers.

"Who're you calling?" Judith asked as Emil continued to flap and thrust.

"The cops," Renie replied. "We're being attacked, aren't—Hello, yes, this is Mrs. Jones at—"

Judith lunged at Renie and wrested the phone out of her hand. "You idiot!" she cried, disconnecting the receiver. "We need to call Mr. and Mrs. Baines. This stupid ostrich belongs to them, remember?"

"Oh." Renie looked sheepish. "I forgot. Let me get the phone book so I can find their number." She reached under a counter by the back door and pulled out the white pages. "Do you know either of their first names?"

"Dave and Emily," Judith replied promptly. "Isn't that what Midge O'Dowd told us?"

"I guess." Renie was down on the floor, scanning the listings under Baines. "Here they are, over on your side of the hill. That's right isn't it?"

"Yes," Judith said, gazing at the window, "but it's wrong to call them."

Renie looked up. "Huh?"

"Emil's gone." She pointed out beyond the backyard where Emil could be seen running down the street.

"Shouldn't we let his owners know he's alive and flapping?" Renie asked.

"Yes," Judith said, sitting back down at the table. "I suppose it wouldn't hurt."

Renie started to dial the Baineses' number.

"Wait!" Judith called out sharply.

"What now?" Renie looked annoyed.

"They live near the O'Dowds, right?" Seeing Renie give a faint nod, she went on: "Let's drop in on them when we go see the O'Dowds. Now."

"Now?" Renie replaced the phone book and stood up. "I have to go to work."

"It's not quite noon," Judith said. "You never start until after that."

Renie sighed. "Okay. I'll leave a note for Bill. But we'd better be back here no later than one-thirty. I've got a deadline, you know."

To Judith's consternation, Dave and Emily Baines weren't home in their one-story Roman brick house four blocks from the O'Dowds and three blocks from Hillside Manor. Leaving a note under the welcome mat about the second sighting of Emil, the cousins drove to the O'Dowds' apartment, where Billy answered the door.

"Not you again," he said with something akin to aversion.

Judith presented her most winning smile. "Please, we just have a couple of questions."

Midge appeared behind Billy. "Ask now," she commanded, jaw jutting. "It's a nice day, you can stand outside."

"All right," Judith said calmly. "We're here to warn you. The police may be about to arrest you for withholding evidence and obstructing justice."

"What?" shrieked Midge, her face turning a deep red.

Judith nodded solemnly. "This is a murder investigation, after all."

"We don't know anything about any wizards and such," Billy declared.

Midge rammed an elbow into her husband's arm. "That woman was a conjurer, not a wizard, you dummy."

Billy shook himself. "Whatever."

"She was an exorcist," Judith said, still very calm. "But that's not the point. I'm talking about Mrs. Meacham, not Mrs. Carrabas."

"Mrs. Meacham!" Midge's high color began to fade. "Why, that was a million years ago. What're you talking about?"

"The two homicides may be linked," Judith said, trying to squelch any doubts in her own mind. "You didn't tell us—that is, the police or my husband—that you not only knew the Meachams, but that you were the ones who were taking care of Anne-Marie the day that her mother disappeared."

"A lot you know," Midge shot back. "We told the police all that stuff when Dotty didn't show up back in forty-six. As for now, nobody's asked us. Except you two pests."

"You're missing the point," Judith said, her calm fraying a bit. "I mentioned that the two crimes may be connected. All we want is some information about Anne-Marie. For instance, how long did you take care of her after her mother disappeared?"

Instead of finally inviting the cousins in, as Judith had hoped, the O'Dowds both moved out onto the small porch, which forced Judith and Renie to descend the single step to the path.

"She stayed two nights," Midge said.

"She only stayed one," Billy put in.

"You're crazy," Midge retorted. "She stayed the night before and the next night, after Dotty disappeared. Don't you remember? The first night, I couldn't get her and Frankie to go to sleep. It was the first time Anne-Marie had ever stayed over. Besides, Danny kept bugging them."

Billy didn't argue this time, and Judith took Midge at her word. Mothers had better memories than fathers when it came to recollections of their children.

"Was it your idea to invite Anne-Marie for the night?" Judith inquired.

Midge grimaced. "I guess so. Or maybe Harry or Dotty suggested it. Honest, I forget."

On the sidewalk a few feet away, a young couple walked by with two pugs on leashes. The morning cloud cover had broken, and the first day of September promised to be warm.

"By the way," Judith asked, "are Frankie and Danny both boys?"

Midge let out a hoot of laughter. "They're girls. Francesca and Danielle."

Billy gave his wife a baleful glance. "Mrs. Fancy Pants here. She had to come up with these high class names. So they end up being Frankie and Danny. Sheesh."

"They got those nicknames because you couldn't spell their given names," Midge asserted. "You can't spell 'cat'."

"I can, too," Billy countered, looking belligerent. "C-A—"

"T," Renie put in, a bored expression on her face. "Can we move along here? I've got work to do."

"That's a good idea," Judith said quickly. "I only have a couple of other questions. Did you ever take care of Anne-Marie after her mother disappeared?"

"No," Midge replied. "Harry sent her to live with an aunt or somebody. What was her name, Billy? I forget."

"Cat," Billy retorted, still belligerent.

"Beth," Midge said, looking triumphant. "Aunt Beth. It just came back to me."

"On which side?" Judith inquired. "Harry's or Dorothy's?"

The O'Dowds exchanged glances: Midge's was puzzled; Billy's was blank. "I'm not sure," Midge said at last. "I never heard Dotty speak of having a sister. Or a brother, either. I think Harry's family was all back east. Ohio, maybe."

"Iowa," Billy put in.

"Perhaps," Judith suggested, "it was a close friend that Anne-Marie called aunt."

Again, the O'Dowds looked at each other, but this time they both appeared troubled.

Midge turned back to the cousins and sighed. "I doubt it. Poor Dotty didn't have any friends, except maybe me. She was kind of . . . odd."

"In what way?" Renie asked.

"Paranoid," Billy said. "At least that's what they used to call it. She thought people were out to get her."

"Now Billy . . ." Midge began.

"Don't try to dress it up," Billy interrupted. "Dotty was dotty and that's it. She thought everybody in that apartment house was trying to steal from her. Not that she had much to take. Oh, there were plenty of jobs for women during the war, but Dotty couldn't work because she wasn't right in her head. Besides, she had to stay home with the little girl."

For once, Midge agreed with her spouse. "That's so. Dotty and Harry got married just before the war. They didn't have much, just newlyweds starting out. Anne-Marie was born right after Harry went in the army. Not that we knew them then—that came later, when our little girls got acquainted in the park."

"But Harry must have had friends," Judith pointed out.

Midge frowned. "I'm not so sure he did. He was going to school on the GI bill and working part-time. Harry was hardly ever home. Maybe that was part of it with Dotty. She was alone too much with Anne-Marie. That trip downtown the day she disappeared was a big outing for her. She was pretty nervous about it, too. I guess that's why I thought it'd be nice for Anne-Marie to sleep over another night. It'd give Harry and Dotty an evening together for his birthday."

"Bull," Billy sneered. "Harry asked you to keep Anne-Marie. He said he couldn't let her see how upset he was about Dorothy."

Midge went on the defensive. "So? I still felt sorry for Dotty."

A picture of Dorothy Meacham was beginning to form in Judith's mind's eye. Young, naïve, afraid, alone. Harry was away in the service for over four years. Dorothy stayed home with their child, going out only for groceries or to the park. The Meachams probably didn't have a car. Not all women drove in those days anyway, and gas was rationed. Judith felt a pang for the lonely woman, waiting for the occasional censored letter to come through from Europe.

"Where was Dorothy from?" Judith asked.

"Here," Midge responded.

"Denver," Billy said, almost in unison with his wife.

They glared at each other. "Actually," Midge said, "I think it was more like Reno."

"Las Vegas," Billy put in.

"Nevada, anyway," Midge said, apparently allowing for compromise. "Yes, that was it, someplace in Nevada. Not Reno, not Vegas, a funny name that began with a 'T.' Harry met her on his travels. He sort of worked his way west and they settled here."

"One last question," Judith said. "Do you know anything about that jewelry chest that was found in the Alhambra?"

"The one they mentioned in the news?" Billy asked. "Not a thing. We sure never found anything tucked away in our apartment."

"Except some mice," Midge added. "They should have allowed cats. The cats would have gotten rid of the mice."

"Cats," Billy repeated. "C-A-T—"

"Thanks so much," Judith interrupted again. "We really appreciate your help. As I said, I have a feeling the two murders may be connected. By the way, how long was it before Harry came back to stay at the apartment?"

"You mean after Dotty disappeared?" Midge said, with an inquiring glance for Billy. "What? A few weeks?"

Billy nodded. "He didn't stay but a few days. The next thing we knew, he was gone without a word."

"You'd have thought he'd have stopped by to thank us for having Anne-Marie," Midge said. "At the time, I figured he was upset. But now . . . well, we don't know if Harry really killed Dotty, do we?"

Judith blinked at Midge. "You're right," she said, faintly awed. "We don't."

TEN

JUDITH HAD FORGOTTEN all about Alfred Ashe. He hadn't appeared for breakfast with the other guests, so she had assumed he was worn out from the previous day's perilous adventures. It was hardly the first time that a guest had chosen to sleep in during a stay at the B&B.

After dropping Renie off, Judith was foiled in her attempt to hurry back home. The hill's burgeoning population created a midday traffic jam throughout the commercial district. The neighborhood's popularity had come at a high price that included more than soaring real estate sales.

"Drat," Judith muttered as she passed Falstaff's Grocery at two miles an hour. "Where do all these people come from?"

Joe's cherished MG wasn't in the driveway or the garage, so Judith assumed he hadn't returned from his morning's endeavors. Gertrude, however, was stumping along the garden path on her walker.

"Where've you been?" she snarled at Judith. "What time zone are you in? Right here, it's one o'clock. My lunch is an hour late."

"I know, Mother," Judith said, hurrying to help

the old lady up the back porch steps. "I'm sorry. I got waylaid."

"By bandits, I hope," Gertrude said with a sneer. "It'd serve you right. Where's Lunkhead?"

"Please, Mother," Judith begged, "can't you call Joe by his name?"

"His name is Joe?" Gertrude looked puzzled. "What happened to Dan?"

"Dan died," Judith said, wondering if her mother was feigning stupidity or was genuinely confused.

"He did, huh?" Gertrude said as they proceeded into the kitchen. "Did I go to the funeral?"

"We had a memorial at our former parish near Thurlow Street," Judith said. "Dan was cremated."

"Before or after he died?"

"Mother . . ."

Gertrude eased herself into a chair at the kitchen table. "You got any sardines? I'm in the mood for sardines, with sweet pickles."

"I think I have both," Judith said. "Let me check on something real quick, okay? I'll be right back."

"I'll bet," Gertrude mumbled as Judith hurried toward the back stairs.

The long, narrow flight not only winded Judith but made her hips ache even more. She paused for breath in the hallway, then proceeded the length of the house to reach Room Two. The door was closed. In Room Three, she heard Phyliss Rackley running the vacuum cleaner.

"Phyliss," Judith called from the doorway. "Phyliss!" she called again, much louder.

Phyliss jumped and turned off the vacuum. "Great Jehoshaphat," the cleaning woman cried. "You scared me. I thought at first you were Lucifer himself."

"I'm not," Judith said with a straight face. "Have you cleaned Room Two yet?"

Phyliss shook her head. "I started from the other end today, with Room Eight. Why are you asking?"

Judith explained that the guest in Room Two hadn't shown up for breakfast, at least not before Judith had left Hillside Manor shortly after nine-thirty.

Phyliss perked up when Judith described Dr. Ashe. "You say he's a chiropractor? Let me know when he wakes up. I've got a few body parts I'd like straightened out."

Judith was afraid that Dr. Ashe might not be waking up at all. Warily, she returned to Room Two and knocked. There was no answer. Judith used her master key to open the door, but discovered that it was unlocked. Taking a deep breath, she gazed into the long, narrow room.

It was empty. The bed had been made. A suitcase and an overnight bag were stowed by the dresser. On the single pillow lay a note written with a black felt-tipped pen. Judith picked it up and read it swiftly.

"Mrs. Flynn—I've gone to the library. Do you have a vacancy for tonight? Thanks. Alfred Ashe, D.C."

Judith heaved a sigh of relief. Alfred hadn't gone to his eternal reward, only to the library. Room Two was vacant until Thursday, the unofficial jump start of the Labor Day weekend, when Hillside Manor would be completely filled.

Curiosity overcame her. Slowly easing down on her knees, she unzipped the overnight bag. It contained the usual items—a shaving kit, socks and underwear, a pair of corduroy bedroom slippers, a couple of health industry magazines.

Next, Judith opened the suitcase. More socks, more underwear, some shirts, two pairs of neatly folded slacks, a cardigan sweater, shoes in flannel bags, a brown leather belt, pajamas, and a bathrobe. Judith reached into the flat inner pocket and pulled out a letter-sized manila envelope. The single word BACKGROUND was written with the same black felt-tipped pen that had been used on the note to Judith.

Gingerly, Judith slipped the dozen or so pages out of the envelope. They were copies of articles from various publications, mostly magazines, but also at least two encyclopedia pieces.

The subject was the internment of Japanese citizens during World War Two. In the corner of an article from a recent literary magazine was a notation written in a fine hand.

"I saw this today while I was waiting at the dentist's. Thought you could read it on the plane. Hiroko."

Judith put the articles back in the envelope, slid the envelope into the pocket, and closed the suitcase. Intrigued, she went downstairs to call Renie.

"What now?" Renie demanded in a crabby voice. "I'm trying to work here."

"Sorry," Judith apologized, though she didn't sound like she meant it, "but I had to bounce an idea off of you."

"Go ahead. I'll hang up. Call me back later when you find out how far you can bounce it."

"Coz . . . please."

"Okay, okay." Renie sighed. "Make it quick."

Judith related what she'd found in Alfred's suitcase. "What do you make of that?" she asked Renie.

"At least you didn't find Alfred sticks up," Renie remarked. "To be frank, I don't make anything of it. Dr. Ashe is doing some research. Didn't you say he'd gone to the library? What's so weird?"

"He said he came here for a chiropractors' meeting," Judith said, annoyed by Renie's lack of enthusiasm.

"So?"

"But he came prepared for something else," Judith persisted. "He brought all these articles on the internment camps with him. Now he's off to the library. I'll bet that attaché case of his is stuffed with more information about the government's shocking behavior toward the Japanese in this country."

"You're probably right," Renie said with a yawn.

"Not to mention his notes from the chiropractor conference. Boy, this is really fascinating. What next, X-rays of his patients?"

"Coz," Judith said sharply, then stopped. "That attaché case . . . Could it have belonged to Mrs. Carrabas?"

"It could," Renie replied with another yawn. "Or to—get this, it's pretty wild—Dr. Ashe."

"Okay, big mouth," Judith said, as exasperated as Renie, "who is Hiroko?"

"Hiroko?" Renie sounded puzzled.

"The person who gave Alfred the article to read on the plane."

"I don't know. Who is Hiroko? That could be a song—'Who is Hiroko? Who can she be? Tra-la-la . . . ' " Renie sang in her perfectly dreadful off-key voice.

"Stop that or I'll have to strangle you," Judith commanded. "I think Hiroko could be Alfred's receptionist or maybe another chiropractor."

"Come on, coz," Renie said, her patience just about gone, "what's your point?"

"I'm not sure." Judith's voice had gone flat.

"Then stop bouncing." Renie clicked off.

Judith was frustrated. She'd flunked her chance to meet Rufus Holmes, she was stymied in talking again to Helen Schnell because she couldn't bring up the jewelry stash, and her vague suspicions about Alfred Ashe were nothing more than a wild guess. For almost an hour, she went through her afternoon routine like a robot, thoughts darting this way and that.

Then inspiration hit. Grabbing the phone, she dialed Aunt Deb's number. The initial chitchat took at least five minutes, but Judith figured it was worth it. Finally, she was able to ask the question uppermost in her mind.

"Aunt Deb," she said, "do either Mr. Whiffel or his sister have all their faculties?"

"Why, dear," Aunt Deb replied in her kindly voice, "I'm not sure they ever did. Don't you recall how I always said that Mr. Whiffel was difficult? He had so many queer ideas, especially about money and religion. It was very hard to get him to attend to business. As for his sister, Jewel, well, she was a retired guidance counselor for the schools, and had about as much common sense as a pigeon. I can only guess how many children she sent down the wrong path. Our prisons are probably full of them."

"Where are the Whiffels living now that they moved out of the Alhambra?" Judith inquired.

"A Christian retirement home up near the hospital district," Aunt Deb replied. "I've never been there, of course. You know how busy Renie is—she can't seem to take her mother many places. Of course, it is hard for her to get me around in my wheelchair."

Since Judith knew that Renie carted Aunt Deb to bridge, to lunch, to coffee klatches, and just about everything else except the sidelines of pro football games, Judith shouldn't have spared her aunt any sympathy. Except that, being softhearted, Judith did.

"How would you like to visit them?" she asked.

"Really?" Aunt Deb sounded shocked. "Oh, dear—I don't think so. It's kind of you to offer, but Jewel is so deaf, and when I think of how stingy Mr. Whiffel always was, I get quite angry. Besides, they never wash their dishes. It's disgusting. Renie practically threw up the last time we visited them at the Alhambra. But then you know how delicate Renie is."

Judith's eyelids fluttered in disbelief. Her cousin might be small, but she was about as delicate as a rhinoceros. "How long did the Whiffels live in the Alhambra?"

"Goodness, forever," Aunt Deb replied. "I worked for Mr. Winston first, then he brought Ewart—Mr. Whiffel—into the practice right out of law school, not long before Renie was born. Even then, Ewart and Jewel and their mother were living at the Alhambra. Mr. Whiffel had died shortly before Ewart finished his law degree. Old Mrs. Whiffel was a tartar. She was such a religious fanatic that she used to send magazines to the office but only after she'd cut out the liquor and cigarette ads, which, in those days, didn't leave much to read. Your Uncle Cliff used to always light up in front of Ewart. One time, he smoked two cigarettes at once. He'd forgotten he already had one going."

"Maybe I'll call them," Judith murmured. A visit to the Whiffels was sounding less and less appealing.

"And gambling!" Aunt Deb exclaimed. "The whole family was dead-set against any kind of gambling. I remember one Friday night, Mr. Whiffel stopped by at our house to drop off some papers I needed to sign. We were playing six-handed pinochle—not for money, of course—and Mr. Whiffel practically had the fan-tods. I was a bit embarrassed, especially when your Uncle Cliff asked Mr. Whiffel if he'd like to play a hand. And of course your mother—you know what a card fiend she is—got her wallet out of her purse and threw a five dollar bill on the table. I must say," Aunt Deb added with a sniff of contempt, "that was about the only time I ever saw Gertrude throw her money around. Really, Judith dear, she's almost as big a skinflint as Mr. Whiffel."

"I think I'll call them," Judith said, grateful to get a word in edgewise. "Do you have the number handy?"

"Yes, of course, it's right in the address book I keep in the pocket of my wheelchair. I never know when I'll feel like calling up an old friend."

Like constantly, Judith thought, hearing the faint sound of her aunt rummaging around at the other end of the line.

"Jewel is quite crippled with arthritis, you know," Aunt Deb was saying. "She doesn't get out much anymore. I sympathize. The last time I spoke with her, she'd had a bad fall. She'd been out to lunch with Helen Schnell, a schoolteacher friend of hers, and Jewel said

Helen was very careless about not hanging on to her tight enough when they were leaving the restaurant by the fountain in the foyer and poor Jewel landed right in the middle of the—"

"There's someone at my door," Judith said, interrupting her aunt and actually telling the truth. "Can I get that number?"

"Of course, dear, it's . . ."

Judith hurriedly scribbled the Whiffels' number on a piece of scratch paper, then carried the phone with her to the front door. "Thanks so much, Aunt Deb. Did you say Helen Schnell?"

"Yes, I did, dear. She taught with your father, I believe. Later, she was at one of the high schools where Jewel was the guidance counselor. Can you imagine what kind of advice Jewel must have given those poor young—"

"Talk to you later, Aunt Deb. Thanks so much." Judith clicked off with one hand and opened the door with the other.

Alfred Ashe, wearing a sheepish expression, stood on the doormat. "I didn't know if I should use my key during the day or just knock," he said, the long eyelashes drooping.

"It's not locked until evening," Judith said with a small smile. "Did you find what you were looking for at the library?"

Alfred gestured with the attaché case. "I did. I went to the one downtown, and everyone was most helpful."

"I used to be a librarian," Judith remarked. "I still have several friends who work in the various libraries around the area. Most of us enjoy helping patrons. We learn while doing, and research is like detective work. I'm not up to speed on all the computer tricks or the databases. Was there anything they couldn't find for you?"

"No," Alfred replied, looking pleased as he flashed

his dimples. "The main thing I wanted wasn't that hard to find. Of course, they keep the old city directories on microfiche."

"Yes," Judith said slowly. "They did that even when I was still working as a librarian over ten years ago. How far back were you searching?"

"Ah . . ." Alfred's glance shifted to the elephant foot umbrella stand. "Just before the Second World War."

Judith forced a big smile. "Ancestor hunting, I'll bet."

Alfred's eyes widened and swerved back to Judith's face. "How did you know?"

Judith let out a little sigh. "Come into the living room, Dr. Ashe. We need to talk, especially if you're going to stay with us another night. And yes, I do have a vacancy. But I'm just a trifle confused about what's going on."

"Well, really," Alfred began, shifting the attaché case from one hand to the other. "It's nothing, I merely—"

"Did anyone try to run you down today?" Judith asked over her shoulder.

Reluctantly, Alfred followed Judith into the living room and perched on the arm of one of the matching sofas. To Judith, it looked as if he were poised for flight.

"Hiroko is from this area," he said, gripping the attaché case with both hands. "She's interested in her family. Yes, I guess you could say I'm on an ancestor hunt."

"Hiroko?" Judith echoed.

"Yes," Dr. Ashe replied with a lift of his head. "Hiroko Hasegawa."

"Hasegawa?" Judith said in surprise. "Wasn't there a family by that name who lived at the Alhambra many years ago?"

"Yes," Alfred said, sounding tense. "That was her family, though she was born a few years later."

Judith's expression grew sympathetic. "They were sent to an internment camp, I heard."

"That's right." Alfred's expression was grim. "Can you imagine such an injustice in this country?"

Judith shook her head. "It was panic, I suppose, after Pearl Harbor was bombed. But that doesn't excuse such stupidity. It's very kind of you to help your friend."

Alfred's long lashes fluttered as he blinked several times in rapid succession. "My friend? Do you mean Hiroko?" He paused as Judith gave a nod. "Hiroko's my wife."

"Oh!" Judith exclaimed and smiled through her embarrassment. "You called her Hiroko Hasegawa, so I thought she must be—"

"She kept her maiden name," Alfred interrupted. "She's an attorney."

"Is searching for Hiroko's family your real reason for coming here?" Judith asked. "That is, you took the tour of the Alhambra and now you're staying at Hillside Manor which is close by."

"Let's say I seized the opportunity," Alfred replied, shifting uncomfortably on the sofa arm.

"Including an opportunity to go back to the Alhambra yesterday afternoon?" Judith inquired.

"Oh." Alfred covered his mouth with his hand and looked out at Judith from under his long lashes. "How did you know?"

Judith tried to look mysterious. "I have my methods."

"Your husband's investigating the murder of Mrs. Carrabas, isn't he?" There was a note of accusation in Alfred's voice.

"Um . . . yes, yes he is." Judith cleared her throat. "What are you looking for, Dr. Ashe?"

"Please, call me Alfred." He paused, his eyes traveling along the plate rail with its collection of Blue Willow, Royal Doulton, Belleek, and Friendly Village pieces. "It's a long story, and perhaps a hopeless one. If you don't mind, I'd rather not discuss it just now. I may be on a wild goose chase."

"Okay." Judith decided to surrender. Temporarily. "Speaking of chases, why would anyone try to kill you?"

Alfred actually blushed. "I'm afraid I misled you, Mrs. Flynn."

"Call me Judith. How come?"

"This is rather painful," Alfred said.

"Don't fuss," Judith soothed. "You wouldn't believe the people who have unloaded on me over the years, from the Thurlow Street Library to this very living room." She left out the slobbering drunks at the Meat & Mingle. Even Judith was sometimes careful of her image.

"Yes," Alfred said slowly. "Yes, you have a sympathetic face. You invite confidences. And you let me stay here last night under false pretenses."

"So tell me about the cars chasing you or not chasing you, as the case may be."

"Well." Alfred set the leather case on his knees and folded his hands on top of it. "I wanted to be closer to the Alhambra. Besides, I'd only reserved my room at the hotel downtown through Sunday night. They've got a conference going on there that started yesterday, so they were full for last night. I didn't feel right about just dropping in on you, so I sort of made up the story about being chased. But," he added on an ominous note, "there are a lot of very bad drivers in this city."

"True," Judith said, and let Alfred's explanation slide. "Okay, the room is yours until Thursday morning."

Alfred beamed at Judith. "Thank you so much. I really appreciate this. I hope to be out of here by tomorrow."

Judith watched Alfred hurry from the living room and wondered why he still wasn't telling her the whole truth.

To Judith's relief, Joe was much more forthcoming when he got home at five-fifteen. Maybe that was because he smelled like whiskey.

"Where've you been?" Judith asked, trying not to sound like a suspicious wife.

"With Woody," Joe replied, stealing one of the oysters Rockefeller Judith was preparing for her guests' social hour. "We stopped at our old haunt to have a drink."

"That's nice," Judith said, and meant it. "How's Woody?"

"Good," Joe replied, swiping another oyster. "He sends his love."

"What's new with the case?" Judith asked.

"Pour me a Scotch and I'll tell you," Joe said.

"Take another oyster and I'll call you Stubby," Judith warned as Joe again eyed the platter.

"Woody and Sancha Rael have talked to almost all of the witnesses except for a couple of tourists who slipped through their fingers and left town," Joe said, lighting a cigar.

"Anything new?" Judith said, making them each a drink.

"Nothing suspicious," Joe replied, checking to make sure the cigar was lighted. "Woody left Alfred Ashe to me. I trust he's still here?"

"He is," Judith said, sitting down. "I talked to him this afternoon. If you ask me, he's hiding something."

Judith went on to explain how Alfred had dodged some of her questions. "I understand his interest in the Alhambra because his wife's family lived there before they were shipped off to the internment camp. But why would he need an old city directory to figure that out? I'm guessing he was looking for someone else, maybe even somebody who lived in the apartment house at the same time that the Hasegawas did."

"Mmm," Joe responded, puffing on his cigar. "Now what does that have to do with Mrs. Carrabas?"

"Nothing, I suppose," Judith admitted. "But I'm just puttering around, trying to figure out what happened with the Meachams."

"A waste of time, Jude-girl," Joe asserted.

Judith offered Joe a coy smile. "You know how I like a

puzzle. And I realize you don't want me getting in your way on the Carrabas case."

Joe made an expansive gesture. "Any input is appreciated. I told you that from the start."

"You're so sweet," Judith said, still demure. "What does Woody hear from the police in California?"

"Aimee Carrabas had recently put her house up for sale," Joe said. "Apparently, she was looking at a place in Newport Beach, which is why she'd asked for that loan."

"Newport Beach is very pricey, isn't it?"

"Very," Joe replied. "The detectives down there talked to the loan officer, who said that they intended to approve the request. The loan would have been for the down payment. It seems that Mrs. Carrabas was due to come into a large sum of money. Her father had recently died, and he'd made a pile in construction. I gather she was his only heir."

"Poor woman," Judith said. "She had everything to look forward to. Not that I suppose she wasn't sorry to lose her father. Is her mother still living?"

Joe shook his head. "She died several years ago—cancer, I think. Mrs. Carrabas was waiting for the estate to go through probate—it was necessary, because the amount was so large—but she'd found this place at Newport Beach, and wanted to snap it up."

Judith was silent for a few moments. "Money is such a good motive," she finally said. "But I don't suppose there's a connection between anyone around here and Mrs. Carrabas down there."

"Not that we've found so far," Joe allowed. "The detectives in Studio City are going through all of Mrs. Carrabas's things, trying to uncover any leads. So far, not even her client file has shown anything that pertains to this area."

"But there's got to be something," Judith declared. "What's new on the treasure trove?"

Joe shrugged. "The experts are still studying the stuff. They like to take their time. The only thing they've told Woody so far is that the gold and silver is genuine, and it's at least sixty years old."

"Prewar," Judith murmured. "That's interesting."

"Is it?" Joe didn't seem to share Judith's enthusiasm.

"You know that it came from the Schnell apartment, I assume," Judith said.

Joe nodded. "Guthrie 'fessed up about that this afternoon." He narrowed his eyes at Judith. "How did you know?"

"A little bird told me," Judith said. "Which reminds me, Renie and I saw Emil on her deck today. We left a note at the Baines house."

Joe gave Judith a dubious look. "You're sleuthing, right?"

"On the Meacham case," Judith put in quickly. "Of course, if I find out anything pertinent to the Carrabas murder, I'm more than willing to share."

"And have you learned something of interest?" Joe inquired.

"Not really," Judith said. "Has Woody heard anything more about the weapon that killed Mrs. Carrabas?"

"As in found it?" Joe shook his head. "Woody's pretty frustrated. There are no real leads. Consider the crime scene. Guthrie's crew, at least the ones who hadn't yet taken a lunch break, were all busy, not to mention making a lot of noise. They've been informed that a tour group is coming through, also that the media are scheduled to show up. If a stranger walks into that courtyard, will they pay any attention even if they notice in the first place? No."

Judith had sat down at the table with her drink. "But did they see anyone, say before our group or the media arrived?"

"No, they insist they didn't." Joe made a face. "Not ideal witnesses, but they weren't expecting a killer."

Judith was silent for a moment, then snapped her fingers. "I almost forgot—after the tour bus pulled up, I saw somebody at an upstairs window."

Joe's gaze sharpened. "Which floor?"

"Third floor, in the front," Judith said. "Plus—and I had forgotten all about this until now—Jeremy Lamar went to the third floor just ahead of me. He took the elevator, so that's how I know. I saw him get into it because I was following him to chew him out for the previous stop here at the B&B."

"But you didn't see him after he got to the third floor?" Joe asked.

"No. I checked the first two apartments on the right after I got off the elevator," Judith recalled. "One was locked and the other one was a mess. Then I went into the one where I found Mrs. Carrabas. There was no sign of Jeremy, though."

Joe was wearing his policeman's bland look. "Would you have heard a shot from the hallway?"

Judith tried to remember. "I didn't hear one, but I suppose the workmen were running their jackhammers or whatever. If Jeremy was just ahead of me, surely I would have seen him in that third unit."

"Not if he was hiding in the closet where you and Renie went afterward," Joe pointed out.

"That's true," Judith said slowly. "But why on earth would Jeremy kill Mrs. Carrabas?"

Joe set the cigar down in an earthenware ashtray and sat back in his captain's chair. "That's the problem, Jude-girl. Why would anyone kill Aimee Carrabas?"

ELEVEN

"I WISH," JUDITH said to Renie over rare beef dip sandwiches at the Boxhedge Broiler, "I'd insisted on seeing Jeremy again at his office the other day. I haven't really talked to him about the murder one-on-one."

"You've given up on Rufus Holmes?" asked Renie, stuffing three French fries into her mouth at once.

"Even I'm not up to chasing him around that fleabag hotel he's holed up in," Judith said. "Besides, if he's such a recluse, he probably wouldn't know all that much about the other tenants in the Alhambra."

"Now—or then?" Renie queried.

"Well . . ." Judith paused, fork poised over her green salad. "He'd have still been a kid when Dorothy Meacham was killed. Maybe he was more normal then."

"Oo hab tu awwit dad hif faind wath obd," Renie said through a mouthful of beef.

"True," Judith said, having finally learned to interpret her cousin's words through a mouthful of food. "I definitely admit that his faint was odd."

Renie rocked a bit in the booth until she swallowed. "Did he really expect to see a wife at the café?"

"I wondered about that, too," Judith said. "Billy O'Dowd told us that Rufus had been married once, if briefly. So maybe he did expect to see the former Mrs. Holmes. I should ask Helen Schnell about that."

"Did you call the Whiffels?" Renie inquired. "Mom was all wrought up over that one. She was hoping you'd actually go there and see what kind of mess they're living in."

Judith sighed. "I put that off, though I shouldn't have. As soon as we get back from getting our plants at the nursery, I'll call. Maybe you should be there, on the other line. They know you much better than they know me."

"Did you call Dr. Alfonso?" Renie asked, looking stern despite a small slice of beef that dangled from her lower lip.

"Yes," Judith said, "but he wasn't in and his nurse was with another patient, so they'll have to call me back."

"Keep after them," Renie urged. "Things tend to fall between the cracks these days when it comes to medicine. Or anything else, really."

Judith didn't argue. Following lunch, the cousins proceeded to Molmo's, a large nursery near the university. Their goal was the annual end-of-summer plant clearance sale. To their surprise, they found a TV crew on hand to catch the floral frenzy.

"Goodness," Judith exclaimed as Renie drove up and down the rows of parked cars trying to find an empty space, "I didn't expect such a crowd in the middle of a workday."

"Molmo's advertised this sale as bigger and better than ever," Renie said, cutting off two nuns in a white sedan and wheeling the Camry into a space vacated by an SUV. "I guess that's why the TV folks showed up."

Sure enough, cameras were catching all the action as frantic gardeners seized pots, flats, baskets, and boxes. Two white-haired women swung their purses at each other as they fought over a fuchsia tree. A middle-aged man and his teenage son faced off with two girls wearing cutoffs and tank tops as they vied for what looked like almost-dead petunias. What appeared to be an entire garden club charged the front entrance, using a shovel as a battering ram. It was chaos, and the cousins cowered next to a trio of ugly stone gnomes.

"Good grief." Renie gasped. "This is awful. There's nothing here I want to risk my life for. Why did we come?"

"To fill in the dark spots of our late summer gardens?" Judith said in a feeble voice. "You're right, this was a bad idea."

"Oops!" gasped Renie, ducking behind Judith. "It's worse than I thought. Here come the nuns."

Surprisingly, the nuns were young and in full habit, an uncommon sight in the modern era of dwindling vocations and the adoption of ordinary clothing. Their veils flapped in the summer breeze as they bore down on the cousins.

"Hey, jerk-offs!" the shorter of the two yelled. "Try that stunt again, and we'll separate your ugly heads from your lumpy bodies!"

"I beg your pardon?" Judith said, taken aback. "Really, we're sorry. It's just that I have a hip problem and—"

"You sure do, Chunky," the other nun shouted. "But it's that rotten little buck-toothed beaver hiding behind your broad butt who ticked us off. How'd you like us to tap out a couple of decades of the rosary on your head with a Molmo's weed whacker?"

"Hold it!" Renie cried, darting out from behind Judith and raising her fists. "That does it! Let's take this out to the parking lot right now!"

"Are you kidding?" the first nun sneered. "That's where this all started. You'll get in your car and run over us. Right, Sister Cherie?"

"Absolutely, Sister Didi," the other nun replied. "We'll let you off with a warning this time."

"Oh, no, you won't," Renie retorted and charged at the retreating nuns. Mercifully, a small train of preschoolers in plastic wagons led by two cheerful teachers cut the cousins off. By the time the little caravan had passed, the nuns had disappeared into the crowd.

"What kind of nuns are those?" Renie demanded, shaking her fists.

"Not the kind who taught at Our Lady, Star of the Sea for so many years," Judith replied. "Goodness."

Judith and Renie waited to make their next move until a sixtyish couple pushed a wheelbarrow full of beauty bark past them. Then they headed for the exit. Unfortunately, their path was barred by Liz Ogilvy, microphone in hand.

"Liz!" Judith gasped, and immediately wished she'd kept her mouth shut.

Liz's green eyes narrowed at the cousins. "You!" she cried, and switched off the microphone. "Listen up," she said, grabbing Judith by the sleeve of her navy blue tee, "it's all your fault I got stuck with this zoo. I don't do features, dammit, I do hard news. But because you gave Mavis a better interview, I'm stuck with this kind of"—she gestured at a man carrying a bag of fertilizer— "stuff."

"Huh?" Judith stared at Liz. "Hey, it's not my fault. I didn't want to give either of you an interview. I was an innocent bystander."

"I guess you were," Liz huffed. "You certainly haven't solved the murder." She took an intimidating step toward Judith. "Or have you?"

"No." Judith gulped. "I haven't."

Next to Liz, and in front of the cameraman who had been trailing her, two twelve-year-old boys tried to give another boy a wedgie. Much squealing, wriggling, and yelling ensued before a hulking Molmo's sales clerk separated the boys just as the victim's pants reached his chin.

"So," Liz said, lowering her voice, "what have you found out?"

"Not very much," Judith admitted. "I've been looking into the Meacham case instead. Just out of curiosity," she added hastily.

"I see." Liz moved even closer, one strong hand on Judith's arm. "Look," she said, dropping her voice to a ragged whisper, "I don't much like covering the Wygelia Wars at Molmo's Nursery. And I don't much like Mavis Lean-Brodie, either. If I tell you something I haven't told anybody else, would you promise to let me know what your husband finds out in advance so I get an exclusive?"

Judith frowned. "An exclusive on what?"

"On any breaks in the story," Liz retorted, looking annoyed. "A lead, a suspect, evidence. I thought you were a mystery maven."

"I never claimed to be any such thing," Judith countered. "That was the media's idea, including yours."

"Then I guess you're not interested in the person I saw leaving the Alhambra right after the murder," Liz said, her voice taunting.

"Who?" Judith asked, eyes wide.

"Never mind." Liz started to move away. "You won't cooperate."

"Hey," Judith said, hands raised in a helpless gesture. "I can't make promises for Joe. I'm not even sure he'll tell me everything. Often, he doesn't reveal a word about his cases until they're solved or closed."

"Fine," Liz said over her shoulder. "See you in Winter Cabbages."

"Wait!" Judith called, grabbing Renie for support and going after Liz. "What if I promise to tell you anything I find out, but can't promise to keep my promise?"

Liz regarded Judith quizzically. "What?" She shook herself. "Okay, okay, I think I get it. First of all, I want the inside dope on that treasure. I had to agree—along with everybody else—to downplay that angle for the moment. But if you hear anything at all, let me know."

"Swastikas," Renie said, looking smug. "Some of the jewelry had swastikas. It's possible that it came off the Hungarian gold train."

Judith tried not to stare at Renie. Liz, however, was all ears.

"What was that?" she asked.

"It was a train that carried paintings and gold confiscated by the Nazis from Hungarian Jews," Renie responded. "Much of the treasure was never found, but believed to have turned up in the homes of certain art-loving American generals."

"Well." Liz flashed a toothy smile at Renie. "Very interesting. Thanks." She turned to Judith. "Okay, so now I owe you. Here's what happened when I got to the Alhambra with the TV crew."

Judith was eager to hear the revelation, but had to wait until Liz disentangled herself from a small child who was holding on to her ankles and screaming. A harassed mother disengaged the child, administered a weary warning, and took off into the crowd.

"When we arrived at the Alhambra," Liz began, "we had to use the stairs because we couldn't all fit into the elevator. I was passing by when the car door opened and a man came out. He looked rather furtive, but I didn't pay any attention because I figured he was probably part of the tour and maybe he'd been put off by whatever spiel Nan Leech or Jeremy Lamar happened to be giving. Anyway, the last I saw of him, he was headed out through the courtyard."

"Was he part of the tour?" Judith asked.

"No," Liz replied. "After I found out about the murder and heard that the police had questioned all of the members on the tour, I learned from Nan Leech that everybody was accounted for—except you two."

Judith grimaced. "We deserted, I guess."

"Whatever." Liz shrugged. "The point is, the man didn't belong to the group or to George Guthrie. I know, because I asked him. Anyway, he didn't look like a workman."

"What did he look like?" Judith asked, her excitement growing.

Liz paused, running her fingers through her short red hair. "I want to be accurate. It was only a glimpse, remember, and it didn't seem important at the time. He was probably sixty, very thin, fairly tall, maybe six feet, and was wearing a short-sleeved knit shirt and dark pants. He didn't have much hair, and what there was of it was gray. Does that give you any ideas?"

Judith glanced at Renie, who looked blank. "Yes," Judith said, "it does."

The idea she had in mind was named Rufus Holmes.

"Rufus, huh?" Renie remarked as they fought their way to the parking lot. "Are you sure?"

"Not a hundred percent," Judith replied. "I didn't get a very good look at him yesterday. I mean, it's sort of hard to tell much about people when they're unconscious."

The cousins both stopped dead in their tracks as they saw the nuns loading the trunk of their car with several large houseplants. Judith heard Renie tense and let out a hiss, like a cobra preparing to strike.

"Don't," she urged, putting a firm hand on her cousin's arm.

"Why not? Nuns or not, they're a couple of creeps."

"Face it, coz," Judith said in a reasonable tone, "you robbed them of their parking place. Nuns expect better treatment. Or at least civility."

"I don't know why," Renie began, then stared as the

nuns started removing their long habits to reveal shorts and halter tops. "Good grief!" Renie shouted. "I'll bet they're not nuns at all! They're phonies, wearing habits just to get better treatment! No wonder they got their shopping done so fast!"

The two women had jumped into the white sedan and were pulling out. As they passed the cousins, Cherie and Didi gave them the finger.

"I should have guessed," Renie muttered as they made their way to the Camry. "Not only didn't they sound like nuns, they sounded like *me*."

Judith laughed. "You've got to admit, it was a pretty good gig."

"I suppose." Renie let out a sigh, then unlocked the car doors. "What were we talking about before we saw Cherie and Didi get rid of their bad habits?"

"Rufus Holmes," Judith said, getting into the passenger seat. "Rufus at the Alhambra. Maybe."

"So why was he there—*if* he was there?" Renie asked, barging out into the main exit lane as three irate motorists honked their horns.

Judith shrugged. "I've no idea. Maybe he wanted to see what progress was being made on his new condo. Maybe he wanted to kill Mrs. Carrabas."

"And the motive?" Renie prompted.

"I couldn't guess," Judith said. "It crossed my mind just now that Rufus's brief marriage might have been to Aimee Carrabas. But if that were the case, why would he have expected to see a live wife at the café downtown?"

"Good point," Renie said. "Of course, the man Liz saw might not be Rufus Holmes. That description could fit any number of men."

"Say," Judith said, with a wry glance for Renie, "where did you come up with that goofy Hungarian gold train idea?"

"In the newspaper," Renie replied as they drove through the busy commercial district that abutted on the university. "Or was it a movie? I forget. Anyway, I thought I'd throw it out there and see if Liz would take the bait. She did, right?"

"Very clever," Judith said with a smile. "I thought you were making it up."

"I don't tell whoppers like you do," Renie declared, running a red light and scattering several pedestrians. "I'm an upright citizen."

"Those people you just grazed with the Camry aren't," Judith noted. "At least one of them is hanging on to a lamp post back there."

"They jumped the gun," Renie retorted. "They see an amber light flash on, so they trot right off the curb. They should wait for the WALK signal, which is delayed at least a second after the red light comes on. I've no patience with people who're in such a big hurry, especially college students. They're probably cutting class or they wouldn't be out wandering around. Where do they think they're going?"

"To the hospital emergency ward?" Judith suggested.

Except for a sour expression, Renie had no response. After they returned to Hillside Manor, Judith headed straight for the telephone to make good on her promise to call the Whiffels. Renie picked up the extension in the living room.

"Miss Whiffel?" Judith said when a high-pitched, quavering voice responded at the other end. "This is Judith Flynn, Deborah Grover's niece. I have Renie on the other—Yes, Serena Grover. Jones. I used to be Judith Grover . . . Yes, there was another name in between . . . McMonigle . . . That's M-C-cap M-O . . . Really? I didn't know you had a family of McMonigles when you taught school . . . No, Dan was from Arizona . . ."

Judith glanced across the coffee table to where Renie was sitting on the other sofa. Her cousin's eyes were rolling upward into her skull and her mouth was agape.

"What I wanted to ask was about the years you lived in the Alhambra Arms," Judith finally managed to wedge into the conversation. "Especially the period right after the war. Do you remember the Meachams?"

There was such a long pause that Judith thought Jewel Whiffel might have hung up. Finally, the other woman spoke:

"The Meachams, did you say? A man and a woman?"

"Yes," Judith said. "A couple."

"With a dear little girl," Jewel added.

"Yes, around four years old by the end of the war. Harry Meacham served in the army."

"Brother didn't go into the service," Jewel said. "He had an overbite."

Judith recalled that Ewart Gladstone Whiffel's overbite was very prominent, possibly capable of felling large trees, though she didn't know why that should have earned him a 4-F rating with the military. Nor did she ask.

"Such lovely people," Jewel was saying. "The wife—I don't recall her name—was quite nice-looking. The husband was . . . tall. Do you know them, too?"

"Dorothy and Harry," Judith said. "No, I don't. In fact, they're both dead. Or may be. Dorothy is. Do you recall anything about that?"

"About what?" Jewel sounded mystified.

"About Dorothy and what happened to her."

"She was blond," Jewel said. "A foreigner, but that can't be helped. Still, she was always pleasant."

Judith frowned at Renie, who appeared to be asleep with the receiver propped between her chin and shoulder. "I thought Dorothy Meacham was a brunette," Judith said, though for all she knew, Harry's first wife's hair could have been primrose pink.

Jewel's reaction was to let loose with a giggle so high-pitched that one more note would have sent it into hearing range only for dogs. "No, no, dear Judith. She was very fair, tall, a strong-looking woman. My late mother called her Brunhilde. It was meant as a compliment, of course. Mother was never unkind."

Unless, Judith thought with a quick glance for Renie, the old girl had caught Brunhilde playing gin rummy. "A good mother, I take it?" Judith remarked.

"I'm sure she was," Jewel replied. "Though I must admit, she . . ."

Again, the long pause made Judith wonder if Jewel Whiffel had hung up. "Yes?" Judith encouraged.

"Oh, dear." Jewel sounded confused. "I don't remember ever seeing her with the little girl. Such a precious child. Was there a nanny?"

"Ah . . ." It was Judith's turn to pause.

"Anne-Marie's mother," Renie put in, her eyes not only fully opened, but wearing what Judith called her cousin's board room face. "Jewel, this is Serena. Tell me about Anne-Marie's mother."

"Anne-Marie?" Jewel sounded vague.

"The Meacham girl, the precious one," Renie said.

"Oh. Well," Jewel began, her quavering voice a bit more certain, "you mean the dark-haired girl with the green eyes. She was nice, but very quiet." Another pause, though brief. "Was she the nanny?"

"No," Renie said. "There was no nanny. Do you know if the blond or the brunette was Anne-Marie's mother?"

"Oh, dear," sighed Jewel, "I really can't recall. Now I'm all mixed up. Maybe the blond woman was a governess. Foreigners often are. Governesses, I should say."

Judith gave Renie a shake of the head. "Never mind, Jewel. I was really calling about your friend, Helen Schnell. She was a student teacher under my father. I understand you still see her."

"Helen!" Jewel's voice brightened. "Such a lovely girl. We have so much in common, both being schoolteachers and spinsters and with such wonderful mothers. We lived right over the Schnells, you see, on the third floor. I never understood," Jewel went on, her voice darkening a bit, "why Mrs. Schnell and my own dear mother weren't better friends. Of course there was an age difference. Mother was older, just as I'm a few years further along than Helen."

Renie flashed the fingers on both hands twice and mouthed the word "plus." Judith calculated that Jewel must be in her nineties. "That's too bad," Judith said. "About your mothers, I mean, especially when you lived right on top of each other. So to speak."

"We," Jewel said carefully, "were on top of them. Of course it might have been the noise that upset Mother. She didn't like noise."

"Noise?" Judith echoed. "I thought the Alhambra was solidly built."

"It was," Jewel responded. "But all the same, Mother and Brother and I could sometimes hear noises directly below us. Sometimes they woke us up. It was very hard on Brother, especially when he'd stay up half the night studying for his law school exams."

"What do you think the Schnells were doing?" Judith asked.

"I have no idea," Jewel replied, then added in a disapproving tone, "dancing, perhaps."

"Jewel," Renie said, still in her professional mode, "do you remember anything peculiar about the Schnells?"

Yet another pause. "Yes. But I'm not clear on what it was."

"Would Ewart know?" Renie asked.

"Brother rarely spoke to people who weren't saved," Jewel said firmly. "The Schnells weren't churchgoers, that is, not Mr. Schnell. Mrs. Schnell and dear Helen went to the Methodist church upon occasion. They were probably saved. Mother should have liked that, but . . . I believe Helen fancies herself an Episcopalian these days."

"Was Mr. Schnell a . . ." Renie made a face. "A heathen?"

"I believe he was," Jewel said. "That's why Brother

wouldn't speak to him. Nor would Mother. Perhaps that's why Mother and Mrs. Schnell weren't close. Mother couldn't understand why a woman would marry a heathen."

"So even after Mr. Schnell was killed in the war," Renie began, "your mother didn't become friendly with—"

"No, no, dear," Jewel interrupted. "Mr. Schnell never went to war. He was killed by the police."

After that, the conversation ended abruptly. Brother wanted his cocoa. Politely, Jewel hung up on the cousins.

"Mr. Schnell had a rap sheet?" Judith said as the cousins stared at each other.

"Maybe it was a mistake," Renie said. "You know, dark night, dark alley, wrong suspect."

"Maybe not." Judith stared at the gypsy phone lying in her lap. "I wonder how far back the police records go?"

"Pretty far, as you ought to know," Renie said. "Ask Joe."

"No," Judith said. "Not Joe. He thinks I'm silly for concentrating on the Meacham murder. Or supposedly concentrating on it. I'll ask Woody."

"How about asking Helen Schnell?" Renie suggested.

Judith frowned at Renie. "As in, 'Hey, Helen, I hear your old man got whacked by the cops back in 'forty-five. How come?' But there are other ways to find out."

"All of which you are well-acquainted with," Renie noted. "Helen must have given you the impression that her father was killed in the war, right?"

"Yes, something about how he was killed shortly before V-E Day. I assumed he died defending his country."

Judith dialed Joe's old work number, which had now been assigned to Woody Price. Woody wasn't in, but Judith left a message.

"I wish Ewart hadn't needed his cocoa just then,"

Judith complained. "The longer we talked, the more Jewel's mind seemed to stay on track."

"I know," Renie said. "It's sad. Old folks spend so much time shut in and alone that their brains get rusty. At least that's what Mom says. According to her, the brain is a muscle which needs exercise like any other part of the body. Sometimes I think it's why she talks on the phone so much. It keeps her mind working. She's much more like you than like me. She loves people and they tell her all their troubles."

Judith looked askance at Renie. "Which, I hope you realize, means that you're more like my mother."

"I know," Renie said with a nod. "Scary, huh?"

"For you," Judith grinned.

Renie shook her head. "Oh, no. For you. You'll have to put up with me. I'll have a wonderful time being an ornery old codger."

"Great." Judith got up from the sofa. "It sounds as if Jewel got the two Mrs. Meachams confused."

"I suspect," said Renie, following Judith out through the dining room and into the kitchen, "Jewel either forgot or didn't realize there *were* two Mrs. Meachams."

"Brunhilde," Judith mused, opening the refrigerator. "Could she have been a war bride?"

"What?" Renie was leaning against the sink counter. "How could she be? Harry was still married when he got out of the service."

Judith stopped with her hand on a package of frozen shrimp. "Of course. Harry was still married to Dorothy. Maybe that's why he killed her."

"A perfect motive," Renie said, then her face fell. "Damn!"

"What's wrong?" Judith asked.

Renie gave her cousin an odd look. "You know—one of those visual memories you don't even know you had? Well, I just had one."

"What was it?" Judith asked, putting the shrimp on the counter and staring at Renie.

"I was just a little girl, maybe three or four at the most," Renie said. "Mother and I took the streetcar to see the Whiffels. Mother wasn't working then, Aunt Ellen had taken her place at the law office. It had to be early on in the war because Aunt Ellen and Auntie Vance hadn't gone to work for the navy yet. It was summer, and Jewel wasn't teaching. We were in the courtyard of the Alhambra and a woman and a little girl came in. Jewel pointed to them and said, 'There's so-and-so. She's close to your age. You two should play together.' It could have been Anne-Marie."

"You're kidding," Judith said, a little breathless.

"No, I'm not. I'd forgotten all about those early visits to the Whiffels," Renie went on in a slightly awed voice. "After the war, when Dad quit working on the oil tankers, I didn't go with Mom anymore to visit. Dad drove her and I stayed here with Grandma and Grandpa Grover. You and I'd play paper dolls."

"Our own version," Judith said, "which usually featured our paper dolls trying to solve a mystery."

Renie laughed. "Isn't that strange? Here we are, a couple of middle-aged matrons, still doing the same thing."

"Did you actually play with Anne-Marie?" Judith asked.

"No. Mother wouldn't let me. She was afraid Anne-Marie might have germs."

"Do you remember what the little girl or the mother looked like?" Judith asked.

"Only an impression," Renie said, frowning. "I think the mother was wearing a hat, one of those dinner-plate styles that sat kind of on the back of the head. It's very vague. I suppose it means they were both nondescript."

"Coz," Judith said, now very serious, "what else do you remember about those visits to the Alhambra?"

"Nothing," Renie said. "I don't think we went more than two or three times. It wasn't easy on the streetcar.

We had to transfer at least once. As I mentioned, I'd forgotten all about that trip until now."

Judith studied Renie for a moment, then put the frozen shrimp into the microwave and hit the defrost button. "You have a tremendous memory when it comes to your youth, especially going way back. Do you think you could delve a bit?"

Renie uttered a little laugh. "I could, but nothing may come of it. I honestly had forgotten about those early visits until now, when I heard Jewel's voice and pictured her not in that retirement home, but the Alhambra. I sure didn't recall that they lived over anybody named Schnell. In fact, I don't remember either Jewel or Ewart mentioning their neighbors. But I've always tried to steer clear of the Whiffels. That oozing, unctuous type of Christianity rubs me the wrong way, particularly when Ewart was so stingy when it came to paying his employees. I almost prefer Phyliss's aggressive brand of 'my way or the hell way.' "

"I understand," Judith said. "But give it a try, anyway. Your memory, that is."

"Sure." Renie headed for the back door. "I've got to go to work, at least for a couple of hours. What's your next move?"

"Helen Schnell," Judith said promptly. "I'm going to invite her over to see the B&B. She may be lonesome."

"What about Rufus Holmes?" Renie inquired. "Have you thought about checking on his marital history, brief though it may be?"

"Yes, but that's a trip to the county courthouse," Judith replied, removing the shrimp from the microwave. "Tomorrow, maybe."

As Renie went out, Sweetums came in. He'd apparently been taking a nap, since the first dry leaves of the season were entangled in his fur. Judith leaned down to remove them, but Sweetums snarled and waved his claws in a menacing gesture.

"Keep it up," she warned. "Maybe Emil will eat you. Ha-ha."

Sweetums showed disdain for Emil as he slunk off to his food dish by the pantry. Judith could hear the cat noisily slurping up his food as she dialed Helen Schnell's number.

Helen was delighted by the invitation. She'd been about to leave for the bookstore on top of the hill, and would stop by on her way back.

Judith got out a loaf of frozen cinnamon bread and put the tea kettle on. A few moments later, Alfred Ashe called to her from the entry hall.

"Dr. Ashe," Judith said, hurrying to greet him, "I mean, Alfred. Hi. What's new?"

Alfred's usual amiable demeanor was absent, replaced by a stony glower. "The American government ought to be ashamed of itself. I've booked a flight on a five o'clock plane back to San Francisco. It seems I've been on a wild goose chase." He tipped his head to one side and narrowed his eyes. "There are all kinds of crooks in this world, aren't there? Maybe murder is the only just retribution."

To Judith's dismay, Alfred stomped upstairs without another word.

TWELVE

JUDITH WAS ON the phone taking a reservation when Alfred Ashe slammed out of Hillside Manor. He'd left his credit card number, so at least he hadn't stiffed Judith out of the money he owed her. She was still wondering what had set the usually good-natured chiropractor off when Helen Schnell arrived, driving an old but well-tended Chevrolet sedan. Judith gave her the brief tour first, since it was going on four o'clock and guests might be arriving soon.

"This is a lovely old home," Helen enthused as they sat down to tea in the front parlor. "I don't believe I've ever seen it tucked away in this cul-de-sac."

"The setting is ideal for a guest house," Judith said. "It's quiet and relatively private. After my first husband died, my mother was living here alone so I moved in with her. She really couldn't cope with such a large place anymore, and my son, Mike, was starting college so I decided to put the property to work for us. The mortgage had been paid off years ago by my grandparents. The major expenses went to update the kitchen with modern appliances and expand the attic into family quarters. Happily, it's turned out well. The first of this year, I made the last payment on the major renovation loan."

Helen nodded with approval as she accepted a piece of cinnamon bread from Judith. "Yes, that must be a good feeling. I'm glad I've been of a saving nature all these years. My monthly payment for the condo won't be any more than my rent, and I'll have more space. Not that I really need it at my age."

"Did either of your parents teach?" Judith inquired in an offhand manner.

"No," Helen replied, applying a small amount of butter to her cinnamon bread. "You know how it was in those days. Wives tended to stay home. Mother was quite deft at embroidery. She even sold some of her work to the local stores."

"And your father?" Judith kept her voice casual.

"He was in the import-export business," Helen answered, nibbling daintily on the cinnamon bread. "He made a good living."

"You know," Judith said, her manner growing more confidential, "we have mutual acquaintances. The Whiffels. I understand you and Jewel are good friends."

"Jewel." Helen smiled fondly. "She's quite a character, isn't she? Next to your father, she was my favorite colleague. Never a dull moment with Jewel."

"Really." Judith tried to sound enthusiastic. "I decided to call her today. It had been so long since we chatted. My cousin's mother—my Aunt Deb—used to work for Mr. Whiffel."

"I daresay!" Helen beamed at Judith. "What a coincidence."

"Yes, I suppose so," Judith agreed. "Jewel said something about a tragedy concerning your father. Now let me think . . ."

The color, or what there was of it, drained from Helen's face and her fingers tightened on her teacup. "What did she say?"

"That he'd been shot by someone," Judith replied. "I

thought she meant in the war, but that wasn't the case. Goodness, I couldn't quite figure it out. Jewel is a bit . . . muddled sometimes."

"Yes," Helen said, nodding vigorously, "she is. Of course, she's over ninety. I marvel that her mind is as good as it is. Why, just the other day we were talking about a student we'd both had some thirty years ago, and she recalled that he'd . . ."

Judith listened patiently. When the anecdote, which also seemed to include Helen's philosophy of education, finally wound down, Judith decided to throw tact out the window.

"How did your father get shot? It must have been terrible."

Helen set the teacup down on the side table and put both hands to her breast. "Shot? Is that what Jewel told you? Oh, my—she's confused. My father was hit by a streetcar."

Undoubtedly, Jewel's mind had been playing tricks on her. Judith was sympathetic with Helen's tragedy. "That's awful. Did it happen in the neighborhood?"

"Yes." Helen looked away, toward the stone fireplace. "At the bottom of the hill. Right by the bus stop in front of the arena."

"I'm so sorry," Judith said, and was at a loss for words.

"Mother and I managed," Helen went on, speaking more rapidly than usual. "We had his life insurance and our savings. Luckily, I had a scholarship all the way through the university."

"Very lucky," Judith remarked.

"We lived simply, even after I graduated and was teaching," Helen said, picking up her teacup again. "Mother continued sewing until her hands got crippled with arthritis."

The conversation wasn't going anywhere. Or maybe it had gone far enough. Judith was temporarily saved by the front doorbell. She excused herself to answer it, and spent the next ten minutes welcoming middle-aged twin sisters from Chicago.

"Sorry," she apologized again to Helen. "The guests usually start coming around this time."

"Oh, dear," Helen said. "I should be going."

"No need." Judith smiled. "As long as you don't mind the interruptions."

"Well . . ." Helen eyed the teapot and the slices of cinnamon bread, which Judith readily proffered. "Thank you so much. I was curious, I must admit. How is your husband doing with the homicide investigation?"

"Slowly," Judith responded, pouring more tea for herself and carefully hiding her surprise at the question. "I gather it's the same with the police. Joe's working closely with them, you see. It's his former partner who's the primary."

"Primary?" Helen's smile was puckish. "As opposed to secondary? As in grade levels? Oh, excuse me—I must have my little education jokes."

Very little, thought Judith, but managed a chuckle that unfortunately sounded like "ar, ar, ar." "It means he's the lead officer. It's like trial lawyers—first and second chair."

"Yes, of course." Helen took a rather large bite of cinnamon bread and waited until she'd finished chewing before speaking again. "It's odd, but I haven't read much in the news about that treasure they found."

"I suppose it wasn't really a treasure," Judith said with what she hoped was a discreet yet probing glance at her guest. "It was probably costume jewelry or something like that."

"Really?" Helen's long, plain face showed surprise. "Then why would anyone hide such a thing?"

"Who knows? People are odd sometimes."

"Still . . ." Helen stopped herself, then uttered an uncharacteristically girlish laugh. "I was hoping it would be something romantic, like stolen Nazi plunder that may have been intended for return to the original owners."

"Stolen by whom?" Judith asked.

Helen looked startled. "By whom? I couldn't say. Soldiers, I suppose."

"Soldiers who served in Europe?" Judith suggested. "Did anyone in the building serve there besides Harry Meacham?"

Helen ruffled her short gray hair. "Let me think. People who had a loved one in the service put a small flag in the windows overlooking the courtyard. They had a star to represent the person."

Judith didn't remember, but she'd heard Renie mention the two stars her grandparents had had, for Uncle Corky and Uncle Al. She did, however, remember Grandpa and Grandma Grover's pride. And their fears. Grandpa suffered a nervous breakdown during the war, and had been hauled off, as Auntie Vance had bluntly put it, to the loony bin. Judith was aware that there were more casualties in World War Two than those on the battlefield.

"On our floor," Helen was saying, "there was Harry Meacham. Oh, and the Quesnells—one of the girls was a WAC and her brother was a Seabee. There were two brothers on five who went into the Marines in the South Pacific. One came back, the other didn't. Mr. Evans on four served in the Coast Guard. On the first floor, Mr. Harrison was in the army, in Europe, but he was killed in the Battle of the Bulge. He left a darling little boy nicknamed Skipper who became an orthopedic surgeon. That's all I remember."

"That's quite remarkable," Judith said.

"Not really." Helen sighed. "I was old enough to understand what was going on, right from the start of the war. Children paid attention to what was happening. You had to, your whole life was changed, even on the home front."

"Do you remember the Hasegawas?" Judith asked.

Helen's face grew even longer, and a faint spot of color appeared in each cheek. "I certainly do. That was a shameful thing. Such lovely people, and sent off like criminals. I wonder whatever became of them."

Judith didn't comment. "One other thing I was curious about," she said, offering the teapot again. "I heard that Rufus Holmes was briefly married. Whatever happened?"

"Rufus." Helen shook her head. "Who knows? I never saw his wife. He'd been on a trip, which was very rare for him, but I think it was one of those annual stockholder meetings. He made all his money in the market, so once in a while he'd attend an annual meeting in New York or San Francisco or Chicago. Rufus is very opinionated, and I suppose he had something he felt the company officials ought to hear. Anyway, this time he was gone for two or three months. When he returned, Mrs. Folger—the woman who used to own the Alhambra—said she thought he'd gotten married but it hadn't worked out. No wonder. Rufus is a very odd duck."

"That was when?" Judith asked.

Helen thought for a moment. "Twenty years ago, perhaps more. Yes, I'm sure it was the late seventies, shortly before divestiture."

"Divestiture?" Judith echoed as the doorbell rang again.

"Yes, the phone company," Helen said hurriedly as Judith stood up. "We had some AT&T stock, but Rufus had Pacific Tel & Tel. He probably went to San Francisco for the annual meeting."

. By the time Judith had greeted her latest guests, an older couple from Missouri, the twins were leaving for a stroll through the neighborhood. Waving them off, she turned to see Helen in the entry hall.

"I really must go," Helen said. "It's been delightful. I'd never seen Mr. Grover's family home before. I always tried to imagine where he lived. Somehow, I pictured a vine-covered brick cottage with his dear wife—he always called her his 'dear wife'– baking constantly."

Judith tried not to wince. Somehow, Helen's image of Donald and Gertrude Grover was skewed. Gertrude had baked twice a year, at Christmas and for Auntie Vance's birthday. In fact, she'd stopped baking the requested angel food cake twenty-odd years ago when Auntie Vance had declared it tasted like the devil. The cake had ended up on the floor, the ceiling, and all over Uncle Corky.

After bidding her guest good-bye, Judith returned to the kitchen. She thought about calling Renie, decided against bothering her cousin, who was probably still working, and sat down at the table to think. Alfred Ashe was very interested in the treasure. Perhaps Rufus Holmes was, too, which was why he'd come back to the Alhambra. Helen had expressed a mild curiosity as well. The treasure had been found in the floor of her former unit. Was it possible that she didn't know it was there? And if she didn't, why not?

Because, Judith reasoned, she hadn't put it there. Someone else had, maybe one of her parents. And why was Helen lying about how her father had died?

Judith couldn't stand it. She grabbed the phone and dialed Renie's number.

"Of course you're not nuts," Renie said after briefly chewing her cousin out for interrupting an alleged moment of genius. "I don't remember exactly what was on the site of the arena, but the original basketball venue wasn't built until the early sixties."

"Thus, Mr. Schnell couldn't have been hit by a streetcar there in 1945," Judith said. "Helen blurted out the first thing she could think of."

"The bus line didn't go that route back then," Renie said. "It followed the old streetcar lines a block over, on Heraldsgate Avenue. Furthermore, all the streetcars were retired not long after the war started. The buses use the main avenue now and the one by the arena because of the one-way streets. But traffic wasn't rerouted until the sixties."

"Good point," said Judith. "I'll bet Mr. Schnell was shot by the police and Helen is ashamed. Do you suppose he was a crook?"

"Usually, if not always, people who get shot by the cops are crooks," Renie noted.

"What kind of crook?" Judith asked.

"Crook crooks," Renie said, sounding irritated. "What do you mean?"

"Crooks who flee," Judith said reasonably. "Bank robbers. Burglars. Muggers. In short, people committing some kind of larceny, perhaps while armed."

"What about murderers?" Renie said.

"No. Not as a rule," Judith responded slowly. "Unless they've killed a cop." Her ears pricked up as she heard Joe's MG in the drive. "Jiggers, it's the cops. Or ex-cop. Joe's home. I'll talk to you later."

Judith had Joe's drink fixed before he came through the back door. She greeted him with a big kiss and an extra hug. Naturally, Joe was suspicious.

"Tired of mucking around in a fifty-year old murder, Jude-girl?" he said with a grin. "Want to pick my brains or merely seduce me?"

"Both," Judith replied, helping him with his summer-weight jacket. "You do the first thing first, and the second one later. If I get the first thing, that is."

"That's bribery," Joe said with a mock frown.

"Come on, Joe," Judith coaxed, "you said you'd share."

"I did. I will." Joe eased himself into his captain's chair. "How about you? Anything new?"

"Dr. Ashe left in a huff," Judith said. "He was angry about the government."

"Which government?" Joe asked, taking a sip of Scotch.

"I'm not sure," Judith replied, sitting down across from Joe. "Generic government, maybe."

Joe shrugged. "Everybody's mad at the government. Maybe he's fighting with Medicare over chiropractic coverage."

"Well," Judith said, listening for the oven timer to sound off so she could start baking her seafood casserole, "I'll admit, I concentrated on the Meachams. But there are a couple of odd things that might be connected."

Judith told Joe about Rufus Holmes's brief marriage and how Liz Ogilvy might have seen him at the Alhambra about the time of the murder. Joe evinced mild interest. She went on to tell him about Helen Schnell's father.

"I called Woody to check on it, but he wasn't in," Judith said as the front doorbell rang. "Hang on, that's probably the last of the guests. They were flying in from Miami."

It wasn't the guests but a harried-looking Jeremy Lamar. "Where's Mr. Flynn?" he asked in a breathless voice.

"In the kitchen," Judith said. "I'll go get—"

Before she could finish, Jeremy flew past her, across the entry hall, and through the dining room. She caught up with him as he collapsed into the kitchen chair she'd just vacated.

"I'm worried," Jeremy said. "Nan Leech has been missing since yesterday. I'm afraid she might have been murdered, too."

Joe offered to make Jeremy a drink. He readily accepted. "Take it easy," Joe said, reaching for the second-best Scotch. "What makes you think something's happened to Nan?"

Jeremy jumped out of the chair and grabbed the glass before Joe could add ice. "Nan is the most dependable person in the world," Jeremy declared after taking a big gulp of Scotch. "Ask George Guthrie. She never missed a day all the years she worked for him. Suddenly she doesn't show up for work this morning. She didn't call, so I phoned her around ten." Jeremy paused and took another swig. "There was no answer, not even a machine. I sent my brother, Dennis, over to her condo but there was no sign of her, even though her car was in the parking area. Dennis had the manager open the door, but no sign of Nan. It's not like her, I tell you. She's utterly reliable." He gulped down the rest of the Scotch and held the empty glass out to Judith.

"Have you called the police?" Joe asked, his voice very calm.

Jeremy shook his head. His boyish features seemed to have aged overnight. "I thought the police wouldn't act until somebody was missing for at least forty-eight hours. That's why I'm here. I want you to find her. I'll pay extra, I promise."

Joe grimaced. "I'm inclined to go along with the police on this. But I can start a search. The airport, the bus depot, the train station. I take it your brother didn't find any signs of violence at the apartment?"

Jeremy shook his head as he accepted the second drink from Judith. "Nothing was disturbed. Nan is a very neat person, so it'd be noticeable if there'd been any . . . mess."

"Okay." Joe got up and went over to the peg where his jacket was hanging. He got out a notebook and returned to the table. "Let's get the basics. I haven't met Nan, so I don't know what she looks like. How about a description?"

Jeremy offered a rough verbal sketch of Nan Leech. "Five-ten, a hundred and fifty pounds, maybe more, blue eyes, kind of short blond hair, maybe touched up, late fifties, not bad-looking, but nothing that stands out."

"That's not a lot of help," Joe noted, "but it's a start. But before I begin checking, I'd like to know why you think Nan might have been murdered."

With a motion so jerky that he almost knocked over his drink, Jeremy raised his hands in a helpless gesture. "Why not? George hired an exorcist who got killed. Maybe somebody's out to sabotage both of us. One by one, we'll all get killed."

Joe shook his head. "That's not likely. Is there any connection, however remote, between Nan Leech and Aimee Carrabas?"

"I don't think they ever met," Jeremy admitted. "But doesn't it seem weird to you that Mrs. Carrabas gets murdered and then Nan disappears?"

"The explanation may be very simple," Joe said. "It often is, with missing persons. Does Nan have family around here?"

"No," Jeremy said. "She was originally from L.A. I think her folks are dead. She never mentioned any brothers or sisters. Of course, she's only worked for me a short time. George would know more about her background."

"She sold real estate before she worked for George," Judith put in. "Her family moved west during the Depression. I believe they came from Texas."

Joe shot his wife an admiring glance. "As usual, my lovely spouse knows more about a virtual stranger than people who've been long-time acquaintances. She has a knack." He reached out and patted Judith on the hip.

Judith gave Joe what she hoped was a grateful smile. "It's a wild guess, but could there be a California connection between the two women?"

"It's a big state," Joe said, the gold flecks dancing in his green eyes. "How long has it been since Nan lived there?"

"I think Nan said twenty-five years," Judith replied, going to the stove and checking on her casserole. "I realize it's a long-shot."

"Maybe she went back to California," Joe suggested. "Or Texas. It could be some sort of family emergency.

Did your brother—Dennis, is it?—look to see if her luggage was missing?"

"No." Jeremy brightened, drank some more Scotch, and stood up. "That's a good idea. Maybe I'll go check out the condo right now. Dennis is a good kid, but he's young and kind of flaky."

Judith remembered Dennis and the stunt with the ghost costume. "He'll grow up. They all do."

Joe had also gotten to his feet. "Let me come along with you," he said to Jeremy. "I'll follow in my car."

Judith started to protest that Joe should wait until after dinner, but the front doorbell rang again. As Joe led Jeremy out the back way, she ushered in the last guests who'd arrived in an airport shuttle. They were tired, cranky, and full of complaints, especially about the long flight from Miami.

"Too many delays," the husband grumbled.

"Terrible food," the wife groused.

"Ugly flight attendants," said the husband. "They looked like men."

"They *were* men," the wife snapped. "Honestly, Elwood, you really should get your eyes checked . . ."

Judith tuned them out on the way up the stairs. She had other things on her mind, such as the possibility of Nan Leech and Aimee Carrabas somehow being connected. Yet she couldn't see how. Mrs. Carrabas had never been in the city before; Nan had left the Los Angeles area a quarter of a century earlier. Millions and millions of people lived in and around L.A. The chances of the two women knowing each other were extremely remote.

After getting the newcomers settled, Judith returned to the kitchen to get out the appetizers. She set the oven back some fifty degrees and went out to inform her mother that dinner would be a little late.

"How late?" Gertrude demanded. "It's already going on six. You know I like my supper at five."

Judith didn't want to chew on that old bone of contention. "Joe's working. He should be back within the hour. If you're really that hungry, I can serve your dinner sooner."

"Supper," Gertrude said stubbornly. "Dinner was at noon in my day. Did you forget we used to lived on a farm?"

"No, Mother," Judith responded docilely. "But you didn't live there very long."

"My father raised cows and chickens," Gertrude said, suddenly looking very faraway. "The cows were poor milk producers. My mother said my father's hands were always too cold. The chickens were Rhode Island Reds. Good eating, those chickens. But dumb." With effort, she turned to look at Judith. "Did I ever tell you how dumb chickens are? They're almost as dumb as the men you keep marrying."

"Thanks, Mother," Judith said dryly.

Gertrude's eyes narrowed. "Where'd that big chicken go?"

"What big chicken?" Judith hoped her mother wasn't referring to Joe.

"The one that was in the backyard the other day," Gertrude said. "It could've fed twenty people."

"That was an ostrich," Judith said. "As far as I know, he's still on the loose."

"Are we having ostrich for supper?" Gertrude asked, her wrinkled face a mask of confusion.

"No, Mother," Judith replied gently. "I made a seafood casserole and a green salad. I'll heat up some garlic bread, too."

"Your father loves garlic," Gertrude said. "It's a wonder he doesn't put garlic on his mush."

Her mother's use of the present tense worried Judith. "Uncle Cliff was the opposite. He hated garlic. He said it made him sick."

"Your Uncle Cliff has some weird ideas sometimes,"

Gertrude said. "All those contraptions he makes. Like the catapult to pick apples. It served him right when it backfired and hit him in the head."

Judith's smile was tremulous. She vividly recalled some of Cliff Grover's so-called contraptions, a few of which actually worked. "I'll go check on the casserole," she said, heading for the door.

"Don't forget to pull down the blackout shades," Gertrude called out. "Your father and Uncle Cliff left early tonight on their air raid watch."

"Okay." Judith quietly closed the door. Her mother seemed worse tonight. Before now, Judith didn't recall Gertrude's mind going back to the war. Maybe it was something in the air, triggered by her own preoccupation with the 1940s. Slowly, she returned to the house. In some ways, she wished she could remember the era as clearly as her mother did. But Judith wasn't quite four years old when peace finally came. She recalled very little, and even that only in small, isolated snatches.

Joe got home just before six-thirty. By then, Judith had not only served Gertrude, but spent a few minutes with the guests during their social hour. The couple from Miami was still complaining; the twins from Chicago were enthusiasts; the other four guests seemed a bit stand-offish, though Judith eventually managed to draw them into the general conversation.

"Well?" Judith said as she and Joe sat down at the kitchen table. "Did Nan do a bunk?"

"It's hard to tell," Joe replied. "Jeremy's brother was right about the place being undisturbed. There were two suitcases in a hall closet, but there was space for at least one or two more. The fridge had some staples, but nothing that looked as if Nan was expecting to fix a meal soon. Apparently, her mail had been taken in yesterday, but not today, which indicates she was home some time Tuesday. There were a couple of bills on her desk postmarked Monday."

"What about clothes?" Judith inquired, passing the salad dressing to Joe.

"It's hard to tell with you women," Joe said, tasting the casserole and giving Judith a thumbs-up sign. "Nan wasn't much of a clothes horse, but I couldn't determine if she'd taken anything out of her closet or drawers."

"Did you find anything personal?" Judith asked. "That is, anything that might lead you to think Nan was frightened or in trouble?"

"From what I did or didn't find," Joe said with a little shake of his head, "Nan Leech is She of the Blameless Life. Which is what worries me."

"Worries you?" Judith repeated. "Why?"

"I think the same has been said of Aimee Carrabas," Joe noted thoughtfully. "An ordinary person, unless you consider being an exorcist out of the ordinary."

"I do, in a way," Judith put in.

"But not in a negative way," Joe pointed out. "She performed a service, like a dry cleaner or a chimney sweep. You've got an evil spirit, Aimee Carrabas will rid you of it. Would you kill her if she failed?"

"Probably not," Judith said. "Anyway, her failures, if there were any, would have been in California."

"Right." Joe bit off a chunk of warm garlic bread. "So," he went on after a pause, "that doesn't seem to be a motive for murdering her here. She had yet to perform her exorcism."

"You're saying someone didn't want to rid the Alhambra of whatever supposed evil was there?"

"No," Joe said. "What I'm saying is that we have one victim who seemingly hasn't done anything to provoke murder. Now we have a second woman who is equally blameless and she's disappeared. You have to wonder what, if any, is the connection."

Judith's eyes widened. "You think Nan really may be dead?"

"I won't go that far," Joe said. "But what I think is that Nan may be afraid for her life. I'd like to know why."

*   *   *

Judith wanted to know why Nan should be so frightened, too. The woman hadn't struck her as someone who'd be easily scared. Nan Leech was too cool, too detached, too self-sufficient. The problem bothered Judith all evening and into the following morning.

Joe, meanwhile, asked Woody to start an official search. Since Nan had been on the scene at the time of Mrs. Carrabas's murder, there was no official balking at the request. Indeed, Woody had considered Nan's disappearance more suspicious than frightening. He told Joe that perhaps she should be considered a suspect.

"Do you agree?" Judith asked Joe before he went off on his appointed rounds Thursday morning.

Joe didn't respond right away. "It's always an attention grabber when a witness goes to ground. But in my experience, it's usually out of fear, not guilt. Nan may know something she isn't telling us. Didn't you say she was vague about how she'd heard of Mrs. Carrabas?"

"Yes," Judith replied, loading the dishwasher with the guests' breakfast things. "It had to do with a phone message left on her desk. And though she wasn't clear how it got there, her confusion was convincing."

Joe gave a nod. "I've been looking at that alleged message all along. It's the only direct connection between Mrs. Carrabas and any of the people who were at the Alhambra at the time of the killing."

"Unless," Judith pointed out, "Mrs. Carrabas used to be Mrs. Holmes."

Joe wiggled a reddish eyebrow at Judith. "Could Ms. Leech have been Mrs. Holmes?"

Judith admitted she hadn't considered the possibility. "Nan's my height, my build, but blond. Rufus wouldn't know that Nan probably dyed her hair in later years. He might expect to see a gray-haired woman." She touched her own short salt-and-pepper locks just as the phone rang.

"Mrs. Flynn?" inquired a woman's businesslike voice at the other end. "Are you the owner of Hillside Manor?"

"Yes," Judith answered. "Are you calling about a reservation?"

"No," said the woman. "I'm calling from Norway General Hospital. We have a patient here who may know you."

"Who?" Judith asked, immediately thinking of Mike. Attacked by an irate camper. Struck by a falling tree. Mauled by a grizzly bear. Forest rangers lived with danger. Judith began to panic.

"His name is Alfred Ashe," the voice said calmly.

Relief was replaced by surprise. "He wants to see me?"

"He doesn't want anything at the moment," the voice said. "Alfred Ashe is in a coma."

THIRTEEN

JOE HAD ALREADY started out the back door. Judith got his attention by banging a teaspoon on the table. He turned with a curious expression, then shut the screen door and waited.

"Let me get this straight, ma'am," Judith said for Joe's benefit. "Alfred Ashe is in a coma at Norway General. You must have found Hillside Manor's number on his person. What on earth happened to poor Alfred?"

"I'm not at liberty to say," the woman responded, sounding rather pleased with herself. "At present, we need to establish Dr. Ashe's medical coverage. We're trying to reach a Hiroko Hasegawa in San Francisco who appears to be his next of kin. However, we're told she's unavailable this morning. Since he had your name and that of your establishment in his wallet, we thought you should be informed. Are you a relative?"

"Yes," Judith said swiftly. "I'm his sister. Judith. Judith Ashe. Before I was married to Mr. Flynn. Please, tell me what happened to him."

Joe was leaning against the doorjamb between the kitchen and the hallway. He let out a big sigh and shook his head in disbelief.

"Perhaps you'd better come to the hospital," the woman said. "We can't give out such information over the phone. Also, it would be better if you were here in person to help us sort out his coverage."

"I'll be right there," Judith said, then rang off and rushed past Joe to get her jacket and purse. "Are you coming with me?" she asked over her shoulder.

"I hadn't planned on it," Joe said dryly. "I was going down to headquarters to check with Woody."

"Maybe you'd better change your plans," Judith said at the back door. "Something terrible must have happened to Alfred."

"He certainly missed his plane," Joe remarked. "Okay, but let's go in separate cars. I still want to hook up with Woody."

It took fifteen minutes to reach Norway General in the hospital district adjacent to downtown. It took ten more minutes to find parking places in the garage across the street. The Flynns rendezvoused at the main desk where they inquired after Alfred Ashe. He was on the fourth floor in the intensive care unit.

As soon as they got out of the elevator, Judith grabbed Joe's arm. "Oh, dear—what will I do if they ask for ID? I can't prove I'm Alfred's sister."

"That's because you aren't," Joe said with a disapproving look. "Leave it to me. As a former cop and a private eye, I can pull some strings. But I wish to hell you'd stop telling such whoppers. Someday you're going to get into serious trouble."

"Joe . . ."

"Can it, Jude-girl. Here comes Nurse Ratchet."

At first glance, the RN who approached the Flynns looked more like Mammy in *Gone With the Wind* than the villainess of *One Flew Over the Cuckoo's Nest*. The name tag on her large bosom read "J. Royce," and on second thought, Judith didn't think she looked nearly as kind as Hattie McDaniel.

Joe went into his act, flashing badges and licenses.

J. Royce scrutinized the pair as if they were Scarlett and Rhett, behaving badly.

"Nurse Glickman said Dr. Ashe's sister was coming," the nurse said in a deep, no-nonsense voice. "Where is she?"

"She couldn't make it," Judith said, and tried to hide behind Joe.

"I'm representing her," Joe said, purposely stepping on Judith's toe. "May we speak with the physician in charge?"

Nurse Royce eyed the couple suspiciously, then wordlessly walked away. A moment later Judith heard her voice booming over the intercom, paging Dr. Bentley.

Five minutes passed before a small man with glasses and thinning gray hair appeared from the end of the hall. J. Royce, who was manning the nurses' station, looked up and nodded at Judith and Joe. The doctor approached and held out his hand.

"Dr. Bentley," he said by way of introduction. "You're . . . ?"

Joe went through his routine again, concluding with a question: "Has my former partner, homicide detective Woodrow Price, been informed of Dr. Ashe's condition?"

"I heard he's on his way," Dr. Bentley replied. "Come, let's go into the doctors' lounge where we can speak privately." He took a brief detour to the nurses' station. "Thank you, Jolene," he said in a deferential manner. Judith guessed that everyone deferred to Jolene Royce. Or else.

The lounge was empty, and Judith was surprised to detect the faint odor of cigarette smoke. Then again, maybe she shouldn't be surprised. Doctors didn't always practice what they preached.

"Let me get this straight," Dr. Bentley began, a glimmer of excitement in his keen blue eyes. "Mr. Flynn, I understand from the police that you've been hired to investigate a murder. I'd like to cooperate in any way I can." The glimmer seemed to become more vivid. "I must confess, I've never been involved in a homicide before."

Joe explained, in precise terms, how he'd been asked to work on the Carrabas case. He also made it clear that his connection with the official investigation was solid.

"Woody, my former partner, still picks my brains," Joe said without false modesty. "We worked as a team for over ten years."

It was at that exact moment that Nurse Royce ushered Woody Price and Sancha Rael into the lounge. Greetings were exchanged, introductions made, and coffee offered from an old-fashioned four-gallon stainless steel coffee maker.

"Detective Price," Dr. Bentley said, his excitement still evident, "maybe you should start. I don't think Mr. Flynn knows what happened to Dr. Ashe."

Judith was bursting. Balancing a coffee mug in her lap, she leaned forward on the leatherette sofa to listen to Woody's account.

"I got a call the minute I stepped into the office at eight o'clock this morning," Woody began in his rich, soft baritone. "The night shift uniforms at the Alhambra had been making their last rounds before they went off duty at seven A.M." He paused to glance in the doctor's direction. "We don't keep officers at the murder site while the construction crew is working. In fact, we were going to pull them off as of today. Until this happened, anyway."

"I left an order for a pair of uniforms to show up at five," Sancha said, apparently not wanting to be left out.

Woody nodded. "Good, Sancha. In any event, when they got to the second floor, the officers found Dr. Ashe unconscious in the former Schnell unit. He'd been struck on the back of the head. An ambulance was called, and he was brought here around seven-thirty." Woody again looked at Dr. Bentley. "How is he doing, Doctor?"

"He's still unconscious," the physician replied. "There was enormous trauma to the back of the skull. However, patients have been known to recover from such a blow. It just takes time."

"How did he get into the building?" Joe asked.

Woody heaved a disgusted sigh. "A little after midnight there was some sort of explosion nearby. The officers on duty rushed off to see what had happened. It was down at the corner, in some bushes. They found remnants of some illegal fireworks, apparently left over from the Fourth of July. They figured it was kids, so they didn't give chase. Now, of course, we assume it was deliberately set off as a diversion so that Dr. Ashe—or someone else—could enter the apartment building."

"You mean like the someone else who hit him on the head?" Judith put in.

Woody nodded. "Obviously, two people sneaked inside. Maybe they came together, maybe not."

"Did you find a weapon?" Joe inquired.

Again, Woody nodded. "We think so. It was a clawhammer. The lab has it now."

"Someone came prepared," Judith murmured.

Woody gave her an off-center smile. "Dr. Ashe was the one who came prepared. He had his attaché case with him, and it was full of tools."

Joe, Woody, and Sancha went off to confer at a nearby coffee shop. Judith could find out later what the trio had discussed. For now, she needed to think about her options. She was less than a mile from the city's historic district, so she took a detour, driving past the Hairsley Arms Hotel that served as Rufus Holmes's temporary address. In the soft morning sunlight, the building didn't look so very threatening. Judith wondered if it would be safe to go inside and ask for Rufus.

She was still considering the possibility when two drunks staggered out of the front entrance. They immediately began to shove each other. Judith stepped on the gas and headed for Heraldsgate Hill. If she came back, it would be with Renie.

Renie. Could she pull off impersonating Alfred Ashe's sister? Would she even try? Or, like Joe, would she chastise Judith for telling a big fat lie? It wouldn't hurt to call Renie and ask.

"Now what?" Renie demanded. "It's not even ten o'clock, I'm just achieving full consciousness. Aha! I found the coffeepot. Go away."

Judith had pulled into the parking lot of a motel on the north side of downtown. She was in the lobby at a pay phone. Inspiration struck.

"You haven't eaten breakfast?" she asked eagerly.

"Hell, no. I haven't even tackled the concept. Maybe Bill can help me. Where is Bill?"

"I'll treat you to breakfast in the coffee shop at the Six Pines Motel."

Renie didn't respond for several moments. "There has to be a catch."

"There is," Judith said ingenuously. "Aren't you curious?"

"Curiosity comes a long time after consciousness," Renie said, then sighed in surrender. "Okay, give me twenty minutes to get dressed and drive down there."

In that twenty minutes, Judith made another phone call, this time to Norway General. To her relief, a young, cheery voice answered the phone on the ICU floor.

"Nurse Millie here," she said. "How can I help you?"

"This is Mrs. Flynn, Millie," Judith began. "I was checking on Alfred Ashe this morning with my—"

The nurse giggled. "My last name is Millie, but that's okay. You can call me Lily. That's my first name."

"Lily Millie?" Judith said. "That's . . . cute."

"It's my married name," the nurse replied. "My husband's first name is Dolph."

"Oh," Judith said, grateful that his name wasn't Billy. "Anyway, my husband and I met with Dr. Bentley and the investigating officers on Dr. Ashe's case. As we were leaving, I heard Nurse Royce mention something about Alfred—Dr. Ashe—having some personal effects. I wonder if I could come by with his sister to collect them for safekeeping."

"Gosh," Lily Millie said in a worried voice, "I think the police took everything with them. Let me ask Nurse Royce."

Judith hung her head. She knew Woody would have collected most of Alfred's belongings as possible evidence. But she'd held out hope that he'd taken only obvious items, such as the attaché case that had probably held the hammer which had been used as an assault weapon.

"I'm really sorry," Nurse Millie said, back on the line. "That nice policeman took everything. All that's left is a little scrap of paper I found when I shook out Dr. Ashe's trousers. Shall I throw it away?"

"No," Judith burst out. "That is, hang on to it, please. It's probably nothing, but his sister might want it."

"I've got it here under a paperweight," Lily Millie said. "If I'm not on the floor, feel free to take it, okay?"

"Yes. Of course. Thanks very much." Judith hung up, and dialed Renie's number again. This time the only answer was her cousin's voice messaging. Renie must have already left.

Judith met Renie in the parking lot. "How about brunch?" she asked in a sheepish voice. "We have to hurry up to the hospital."

"What for?" Renie asked in a querulous tone. "I'm starving."

"Don't you want to know why we're going to the hospital?"

Renie shook her head. "Not unless they're treating me for malnutrition."

"Okay, okay," Judith snapped, also growing testy. "Here's the deal . . ."

She had gotten halfway through the explanation before Renie made a slashing motion with her hand.

"Stop. I get it. Alas. I'm supposed to be Alfred's sister and find a message under a paperweight. I'll do it, but we're heading straight for the nearest Stacks o' Flapjacks afterward. I believe that would be about four blocks away from Norway General. I'll meet you there. Order me the silver dollar pancakes with a side of ham and one egg over easy. Bye." Renie recklessly reversed and roared out of the motel parking lot.

Renie's order was just arriving when she staggered into Stacks o' Flapjacks almost half an hour later. Judith stared at her cousin, who looked disheveled and out of breath. There was a big tear in Renie's Wisconsin Badger tee shirt and the strap on one of her sandals was broken.

"Here," Renie said, slapping a wrinkled piece of paper down on the Formica tabletop. "I hope you're satisfied."

"What happened?" Judith asked, wide-eyed.

"I went one-on-one with somebody named Royce. I lost." Renie began gobbling silver dollar pancakes.

"You didn't lose this," Judith said, picking up the slip of paper which was yellow with age and sent off a damp aroma.

"True. I stuffed it down my front. Royce assaulted me just afterward."

"Are you all right?" Judith asked, still aghast.

"Do I look all right?" Renie swallowed a pancake virtually whole. "I should have checked myself into emergency."

"Exactly what happened?" Judith inquired, guilt flowing over her in much the same way that Renie was pouring syrup on her hotcakes.

"I told you," Renie said. "I was at the desk. I grabbed the note. Nurse Royce came along and looked as if she were going to grab me. In my rush to escape, I put my foot in the wastebasket, and fell over—right into Nurse Royce. She must have thought I was on the attack." Renie's brown eyes grew very wide. "The next thing that happened was really gruesome."

"What?" Judith demanded, her eyes as wide as
Renie's.

"She picked me up by the scruff of the neck and tried
to jam me all the way into the wastebasket. I got stuck.
She picked me up again, wastebasket and all, and threw
me into the recycling bin. At that point, the only thing
sticking out was my feet. *Were* my feet," Renie corrected
herself. "Nurse Royce stomped off and I had one hell of
a time getting out of that damned bin. I hope they don't
keep body parts in that thing. Do I smell funny?"

"No, no, of course not," Judith assured her cousin.
"I'm so sorry."

"No, you're not. At least I didn't have to pretend I was
Alfred's sister. Man, Nurse Royce is one tough momma."

"I really am sorry," Judith insisted. "I should have
done it myself."

"Yes, you should," Renie replied, pointing at the piece
of paper with her fork. "So did I offer my poor small
body up in vain?"

Judith smoothed the paper out on the table. It was
faintly lined, and looked as if it had come out of a small
notebook. "Hunh. This is interesting. It says . . . Here,
read it for yourself." She shoved the paper in Renie's
direction.

104—Graingers?
201—Hedstrom OK
102—McMillan
304—Holmes?
206—Hasegawa OK
505—Paretti
Cavendish Court #5, #9
Sound View Apts. 208 & 412
The Montana 1-C, 1-E, 3-B

Below the list, which had faded with age, was a single
name, written in a different, and much fresher hand:
Meacham.

"It's apartment houses and units," Renie said, returning the slip of paper to Judith. "Any idea what it means?"

"Maybe," Judith replied, again studying the list. "The first set of numbers must be for the Alhambra, since the Hasegawas and Rufus Holmes—or Rufus and his parents—are on it. Do the other three names sound familiar?"

"You mean the ones that sound like other apartments?" Renie asked. "Yes, they do. The Montana is still there on Heraldsgate Avenue. You've driven past it a zillion times. Cavendish Court is now condos. It's about halfway up the hill, east of the avenue. I'm not sure about the Sound View Apartments. They may be gone. I vaguely remember that building as being at the bottom of the hill where so much of the old stuff has been torn down."

"I do know the Montana," Judith said. "It's sort of California Mission style, with trailing vines growing over the balconies. So this could simply be a list of apartments that, say, someone looking for a place to live might keep."

Renie picked up the paper and sniffed. "They'd keep it for almost sixty years? Isn't that how you'd date it? The Hasegawas got hauled off in forty-two."

"Obviously," Judith said, "it wasn't kept in a usual place for such things. Otherwise, the paper wouldn't be so beat-up or smell like mold. I figure that Alfred found it while he was searching the Schnell apartment."

"And why would Alfred be doing such a thing?" Renie inquired, polishing off her egg.

"Notice who isn't on this list," Judith said. "The Whiffels, for example. The Meachams. The Schnells."

"But you think Alfred found that piece of paper in the Schnell apartment?"

"Yes. I'm willing to bet he found it under the floor, where the so-called treasure was hidden." Judith sat back in the booth, arms folded across her chest. "Maybe my usual logic has deserted me, but see if this sounds too crazy. The Whiffels aren't on that list because they were incredible tightwads who saved every dime they earned. Tell me, did you ever see anything in their apartment that was worth stealing?"

"Never," Renie replied, a glimmer of comprehension showing in her eyes. "It was all cheap furniture and almost-dead houseplants."

"What did I say earlier about the kind of crook who gets shot by the cops? Someone who is fleeing, right?"

Renie grinned. "Like a robber?"

Judith gave a single nod. "Like that. Interestingly enough, at least two of these buildings—the Alhambra and the Montana—have balconies for easy cat burglar access. By the way, could the Sound View Apartments have stood where the basketball arena is now located?"

Renie thought for a moment. "You're right. That was where they were and that was why they were torn down."

"Okay." Judith picked up the slip of paper and waved it at Renie. "I'm almost certain that Mr. Schnell was a burglar. He was shot fleeing from the police after he tried to knock over the Sound View Apartments. What do you think about that, coz?"

Renie was silent for a few moments while she finished her breakfast. "About those swastikas," she finally said.

"Huh?"

"They aren't Nazi swastikas," Renie said. "I've been doing this Native American jewelry display, right? I meant to bring this up earlier, but we got interrupted. The swastika had been used by several ethnic groups before the Nazis glommed onto it. I'll bet those silver pieces came from the Navajos or some other tribe in the Southwest. It may have been purchased by somebody who liked the style. That type of Native American jewelry is extremely popular. It can also be very expensive."

Judith looked bemused. "Why didn't I think of that?"

"Even you can't think of everything," Renie said drolly. "So we've fingered Mr. Schnell as a burglar. Does Helen know it?"

"She must," Judith replied. "Frankly, she sounded sort of iffy when I asked her what her father did for a living. Import-export, she said. In a way, that's right. Mr. Schnell would import something from somebody else's home, and export it to a fence for profit."

"The gold and silver must have been leftovers," Renie noted. "That stuff probably had been under the floor since Schnell got whacked."

"No wonder Helen hasn't put in a claim," Judith remarked. "Even if she knew it was there, she doesn't want the cops asking where the jewelry came from."

"So who conked poor Alfred over the head?" Renie inquired. "Helen?"

Judith winced. "It's possible. But I hate to think it. I like Helen. It's not her fault her father was a crook."

"You don't know for sure that he was a crook," Renie pointed out.

"I'll find out," Judith replied. "Joe was going to search the records today."

The check arrived. Renie flipped it to Judith. "Thanks. That was tasty."

"My pleasure," Judith said, calculating the tip. "Now let me tell you how to get to our next stop."

Renie drew back in the booth. "What next stop?"

"The Hairsley Arms Hotel," Judith replied. "Unfortunately, several letters are missing from the sign. All you'll see is HAIR___Y ARM_ HO_EL."

"That's disgusting," Renie declared. "I just finished eating. I'm not going to any such place. I'm going home to dust."

Judith waved the bill at Renie. "I bought you, remember?"

"You bought me to get beat up by Nurse Royce," Renie reminded her cousin. "Now you want to double-dip?"

"Yes, I suppose you could say that," Judith said, gazing at the ceiling.

"Forget it," Renie snapped, on her feet and heading for the exit.

Judith was right behind her. "I'll buy lunch at Papaya Pete's."

"I just ate." Renie kept going.

Judith threw a ten and a five down by the cash register and hurried as fast as her hips would permit. "Wait!" she yelled to Renie, who was unlocking the Camry's door. "Let me explain."

Renie opened the car door but didn't get in. "Okay, okay. What idiotic idea have you got now?"

"Rufus Holmes," Judith said, and proceeded to explain why she felt she needed reinforcements before calling on him in his temporary residence.

"You don't need me," Renie insisted. "You need a gun."

"Please, coz . . ."

"Damn!" Renie slapped her hands together, then flinched. "Ow! I forgot that I hurt in various places after wrestling with Royce. Okay, I'll meet you there. What do we do, park on the street and watch our cars get stripped?"

Judith explained that there was a garage about two blocks away. Ten minutes later, the cousins were walking in the direction of Rufus's hotel.

"When do we get panhandled?" Renie asked. "Where are the perverts? The muggers? The armed lunatics who assault innocent passersby?"

"It's not that bad," Judith retorted. "In fact, here's the café where I waited for Rufus. It's quite respectable, even somewhat trendy, I believe."

Renie paused to peer through the window. "You're right, people are dressed and everything in there."

"Of course," Judith said, glancing inside. "If I recall correctly, Joe and Woody used to—Hey! There's Rufus!"

Rufus Holmes sat near the back of the restaurant at a small wooden table. He appeared absorbed in a book, his back turned to the half-dozen customers seated at the counter. Judith dashed through the door and marched straight up to her prey.

"Rufus," she said, sitting down in the vacant chair across from him, "are you all right? I was so worried about you the other day when you passed out."

Rufus took off his glasses and peered closely at Judith. "Who are you?" he demanded, then clutched at his throat with long, thin fingers. "You're not . . . ?"

"Who do you think I am?" Judith asked softly as Renie wandered around by the counter.

Rufus peered even harder, his face not more than six inches from Judith's. "I don't know," he finally said, and slumped back in his chair.

"I do," Judith said, still speaking softly. "You thought I was your ex-wife. Isn't that who you expected to see?"

Rufus's pale gray eyes narrowed again, this time in suspicion. "Go away. You're trying to torture me."

A pang of guilt struck Judith. Maybe that's what she was doing. Rufus, after all, was a stranger, and while he might be reclusive, that didn't mean he wasn't a decent person.

"I'm sorry," Judith said, noticing that Rufus had only a cup of coffee on the table. "Let me buy you lunch and I'll explain."

"It's too early for lunch," Rufus said. "I don't eat lunch until noon. You have to keep good habits to stay healthy at my age."

"It's twenty to twelve," Judith pointed out.

"It's not noon," Rufus said doggedly. "Besides, don't you think I can afford to pay for my own lunch?"

"I think you can probably afford to pay for this entire café," Judith said. "I've heard you're a real whiz with money."

"Says who?" Rufus countered.

"Says Helen Schnell, your neighbor," Judith replied, giving Renie a high sign to join them. "She's a great admirer of your financial acumen."

Rufus looked up sharply as Renie pulled a chair over to the table and sat down. "What's this? Is everybody ganging up on me?"

Sensing that Rufus was about to bolt, Judith put out a soothing hand. "No, Rufus, not at all. I'm Mrs. Flynn, and this is my cousin, Mrs. Jones. We're friends of Helen Schnell. I must say, you're both very shrewd to be able to buy back into the Alhambra."

"Are we?" Rufus ignored Renie and avoided Judith's gaze.

"Is there a problem?" Judith asked.

"None of your damned business," Rufus snarled. "Why are you harassing me?" He turned around in his chair. "Where's Alva? She never lets people bother me when I come in here."

"Alva's probably in the kitchen," Judith said, "cooking lunch. Honestly, we don't mean to bother you. We just wanted to ask a couple of questions about the Alhambra."

Rufus again eyed Judith and now Renie with suspicion. "You thinking about buying into the place, too?"

"Possibly," Judith said. "Do you think it's worth the money?"

"No," Rufus responded. "But that's not the point as far as I'm concerned. I don't want to live anywhere else. I never have. Neither has Miss Schnell. So what? It's worth it to folks like us."

Judith nodded sympathetically. "I understand. Still, the Alhambra hasn't always been a happy place for some of its tenants. Like the Hasegawas, for example."

"The Japs?" Rufus said. "I don't recall. I was just a kid."

"The Meachams," Judith said.

"Oh, them." Rufus dismissed the Meachams with a

wave of one hand. "One of those wartime marriages. They never last."

"But one of them doesn't usually end up sealed in a wall," Renie noted.

Rufus turned to Renie. "Oh, so you *can* talk? I thought you were this other one's stooge."

"I am," Renie said in a hapless voice.

Rufus closed the book he'd been reading, and Judith noticed that it was entitled *The Guilty Rich*. "First off, I don't watch TV or read the newspapers. Bunch of sensationalism. Now I've got to be going, or I'll be late for lunch."

"You aren't eating here?" Judith inquired.

Rufus shook his head. "I feel like Chinese. I'm going down the street to Fu Man Chew's."

"Then let me treat," Judith said. "I still have some questions about the apartment house."

"I'm doing takeout," Rufus declared. "I've had enough sociability to last me a week."

"Please," Judith begged. "Just a couple more minutes?"

Rufus made a face. "Make it quick. I'm getting hungry."

Judith gave Rufus a grateful smile. "What do you remember about Harry and Dorothy Meacham? Or a blond woman who showed up with Harry later?"

"Not a damned thing," Rufus said. "I was a kid, I didn't pay much attention to grown-ups. Or to other kids, if comes to that. I like my own company just fine."

"But eventually, you married," Judith pointed out.

"It was a big mistake," Rufus said grimly. "Ritzy didn't approve of the way I made my money."

"Ritzy?" Judith said. "That was your wife's name?"

Giving a single nod, Rufus scowled at Judith. "That was her nickname, short for Fritzy Ritz, like the funny paper girl. Ritzy was superstitious as hell. Once she found out how I'd made my pile, she refused to come north with me from California. That was the end of it."

Renie waved a hand in Rufus's face. "Hey, remember me? The stooge? I thought you got rich through investments."

"I did," Rufus replied, taking his book from the table and standing up. "It was my original nest egg that bothered Ritzy. She called it blood money." He glanced at the book under his arm. "That's always bothered me. It was no such thing. I came by it honestly, the old-fashioned way. I inherited it."

Rufus Holmes pushed his chair out of the way and moved swiftly to the café exit.

FOURTEEN

GREG, THE WAITER, finally showed up to ask the cousins if they'd seen the menu. Renie informed him that they didn't need to, they were leaving. When Greg apologized for the slow service, Judith explained that they had come only to visit with an old friend. Mollified, Greg moved on to another table as the café began to fill up with the lunchtime crowd.

Judith and Renie barely got out the door when they spotted Joe and Woody heading in their direction.

"What now?" Joe asked, vaguely irritated. "I thought my lovely bride was going home after the hospital visit."

"I had some things to do," Judith murmured. "Did you find out about Mr. Schnell?"

Woody smiled at Judith. "You really are amazing," he said. "I don't care what Joe says. Charlie Schnell was indeed shot and killed while fleeing the old Sound View Apartments. He'd surprised an elderly woman who put up a struggle. The neighbors heard the ruckus and called the police. There was a patrol car just a block away. Charlie was armed and holding the woman hostage. He refused to come out at first, but he finally dragged the poor woman to the street level, then pushed her away and fled on foot. That's when he was shot. The police in those days were quite a bit more trigger-happy than they are now. It's believed that he was responsible for a series of burglaries over at least a ten-year period."

"Wow!" Judith grinned back at Woody. "That's terrific news." She stopped, restraining her enthusiasm. "Not for the Schnells, of course. I mean, not when Mr. Schnell got killed."

Joe was staring at Renie. "What happened to you? Did you finally run over yourself with your car?"

"Very funny," Renie shot back. "I met Nurse Royce."

"Oh, yes—the formidable Nurse Royce." Joe was trying not to smile, but failing. Briefly. Suddenly, he scowled, not at Renie but at Judith. "Why was Renie at the hospital this morning? Was that your idea?"

"Well—yes," Judith admitted. "One of the other nurses found a piece of paper in Dr. Ashe's trousers." Judith rummaged in her handbag, found the paper, and handed it to Joe. "It sort of confirms that Mr. Schnell was a burglar, doesn't it?"

Woody looked over Joe's shoulder. "Gosh, this is really old. It even smells funny." He scanned the names on the list. "Yes, I think those other apartment houses were mentioned in Schnell's file. But what's this 'Meacham' at the bottom?"

Judith snatched the paper away from Joe. "Good question. I assume Dr. Ashe wrote that, since it's very recent. He must have found this in the Schnell unit before he got knocked out."

Woody nodded. "That makes sense. So do the tools in his attaché case. He'd brought them along so that he could search under the floor or in the walls or wherever. But what was he looking for?"

"Restitution, maybe," Judith said, stepping aside as a quartet of businessmen walked past the little group.

"Did you notice the Hasegawas on that list? Dr. Ashe is married to Hiroko Hasegawa. She was born after the war. I figure he came up here to check out her roots while he was attending the chiropractic conference. In doing so, he took the tour and learned that some so-called treasure had been found in the Alhambra. Hiroko's family must have been one of Charlie Schnell's victims. Maybe that treasure belongs to the Hasegawas. Maybe Dr. Ashe thought there was more, and was searching for it."

Joe and Woody exchanged quick glances. "That's possible," Joe said. "But it's not a motive for murdering Aimee Carrabas."

Judith smiled sweetly at Joe. "Did I say I was investigating the Carrabas case? That's your job. I'm working in the past, on the Meacham murder."

"The Meacham murder was unofficially solved," Joe declared, eyeing his wife suspiciously. "I thought you were looking for a connection."

"Well—I was," Judith said. "I am. I guess." She turned an appealing look on Woody. "But how could the police have been sure that Harry killed Dorothy? Did they have proof or were they just guessing?"

Woody offered Judith a kindhearted smile. "Since the body was found only a month ago, and there was no trace of Harry Meacham after he left town, the case is officially open. But because of circumstantial evidence, we assume that the spouse is the prime suspect."

Judith nodded slowly. "Yes, I see." An idea suddenly struck her. "Woody, did Aimee Carrabas have any living relatives?"

"No," Woody replied, looking bemused. "Her mother, Elizabeth Ritter, died recently in a nursing home out in the San Fernando Valley. Her father had been dead for several years."

"Did Mrs. Ritter have a will?" Judith asked, ignoring Joe's impatient sighs.

"She did," Woody said, still regarding Judith with mild curiosity. "She left everything to Aimee. The estate is quite large, which is why it has to go through probate."

"Of course." Judith started to back away, then stopped. "Are you two having lunch here?" she asked, gesturing toward the café.

"That's right," Joe replied. "Do we need permission?"

"No," Judith said meekly. "But you might consider Fu Man Chew's down the street. You'll find Rufus Holmes there, waiting for takeout. Bye."

The cousins made a swift getaway. They had to stop at the corner for the traffic light, and Judith glanced over her shoulder. Joe and Woody were still outside the café, apparently debating something. The light changed and Judith moved quickly across the street.

"Hold up," Renie yelled. "I thought your hips hurt."

"They do," Judith said. "I figure Joe and Woody are going to Fu Man Chew's but Joe doesn't want me to know it. Ergo, I want to get out of sight so they can arrive before Rufus leaves with his order."

"How will they know who Rufus is?" Renie asked, hurrying to catch up.

Judith gave her a cousin a wry little smile. "Because they're cops, that's how."

Renie had been adamant about not going to see George Guthrie. Since she had her own car, she was heading uptown to the art museum to show the staff how the Native American project was progressing. Then, she promised, she'd meet Judith at Papaya Pete's around one-thirty.

Judith didn't bother considering how Renie dared to show up at the art museum in her disheveled state. Though her closet was stuffed with designer clothes, Renie often showed an utter disregard bordering on contempt for her public appearance. Judith merely wondered how Renie managed to get away with it.

Rory, the receptionist, greeted Judith with a tentative smile. "You're . . . ?" he said, then frowned.

"Mrs. Flynn," Judith replied. "I was here the other day to see Mr. Guthrie. Is he in?"

"Yes and no," Rory answered, still frowning. "I mean, he's not available. He's in a big meeting that'll probably last all afternoon."

"A new project?" Judith suggested in her friendliest manner.

Rory's hands twitched nervously on the desk. "Not exactly. I'll let Mr. Guthrie know you stopped by."

If Rory was hinting dismissal, Judith was ignoring him. "How soon will the Alhambra's renovations be completed?"

"The finish date is the first of the year," Rory said glumly. "But with all these delays in the past week, we may be looking at February."

"That's not unusual, is it?" Judith inquired. "My Uncle Corky used to be in construction. Between weather conditions, strikes, and other unforeseen occurrences, it always seemed as if completion dates got changed."

"That's true," Rory said. "It's just that—" He stopped as a tall man in an Armani suit came hurrying out of George's office. "Mr. Stensrud?" Rory gulped.

The man paused at the reception desk. "I've got a one o'clock appointment with the city I can't miss. George is on his own for the next hour. Whatever you do, don't let him walk out on these clowns," he said, gesturing in the direction of the inner office. "He's pretty hot under the collar."

"Yes, Mr. Stensrud," Rory said with a jerky nod. "I'll do my best. But you know how upset he gets with these zoning officials."

Stensrud rolled his eyes. "Of course I do. That's why he pays me big bucks to keep him out of trouble. See you later." He swerved abruptly and looked at Judith. "Excuse me. Are you a client?"

"Of yours?" Judith retorted, assuming Stensrud was an attorney.

Stensrud shook his head. "No, I meant of George's."

"No," Judith said. "I'm . . . sort of a friend."

"Good." Stensrud patted Judith on the arm. "No harm done, then. I'm off." He was out the door in three long strides.

"Lawyers are usually more discreet," Judith said with a little smile.

Rory seemed disconcerted. "Yes, of course. But Mr. Stensrud . . . Well, he can be blunt. He's a very aggressive type of attorney, which is good."

"That's helpful for George," Judith remarked. "Construction projects are so controversial these days."

Apparently assuming he'd found a kindred spirit, Rory eyed Judith with approbation. "Mr. Stensrud gives Mr. Guthrie excellent representation. You're right, when your client is a builder, you have to be tough to go up against all these zoning commissions and environmental agencies."

"Of course," Judith said, still in her friendly mode. "Builders are in a bind these days. There's so much in-city construction. People want to live close to downtown, but housing developments are restricted, not just because of a shortage of space, but because of all the . . . legal ramifications." Judith wasn't sure what she was talking about, but thought it sounded plausible.

Indeed, Rory agreed wholeheartedly. "Absolutely," he declared, growing expansive. "I haven't worked here that long, but already I can see what Mr. Guthrie's up against." He gestured toward the inner office. "Right now, he's in there fighting for his projects. Don't these negative types realize that construction is good for the community? It provides jobs, for one thing. I had some different ideas before Mr. Guthrie hired me, but I learned real quick that I was dead wrong. Take the Alhambra, for example. The Heraldsgate Hill Historical

Society put up a big fuss about the renovation, but Mr. Guthrie hasn't hurt the exterior at all. In fact, he's improved the place. It was overdue for some big improvements."

Judith looked puzzled. "I didn't realize the historical society had protested the changes."

"Oh, yes," Rory asserted. "I was a member, in fact. I live over on the side of the hill above the lake. I majored in history at the university, so I thought it might be kind of cool to join the historical society. There was quite a bit of news about it, especially in the weekly newspaper."

Judith winced. With her busy schedule, weeks went by when she didn't look at anything in the community paper except Falstaff's Grocery specials.

"I guess I missed that," she admitted. "When was it?"

Rory reflected briefly. "In the late winter or early spring. Naturally, I sided with the O'Dowds and some of the other members at first, but after I got this job, I quit the society altogether. They're just a bunch of troublemakers."

"The O'Dowds?" Judith said. "Do you mean the couple who used to lived in the Alhambra?"

"That's right," Rory said. "Billy and Midge. In retrospect, I can see that it was sour grapes with them. They couldn't afford to buy a condo and didn't want to move. They were just stonewalling."

"Yes," Judith murmured, her brain kicking into high gear. "Of course. Stonewalling. Well," she said, her voice turning brisk, "I'd better be on my way. I'll catch Mr. Guthrie later. Thanks, Rory."

Uptown, in the luxury hotel that featured the exotic Papaya Pete's Restaurant, Judith had to wait almost half an hour for Renie. In fact, she had just about given up and was going to call the art museum when Renie stomped into the restaurant wearing a gray wool dress, sling-back pumps, and a gray jacket trimmed in Norwegian fox.

"What on earth . . . ?" Judith exclaimed. "It's seventy-five degrees outside. Why are you dressed for winter? And where did you get those clothes?"

"I bought them at Nordquist's," Renie replied in an annoyed voice as she shed the fur-trimmed coat. "I got here early, and they wouldn't let me in. They said I looked like a bum. I wasn't up to another wrestling match, so I marched up the street to Nordquist's and bought something more suitable."

Judith gaped. "That must have set you back a grand."

"Ha!" Renie batted at one of the artificial palm fronds that was drooping dangerously near her shoulder. "That was just for the coat. The dress and the shoes were another eight hundred bucks. I think I'll send the bill to that snotty maître d'."

"Goodness." Judith was flabbergasted. "You should have sent word in to me, and I'd have left to meet you someplace else."

"No." Renie's short chin jutted as far as her physiognomy would permit. "It's the principle of the thing."

"The principle is worth almost two grand?" Judith shook her head in dismay. "That price tag is too high for me."

"I need some new fall clothes," Renie said with a shrug. "Where's the waiter? The drinks around here seem to be flowing like glue."

Judith decided to abandon the topic of Renie's wardrobe extravagance, which always stupefied her anyway. As soon as they'd gotten the attention of their server and each ordered one of the house's tropical specialties, Judith confronted Renie about the Heraldsgate Hill Historical Society.

"You were the one who was supposed to know all about the Alhambra and its background," Judith declared. "Why didn't you tell me about the society's protest and the O'Dowds being members?"

Renie looked blank. "Because I didn't know? Because the kid who used to deliver the weekly took Bill's generous tips and enrolled at Harvard? Because we haven't had a paper delivered in over a year? That reminds me, I should call circulation."

"Oh," Judith said, subdued. "I forgot you haven't been getting the paper."

"So did I," Renie said, now hidden by the large menu. "Which is why I also keep forgetting to call. I always think of it at times like this, when phoning isn't convenient. Then I forget again."

Judith uttered a small sigh. "Okay, I forgive you. But this is very interesting about the O'Dowds—and others— who opposed Guthrie's project from the get-go. It opens up a whole new line of possibilities."

Renie waited to respond until the waiter had delivered their drinks. "A Papaya Pile Driver for you, miss," he said to Judith, "and a Waikiki Whammy for you," he added, setting a fruit-laden glass in front of Renie. "Didn't I see you at the entrance much earlier, miss? You look very familiar and yet . . ." His voice trailed off.

"That was my evil twin," Renie said. "The one who goes around violating dress codes and wins huge discrimination settlements against upscale restaurants."

"Oh." The waiter managed a faint smile. "Of course." He bowed and left the table.

"Are you saying," Renie began, "that some disgruntled historical society member knocked off Guthrie's exorcist in a fit of pique?"

"Well . . . not exactly," Judith temporized. "I guess I'm saying that what amounts to getting evicted could be a motive. I suppose," she went on, deflating a bit, "that Woody has checked that out already. Joe hasn't mentioned it, though. I'll have to ask him when he gets home."

"The O'Dowds weren't the only ones," Renie said after a lengthy pause.

"That's true," Judith agreed. "There were what? Thirty units more or less in the original floor plan? That means there may be several more disgruntled people."

"That's too many suspects," Renie remarked. "You know I'm weak at math."

"I'll bet Woody is interviewing all of them," Judith said, invigorated once more. "Why didn't I think of this before? Murdering Mrs. Carrabas just might put a damper on George's sales."

"Haven't you discovered that homicide is a marketing tool?" Renie asked dryly.

"No, I haven't," Judith retorted. "It's a wonder that the fortune-teller's murder didn't sink me. I hadn't been in business very long, and I was sure my reputation was ruined before I even had a reputation."

"But it wasn't," Renie pointed out, devouring a slice of pineapple.

"No," Judith admitted. "It brought attention to the B&B, even if it was the wrong kind. Still, it probably scared off some potential customers."

"Maybe," Renie allowed. "But there are people who actively search out inns that have a resident ghost."

"I don't claim to have one," Judith declared. "Besides, there's a big difference between a ghost and a recent homicide. Especially when another body had been discovered sealed up in the wall."

"Okay," Renie said. "I'll give you that."

The waiter approached to take their orders. "So," Renie continued, after the cousins had both selected the chicken curry, "maybe some squeamish folks would look askance at the Alhambra as their next address. The prices certainly make me squeamish."

"That's not quite the motive I had in mind," Judith said, wondering just how many different kinds of alcohol were in her Pile Driver. She could taste rum, gin, vodka, and something else. Maybe lighter fluid. If she ordered a second round, the bartender could use antifreeze and she wouldn't know the difference. "I was thinking more of spite. You know, like with the O'Dowds. They might bump off Mrs. Carrabas just to embarrass George Guthrie as well as to slow condo sales."

"That's what I meant," Renie said, somewhat vaguely. "Isn't it? Hey, did I order a Whammy or a Double Whammy?"

"How should I know?" Judith responded in a rather testy tone. "I'd forgotten how strong these specialty drinks are." She gazed around the dining room, which had almost emptied out at going on two o'clock. "Are those palm trees moving over there in the corner?"

"Those aren't palm trees," Renie replied. "They're busboys."

"Hunh." Judith took another sip of her drink. "They'd better serve us pretty quick. I haven't eaten since eight o'clock."

"Here come the salads," Renie said.

"That's a dessert cart for the table with all the old ladies," Judith countered.

Renie twisted around so far that she practically fell out of her chair. "What old ladies?"

Judith blinked. "I guess they aren't old ladies. The white sails on those model ships look like hair."

"So where'd our salads go?" Renie asked, awkwardly managing to face front again.

"I don't know," Judith admitted, then lowered her voice. "Let's try to act dignified. You've already been thrown out of here once today."

"Good idea," Renie agreed, her eyes slightly crossed. "Dignity, I mean. You can't go wrong with dignity."

"Not at all," Judith said, reaching for her glass and picking up the candleholder instead. "Oops!"

Renie giggled. "You might have set your face on fire. That would have been really funny." She giggled some more.

"Hey!" Judith said in a stage whisper. "Let's not tell them what I just saw by the entrance."

"Which was what? I don't think I can turn around again," said Renie.

"A giant bird." Judith looked very pleased with herself.

"Really." Renie didn't sound surprised.

Judith nodded solemnly. "It ran right through the foyer. It looked like—" She stopped, frowning in concentration. "It looked like Emil!" she cried in a more natural voice.

Both cousins stood up, almost knocking over the table. Just as they stared in the direction of the entrance, Emil raced by again, this time with a uniformed doorman in pursuit.

Renie made an uncoordinated gesture with one hand and sat down. "Let's ignore Emil."

Judith nodded again. "That's smart. We won't tell them we know Emil. They probably wouldn't believe us."

Renie winced as she half-fell into her chair. "Actually," she said, somewhat subdued, "I think they would."

By the time the cousins left Papaya Pete's, they were sober. A large lunch and several cups of coffee had restored them. They did not, however, inquire after Emil. Perhaps he had been captured and finally returned to his owners. At least that's what Judith and Renie wanted to believe.

For what was left of the afternoon, Judith turned into a dervish, trying to catch up with the work she'd missed while playing detective. One set of guests, a couple from Samoa, had arrived just ten minutes after she got back to the B&B. They would be staying throughout the long Labor Day weekend, on the initial leg of a first-time visit to the United States.

The mail had brought not only the usual bills and circulars, but the first Christmas catalogue of the season. Judith grimaced and ditched it in a drawer.

Joe arrived home before five, looking tired. Judith poured him a cocktail, but stayed with the diet soda she'd been nursing for the last hour. After he'd begun to relax a bit, she quizzed him about his day.

Joe gave his wife a baleful look. "We missed Rufus Holmes at Fu Man Chew's. He's a regular there, and he always goes out the back door to avoid the crowds."

Nothing really new had come out of the meeting with Woody and Sancha. "I went through the Alhambra again with them," Joe said. "It definitely looks as if Alfred had been trying to pry up more floorboards. He's still out of it, by the way."

"Poor Alfred," Judith said. "Have you any idea who hit him over the head?"

Joe looked enigmatic. "Do you?"

Judith flinched. "Well . . . I hate to say it, but I think it could have been Helen Schnell."

"Good guess," Joe said. "It was her old unit, her old man was a burglar, she has a reputation to uphold."

"Did you talk to her?" Judith asked as the phone rang.

"Woody did," Joe said. "Of course she denied it."

"Of course." Judith said hello into the phone.

Jeremy Lamar was at the other end, sounding chagrined. "Is Mr. Flynn there?"

"Yes, hold on," Judith said, handing the receiver to Joe.

Joe propped the phone between his chin and shoulder. "Yes," he said, then paused. "Really?" He winked at Judith. "Of course . . . No, but so far we've just done the routine checks . . . Sure. I'm pleased, too. Thanks, Jeremy." Joe hung up.

"What was that all about?" Judith asked, sitting down at the table.

Joe grinned. "Nan Leech has been found. Apparently, she was never lost. According to her, she mentioned to Jeremy that she was taking a day or two off. She called him just before five today to see if there was anything she should know about in advance of coming into work tomorrow. Jeremy is very embarrassed. He says he simply didn't hear Nan say anything about a vacation."

"Do you believe her?" Judith asked. "Do you believe him?"

Joe shrugged. "I can't say. Woody told me that apparently there was no sign of her at any of the usual checkpoints. That indicated she was still in town since her car was parked at her condo. Maybe she was with some guy."

Judith shot her husband an arch little look. "Some guy like Alfred Ashe?"

Joe scowled. "I don't see that. How do you figure?"

Judith raised her hands in a helpless gesture. "I don't know. It just popped into my head."

"I'm sure Woody isn't counting anybody out as a murder suspect," Joe said. "He thinks—and I agree—that as far as Alfred is concerned, he agreed to meet someone at the Alhambra. That fireworks stunt allowed both of them to get inside the building."

"And how did Alfred's attacker get out?" Judith inquired.

Joe gave Judith a lopsided grin. "I was wondering when you'd ask that. The back way, I suppose. And don't forget all those balconies. Let's face it, the uniforms didn't exactly make the rounds every fifteen minutes, at least not after the first night. An elephant could have sneaked in through the back."

"Or an ostrich?" Judith remarked.

"That, too," said Joe.

While Joe was watching a baseball game on TV, Judith called Renie around eight o'clock and brought her cousin up to date.

Renie yawned in Judith's ear. "That's it?"

"Isn't that enough?" Judith shot back. "Especially the part about Nan Leech being okay."

"Says who?"

Judith was taken aback. "Says Jeremy, her boss and concerned citizen."

"You only have his word for it," Renie noted. "Have you talked to Nan?"

"No," Judith retorted, "but I could if I wanted to."

"Then why don't you? Maybe she's not watching the ball game. I am." Renie hung up.

Judith got mad. She hit the redial button.

"What now?" Renie growled. "I know it's you, I have Caller ID."

"And no manners," Judith huffed. "Let me finish telling you about the canvass."

"Canvas? You're sleeping in a tent? Isn't it a little late in the season for that?"

"This won't take a minute," Judith said, ignoring her cousin's remarks. It actually took closer to two minutes to relate how Woody and Sancha had been interrogating former Alhambra tenants. "So," Judith said in summation, "of the thirty people they've been able to talk to, all of them have alibis for the time of the murder. The police are still tracking down two others, but there's no reason to consider them suspects . . ."

Instead of responding, Renie swore, using words she had learned at her seagoing father's knee.

"What happened?" Judith asked in alarm.

"Bases juiced," Renie snarled, "nobody out—and we still ended up stranding those guys. Two fanned and one infield fly." There was more swearing.

"So far, there's no indication of a vendetta against George Guthrie," Judith said, stretching out her tired legs under the desk Joe had installed in the third floor family room. "There aren't many serious suspects," she added, idly going through the papers on Joe's desk. "I mean, among the ex-tenants. The O'Dowds were on the scene, of course. So, perhaps, was Rufus Holmes."

"I still say it's a stretch from outraged tenant to homicidal nut," Renie commented.

"I'm not arguing," Judith said, noting that Joe's

Carrabas case file seemed remarkably empty. "It's probably even a longer stretch from the Meacham killing to
this one. Say, do you suppose Joe puts all his case data
on disk?"

"I'm sure he would," Renie said. "Why?"

"He's only got this stuff organized in the last three
months," Judith said, quietly opening drawers and
peering into the single filing cabinet. "I've been so busy
with summer guests that I've never really looked at his
setup. I should take more interest."

Renie let out a shriek and then a cackle. "Double play.
All right!"

Judith sighed. "It's going to be a losing season. Calm
down."

"I'm calm. Where were we? Oh—well, you've never
been that curious about his caseload until now," Renie
pointed out with a snicker. "How excited do you get
over a missing Pomeranian named Yogurt?"

"It was Yeltsin," Judith said. "And I'm not actually
snooping."

"Yes, you are. I'll bet it's all in the computer, both on
the hard drive and on disk. There's probably a secret
word, something he could never forget, not even in his
dreams."

"Like 'Judith'?"

"Like 'Gertrude,' " said Renie and hung up.

Judith did call Nan Leech the next morning, after
she'd gotten the guests taken care of and had greeted
Phyliss Rackley. Nan was at her post, sounding efficient
and irritable.

"You worried everyone," Judith said, exuding empa-
thy. "We thought something had happened to you."

"Happened to me?" Nan sounded incredulous. "Why
would you think that?"

"Well . . . one person is already dead and another has
been assaulted," Judith pointed out.

"Neither of those things pertain to me," Nan declared.

"Everybody needs an occasional break to attend to their personal lives. However, I was sorry to hear about Dr. Ashe. I understand he's still in a coma this morning."

"I hadn't heard," Judith said. "Poor man. Did you meet him during the tour?"

"Only after Mrs. Carrabas's body had been found," Nan replied, adding in an accusatory tone, "by *you*. While we were waiting to be interviewed by the police, Dr. Ashe kept asking both Jeremy and me a million questions. Obviously, he had more than a passing interest in the Alhambra."

"What was he asking about?" Judith inquired casually.

"Mainly the treasure," Nan replied, sounding impatient. "I don't remember exactly. It was chaos, trying to keep everybody calm and under control until the police could conclude their individual interviews. It's no wonder I needed some time off."

Judith decided to press her luck with Nan. "Did anything interesting come out of those interviews?"

"How would I know?" Nan retorted. "They were conducted in a separate room."

"Of course," Judith remarked. "Tell me, has the murder affected Jeremy's tour business?"

"The mystery tour is full for the next three weeks and the Halloween tours are almost booked, too," Nan said. "I have to say that the unfortunate death of Mrs. Carrabas has been a boon to business. Now if you'll excuse me, I have to get down to just that. Business."

Judith stood by the sink with the phone in her hand for several minutes. Aimee Carrabas's homicide had been a plus for Jeremy Lamar, possibly a minus for George Guthrie. Was there a motive involved between cause and effect? Jeremy had benefited from the tragedy, at least in the short term. George, despite his initial idea to create publicity for his project, might suffer in the long run. But who would seek his misfortune by killing an innocent person?

"The Devil works in mysterious ways," Phyliss Rackley announced as she entered the kitchen from the back stairs. "That furry four-legged Limb of Satan got into Room Two and shredded your lace curtains."

"No!" Judith burst out. "Where is the little wretch?"

"Lucifer swept him up and carried him out the window," Phyliss said.

"What?" Judith demanded, already halfway to the stairs.

Phyliss nodded solemnly. "He's gone. He's probably in the Fiery Furnace. Or the Boiling Cauldron. Good riddance, I say. Now maybe you and Mr. Flynn can still be saved. Your mother remains in doubt."

With a dark look at Phyliss, Judith hurried up the stairs and down the hall to Room Two. Sure enough, the lace curtains were ripped in several places and the window was open. Over the years, Sweetums had been trained not to go onto the second floor and bother the guests. Or perhaps Judith was trained to keep an eye on the unruly cat when guests were in their rooms. The problem was that some of her clientele were cat lovers, and coaxed Sweetums upstairs. Or so Judith rationalized.

It was unlikely that Lucifer had swept Sweetums away. Obviously, Phyliss had opened the window to air out the room. A huge camellia bush grew halfway up the exterior wall of the second story. It was an easy jump for Sweetums. Judith looked outside, where she saw an orange-and-white form slinking through the dahlias. Lucifer was nowhere in sight.

With a sigh, she took down the curtain panel that Sweetums had ripped. Fortunately, it could be mended. She'd have to do it before her guests started arriving. The room was taken by a widow who was traveling with her sister and brother-in-law.

Adjusting the curtain rod, Judith lost her balance and banged against the chest of drawers next to the window. As she caught herself, her arm flew up, dislodging the dresser scarf. A piece of paper fluttered to the floor.

Judith picked it up and stared. Two words were written on the notebook-sized paper: "Meacham" and "Revenge?"

The handwriting and the ink were the same as that of the word "Meacham" written on the old, faded slip of paper that Renie had retrieved from the hospital.

It figured. The last occupant of Room Two had been Alfred Ashe.

FIFTEEN

"IT KEEPS COMING back to Alfred Ashe," Judith asserted over the phone to Renie. "The link has to be the Hasegawas, of course. But why?"

"What do you mean, why?" Renie shot back. "They're his in-laws. They got sent off to a detention camp. He's helping his wife find her—"

"Treasure," Judith interrupted. "What do you bet that Charlie Schnell stole that jewelry from the Hasegawas?"

"I was going to say roots," Renie murmured, "but you're right. So why does Alfred keep making notes about the Meachams?"

" 'Meachams' with a question mark this time," Judith noted. "The Hasegawas knew the Meachams, they were neighbors. I wonder if Mrs. Ashe's—or Hiroko Hasegawa's—parents are still alive?"

"Ask her," Renie said. "I imagine she'll be coming up here from San Francisco to sit by her husband's bed."

"You're right," Judith replied. "I think I'll try to reach her right now."

Hiroko Hasegawa belonged to a large firm that sounded as if it covered the ethnic map: Olson,

Epstein, La Fleur, Chang, Lincoln, Habib, Brownbear, Cassetti, Hasegawa, Quandi, Fabersham, and Smith had offices in the heart of San Francisco's financial district. They also, Judith figured, had a very large letterhead.

An austere female voice took Judith's call. "Ms. Hasegawa is unavailable," said the voice. "May I tell her who's calling?"

Judith identified herself, adding that she was a friend of Ms. Hasegawa's husband. "I'd like to know if Hiroko is coming here to be with her husband."

"I'm sorry, Mrs. Flynn," the voice said in a tone that conveyed no regret whatsoever, "but I'm not at liberty to reveal Ms. Hasegawa's personal plans. At the moment, she's in court on a very important case."

"Oh, of course," Judith said in her most confidential manner. "I know she'll come out on top. It's vital that she does."

"You know about it?" the voice said, a trifle shaken.

"Of course," Judith replied, lying through her teeth. "I told you, Alfred and I are very close. He was staying with my husband and me up until he suffered his accident."

"Then you know who has right on their side," the voice said, warming audibly. "The injustice of it all! And of course Hiroko has a personal stake, since her parents and her two older siblings were shipped off to one of those awful camps. The government owes them much more than money, but what else can you ask for but restitution at this point?"

"Yes," Judith said, enlightened. "Yes, it's the least— and unfortunately the most—that can be done. Which reminds me, I've misplaced Hiroko's brother's address."

"Goodness," the voice said, sounding chagrined, "I don't have either of her brothers' addresses, not since Ozawa moved to London and Hashimoto was transferred to Buenos Aires."

"Oh." Judith may have gotten lucky guessing that

Hiroko had at least one brother, but she wasn't about to
try to track down people living abroad. Nor did she
push her luck by inquiring after a sister. "That's all
right. Let's just hope that Alfred's condition improves."

"We're all pulling for him," the voice said. "By the
way, Hiroko's parents have their sons' new addresses.
Would you like their number?"

"Yes, yes, I would," Judith said, brightening.

"It's four-one-five . . ." the voice began as Judith
grabbed a piece of paper and began writing.

Three minutes later, Judith was speaking with a
sprightly voiced woman in San Francisco who assured
her caller that she was Mrs. Hasegawa. "You're a detective?" she asked with the faintest of accents. "Do you
know who hurt poor Alfred?"

"Not yet," Judith confessed. "My husband's working
on the case. I sort of . . . help. But the doctor is quite
optimistic."

"Good," Mrs. Hasegawa said. "Alfred has a very hard
head. I've told him so many times."

"What I'm really calling about," Judith went on as
Phyliss appeared from the basement, "is in regard to a
previous murder investigation at the Alhambra."

"Murder!" Phyliss burst out. "Carnage! Bloodbaths!
Are you perjuring your soul with some of those big
whoppers again, Mrs. Flynn?"

Judith made a face at Phyliss and shook her head in
denial. In San Francisco, Mrs. Hasegawa was making
some strange noises of her own. "The Alhambra!" she
exclaimed. "Such a nice place! I never want to see it
again!"

Momentarily, Judith felt as if she were talking to
Arlene Rankers, who was often given to contradicting
herself in the same breath. "Is that so? How come?"

"There were some very bad people living there," Mrs.
Hasegawa declared. "Thieves. Adulterers. Traitors."

"Really?" Judith's surprise was genuine.

"That's right. Of course, you live in an apartment house, you live with all sorts of odd people. Take the Whiffels, for instance."

The Whiffels were the last tenants that Judith wanted to discuss, but she patiently listened to Mrs. Hasegawa's assessment of the family's religious mania. Obviously, such obsessions were still alive and well as Phyliss passed through the kitchen, announcing that Satan had blown a fuse in the dryer, but the Angel Gabriel had tripped the circuit and all was well.

"What about the Meachams?" Judith asked when Mrs. Hasegawa was finally done with the Whiffels.

"Very strange doings," the old lady declared. "That man had two wives."

"Oh?"

"That's right. One blond, one brunette," said Mrs. Hasegawa. "Both were quite good-looking, in their way. I thought it was scandalous. I said so. Anyway, that's probably why Mr. Meacham told the authorities we were Japanese spies."

"He did?" Judith gasped. "How awful!"

"How wrong," Mrs. Hasegawa asserted. "We'd both come to this country when we were very young, we were both citizens, we loved America. Why, my husband and I practically went to every baseball game during the summer. Of course, the team was only Triple AAA back then, but the quality of the players was big league. All this expansion! It's diluted the game. How often do you see a pitcher go nine innings these days?"

"Only when the team hasn't got a bullpen," Judith said, then got the conversation back on track. "Are you sure it was Harry Meacham who accused you of being spies?"

"Yes," the older woman answered. "Who else? I think he did it to cover up for his wife—the blond wife—who was probably a German agent. To divert attention, you know."

"The blond Mrs. Meacham was German? By birth?" Judith queried, trying to sort through Mrs. Hasegawa's information and allegations.

"Yes, indeed," Mrs. Hasegawa said firmly. "Alfred confirmed this on the phone. He looked her up in an old reverse directory at the library. Then he checked through one of those genealogical things. She was born in Berlin, wouldn't you know it? I always figured her for a spy. She had an accent, very slight, but there it was. Anyway, I ought to know, I still have a bit of an accent myself. Imagine—after over sixty years."

"It's hardly noticeable," Judith commented as Phyliss returned again from the basement.

"Beelzebub put those new red towels in the washer and your husband's undies are all pink," she said as she bustled through the kitchen and into the dining room.

Judith kept from groaning out loud. Joe wouldn't like having pink underwear. "Tell me," Judith said into the receiver, "how did Harry Meacham manage with two wives?"

Mrs. Hasegawa snickered. "Very carefully, I assure you. He moved in with the blond—Beth, he called her— a year or two before the war. They had a unit on the top floor, in 503. Then what do you know, the summer before Pearl Harbor, he shows up with Dorothy, who's pregnant. They move into the second floor, 204, I think it was. My husband and I couldn't believe it. Beth seemed to have disappeared. We figured that she and Harry had gotten a divorce. Anyway, Harry joined the army, and we were shipped off to Idaho. The government decided we weren't spies, but we still had to leave everything and move away. Anyway, at least we didn't end up in prison."

"You're sure it was Harry who was the so-called informer?" Judith asked.

"Who else?" Mrs. Hasegawa retorted. "I'd made the mistake of criticizing him and his women one day in the courtyard when I was talking to Mrs. Folger, the manager. Harry Meacham was just on the other side of the fountain. I didn't see him until it was too late."

Judith remained vaguely skeptical. Mrs. Hasegawa might be paranoid, and with good reason.

"I know about the body in the wall," Mrs. Hasegawa said. "We still have friends in your area. They sent us the newspaper clippings about it. Isn't that something? Not that I'd put it past Harry. You see, Mrs. Folger—she was the manager—kept in touch with me after we were sent to that awful camp. Have you ever tried to sweep a dirt floor? Anyway," she continued, barely pausing for breath, "she told us about the little girl that Harry and Dorothy had had just after we were sent packing. Very cute, very sweet. Harry came home on leave a couple of times. Dorothy doted on their little girl—now what was her name?"

"Anne-Marie," Judith put in.

"Yes, Anne-Marie. Anyway, Harry finally came back after the war. Eventually, we were freed, but because of all the bad memories, we decided to move to San Francisco. My husband had family here, a brother and an aunt and an uncle. But I kept in touch with Mrs. Folger—she kept track of what was going on in the building, it was her business to know. She wasn't like that snoopy Mrs. Schnell who was always nosing around. Why, once I caught her going through our bedroom drawers while she thought I was making tea. How long does it take to make tea? I never learned all that tea ceremony stuff. The government should have known that anybody who didn't know the tea ceremony didn't care much for the old country. When I was a little girl in the twenties, I wanted to be a flapper, with rolled stockings and a gin flask on my hip. By the time I was old enough, it was the thirties and I got married. I never got to flap."

Mrs. Hasegawa finally ran out of breath. "So you were saying about the Meachams after the war?" Judith coaxed.

"I was? Oh—yes, I guess so. Anyway, Mrs. Folger told

me about Dorothy disappearing. My husband and I figured it made sense, in a peculiar sort of way. She'd been
left alone for so long, maybe she'd found somebody
else. Of course, we couldn't figure out why she'd leave
her little girl. That seemed queer. Anyway, the next
thing we hear from Mrs. Folger is that Beth, the blond,
has shown up again."

"Where had she been during the war?" Judith asked,
taking advantage of a brief pause at the other end.

"I don't know," Mrs. Hasegawa replied, sounding
faintly indignant that such a piece of information could
have passed her by. "Mrs. Folger didn't know, either.
She'd moved out about the same time that Harry and
Dorothy moved in. That's why we figured that Harry
and Beth had divorced. So maybe she got him back on
the rebound, maybe he married her twice. Maybe," the
old lady added darkly, "Harry and Beth were never
married at all. Or maybe Harry and Dorothy weren't
married. You didn't broadcast such things in those days.
Now everybody lives together in one big pig pile and
they don't care who knows it."

"That's true," Judith remarked. "Did anyone know
where Beth went?"

"Not far, it would seem," Mrs. Hasegawa huffed.
"Although my husband figured she'd gone back to Germany to become one of those horrible Nazis. I told him
he was crazy. I figured she stayed right in town, waiting
for Harry to come back."

"From the war?" Judith asked. "Or from Dorothy?"

"Both," Mrs. Hasegawa replied. "Only Dorothy
didn't see it that way, which, I figure, is why she ended
up inside that wall at the Alhambra."

Mrs. Hasegawa didn't have much more to add. She
couldn't recall Beth's last name, though she thought it
might come to her, and asked for Judith's number in
case she remembered. Perhaps, Mrs. Hasegawa suggested, if Hiroko couldn't get away to be with Alfred,

Judith could act as the personal contact in town to keep the family apprised of any change in her son-in-law's condition. Judith said she'd be glad to do whatever she could.

The phone rang just as soon as Judith hung up. The caller requested a reservation for the Thanksgiving weekend. Judith took down the information and smiled to herself. For most of the major holidays, the B&B was always full, and at least half of the reservations were holdovers from previous years. In ten years, she had built up a loyal clientele, not just for holidays, but during other parts of the year as well. Repeat business was good business. Judith allowed herself to enjoy a small sense of pride.

But upkeep was vital. After Joe had retired from the police department and before he'd decided to work part-time as a private investigator, Judith had hoped he'd be able to do many of the odd jobs around the house. That hadn't panned out. With fall coming on, she should tend to some needed repairs. Judith was looking up the number for her aged but highly competent carpenter, Skjoval Tolvang, when the phone rang again.

"This is Nurse Millie from Norway General," said the chipper voice at the other end. "Dr. Bentley asked me to call and let you know that Dr. Ashe has regained consciousness."

"Oh!" Judith cried. "That's wonderful news! Will he be all right?"

"He's in guarded condition," Nurse Millie replied. "But Dr. Bentley feels his prognosis is good."

"I'm so glad," Judith said. "Can he speak?"

"Oh, no, he has to remain perfectly quiet for at least the next twenty-four hours," Nurse Millie said. "Absolutely no visitors are allowed."

"Oh." The enthusiasm fled from Judith's voice. "Well . . . certainly. I understand," she said, cranking up all the charity she could muster. "Thanks so much for calling. I'll let his family know about this. Or have they already been notified?"

"We left word at the courthouse for his wife in San Francisco," Nurse Millie responded. "Apparently, she's in the courtroom but is expected out soon for the lunch recess."

"Good," Judith said. "I'm sure she'll be immensely relieved. Thanks so much."

Judith immediately dialed Mrs. Hasegawa's number, but this time there was no answer, just a machine message in a rather gruff male voice saying, "We're gone. Leave your number. Please." Judith decided not to say anything, but to wait until she got through to Mrs. Hasegawa.

For several minutes, Judith sat at the kitchen counter, staring at her computer screen and thinking. At last, she picked up the telephone and dialed Renie's number.

"No," Renie said emphatically. "I do not want to traipse around with a real estate person pretending to buy a condo I don't want or need. I want to spend at least one day working at my desk and leading a life of truth and integrity. No pretense, no sham. Go away."

"Coz . . ."

"Stop it."

"It's almost lunchtime."

"I ate breakfast at ten-thirty. Please hang up."

"Okay."

Judith hung up. The phone rang almost immediately.

"Ha!" Judith exclaimed. "You are a sucker."

"No, I'm not," Renie asserted. "I just thought of something. Take Arlene with you. Her daughter's in real estate. You know how Arlene loves to find out who's asking what prices for which property."

It wasn't a bad idea. Judith rang off and called Arlene.

"I can't go," she told Judith on a note of regret. "We're painting the guest room in the basement. What time shall we leave?"

"Uh . . ." It took Judith only a moment to readjust her thinking to her neighbor's whimsies. "Now?"

"Give me fifteen minutes. The Alhambra, you say? I've been dying to get in there, but I understand they're only showing mock-ups."

"That's right," Judith agreed. "They're a long way off from completion."

"All those bodies," Arlene murmured. "Carl and I were out of town over the weekend. Did I tell you that? Of course I did. We went to visit my cousins down south. They raise chickens, you know. All the chickens died last month. Nobody knows why. I'll meet you in the driveway in half an hour."

Though Judith's head was swimming, she smiled. Conversations with Arlene could be disconcerting, even confusing, but the Rankerses were wonderful neighbors. Judith sought out Phyliss to give her last-minute instructions, then searched through the recycling bin to find the previous Sunday's real estate listings. Sure enough, there was an ad for the Alhambra. One of Heraldsgate Hill's crackerjack agents, Geoff Blitz, was handling the property.

Luckily, Geoff was in, apparently on his lunch break. He would be delighted to show Mrs. Flynn and Mrs. Rankers through the Alhambra. Was Mrs. Rankers, by any chance, related to Cathy Rankers of Rankers & Rankers?

Judith explained that she was, but was only coming along for moral support. The hint of suspicion in Geoff's voice didn't quite disappear.

Arlene was ready in twenty minutes, not fifteen or thirty, as she had indicated. Though she had changed her clothes, there were a few patches of periwinkle-blue paint on her arms and hands.

"How do you like it?" Arlene asked as they headed for the bottom of the hill.

"It's nice," Judith said. "Soothing."

"Really?" Arlene frowned. "I was hoping for something more disturbing. You know, so the guests want to leave sooner."

"That isn't exactly what I'd have in mind," Judith remarked.

Arlene laughed. "No, of course not. But you know what Carl's relatives are like. I love them to pieces, but I don't much like being around them. Maybe we could add some red dots."

Judith decided to get off the subject before they arrived at the Alhambra. "Tell me," she said, respectful of Arlene's vast network of neighborhood knowledge, "what do you know about the building and its tenants?"

Arlene's pretty face looked downcast. "Not much, really. I've never been very interested in the bottom of the hill. I mean, you get down that far, and you're not even exactly *on* the hill, are you? It's kind of a no-man's-land. Some of the people around there go to Our Lady, Star of the Sea, some of the others go to the parish by the center. Then there are all those other people who aren't Catholics. They can't help it, of course, but it's hard to keep track of them. It's all very vague."

Oddly enough, that made sense to Judith. Perhaps it was why she, too, tended to ignore happenings on the lower side of the hill. It was borderline commercial, and thus not a close-knit neighborhood.

"You have to remember," Arlene was saying, "that Carl and I just got back yesterday. We didn't plan to stay that long, but my cousin insisted we go to all the outlet malls around their place. He and his wife wanted to buy some more chickens."

"At an outlet mall?" Judith asked in surprise.

Again, Arlene laughed. "No, no, Judith, of course not! At the poultry place. In fact, my cousin had ordered three dozen chickens. The only problem was, he didn't specify that they should be alive. I guess he should have contacted the hatchery instead. Anyway, we stayed on to help them straighten out the mess. It's a good thing they have a big freezer."

The Guthrie construction crew was back on the job, and there was no sign of the police. Maybe Woody had finished with the Alhambra as a crime scene. It had been a week since the murder. He probably felt that the search had been as thorough as possible, given the building's state of disarray.

Geoff Blitz, standing by a sleek Range Rover, was waiting for Judith and Arlene. He looked surprisingly young, though Judith knew he had to be in his thirties at least. No doubt the boyish quality in his handsome face helped sell real estate.

"I can only give you an overview of the property," Geoff said after the introductions were concluded. "Most of the potential buyers just drive by to get a sense of the location and the structure itself. Here," he said, reaching into the passenger seat of his Range Rover, "you'd better wear these hard hats."

All three of them put on the hats. Judith thought hers was uncomfortable and heavy, maybe like wearing a football helmet. Still, if Alfred Ashe had worn one, perhaps he wouldn't be lying in Norway General with a very sore head.

"So what we usually do," Geoff said, leading the way into the noisy courtyard, "is look at the mock-ups at the office. We'll stop there after we get through here." He paused to shout a greeting at someone named Glenn, who may have been the foreman. "I'll take you up to the second floor, where most of the initial renovations have already been made."

"How are your sales running?" Arlene asked as they exited the elevator. Her curly red-gold head was turning in every direction but backward.

"Quite well," Geoff answered. "Of course, it's early days. So many people have no imagination when it comes to visualizing what the units will actually look like. Even the mock-ups don't grab some of them." The realtor winked at Judith. "I'm sure you're not like that. I'll bet you have plenty of imagination."

"Ah . . . I guess I do," Judith said, trying to avoid looking Geoff in the eye. "Could we view a unit with an eastern exposure?"

"Of course," Geoff replied. "We'll check out 205."

"I wouldn't think," Arlene said as they headed along the open-sided corridor, "it'd be so easy to sell these places after those bodies were found."

Judith winced. She hadn't expected a frontal assault from Arlene. She should have known better.

Geoff chuckled in a careless manner. "People don't read the newspapers these days, and they watch TV with half an eye. Everybody's caught in their own little world, concentrating on keeping everybody else out. That's why condos are so popular, I think. You may live cheek-by-jowl to your next-door neighbor, but if you're lucky, you'll never meet him—or her—in the elevator."

Judith stared at Geoff. "Isn't that kind of cynical for a salesman?"

Geoff shrugged. "It's realistic. It's the way things are. We can't be dreamers when we're selling properties. We have to appeal to what the potential buyer wants, deep down. How do you feel about privacy, Mrs. Flynn?"

"It's very personal with me," Judith said frankly. "That is, my thoughts, my feelings are my own. But in terms of people—well, I like people."

"Yes," Geoff said slowly, his blue eyes very sharp. "I can see that. But you're kind of unusual these days. I salute you." He turned away to open the door to 205.

It was the old Schnell unit, and it didn't look much different from when Judith had seen it last. She didn't know what she expected to find. Maybe nothing. Perhaps she had come only to soak up the atmosphere and to see if the Alhambra's walls could tell her any secrets.

Geoff went into his spiel, which Judith only half-heard. She was thinking about Mr. and Mrs. Schnell and

Helen, as a young girl. Had she known what her father was up to when he left in the middle of the night? Had Mrs. Schnell known?

Yes, Judith thought, Helen's mother had not only known but abetted her husband. Mrs. Hasegawa had talked about how snoopy Mrs. Schnell had been. Helen herself had said that her mother knew everything about the building's tenants. While calling on the neighbors, the old girl had cased the joint, as they say, and reported back to her husband about where he could find the loot.

". . . are up to you," Geoff was saying as they stood in the doorway to the kitchen where the floor had now been completely torn up.

"Up to me?" Judith said with a start. "Yes, that's fine."

"We're going to leave as much interior work as we can up to the buyer," Geoff added with a smile.

"Yes, that's fine, too," Judith agreed. "How many units have been sold?"

"Four," Geoff replied.

"Which leaves how many?" Arlene queried, her expression pugnacious.

"Fourteen," Geoff said. "The fifth floor is being divided into two penthouses." He smiled at Judith. "They're both available. The views will be breathtaking."

So, Judith figured, would be the prices. "How much is this one?"

"Four fifty," Geoff replied blithely. "The view here is actually very good. It would be even better if Mr. Guthrie had been allowed to reconfigure the windows, but the historical society and some of the other busybodies won't budge on changing the exterior. So far, that is. Can't you just envision floor-to-ceiling windows?"

"Yes, I suppose," Judith said somewhat vaguely. All she could really envision was Charlie Schnell climbing up the vine-covered side of the building and entering the units via those very convenient balconies.

"Four," Arlene said in a tone of disgust. "That's not

very many to presell at this point. It's Labor Day. Everybody knows that the market goes flat for at least a month or more after that. Then, just as it's picking up, the holiday season starts. Mid-November to early January are absolutely dead in the real estate business. Just ask Cathy. You and Mr. Guthrie don't have a lot of time to unload this place, especially at the prices you're asking."

If Geoff took umbrage, he didn't show it. Instead, he chuckled. "Now, Mrs. Rankers, we've got a good seven months. The people who buy into the Alhambra aren't just buying four walls and a roof, they're getting a piece of Heraldsgate Hill history."

"They're getting robbed," Arlene huffed. "I wouldn't buy into this place for a million dollars."

"That," Geoff said with a trace of asperity, "is what the penthouse would cost you, Mrs. Rankers. I hope you're not trying to influence Mrs. Flynn here."

Arlene turned wide, innocent eyes on Geoff. "Of course not! Why would I do such a thing? Judith would just love living here. There's even room for her mother. They could let her out of the toolshed."

"Arlene . . ." Judith said through clenched teeth. "Remember, my husband has to see everything before we even start to make a decision."

"Men!" Arlene waved a dismissive hand. "What do they know? Turn on the TV, put the remote in one hand and a beer in the other, and they could live on the moon." She grabbed Judith by the arm and spoke into her ear. "Take it. It's a steal."

"But Arlene . . ."

"Maybe," Geoff said, "we should go to the office so I can show you the mock-ups."

Judith glanced at her watch. It was going on one o'clock. Gertrude would be having a fit because her lunch hadn't been served. "Can I do that later this afternoon? Say around three?"

Geoff Blitz had probably heard such kiss-off lines a

thousand times. If he was annoyed or disappointed, it didn't show. "I'll be there," he said.

"So will Judith," Arlene declared. "I'll be with her. I wouldn't want her weaseling out at this stage of the game."

The walls hadn't talked to Judith, but Arlene certainly had talked—too much.

"Damn," Judith said when they got back into the car, "I thought you were going along with me. You know perfectly well I have no intention of buying a condo in the Alhambra."

"But Judith," Arlene protested, "it's a real bargain. They're asking four-fifty, but they'll come down, especially if you make them sweat it out for a couple of weeks. I'd say you could get it for four and a quarter. And think about what you could do with the kitchen! Weren't you impressed?"

"I hardly heard a word Geoff said," Judith retorted. "Come on, Arlene, you know Joe and I aren't going anywhere."

Arlene was looking mulish. "You're making a big mistake."

Judith sighed. It was useless to argue with Arlene. In any event, she was off on another tangent, finally quizzing Judith about the murders.

"I had no idea you were involved!" Arlene shrieked. "Why didn't you tell me? How could I not have known?"

"Because you were out of town, that's why," Judith said, "and we haven't talked since you got back."

"Still . . ." Arlene murmured, looking stricken. "Oh, Judith, now I understand!"

"Good," Judith said as she pulled into the cul-de-sac in front of the Rankerses' house.

Arlene was laughing. "You were sleuthing. How clever of you. I should have guessed." She got out of the car, then leaned down to poke her head back inside. "Don't forget, three o'clock. I'll be ready. You're going to love living in the Alhambra." Arlene closed the door and marched off toward her front porch.

After Judith had fed her irate mother, she made another attempt to call Mrs. Hasegawa. This time the old lady answered on the first ring.

"We went to the grocery store," she said. "We walk. Traffic is so terrible here. My husband and I almost never drive. Isn't that good news about Alfred?"

"You heard?" Judith said.

"Yes, Hiroko called from the courthouse. She's so upset, so worried. But she doesn't dare leave. This case is huge. It should go to the Supreme Court."

"It should," Judith agreed. "In fact, it should have happened years ago."

"Yes," Mrs. Hasegawa said. "Not that much can be done. So sad for so many people. Oh—by the way, I remembered that Beth's name. It was Ritter."

"Ritter?" Judith echoed.

"Yes," Mrs. Hasegawa said, and spelled it out.

Judith was momentarily speechless.

Ritter had been Aimee Carrabas's maiden name.

SIXTEEN

JUDITH DIDN'T CARE how immersed Renie was in her work. At last there was a glimmer of light shining in the Carrabas case. "You have to come over," Judith asserted. "Now, before I end up buying a condo at the Alhambra."

"No."

"Okay, I'll come over to your house."

"No."

"You can't stop me."

"Yes."

"You won't."

This time, there was a long pause and a heavy sigh. "No."

"I'll be there in five minutes."

Judith was as good as her word. Renie, looking beleaguered and holding what appeared to be a thirty-foot printout, met her at the door.

"This better be good," Renie warned, rattling the paper. "Real good."

"It is," Judith promised, "and I won't take long. I can't, my guests will start coming pretty soon. They always seem to arrive early on a holiday weekend."

Renie ushered Judith into the living room. Bill

was at the dining room table, finishing his leisurely
lunch.

"Hi, Judith," he said, not glancing up from his book.

"Hi, Bill," Judith said brightly. "I hope I'm not interrupting."

"You're not." Bill's gaze remained riveted on the
book. If Joe veered between patronization and annoy-
ance with Judith's amateur sleuthing, Bill simply
ignored his wife's involvement. Unlike Joe, Bill was a
master of detachment.

Judith sat down in Bill's chair in the living room. The
Jones sofa and easy chair were too low; they made her
hips ache when she tried to get up.

"Let's hear it," Renie ordered from the sofa, her feet
propped up on a big green leather ottoman.

Judith breezed through the part about going to the
Alhambra with Arlene and Geoff Blitz. She concentrated
instead on her conversations with Mrs. Hasegawa.
Renie's expression showed a flicker of interest.

"She sounds like a hoot," Renie remarked.

"She is, in her way," Judith said. "But here's the
kicker. Beth's last name was Ritter."

Renie looked blank. "So?"

"That was Mrs. Carrabas's maiden name," Judith
explained. "The old lady who died in the nursing home
in California was Elizabeth Ritter. Elizabeth? Beth?
What do you think of that?"

"Hunh." Renie gave a little shake of her head. "So it
would appear that there is a connection between Mrs.
Carrabas and the Alhambra after all. I'll be darned."

"It can't be a coincidence," Judith declared.

"Well," Renie pointed out, "it can. But it's a lead, I
guess. Have you told Joe?"

"He's not home," Judith said, the excitement still ris-
ing in her voice. "I wish he'd get a cell phone. You'd
think he'd need it in his business."

"Hunh," Renie repeated. "So what are you thinking?"

Judith grew thoughtful. "I'm not sure. Harry must

have had a child by both Beth and Dorothy. Both girls. Unless Mrs. Carrabas was Anne-Marie. But why would she take the last name of Ritter unless Beth was her mother?"

"Why would she take the name of Ritter at all?" Renie asked. "It was her mother's name, not Harry's."

"Maybe she was illegitimate," Judith suggested. "Maybe Harry never married Beth."

"Why not, if Dorothy was dead?" Renie said. "Wouldn't Aimee be younger than Anne-Marie?"

"That's right," Judith murmured. "The police gave her age as fifty-two. I assume they took it from official records. Anne-Marie would be older, fifty-seven or fifty-eight. Aimee would have been born a few years after the war."

"So you think Aimee Carrabas is Harry Meacham's daughter by Elizabeth Ritter," Renie said in a thoughtful tone.

"What do you think?" Judith asked.

"Gosh—I don't know," Renie replied. "Why would she want to come up here to the Alhambra? Aimee wasn't Dorothy's daughter, so I have to assume she wouldn't be particularly interested in the discovery of the body in the wall."

Judith tipped her head to one side. "Wouldn't she want to know if her father was a murderer?"

Renie didn't answer right away. The house was silent, except for Bill, turning the pages of his book and munching on chocolate chip cookies.

"You mean that when George Guthrie called her about the exorcism," Renie said slowly, "he told her that the dead body had been identified as Dorothy Meacham. Aimee probably knew that her father's first wife—or second wife, depending on when and if he married Elizabeth—was named Dorothy. So Aimee jumped at the chance to come to the Alhambra and learn more."

Judith nodded, also in slow motion. "Harry must be dead. Maybe Elizabeth kept her maiden name. For some

reason, she wanted her daughter to have it." Judith
stopped, snapping her fingers. "What if Harry took
Elizabeth's name when he married her? Maybe he did it
because he thought that Dorothy's body had already
been found. Does that make sense?"

Renie gave herself a good shake. "Sense? Where's the
sense? Who's got the sense? I'm getting confused.
You've included everybody but Ish K. Bibble."

Judith tried to be patient, even offering Renie a sympathetic glance. "It's like this. Harry was dating or perhaps married to Elizabeth—or Beth, as she was
familiarly known—before the war. Somehow he met
Dorothy and got her pregnant. They got married and
moved into the Alhambra. Beth nobly and discreetly
steps aside. Or Beth and Harry have a huge fight and
break up. Along comes Pearl Harbor a short time later,
and Harry immediately joins the army. Now I know a
lot of men did that, but in Harry's case, maybe things
had gotten a bit hot for him on the home front. He was
caught between Beth and Dorothy, and may have committed bigamy. So off he goes, and Dorothy has the
baby, Anne-Marie. When he gets out of the service, he
feels an obligation to move back in with Dorothy and
their child. But he's still in love with Beth and she wants
him back. Thus, Dorothy must go. So she ends up inside
the wall, and Harry and Beth leave town. Maybe Anne-
Marie joins them or goes to live with those relatives
nobody can identify. Do you get it now?"

Renie's shoulders had slumped, but she nodded.
"Yes. Harry wanted to disappear. What better way than
to give himself a new name by taking Beth's?"

"Anne-Marie would have taken the name of Ritter,
too," Judith said, suddenly thoughtful. "Why haven't
the police turned her up somewhere?"

Renie shrugged. "Maybe she's dead."

"There should still be records," Judith mused. "Could
I be wrong about all this?"

"I don't think so," Renie replied. "It may be an oversight. Maybe, when the California authorities were digging into Aimee Ritter Carrabas's background, they missed something."

"Y-e-s." Judith said slowly. "That's probably the case. And records do get lost or misplaced." She was silent for a moment, and then, with an eye on Bill, she quietly clapped her hands. "I think we've come pretty close to the truth. Look at it this way—Aimee came here to find out more about her father and his first wife. The timing, the opportunity were too good to miss. Now we'll get Woody to see if there's any record of a Harry Ritter."

"He must be dead," Renie noted. "California's a community property state, like we are. If Aimee Carrabas had to wait for her mother's will to go through probate, it probably meant that her father was already dead. His estate would have gone to his wife. So what's the point of checking him out now?"

"Ah . . ." Judith looked up at the ceiling. "Well . . . we could find out what happened to him after he left here."

"He married Elizabeth Ritter," Renie said. "They had a child, Aimee. What else do you need to know? He didn't kill Beth, so he's no Bluebeard."

Judith lowered her gaze and her eyes grew large. "Maybe he didn't kill Dorothy, either." She leaned forward on the sofa. "Maybe Beth killed her. Why do we assume that Harry was the villain of this piece? Beth had him first, before Dorothy. Maybe she got tired of waiting to get him back."

"She waited a long time," Renie said. "Almost five years. How many women would be that patient?"

Judith gave her cousin a reproachful smile. "I waited more than four times that long. Some men are worth it."

Renie laughed and shook her head. "Sorry. I wasn't thinking." She raised her voice and spoke in Bill's direction. "You're worth it, too."

Bill didn't look up from his book. "Worth what?"

"Never mind."

Bill kept reading.

"Another thing about Bill," Renie said. "He doesn't eavesdrop."

Judith's cell phone went off. She jumped and stared at Renie. "Is that mine? I never get used to it."

"That's because you never turn it on," Renie said. "What's the occasion?"

The phone kept ringing as Judith dug into her handbag. "I must have hit the power button by mistake. Ah—there it is. Goodness, I hope it's not Mother."

The voice at the other end belonged to Jeremy Lamar. "Mrs. Flynn? I hate to bother you, but your cleaning woman gave me this number. I was actually trying to get hold of your husband."

"He doesn't have a cell phone," Judith said. "I'm getting him one for Christmas."

"Oh. That's nice," Jeremy said. "Maybe I should have called Detective Price, but Mr. Flynn is working for George and me, so I . . . Are you sure you'll give him this message right away?"

"Of course," Judith responded. "What's the message?"

"Well . . ." Jeremy sounded disconcerted. "It's about Rufus Holmes. I was over at the Alhambra a little while ago, talking to the construction foreman about whether or not we should keep the site on our mystery tour list, and Mr. Holmes showed up. I guess he wanted to check on the progress of his condo. The foreman said Rufus comes around every so often, usually in the early afternoon. Anyway, George and I were just finishing up, so we asked him to wait a couple of minutes. We were deciding that since the Carrabas murder was so recent, it might be in bad taste to include the Alhambra. Anyway, George said something about 'poor Aimee' and with that, Mr. Holmes keeled over with a heart attack. At least that's what the medics called it. The ambulance took him to Bayview Hospital. I thought Mr. Flynn would want to know."

Judith's jaw dropped. "Will he be okay?"

"I don't know," Jeremy replied. "It happened less than thirty minutes ago. I just got back to the office. Excuse me, I really must run."

Judith fumbled with the small buttons and finally managed to turn the phone off. Renie's frown grew deeper as she listened to her cousin's explanation.

"Rufus passed out when he saw you weren't his ex-wife," Renie said when Judith had finished. "Then he hears about Aimee and has a heart attack. What do you deduce, my kinswoman sleuth?"

"That he thought I was his ex and was shaken to see that I wasn't," Judith said slowly. "That he didn't know anything had happened to said ex. He may have been at the Alhambra at the time of the murder—perhaps he was the person I saw at the window. But Liz Ogilvy said the man she glimpsed was leaving when the TV crews arrived. Rufus, as you may recall, doesn't watch TV or read newspapers. He probably never knew about the murder at the Alhambra, let alone who was killed. But maybe he knew Aimee Carrabas was coming to town. Maybe . . ." Her voice trailed off.

"Maybe Rufus killed Aimee?" Renie offered.

Judith hesitated, then shook her head. "No. If he had, he'd know she was dead."

"True," Renie remarked dryly.

"He must not have found her," Judith mused. "If he had, she might not have gotten killed. Oh, dear—this is all very confusing. I may be off on a tangent. But why else would Rufus keel over with a heart attack if he hadn't been shocked by Aimee's death?"

"That makes sense," Renie agreed. She sat up straighter on the sofa and tucked her feet underneath her bottom. "Oh, no—you're not thinking about another hospital visit, are you? Count me out."

"No, no," Judith assured her cousin. "There's no point. Goodness, Rufus may be in a bad way."

"At least you can eliminate him as a suspect," Renie pointed out.

Judith gazed at her cousin. "In the matter of Mrs. Carrabas, yes. But," she added, standing up, "not necessarily in the attack on Alfred Ashe. Hasn't it occurred to you that Rufus also may have been looking for something in the Alhambra?"

"Like what?" Renie asked.

Judith stood up and shrugged. "Beats me. If we didn't know that Charlie Schnell was the burglar, I'd finger Rufus's dad. That book he was reading, *The Guilty Rich*, indicates that despite his bravado over inheriting his money, it may have been acquired by some illegal means."

"Hmm." Renie had also gotten to her feet and was looking thoughtful. "Maybe crooked investments or fleecing other people?"

"Maybe."

"Like the Whiffels?"

Judith frowned at Renie. "I thought they were wise investors."

"They were, maybe still are," Renie replied, "but they might know about a scam. If they remember."

"I'm probably on the wrong track this time," Judith said, starting for the door. "Really, Mrs. Hasegawa was right—the Alhambra was full of crooks and killers and adulterers and God only knows what else." She paused at the edge of the entrance hall. "Bye, Bill."

Bill didn't look up. "Bye, Judith."

At the door, Judith gave Renie a quirky little smile. "He really doesn't eavesdrop, does he?"

Renie grinned. "With three noisy kids and a rather loud wife, Bill's trained himself to tune us out. It's self-preservation. Do you blame him?"

"Well . . ." Judith made a face. "I might, but Joe wouldn't."

"It's a guy thing," Renie said. "Like the CIA, except in reverse. They only want to know what they need to know."

"They're missing out on a lot of things, though," Judith remarked.

Renie blinked at Judith. "Are they?"

Judith thought about it for a moment. "No," she finally said. "I guess not. Maybe they're the lucky ones."

For once, Judith dreaded the long weekend. Usually, she enjoyed the extended stays of her guests, unless, of course, they turned out to be obnoxious. But this particular Labor Day weekend loomed like a large detour sign. It wasn't going to be easy to pay the proper attention to her visitors and try to solve two murder cases at the same time.

Of course she couldn't admit as much to Joe. When he returned home that Friday evening just before five-thirty, Judith was in the midst of preparing the appetizers. She told him at once about Rufus Holmes and why she thought he'd had a heart attack.

Joe looked askance. "Isn't that a bit of a stretch, Jude-girl?" he asked, easing himself into his captain's chair at the kitchen table.

"No," Judith said defensively. "It makes perfect sense to me."

Joe shrugged, then popped the top on a can of beer. The day had grown warm, even sultry. He had no hankering for his usual Scotch. "Your logic usually works, I have to admit, but this time . . ." He shook his head and took a swig of beer. "What else have you been up to?" he asked with a touch of suspicion.

"Nothing," Judith answered too swiftly. She certainly wasn't going to tell him about the bogus inquiry into the Alhambra condos. There had been three calls from Geoff Blitz and two from Arlene that afternoon. Judith had strained herself to think up excuses for Geoff, and had tried to make Arlene see reason. The former had worked; the latter had failed. It usually did.

Along with the heat, Joe seemed to be suffering from frustration. The investigation was stalled. Woody and Sancha felt as if they were up against one of the Alhambra's reinforced concrete walls. Judith took pity on her husband.

"I'll level with you," she said. The guests had been served and she'd spent a few minutes chatting, even though this particular group didn't seem very friendly. Indeed, a woman from Wyoming had asked that Sweetums be forcibly removed. She was allergic to cats. Sweetums promptly threw up on her shoes.

"Aimee Carrabas is Harry Meacham's daughter," Judith announced, and felt rather pleased with herself.

Joe glanced up from the front section of the evening newspaper. "Who?"

Judith scowled. "Harry Meacham, the man who was believed to have killed his wife, Dorothy, at the Alhambra after the war. Except maybe he didn't. I mean, I have another suspect."

Joe put the paper down. "This is the old case that's been keeping you amused?"

And out of my hair, Judith could hear her husband saying to himself. "Yes. The body in the wall. Dorothy Meacham."

Joe looked skeptical. "Are you sure?"

"Fairly sure," Judith said, and explained what she had figured out from the information Mrs. Hasegawa had given her.

Joe sipped at his second beer while Judith tossed the chicken salad she'd made for dinner. "Woody can run Harry Ritter through the California computer," Joe said, more to himself than to his wife. "Of course, he might have changed the 'Harry,' too. Harry can stand alone or be a nickname for Henry or Harold or even some more exotic names."

"Is that information helpful?" Judith asked innocently.

Joe let out an exasperated sigh. "Sure. Were you really going to keep it a secret?"

"No," Judith said, dishing up a plate for her mother and adding a slice of warm French bread. "I hesitated because you thought I was silly for digging into the old Meacham murder."

As Judith headed for the toolshed, Joe still wasn't looking very happy. Neither was Gertrude.

"What's that? Rabbit food? We don't have a rabbit. If we did, I'd eat him."

"Renie and Bill have a rabbit," Judith pointed out, placing a glass of lemonade next to Gertrude's salad. "They wouldn't dream of eating Clarence. They treat him as if he were another child. Clarence has a satin leash. Or did, until he ate it."

"Stupid," Gertrude grumbled. "Those Joneses are stupid. When was the last time any of their kids came to visit their poor old auntie?"

"They're probably worn out from visiting their poor old granny," Judith said. "You know that Aunt Deb can be sort of . . . demanding."

"Spoiled," Gertrude huffed. "Deb's spoiled rotten."

Judith had heard Aunt Deb say the same thing about Gertrude. Often. "Yes, Mother," Judith said dutifully. "Look, there's plenty of lovely chicken breast in the salad."

"There is?" Gertrude peered among the lettuce and celery and crisp chow mein noodles. "This must have been one flat-chested chicken. I don't see much meat in my portion."

"It's there," Judith insisted. "You just have to find it with your fork."

"What is this?" Gertrude demanded, her small eyes fixed on Judith. "Hunt and peck? Why're you hiding the chicken? Why can't it be right on top? Why can't I find it?"

Judith let out a big sigh. "Because you haven't

looked." *Because if I didn't mix it all up, you wouldn't eat the greens.*

Gertrude began picking through the lettuce. "You're late again."

"I know, Mother," Judith said, edging for the door. "This is the Labor Day weekend. We're full up, and I've been really busy."

"When am I going to be on TV again?" Gertrude asked.

"TV? Oh." So much had happened in the past week, that Judith had almost forgotten about the sorry episode on the news. She hoped everybody else had, too. "Not right away."

"I've been reading about that murder you got mixed up in at the Alhambra," Gertrude said, finally finding a piece of chicken large enough for her liking. "The woman who got killed was no better than she should be."

Judith frowned at her mother. "What do you mean? How do you know about Mrs. Carrabas?"

Gertrude was chomping on her chicken. "I don't know about any Mrs. Casabas. Now you take a good melon, a real juicy, tasty one, and I don't mind that. When was the last time we had cantaloupe?"

"At lunch," Judith retorted. "What are you talking about?"

"Cantaloupe. Did you know Uncle Cliff put salt on his?"

"Renie still does," Judith said impatiently. "We were talking about Mrs. Carrabas. The woman who was killed at the Alhambra."

Gertrude had found more chicken. "Not her," she said crossly. "The other one. Dorothy Blair."

Judith moved back toward the card table. "Dorothy Blair? Or Dorothy Meacham?"

"Blair was her maiden name," Gertrude said. "She married somebody named Meacham because she had to. No wonder she got herself done in. She was probably running around with sailors during the war."

Judith sank down on the arm of her mother's chair. "You knew Dorothy Meacham?" she asked incredulously.

"Yep." Gertrude paused to take a bit of bread. "She worked as a checker at the grocery store at the bottom of the hill. Your father liked their meat, so we used to shop there sometimes. Dorothy was always flirting with the fellows who came in. Oh, she had an eye for the men. And vice versa. No wonder she got in trouble. She was lucky that Harry or whatever-his-name-was married her."

Because Gertrude could forget she'd had cantaloupe for lunch, or that she'd had lunch at all, Judith sometimes forgot that her mother remembered a great many other things, usually from the distant past. There were occasions when Judith realized her mother still was the sharpest tool in the toolshed.

Gertrude had spent most of her life on Heraldsgate Hill, except for the early years of her marriage when Donald Grover had accepted his first teaching assignment out of town. Gertrude's family, the Hoffmans, had lived in one of the older homes at the bottom of the hill that had been torn down to make way for more commercial enterprises.

"Is that the only way you knew Dorothy?" Judith asked eagerly. "Through the grocery store?"

Gertrude nodded and ate more bread. "She wasn't a local girl. Your father and I wondered if she hadn't followed some man out here, and he ran off. So Dorothy was stuck. But not for long. She didn't work at the store for more than a year before she got in the family way. The next thing we knew, she got married. He was a soldier. I remember seeing them once in the store, shopping together. Dorothy was as big as a house by then."

"You never saw her after that?" Judith inquired.

"No," Gertrude replied. "Your father and I weren't around here much during the war, remember? We were living up on the Peninsula until forty-six. It was hard to travel back and forth on the ferries because of all the gas rationing and such. We were lucky to get into town more than once every two or three months."

Judith had a vague memory of those trips. Her parents had owned a black Model A Ford, which they weren't able to replace until 1949. She did, however, vividly recall Donald Grover's pride when he finally bought a brand new Chevrolet sedan.

"Grandma Grover knew them," Gertrude remarked, breaking Judith out of her brief reverie.

"She did?" Judith stared at her mother.

Gertrude nodded matter-of-factly. "Grandma did a lot of sewing for folks around here during the war. She always sewed for the family, but clothes were rationed, too, and she and Grandpa could use the extra money. Besides, it helped take her mind off worrying about Uncle Al and Uncle Corky in the service. I'm pretty sure she mentioned making a couple of pinafores for the little Meacham girl. She made them for you and Serena and your cousin Sue, remember?"

Judith did. The cotton garments, with their cheerful patterns, were always sewn with enough seam allowance so that growing girls could wear them for at least a couple of years. Judith had especially loved the rickrack that decorated the shoulder ruffles.

"Is there anything else you remember?" Judith persisted.

Gertrude, who had eaten most of the chicken but virtually none of the greens, was now munching on an oatmeal cookie. "Isn't that enough?" she snapped. "What're you doing, writing their life story for *The Woman's Home Companion*?"

Judith didn't bother to tell her mother that *The Woman's Home Companion* had ceased publication almost a half-century earlier. Instead, she reflected on everything that Gertrude had told her. Everything fit. Except Beth, who was part of the equation. "Did you ever see her husband with another woman? A tall blond?"

"That would be Beth," Gertrude said blithely. "She worked at the stationery store. Foreign woman, nice-looking. But I heard she could be difficult, like most foreigners."

"You knew Beth Ritter?" Judith was dumbfounded.

"Was that her last name?" The lines in Gertrude's face grew even more wrinkled in concentration. "Hunh. Maybe it was. I don't know if I ever knew it. And I can't say I knew her. She waited on me a few times. I knew Mr. Oakley, who owned the store. Nice man, but a strange color, sort of orange. Liver, I suppose."

"But you knew that Beth and Harry were . . . a couple?" Judith prodded.

"Yep, your dad and I would see them on the avenue. He must have broken up with Beth to marry Dorothy." Gertrude paused, rubbing at her forehead. "That's funny, I thought Harry and Beth were married. Maybe they were. Maybe they got a divorce. No, that doesn't sound right. I saw them once, after the war, on the bus. Beth was still wearing her wedding ring. It was just a plain gold band, and I thought that was kind of funny. Couldn't Harry afford a better one? But she'd had it before the war, so I figured he'd bought it for her during the Depression. Maybe he couldn't afford anything better, like a set, with a diamond."

"Are you sure about all this?" Judith asked.

Gertrude turned and glowered at her daughter. "Am I sure? Of course I'm sure. Do you think I've lost my memory?"

"No," Judith said slowly, giving her mother a hug. "What I think is that Harry Meacham was a bigamist."

SEVENTEEN

THAT NIGHT, JUDITH lay awake long past midnight. Partly, it was because of the muggy weather. The main reason, however, was that she was cudgeling her brain to find the missing link in the Meacham and Carrabas murders. For Judith was convinced there was a connection, and that connection was a human being, possibly a killer.

Faces floated before her mind's eye: Rufus Holmes, Helen Schnell, George Guthrie, Midge and Billy O'Dowd, Nan Leech, Jeremy Lamar, Alfred Ashe.

But nothing inspired her. At last, around one o'clock, she drifted off to sleep. To her utter horror, she awoke at ten minutes to nine. Judith couldn't remember when she had overslept and neglected her guests' breakfasts.

Joe was nowhere in sight. Judith limped into the shower, hurried out, and hastily dressed. Between the third and second floors, she discovered she'd put her slacks on backwards. Making the change as quickly as possible, she finally reached the first floor and had to stop in the kitchen hallway because her hips were so painful. Seeing Joe at the sink, Judith heaved a sigh of relief.

"They liked the blueberry pancakes," he said. "I made the eggs my special way."

"Oh, Joe!" Judith hugged and kissed her husband.

"You were dead to the world," Joe said. "You're wearing yourself out on those bum hips. When's that appointment with Dr. Alfonso?"

Before Judith could answer, the phone rang. To her surprise, it was Liz Ogilvy.

"Listen up," Liz said in her aggressive manner, "what have you got for me on this Carrabas thing? I'm sick of Mavis getting all the gravy. Granted, it's pretty thin stuff, but she's the one with the police contacts. I'm frozen out, and you can help me."

Thinking it wise to continue the conversation out of Joe's hearing range, Judith wandered out into the dining room. Unfortunately, the couple from Wyoming was at the table, along with the husband and wife from Samoa. Flashing a smile, Judith kept going.

"I don't have much," she said to Liz when she'd reached the sanctuary of the front parlor. "But that may change in the next twenty-four hours."

"Really?" Some of the harshness went out of Liz's voice. "Or are you conning me?"

"Not at all," Judith said. "However, I would like to cut a deal with you."

Liz turned suspicious. "I thought so. What is it?"

"If I give you a scoop," Judith began as she sat down on the windowseat to rest her hips, "will you do a small feature on Hillside Manor showing it as a pleasant, hospitable inn instead of a den of iniquity?"

"It's the wrong time of year," Liz declared. "We do travel features in the spring and summer."

"Oh." Judith paused. "Then I guess I can't tell you anything."

"Hold it," Liz commanded. "We could do it for Thanksgiving. But you'd have to trust me on that. It wouldn't air until the third week of November. That's over two months away."

Judith considered the offer. She didn't trust Liz for a variety of reasons, some of which weren't necessarily personal. "No," she said in a firm voice. "That won't do. You don't produce the shows. You can't promise anything so far off in the future. Why can't you make it an end-of-tourist season thing, showing how local residents can get reduced rates for getaways?"

This time it was Liz who paused. "That sounds like an ad, not a feature."

"Think about it," Judith said. "Everybody in this town has visitors during the summer. We're a tourist mecca, we get taken advantage of. By the middle of September, we're all worn out from hosting friends and relatives. Now it's our turn to take a break. I think it'd be kind of cute."

Liz emitted a short, sharp laugh. "Maybe you ought to be a TV producer. That's not the nuttiest idea I ever heard."

"Good," Judith said, pleased with herself. "I've got a houseful of guests and my husband's home today. Why don't I meet you someplace this afternoon?"

"How about at Toujours La Tour?" Liz suggested. "They're open, of course, for the holiday weekend. I have to talk to Jeremy Lamar about doing a Halloween feature. You're not the only one who's been upset about the mystery bus's maiden voyage."

"Yes, I know," Judith agreed. "Okay, I'll see you around two."

Liz was amenable. Judith returned to the kitchen and volunteered to help Joe. He insisted that she go about her other business, since Phyliss had the weekend off.

Judith didn't argue. But she worried. All she could really offer Liz was the possible connection between the Meacham and the Carrabas homicides. It wouldn't be breaking trust with Joe, since it was she who had discovered the link. Still, she didn't feel quite right.

Around ten-thirty, she decided to call Mrs. Hasegawa in San Francisco. The older woman seemed pleased to hear from Judith.

"We're told Alfred is doing much better," she said. "Hiroko flew up there last night, but even she isn't allowed to speak to him until tomorrow."

Judith had no idea that Mrs. Ashe—or Ms. Hasegawa, as she preferred professionally—had arrived in town. "Do they have children?" Judith inquired.

"Twin boys, not identical in any way," Mrs. Hasegawa answered with pride in her voice. "They're college freshman this year, one at Cal, the other at Stanford."

"They must be very bright," Judith said, then moved directly to the reason for her call. "You mentioned that there were crooks in the Alhambra. Were you referring to anyone in particular?"

"Indeed I was," Mrs. Hasegawa responded, sounding indignant. No doubt the memories were as fresh in her mind as the morning's headlines. "Con artists, too. But you have to remember when we first moved in, the Depression was still going on. People had to survive. We owned a small grocery store at the bottom of the hill. So many customers bought on credit, which made it very hard for us. But my husband and I couldn't say no, especially if there were children."

"I can imagine your generosity," Judith remarked. And how the government repaid it, she thought. "I gather some of your neighbors weren't so kindly disposed. You mentioned scams in the building?"

"More than scams," Mrs. Hasegawa declared. "That Charlie Schnell was a thief, I'm sure of it. And Orrin Holmes—well, he was the con artist. He sold phony stocks. My husband and I were never gullible enough to buy any, but I figure plenty of the others were. Stupid, too. Several people actually believed him when he said the stocks had collapsed and the money was gone. Orrin Holmes ran off with it."

"He didn't run very far," Judith pointed out. "Didn't he always live in the Alhambra?"

"That was a manner of speaking," Mrs. Hasegawa said. "Yes, I believe he died in the Alhambra not too many years after the war. His heart. Not that he had one. Why, I know for a fact that he swindled at least ten thousand dollars from the Whiffels. And the son was a lawyer, too! Wouldn't you think he'd have sued Orrin Holmes?"

"Why didn't he?" Judith asked.

"Because," Mrs. Hasegawa said and then stopped for a moment. "It was ridiculous. Mr. Whiffel—the father— was dead by then, and Ewart just out of law school. Mrs. Whiffel confronted Orrin, and guess what he did? He asked her how he could be saved. Mrs. Whiffel was so overcome that she forgave him and started giving him Bible lessons. I figure those were the most expensive Bible lessons since the Crucifixion. Mrs. Whiffel was a very silly woman, though I shouldn't say so, being a Congregationalist myself."

"So Mr. Holmes was never caught," Judith remarked.

"Not that I ever heard," Mrs. Hasegawa said. "Maybe it was small potatoes compared to some. You must remember, after the war there was so much else going on, including black market goods and labor unrest and housing shortages and . . . Well, I figure that even if they were on his trail, the grave robbed the authorities of justice. Consider, too, that so many people are proud. They won't admit they've been taken in."

"That's true," Judith agreed. "It's embarrassing to be shown up as a pigeon."

"Pigeon is the word," Mrs. Hasegawa declared. "We lost so much ourselves, but not through our own fault. We were robbed, even though we weren't stupid. We were just . . . Japanese."

Judith agreed that wasn't stupid—or a crime. "I hate to be so blunt," she said in a humble voice, "but did you lose some of your possessions when you were sent away?"

A painful sigh crept over the phone line. "We weren't able to take everything with us. There wouldn't be room, we were told, and there wasn't much time to make arrangements. I had bought a beautiful jewelry case, very cheap, at a pawnshop during the Depression. It was hand-carved, exquisite. I imagine it had originally cost hundreds of dollars, but the pawnshop owner sold it to me for fifty. That was a large sum even then, but the shopkeeper was a customer of ours and we'd been kind to him. The box had been sitting in the shop for five years. He let me pay for it in trade at our grocery store. In it, I kept the pearls my husband had given me on our wedding day and a few less expensive pieces. I asked Mrs. Whiffel to save the case and its contents for me until we returned. Only later did I learn she'd given it to Dorothy Meacham. Mrs. Whiffel, it seemed, thought that jewelry and jewelry cases were vain. That's really why we had it in for the Meachams, I suppose. When we got out of the camp, they were gone—and so was my jewelry box. It's never turned up and probably never will. Harry and that Beth must have taken it with them."

"I see," Judith said in a saddened voice. "I understand why you might consider them . . . untrustworthy."

"And not just them," Mrs. Hasegawa declared in a heated tone. "My other jewelry just plain disappeared, even before we moved. My husband and I had relatives in the Southwest. I bought some lovely pieces of silver— also quite cheap then—from the Navajos. There were some other gold items and two brooches set with stones and . . . oh, I forget. Just the kind of things a woman fancies. Remember, prices were very low in the thirties— but those same things today would be worth a great deal of money. Someone stole them from the apartment while we were still living there. We notified the police, but nothing came of it. There had been a number of burglaries in the neighborhood. But that was common, too, with so many people out of work. It was a time of desperation and despair. Still, I had my suspicions, and they weren't directed at anyone quite so pitiful."

"Charlie Schnell?" Judith said.

Mrs. Hasegawa sniffed with disdain. "You make a good detective, Mrs. Flynn."

After hanging up, Judith thought about money. It was always such a good motive. Sitting at the kitchen counter, she began to make a list.

"MONEY OR OTHER SOURCES OF WEALTH," Judith wrote in capital letters at the top of the legal-sized yellow tablet.

1. *Holmes swindle with bogus stocks—revenge? Who? The Whiffels? No. Too pious, too meek.*
2. *Gold and silver jewelry—retrieval, by Alfred Ashe, for the Hasegawas. Revenge? Retribution? No. Too . . .*

Judith paused. The disappearance of the jewelry case and the gold and silver items didn't seem like a motive for murder. Especially not after more than half a century. Judith thought that Mrs. Hasegawa was wrong about Harry Meacham reporting that they were Japanese spies. It seemed far more likely that their accuser had been Charlie Schnell. If he'd robbed them once while they were still at the Alhambra, he'd have a field day if they were gone and had left valuables behind.

3. *Burglaries by Schnell. Hasegawas victims. Who else?*

Just about anybody in the building and the surrounding neighborhood, Judith figured. But many of the tenants from sixty years ago were probably dead. Would their descendants seek revenge after all this time? It didn't seem likely, and why kill Mrs. Carrabas? For all that Judith wanted to see a connection between the two murders in the Alhambra, no real light had been shed by Mrs. Hasegawa's revelations.

Mrs. Manuaoloposo entered the kitchen with a shy smile on her round, pretty face. "We're about to leave for the football game," she said. "I hate to bother you, but . . ."

The Manuaoloposos had come from Samoa to watch their son play for the university in the team's season opener. Judith had offered to put a picnic lunch together for the couple.

"Oh, dear!" Judith exclaimed, jumping up from the chair. "Can you give me five minutes?"

Mrs. Manuaoloposos obliged. Hurriedly, Judith used the leftover chicken from the salad of the previous night to make sandwiches, included carrots and celery sticks, a bag of chips, a half-dozen oatmeal cookies, and a thermos of coffee. Feeling guilty for her oversight, she added a bottle of white zinfandel and two plastic glasses.

"Don't let the ushers catch you with this," she warned her guest as she handed over the wicker hamper. "They're cracking down on alcohol in the stadium."

Mrs. Manuaoloposos nodded. "I understand. Do they really check us old folks?"

Since Mrs. Manuaoloposos looked all of forty, Judith had to smile. "Well . . . you have player tickets, right? They're probably more lenient in that section."

"I hope so," Mrs. Manuaoloposos replied. "Most of us parents could use a sedative when our sons get hurt or make a mistake on the field. We Samoans set great store by honor. I don't suppose," she added, her dark eyes limpid, "that you have just a bit of gin?"

Judith filled a pint jelly jar and tucked it into the picnic hamper. A grateful Mrs. Manuaoloposos graciously thanked her hostess and departed.

Judith returned to her list. Money could be a factor with George Guthrie. He could have been set up. But who would do such a thing? A rival developer or real estate magnate? Judith had no idea, but surely Woody and Joe would know.

Money. Who had it, who didn't? Helen Schnell had enough money to buy a condo in the Alhambra. So did Rufus Holmes. Both had acquired their original nest eggs through ill-gotten gains. It was no wonder that Rufus was reading a book called *The Guilty Rich*. Would either of them attack Alfred Ashe to keep their fathers' secrets? Conversely, why would Helen or Rufus kill Aimee Carrabas?

Aimee was coming into money. Aimee was Beth and Harry's daughter. Elizabeth Ritter had died in a nursing home, which indicated that there must have been a great deal of money in the estate. Judith didn't know how long the old lady had been there, but if it was more than a few weeks, her bills would have milked the average family's savings.

Judith went outside where Joe was tinkering with his beloved MG in the garage. "Did Woody check with the California police about an Anne-Marie Ritter?" she asked of Joe's feet, which stuck out from under the car.

"What?" The response was muffled and irritable.

Judith started to drop down to her knees, felt her hips make odd noises, and stood up again. "What about Anne-Marie Ritter or Anne-Marie Meacham?" Judith persisted.

"Not now," Joe barked. "I'm busy."

Judith bit her lip, stomped back into the house, and dialed Renie's number. "My husband's an idiot," she announced.

"Right," Renie said calmly. "What did he do this time?"

"He won't come out from under that damned old car of his," Judith said, pouting a bit. "Do you know how old that thing is? He had it over thirty years ago, before we were engaged."

"It's a classic MG," Renie said, still calm. "Men love cars."

"Bill doesn't dote on yours," Judith said accusingly.

"Yes, he does," Renie replied. "Bill's not mechanical, but Cammy—and all the cars we've ever owned—must be spotless, inside and out. They get more checkups than I do. Come on, coz, it's another guy thing."

"I suppose," Judith muttered. "But Joe's taking the day off. Wouldn't you think he'd be committed to the murder investigation?"

"It's a holiday weekend," Renie said. "Isn't he semi-retired? Cut him some slack."

"All I could see were his feet," Judith said. "If he hadn't grumped at me, it could have been Cecil the mailman under there."

"So what?" Renie remained unmoved.

"So—" Judith stopped herself. "Hey—I just had a brainstorm. What if Aimee Carrabas isn't Aimee Carrabas?"

"What?" At last, Renie's calm cracked.

"How do we know that was Aimee who was shot at the Alhambra?" Judith demanded in an excited tone.

"Because . . ." Now Renie paused. "You mean, her personal effects were planted?"

"That's right," Judith replied. "What if she's really Anne-Marie? What if there is no other daughter of Harry's? What if Aimee is actually some sort of nickname for Anne-Marie? Think about it. It could be a combination of the two, a nickname."

"But the birth records show she was Aimee," Renie pointed out.

"They might have been legally changed. Does a name like Anne-Marie resonate with exorcism talent to you?"

"Not particularly," Renie admitted. "But I don't hang out with a lot of exorcists. For all I know, there's one

named Jane someplace. Besides, didn't the birth certificate state that Aimee was fifty-two years old?"

"It might be wrong," Judith said.

"Why don't you take the day off?" Renie said after a
brief pause. "Aren't you kind of busy with your
guests?"

"Not right now," Judith said, sounding defensive.
"They've all gone off to football games and shopping
expeditions and harbor tours and . . . Which reminds
me, want to go with me to meet Liz Ogilvy at Toujours
La Tour?"

"No. No. And no," Renie said. "Bill and I are going
door shopping. We want to replace this ugly sucker that
we've put up with for almost thirty years. It'd be nice if
the previous owner hadn't kicked in the original. I'll bet
it was quite handsome, if flimsy. Even when they redid
the kitchen, they used the cheapest stuff they could find
and we've had to put in all new appliances over the
years. By the way," Renie added, "what is Liz Ogilvy
doing at Toujours La Tour anyway? In fact, what are
you doing with Liz Ogilvy?"

"Never mind," Judith said in a huffy voice. "You
won't go, you don't care."

"I guess I don't," Renie said agreeably. "At least not
now. Bill and I are off to Hank's Lumber. See you in
church."

Still pouting a bit, Judith accomplished some light
housekeeping in the next hour, made lunch, took three
new reservations, and chased Sweetums around the
house in an attempt to rescue a rather vast pair of
underpants that the little wretch had stolen from the
Wyoming woman's room. Instinctively, cats knew who
hated them most, and always set out to even the score.

At a quarter of two, Judith was almost out the back
door when the phone rang.

"This is Nurse Royce," said the intimidating voice
from Norway General. "Dr. Bentley insisted I call to tell
you that Dr. Ashe's wife has had him removed from this

hospital strictly against orders. He felt you and your husband should know."

"Good grief!" Judith exclaimed. "Why did she do that?"

"I gather she wanted him flown back to San Francisco," Nurse Royce said in an indignant tone. "She's some kind of high-powered attorney, who was waving a bunch of legal papers around. I wasn't here at the time. If I had been . . . Well, what's done is done."

Judith envisioned Hiroko Hasegawa pinned against a wall and looking about as flat as a pizza. "Yes, well, I hope the move doesn't cause a setback for Dr. Ashe."

"That's their problem now," Nurse Royce declared. "They were warned."

Judith thanked Nurse Royce and hung up. At precisely two o'clock, she arrived at Toujours La Tour. Even there, election signs were stuck into the landscaping along the sidewalk on sturdy two-by-fours: "Rappaport for Port Commissioner," "Long Duc for City Council," "Save the Salmon," "Stop the Violence," and "Spare a Tree for You and Me." Judith wondered if she could keep all the candidates and issues straight by the time she went to the polls.

There was no KINE-TV vehicle parked in the lot, so Judith assumed that Liz hadn't shown up yet. The tour trolley was gone, no doubt off on a sightseeing run with Labor Day visitors.

The door to the building was open, but as Judith stepped inside she noticed that there were no lights on. Maybe Dennis was practicing for his Halloween spook show. Enough light came through the open entrance so that Judith could see the door to the inner offices. She turned the knob and went inside. Although the draperies had been closed and the reception area was also dark, she eventually found the light-switch. Blinking against the sudden brightness, she sat down at Nan Leech's desk.

A half-dozen messages dated from late Friday after-

noon were laid out in an orderly fashion. They were all
for Jeremy Lamar, and each one was marked urgent. A
Miami travel agency. Squeals on Wheels Bus Tours in
Chicago. A teachers group from Denver. Another travel
agency, this one with a Dallas number.

Judith smiled grimly. Apparently the discovery of
two dead bodies during the Toujours La Tour visit had
made the national media. The macabre was good business. She hoped that Jeremy wasn't wishing for an
encore.

A sudden noise from somewhere in the distance
made Judith jump. She thought it had come from
Jeremy's inner office, but she couldn't be sure. Sitting
perfectly still, she listened to see if she could hear anything else. But only silence filled the reception area.

After fifteen minutes of reading tour brochures,
studying the routes on maps spread out on the walls,
and eating a half-dozen jellybeans from a candy dish on
Nan's desk, Judith went outside to see if Liz Ogilvy had
arrived. Maybe she wouldn't be driving a KINE-TV
vehicle on a weekend. But there were no newcomers in
the parking lot. Judith went back inside and dialed the
TV station's number.

Liz wasn't in. In fact, the bored voice at the other end
said she hadn't been in all day. Would Judith like to
leave a message?

"Yes," Judith said in a firm voice. "I would. She was
supposed to meet me at Toujours La Tour twenty minutes ago. Please get hold of her and tell her I know who
killed Aimee Carrabas. If she doesn't show in half an
hour, our deal is off."

Judith hung up. The ruse should work, though she
wasn't exactly sure how she was going to get around the
big whopper she'd relayed to Liz. Judith was about to
check the parking lot again when the lights went out.

"Drat!" she murmured, heading for the door with a
sense of trepidation.

She'd taken only a few steps when she heard the door close.

"Who's there?" she called, her voice wavering slightly.

There was no response. Maybe the wind had blown the door shut. But there hadn't been any wind the past few days. Summer was waning on a humid, airless note.

Judith realized then that she had begun to perspire. Was it the heat? Or fear?

A noise, very close by, made her jump. "Who is it?" she demanded, hoping to keep the panic out of her voice.

Again, no one answered. As her eyes adjusted to the darkness, she realized that the closed drapes permitted just enough light to make out shapes in the reception area. She could see Nan's desk, the filing cabinets—and that eerie, ghostly figure hovering near the door. She'd seen it before, on her earlier visit to Toujours la Tour. Even so, the apparition was frightening.

"Dennis?" She gulped. "Dennis?"

The figure swayed closer. Judith could see the awful mask just a few feet away.

"This isn't funny, Dennis," she said, trying to sound severe. "Jeremy wouldn't approve of you trying to scare someone."

The filmy right sleeve of the billowing garment pointed at Judith. "You fool," said a muffled voice from behind the mask. "You reckless, silly fool."

"Dennis?" Judith gulped. Not Dennis. This was no joke. "Who are you?" Judith demanded, the words sounding ragged in her ears as she instinctively backed away.

It was then that she saw the gun under the folds of the ghostly fabric. It was the killer, Judith was certain of it, and she had no idea who lurked behind the mask.

I can't die without knowing, she thought frantically.

"How did you find out?" the voice demanded.

"I . . . didn't," Judith confessed. "I don't know anything. If you go away, I still won't know who you are."

The gun moved up a notch, pointing straight at Judith's heart. "I heard you on the phone. You said you knew the killer's identity. Do you think I'm stupid?"

"I was lying," Judith admitted, and cursed herself for telling such tales out of hand. "I do that. I lie sometimes. I . . ." Her voice was swallowed up as she gulped for breath.

"I don't believe you," the voice said. "You're lying now, not on the phone."

Judith was too frightened, too rattled to consider the irony, except in a hazy, disjointed way. She'd told her share of fibs and even the occasional outright lie, but now her life depended on the truth, and it wasn't believed.

"Really," Judith began, shaking all over. "How could I know? You've been so . . . clever."

She heard the click of the safety being removed. The hand that held the gun was gloved and very steady. "You can't fool me," said the voice. "You should never have gotten involved. You went after me because I insulted your stupid bed-and-breakfast. Why couldn't you have left it alone?"

Despite her terror, Judith was confused. Or maybe she couldn't think straight because she was so terrified. She opened her mouth to speak just as the door flew open behind the spectral apparition.

Judith's would-be killer started to swerve around but was impeded by the folds of heavy fabric. The figure in the doorway swung an election sign with lethal accuracy. The ghost went down in a cloud of gauzy white cloth.

"Renie!" Judith screamed. "Thank God!"

But Renie had also gone down, carried by her own momentum. The gun and the election sign both fell to the floor.

"My shoulder!" she cried, writhing in pain. "I've dislocated it!"

"Coz!" Judith tried to get down on her knees, but the pain was too great. "Oh, coz! I'll call 911."

"You do that," Renie said between clenched teeth.

Judith hit the light switch and grabbed the phone. When she had delivered her frantic message, she turned to see Renie getting up.

"Don't move!" Judith exclaimed. "Wait for the medics!"

But Renie was shaking her head, a sheepish grin on her face. "I saw Mel Gibson in *Lethal Weapon* put his shoulder back in. In fact, I've seen it five times, it's one of Bill's favorites. I hurt, but it's bearable."

Judith regarded Renie with awe, then stared down at the unconscious figure on the floor. "Who is this?" she asked in a shaky whisper.

"Have a look," Renie murmured, rubbing her right shoulder.

Judith leaned down just far enough to remove the mask, which covered the entire head. Renie edged closer.

The cousins stared down into the unconscious face of Nan Leech.

EIGHTEEN

"YOU HOLD THE gun," Renie said. "I'll get the sign."

Judith stared at the sign's red-on-white lettering, which read, "Stop the Violence." She couldn't help but grin. "Should we tie her up?" she inquired of her cousin after making sure that Nan was unconscious.

"We've got the gun." Renie shrugged. "Don't tell me you'd be afraid to use it."

"I don't know how, and I wouldn't want to if I did," Judith said. "I'd rather you used that sign again."

"I can't," Renie said. "My shoulder hurts too much. We could sit on her."

Judith nodded. "We could, except I might not be able to get up again. I don't think she'll be coming around for a while."

Renie's eyes widened. "Did I kill her?"

"No, that mask thing protected her head." Judith suddenly stared at Renie. "How on earth did you happen to show up with that election sign?"

"Oh." Renie's laugh was a trifle lame. "After you and I spoke on the phone, Bill and I headed out to Hank's Lumber. We were talking about all the improvements we'd made in our house during the last thirty years. Then I got to thinking about the renovations you'd done to start up the B&B, and I remembered Grandma and Grandpa Grover's old wood-burning gas range, and how Grandpa almost set the house on fire one Christmas Eve because he put too much used wrapping paper in it, and Uncle Corky poured a bottle of vodka on the fire which only made it worse and—"

"Coz," Judith broke in as Renie began to grow dreamy-eyed, "get to the point."

"Sorry." She glanced at the motionless form of Nan Leech. "It's weird, isn't it? We've been in this kind of situation so often that we've gotten callous. Or are we just numb?"

Judith considered the question. "I'm not sure. I was certainly terrified. I thought I was about to get shot."

"But you've been there before, too," Renie noted. "So have I. Has urban life hardened us this much?"

"No," Judith said slowly. "I mean, maybe, in a way. We were raised to always find the lighter and brighter side of everything. I suppose it was because of the hard times Grandma and Grandpa had trying to support six kids on almost no money. Then the Depression and the war . . . All those things get passed down to shape the way we think and feel. We add our own experiences—which, let's face it, have been a little bizarre—and here we are. Now tell me what clued you in or I'll have to shoot *you*."

"Okay, okay," Renie said with a glance at the gun that lay next to Judith's feet. "It was that old stove. Do you remember when the tour trolley pulled up at Hillside Manor and Nan went into her spiel? She mentioned how the house looked, with chintz and oak and all that—which, of course, she could have seen in the photos from the brochure I designed for you. But she also said something about the old-fashioned gas range. It didn't sink into my brain at the time, and maybe you were too angry to notice. Then suddenly, this afternoon, I realized she couldn't have known about the old stove unless she'd been inside the house before it was converted into a B&B. In fact, the original stove had been replaced forty years ago when Auntie Vance worked for that appliance company. Thus, Nan Leech, who claimed to have moved here from California twenty-odd years ago, had been in the house a half-century earlier. I realized that she could be Anne-Marie Meacham."

Judith had grown bug-eyed. "My God," she breathed. "Anne-Marie. Nan. Of course! How could I have been so blind?"

"Because you were so mad," Renie declared. "All you could do was zero in on the terrible things Nan was saying about the B&B."

Judith was shaking her head. "And it almost got me killed. Not to mention preventing me from concentrating on important clues." She glanced again at Nan, who still wasn't moving. "Where are the cops and the medics? What's taking them so long?"

"I was afraid you might be in trouble so I called them before I got here." Renie cocked an ear toward the door. "I don't hear anything out there."

Judith made a face. "Maybe I should call again." She picked up the phone and punched in the emergency number. "We've already called for help twice," she said in an emphatic tone. "This is a medical and a criminal situation. We have a killer pinned down and people are injured. What's going on?"

Judith listened, clapped a hand to her head, and put the phone down. "The visiting football team's marching band got loose at halftime and started a riot. All units have been summoned, since over seventy thousand people are involved, including one really screwed-up tuba player. He chased the university's mascot all the way to the upper deck."

Renie held her head. "Great."

"I should call Joe," Judith said.

"Why? He's not a doctor. On the other hand," Renie went on, "I could call Bill. He could counsel the nutty tuba player."

"Joe was under the MG when I left. He's probably still there," Judith said, then paused. "So what do you figure? Nan killed Aimee because . . . ?"

"They're half-sisters, right?" Renie offered. "Jealousy, maybe?"

Nan had started to stir. Judith and Renie exchanged quick, worried glances. Renie pointed to the gun. "Hold it. Point it. Menace her."

Gingerly, Judith picked up the weapon. "I'm ruining fingerprints. No, I'm not. She's wearing gloves."

"Nice ones," Renie said, observing Nan's outstretched hands. "From Nordquist's, I'll bet."

Nan was moving slightly on the floor, and her eyelids were beginning to flicker. She groaned and tried to lift her right arm.

"Where the hell is Liz Ogilvy?" Judith said in a low voice, placing the gun beside her on the desk. "She's missing the news story of her life."

"Probably at the stadium," Renie replied, "trying to avoid flying pom-poms."

Nan made a noise that sounded like "aargh."

Judith leaned down. "Nan, can you speak?"

"You," Nan said, her voice thick and her eyes half-open.

"We've sent for help," Judith said.

"Fool," Nan replied, slowly twisting her neck.

"Why did you kill your sister?" Judith asked, trying to sound sympathetic. "What did she do to you?"

"Fool," Nan repeated, and finally opened her eyes.

"You must have hated her," Judith said. "Why?"

Struggling to sit up, Nan didn't respond for at least a full minute. "They got rid of me," she finally said in a groggy voice. "They sent me away."

"Who did?" Judith asked.

"You did, with that German bitch. You only wanted Aimee." Nan's eyes were glazed and she seemed to be talking to someone who wasn't there. "You, my own father, killed my mother. I always knew. You were never sad, you only pretended. Children know when grown-ups pretend. And then we went to California with *her*."

"Beth?" Judy put in.

Nan gave a semblance of a nod. "You got her pregnant.

You never seemed to care that she was always mean to me. When the baby was on the way, she got worse. So you gave me away, to a couple named Leech. They adopted me. But I never got over all the horrible things that had happened, especially when you killed my mother."

Judith and Renie exchanged flabbergasted glances. "Poor Nan," Judith said aloud, and meant it. "Why didn't she go to the police when she got older?"

Nan's mouth formed into a sneer, but her eyes still weren't focused on either of the cousins. "*How* old? I didn't know my father had sealed up my mother in that wall. I thought he'd dumped her body somewhere—the bay, a river, a lake. I'd heard that my father died about two years ago. I never knew about my mother's body until George Guthrie started renovating the Alhambra. I was so shocked and upset that I quit my job with him and, ironically, ended up here at Toujours La Tour. It was like I couldn't escape the horror, even after over fifty years."

Judith had a sudden insight. "You arranged for Aimee to exorcise the Alhambra, didn't you, Nan?"

There was a touch of cruelty in Nan's smile. Finally, she looked at Judith. "Of course. I suggested it to George. It was my farewell gesture. My adoptive parents, the Leeches, are both dead now, too, but I still have some contacts in Orange County. One of them, the same person who'd told me my father had died, also said that Aimee had become an exorcist."

Nan stopped suddenly, her eyes no longer glazed. "Good God," she murmured, holding her head. "What have I said?"

"An extremely tragic story," Judith responded with heartfelt sympathy. "You've been treated with great cruelty."

"Yes," Nan said slowly, fingering her chin. "Yes, I have."

"You must have resented Aimee terribly," Renie put in.

"I never really knew Aimee," Nan said, still speaking slowly. "I knew she'd ruined my life. Oh, the Leeches were decent people, but they'd come to California during the Depression, dirt-poor. They were uneducated and very religious, the Bible-thumping type. Their two children died before they ever left west Texas. They'd given up having another baby, and then my father offered to give them me. The Leeches were happy about it, they'd made some money in the defense plants during the war. But they were older by then, in their forties. I don't think they understood what it meant to take on a six-year-old girl with constant nightmares."

Judith was feeling very sorry for Nan Leech. Or at least for Anne-Marie Meacham, cast off by an abusive stepmother and a villainous father who had murdered her mother. "I can't imagine what it must have been like for you," Judith said.

"I didn't let on who I was when I contacted Aimee," Nan continued, her voice gathering momentum. "At first, she turned me down. Her mother—that bitch, Beth—had recently died, and Aimee had personal business to attend to. I mentioned that we were scheduling a month in advance. Surely she'd be able to wind up her affairs by then? She laughed and said it was a rather large estate, and it would take months before everything was settled."

Nan paused, her face hardening. "You must know that up to this point, I had no intention of killing Aimee. But when she began bragging about her inheritance, I was outraged. My father had gotten rich. He'd made a fortune in southern California real estate. Meanwhile, my adoptive father had gone on disability at fifty-one, and died four years later."

"So why did you bring a gun along to the Alhambra?" Renie inquired, gingerly flexing her shoulder.

"I always carry a gun," Nan responded. "I have a carry permit. I live alone, I want protection. And you never know what to expect when you're out at night with a bunch of tourists who may or may not be crazy or drunk or both. Besides, we go to some pretty danger-

ous parts of town on the mystery tour. You never know
who might pose a threat to the sightseers themselves."

"But you didn't plan to shoot Aimee," Judith noted.
"What happened?"

Nan started to shake her head, then winced and
clutched the top of her skull. "God, I ache all over!"
Awkwardly, she turned toward Renie. "Why didn't you
just kill me and get it over with?"

"I tried," Renie shrugged. "That mask rig is like a
football helmet."

"It *is* a football helmet," Nan declared. "Dennis used
it for the mask's foundation." She turned back to Judith.
"As soon as we arrived, I left the trolley to meet Aimee.
I was terribly curious, of course. She was already in the
unit where she was going to perform her exorcism.
George, I think, had taken her up there. I couldn't resist.
I told her who I was. She laughed and said she didn't
believe me. Her parents had never mentioned another
child. Never. I started to get angry."

"I can see why," Judith said.

"I told her I could prove it," Nan went on. "I had a
copy of my birth certificate with me. I showed it to her,
but she still laughed, though not quite as hard. Then I
said I was entitled to half the estate. That's when she got
really nasty. Aimee said I was an impostor, and even if I
weren't, she couldn't see why she should share. Legally,
I wasn't a Meacham. In fact, my father had changed his
name to Ritter—Beth's last name—when they moved to
California. My parents had never been in a legal union
because my father had married Aimee's mother long
before the war. I was a bastard. 'Look at you,' she said,
still laughing, 'you're a tour guide, eking out a living by
carting around a bunch of silly people looking for a
thrill in their otherwise mundane lives. I've made something of myself. You're nothing to me and nothing to
anybody else'." Nan's face had grown very grim and
her eyes glittered with hatred. "That's when I decided
to kill her. I couldn't help it. All the rejection came flood-

ing back, there in that very building where my father had killed my mother. I got out the gun and shot her twice. She stopped laughing then."

Neither of the cousins spoke for several moments. A series of images passed through Judith's mind's eye: Little Anne-Marie and her mother, Dorothy, living alone through the war years; her father's return and the brutal slaying of her mother; Beth replacing Dorothy and the flight to California; the news that Harry's wife was going to have a baby and Anne-Marie would have to go; the new family, ignorant and stern, perhaps unable to show their adopted daughter either love or laughter. Sometimes people took children in for all the wrong reasons.

"Why," Renie said, breaking the silence, "did you ever move back up here in the first place?"

"I hated California," Nan declared. "To me, it was a symbol of exile and abandonment. The only happiness I'd ever known was here, when I was very young with my mother. I felt obligated to stay in California until my adoptive mother died. She was really a helpless, pitiful kind of creature."

"That was very kind of you," Judith remarked. "I wonder if a jury wouldn't be lenient when they hear what you've been through all these years."

Nan made a dismissive gesture with one gloved hand. "I've learned not to rely on or to trust anyone. If your father betrays you, who will ever stand up for you?"

"You have to give people a chance," Judith said rather lamely.

"You're terribly naïve," Nan asserted, finally shedding the ghost costume and tossing it into a corner.

"Hey," Renie said, "are you the one who conked Dr. Ashe over the head?"

Nan laughed, again an unpleasant sound. "Yes. I knew he'd been snooping around, looking for something which I learned was family heirlooms. That didn't matter to me, he could cart off the whole building for all I cared. But after I shot Aimee, I had to get rid of the gun.

I knew where the original stash of gold and silver had been found in the former Schnell apartment. That was where I'd ditched the gun and Aimee's belongings from the bureau drawer. There was no time to search through her things—I wanted to see if she had anything with her that related to her inheritance. I never got a chance to retrieve the items that day. Then I'd heard Dr. Ashe had been acting kind of strange, and I had to talk to him to make sure he hadn't found it."

Nan paused to twist her neck this way and that. "That's why I disappeared for a bit. I needed the time to figure out how to set Alfred up. I'd hoped that I could just talk to him and find out what he found under the floor. But he was so cagey on the phone that I got suspicious. I finally arranged to meet him at the Alhambra. Naturally, I had to stage a diversion—those fireworks—so that we could get inside without being noticed. He took me straight up to the Schnell apartment, and my worst fears were confirmed when he started rooting around under the floorboards. I figured he'd found the gun and Aimee's things, but left them there for some weird reason. Then I panicked. Those walls—partially exposed—the proximity to where my mother had died—it all came crashing down on me and I must have come undone. I hit Alfred Ashe over the head with one of his tools, got the gun and Aimee's belongings, then fled. I was sure I'd killed him. I tried to take his pulse, but couldn't find one—I must not have done it right. I never took first aid."

Nan paused to utter a jagged little laugh. "I should have joined the Girl Scouts, I guess. Don't they teach lifesaving and such? Anyway, Alfred survived. The irony was that I don't think he actually found anything. And when he comes to, he can identify me as his assailant, but not as a killer."

"Hey," Renie broke in, "answer a different question. All along, I wondered why Judith saw Jeremy going up to the third floor before she discovered the body. Do you know what he was really up to?"

Nan's expression conveyed disdain for both Renie and her query. "Of course. He was making sure that none of the workmen were up there interfering with the media. Jeremy and George didn't want any glitches." Nan narrowed her eyes at Renie. "Surely you didn't suspect that twerp Jeremy capable of carrying out a murder like Aimee's?"

Except for a snort from Renie, the cousins ignored the question. "Why," Judith asked slowly, "are you telling us all of this now?"

Again, Nan laughed. "Why not? You figured out I did it, though I don't know how."

"But I didn't actually . . ." Judith started to protest.

"Besides," Nan broke in, "I'm still going to get away with it." In a lightning move, she dove for the gun by Judith's hand.

"Hey!" Judith cried, but her reactions were too slow for the desperate woman. Nan had the gun in both hands, and the cousins were trapped.

"It felt good letting it all out," Nan said in a rapid voice. "I've kept it bottled up too long, like my mother being shut up inside that damned wall. I'm sorry I have to do this, but I simply can't go to jail. You two are too smart for your own —"

A figure even more frightening and formidable tore into the office, plowing straight into Nan and knocking her to the floor. Once more, she lost the grip on the gun as Emil the ostrich began to peck at her head and shoulders.

"Help!" Nan screamed. "Help me! What is this thing? Get it off me!"

Judith regarded the creature's attack with dismay; Renie looked bemused. Nan writhed under the ostrich's assault, trying to crawl free. The bird's beak was strong. He had begun to draw blood from Nan's neck.

Renie strolled over to the desk and scooped up a handful of jelly beans. "Here, Emil, how about some sweets?"

To Judith's amazement, Emil raised his head, the long neck stretched out toward the candy dish. Just as he was

about to lunge for either Renie or the jelly beans—
Judith couldn't be sure which—Liz Ogilvy and the
KINE-TV crew charged through the door.

"*What . . . ?*" Liz cried in a startled voice. She signaled
to the camera crew. "Roll those suckers! This looks like
news!"

Emil's head went up. Suddenly he looked frightened,
and set off at a trot through the door, scattering at least
three TV crew members. No sooner had the ostrich
made his exit than a herd of emergency personnel,
including four uniformed police officers, rushed inside.

"She's on the floor!" Judith shouted. "The one with
the peck marks!"

" 'She'?" the older of the two officers responded.
"Who *is* she?"

"Nan Leech," Judith said hurriedly, as she tried to
edge toward the door. "She's responsible for the murder
at the Alhambra Arms."

The older officer stared down at Nan, then gave Judith
a skeptical look. "Hold on, how do you know . . . ?"

"That woman on the floor is the tour guide!" Liz
exclaimed.

The other officer turned to Liz. "You know her?"

"I met her . . ." Liz began as Judith and Renie quietly
left the room.

"Holy cats," Renie said as they got outside and saw at
least five emergency vehicles parked by the tour office.
"They must have subdued the tuba player."

"I need some peace and quiet," Judith murmured. "I
wouldn't mind a drink, either."

The cousins moved closer to the sidewalk. "You'll
have to give the police your statement," Renie said. "So
will I. We'd better wait until—" She stopped as the tour
trolley came into view. "Oh, oh. These folks are in for a
real sightseeing adventure."

Judith and Renie moved away from the entrance drive
to avoid getting hit by the trolley. A glance at the parking
strip revealed Emil, his head stuck in the ground.

"Is that where you pulled up the sign?" Judith asked.

"Yes." Renie grinned at the ostrich's rear end. "A ready-made sanctuary for our Emil. What would we have done without him?"

Another car, one which looked familiar to Judith, was pulling in behind the trolley. "That's Woody's Acura," she said. The doors opened on both sides of the car. "That's Woody." Judith gulped. "And Joe."

Joe had changed from his mechanic's togs into a beige linen sport coat and brown slacks. He looked very professional. And utterly astounded.

"Jude-girl!" he shouted. "What the hell are you doing here?"

"Hi," Judith said in a feeble voice. "We're here with Emil."

"Emil?" Joe was striding over to the cousins. He took one look at the ostrich, scowled at Judith, and turned on his heel to follow Woody inside the office building.

The tourists were pouring out of the trolley, voices raised, gestures flying, and chasing after Jeremy Lamar, who was racing through the front door. He was repulsed, along with the tour group. One of the uniforms ordered the sightseers back on the bus. Jeremy remained behind, arguing with the officers.

Traffic, which had been fairly heavy on this holiday weekend, began to slow to a crawl as drivers stopped to stare at the emergency vehicles—and Emil.

"Woody must have been alerted to the 911 call," Judith said. "He must have picked up Joe on his way here."

"What do we do now?" Renie asked as some of the drivers began honking at Emil.

"Nothing," Judith said, nodding toward the parking area. "Our cars are boxed in. Besides, we still have to give our statements."

"Rats," Renie said, her gaze wandering down the street toward T. S. McSnort's. "Why don't we wait for them in the bar? It's hot out here and it's noisy, and if Emil ever gets his head out of that hole, he might go for *us*."

Judith turned around to look at the Toujours La Tour office. Jeremy was still engaged in a heated exchange with the uniforms. The tour group had returned to the trolley, but it was obvious that they were growing restive. Apparently, they thought the emergency personnel were all part of the tour's climax.

"I wonder if Jeremy will make a success of this enterprise," Judith mused.

"If he does," Renie responded, "he'll need a new secretary."

Jeremy had finally turned away in disgust and got back on the bus. The trolley took off with a rattle and a roar, then barged into traffic. Apparently, the tourists were being taken to a different venue.

Judith and Renie looked at each other and shrugged. Emil remained stuck in the dirt.

"I wonder how long he'll stay there," Renie remarked and started to point toward the bird. "Should we call his owners to . . . aaahh!" Her face contorted and her arm fell uselessly to her side. "Damn!" she cried, close to tears. "I dislocated my shoulder again!"

"Oh, poor coz," Judith exclaimed in sympathy, "let me help you!" She lunged at Renie, tripped over an uneven place in the sidewalk, and fell to the ground with a cry of anguish. "My hips! They feel like . . . they're gone!"

At that moment, two medics wandered out from the tour office. Judith barely saw them out of the corner of her eye. "Help!" she called in a feeble voice, but the traffic drowned her out.

"Help!" Renie shouted, adding a string of profanity that would have shocked even the most broad-minded.

The medics, one male and one female, hurried to the cousins. "Are you the victims?" the female asked, kneeling down beside Judith and Renie.

"In a way," Judith managed to get out between clenched teeth. "I think I dislocated at least one hip."

"Shoulder here," Renie gasped, then swore another blue streak.

"Let's get a second ambulance," the male medic said to his female coworker. "I don't think we can fit them both into one vehicle."

"Yes, you can," Judith panted.

"We . . . do . . . everything . . . together," Renie murmured between bouts of pain.

The medics exchanged quick glances. "Okay, it's possible. The shoulder is kind of small. The hips are bigger."

"Uunh," Judith mumbled, taking the comment personally.

Five minutes and considerable agony later, the cousins were loaded into the medics' van. The siren went on, the lights flashed, and they pulled out of the Toujours La Tour parking lot.

A second ambulance had, in fact, been summoned for Nan Leech, whose head injury and ostrich bites required medical attention. As the vehicle drove away, Joe and Woody stood in the parking lot.

"Thanks for letting me in on this," Joe said.

"No problem," Woody responded. "All I had to do was swing up the hill to collect you. Once we'd checked out the known suspects and learned that George Guthrie, Nan Leech, and Rufus Holmes all had carry permits for concealed weapons, it was a process of elimination. We discovered that Guthrie and Holmes both had .38s. Of course anyone could have an illegal firearm, but Nan was the one suspect we hadn't yet checked out, so it was possible that the 9 mm handgun was registered to her, and we'd have to bring her in for questioning. I figured I might as well have you come with me, instead of filling you in later. Sancha should be here any minute. I filled her in on the phone, but she lives over near the university. She's probably stuck in traffic. Maybe I'll let her interrogate Judith and Serena. Sancha may be miffed because she wasn't on the spot." Woody's head swiveled around to scour the parking area. "Where *are* Judith and Renie?"

Joe also searched the lot. "I don't know. Their cars are still here. So's the ostrich." He gestured toward Emil.

"They wouldn't have gone very far," Woody remarked, though there was a note of doubt in his voice. "Maybe they walked over by the big fountain so they could sit down."

"They'll be back," Joe said with confidence. "My dear wife and her cousin never stray too far from a crime scene," he added, then frowned. "I wonder how Jude-girl figured this one out?"

Woody chuckled softly. "She's pretty clever when it comes to seeing through people."

"True," Joe agreed. "But officially, you solved the case. With the gun, I mean. You can match the slugs to it."

"Right," Woody said. "I wasted some time, though, by going to Nan's condo instead of coming here first. I should have realized that these tours operate on weekends. But at least I had a search warrant and got the gun from her home."

Joe was now pacing up and down the sidewalk. "Where the hell are those two? It's not like them to just up and disappear."

"They'll show up," Woody said. "After all, what could have happened to them?"

Joe laughed. "Not much. Not after what went down in the office with Nan and the ostrich. No," he added, "you're right. It's a crazy thing, but those two women keep getting into hot water, and yet they always come out on top. I'm sure they're both just fine."

At last, Emil yanked his head out of the hole. The ostrich stared at Joe and Woody. He looked as if he wanted to tell them something.

If you're a frequent visitor to
Mary Daheim's delightful
Bed-and-Breakfast series,
you'll be pleased to know that

SUTURE SELF
A Bed-and-Breakfast Mystery

is now available in hardcover
from William Morrow.

Hang onto your gurney,
check your vital signs at the door,
and turn the page for a sneak peek
as Judith and Renie take on
Big Bad Medicine in

SUTURE SELF

JUDITH McMONIGLE FLYNN took one look at the newspaper headline, released the brake on her wheelchair, and rolled into the kitchen.

"I'm not sure it's safe to go into the hospital," she said to her husband, Joe Flynn. "Look at this."

Joe, who had just come in through the back door, hung his all-weather jacket on a peg in the hallway and stared at the big, bold front page headline.

ACTRESS DIES FOLLOWING ROUTINE SURGERY
JOHN FREMONT SUCCUMBS
AFTER MINOR FOOT OPERATION

"Who's John Fremont?" Joe asked after kissing his wife on the cheek. "The explorer? No wonder he wrecked his feet, going over all those mountains. Hunh. I thought he was already dead."

"He's been dead for over a hundred years," Judith replied. "It's a—"

"A shame the local newspaper doesn't jump on those stories faster," Joe interrupted. "What's Queen Victoria up to this week?"

Judith made a face at Joe. "It's a typo," she said in a testy voice. "It's supposed to be Joan Fremont. See, there

299

it is in the lead. You know who she is—we've seen her in several local stage productions. She is—was—a wonderful actress."

Joe frowned as he read deeper into the story. "Jeez, don't these people proofread anymore?"

"That's not my point," Judith asserted. "That's the second well-known person in three weeks to peg out at Good Cheer Hospital. I'm getting scared to go in next Monday for my hip replacement."

Joe opened the cupboard and got out a bottle of Scotch. "You mean Somosa, the pitcher? That's no mystery. He was full of amphetamines." With an air of apology, Joe gestured with the bottle. "Sorry, I hate to drink in front of you, but I spent ten hours sitting on my butt for that damned insurance stakeout."

"Never mind." Judith sighed with a martyred air that would have made her Aunt Deb proud. "I'm used to sacrifice and self-denial. After a month in this stupid wheelchair and taking all those pain pills, I suppose I should be looking forward to surgery and getting back to a normal life. How'd the stakeout go?"

"It didn't," Joe replied, dumping ice cubes into a glass. "The guy didn't budge from his sofa except to go to the can. Then he used a walker. Maybe he's legit. The insurance company expected him to play a set of tennis or jump over high hurdles or do the rumba. I hate these alleged insurance fraud assignments."

"They pay well," Judith pointed out, giving the amber liquid in Joe's glass a longing look.

"Oh, yeah," Joe agreed, sitting down at the kitchen table. "We can use the money with the B&B shut down for five weeks. I'm expensive to keep, and you're not delivering."

Teasing or not, the comment nettled Judith. Just after Christmas, her right hip had deteriorated to the point that she'd been confined to a wheelchair. With the help of Joe and their neighbors, Carl and Arlene Rankers, Judith had managed to keep Hillside Manor running smoothly through the New Year's weekend. But Carl and Arlene had left January fifth for a month in Palm Desert. And even though Joe was retired from the police force, his part-time private investigations had become almost a full-time job. It had been a difficult decision for Judith, but she had been forced to cancel all reservations after the first part of January until St. Valentine's Day. Her only consolation was that the weeks in question were the slowest time of the year for the bed-and-breakfast industry.

"We've lost at least four grand," Judith said in a morose tone.

Joe gave a slight shake of his head. "Dubious. The weather around here this winter isn't exactly enticing to visitors."

Judith glanced up at the window over the kitchen sink. It was raining. It seemed to have been raining for months. Fifty degrees and raining. No sun breaks, no snow, just relentless rain and gloomy, glowering skies. Day after day of gray, gray, and grayer. Even a Pacific Northwest native like Judith had an occasional hankering for a patch of blue sky.

"People still visit people," Judith said, unwilling to let herself be cheered.

Joe gave a solemn shake of his head. "Not in January. Everybody's broke."

"Including us," Judith said. "Because of me. Renie and Bill are broke, too," she added, referring to her cousin and her cousin's husband. "Renie can't work with her bad shoulder. This is the busiest time of year for her, with all the annual reports. She usually designs at least a half-dozen, which means big bucks. Now she's out of commission until April."

"When's her surgery?" Joe inquired.

"A week after mine," Judith replied. "January fifteenth. We'll be like ships passing in the night. Or should I say sinking?" Judith emitted another heavy sigh as she rolled over to the sink and took a Percocet.

Then, Judith took another Percocet. It couldn't hurt. Besides, she ached twice as much as she had the previous day.

As a distraction, Judith read the rest of the story about Joan Fremont. The actress had been admitted to Good Cheer Hospital the previous day. Her surgery, pronounced successful, had been performed that afternoon. But at ten-thirty this morning, Joan had died suddenly and without warning. She left behind two grown children and her husband, Addison Kirby, the city hall reporter for the evening newspaper.

"No wonder her name got misspelled," Judith remarked. "Joan's husband works for the paper. The staff must be shaken by her death."

"Oh?" Joe raised rust-colored eyebrows above the sports section. "Kirby, huh? I've run into him a few times at city hall. Nice guy, but sort of aloof."

Judith put the newspaper's front section down on the table. "They'll investigate, I assume?"

"Oh, sure," Joe responded, his gaze back on the sports page. "They did with Joaquin Somosa, they will with Joan Fremont. It's almost automatic when someone relatively young and in otherwise good health dies in a hospital. The county medical examiner has jurisdiction."

Judith rolled to the stove. "I made beef noodle bake. It's almost done. I've fixed a salad, and there are some rolls I'll heat up. Then you can take Mother's portion out to the toolshed."

Joe grimaced. "Can't I phone it in to her?"

"Joe—" Judith stopped. Serving Gertrude's meals was a bone of contention since Judith had become wheelchair-bound. Joe Flynn and Gertrude Grover didn't get along. An understatement, Judith thought. How else to put it? If duels were still legal, they would have skewered each other out by the birdbath a long time ago.

The phone rang just as Judith slipped the foil-wrapped rolls into the oven. Fumbling a bit, she pulled the cordless receiver out of the gingham pocket on her wheelchair.

"Coz?" said Renie, who sounded excited. "Guess what."

"What? Make it quick, I've got my head in the oven."

"Coz!" Renie cried. "Nothing's that bad! Hang in there, you're only a few days away from surgery. You'll be fine."

"I mean I'm trying to put dinner together," Judith said, sounding cross. Her usual easygoing manner had begun to fray in the past few weeks.

"Oh." Renie paused. "Good. I mean . . . Never mind. I called to tell you that Dr. Ming's office just phoned to say that they'd had a surgery cancellation on Monday and I can go in a whole week early. Isn't that great? We'll be in the hospital together."

Judith brightened. "Really? That's wonderful." She paused. "I think."

"You think?" Now Renie sounded annoyed. "We could share a room. We could encourage each other's recovery. We could make fun of the hospital staff and the other patients. We could have some laughs."

"Yes, yes, of course," Judith said as she closed the oven door. "It's just that . . . Have you seen tonight's paper?"

"Ours hasn't come yet," Renie replied. "You know we always have a later delivery on this side of Heraldsgate Hill."

"Well," Judith began, then caught Joe's warning glance. "It's nothing, really. You can see for yourself when the paper comes."

"Coz." Renie sounded stern. "Tell me now or I'll have to hit you with my good arm. You can't run away from me, remember?"

Judith sighed. "There's been another unexpected death at Good Cheer Hospital. Joan Fremont, the actress."

"Joan Fremont!" Renie shrieked. "Oh, no! Wait till I tell Bill. I think he's always had a crush on her. What happened?"

Ignoring Joe's baleful look, Judith picked up the front section of the paper and read the story to Renie.

"That's terrible," Renie responded in a shocked voice. "She was so talented. And young. Well—younger than we are. A little bit, anyway. She'd probably had work done, being an actress."

"That's two deaths in three weeks," Judith noted.

"Joaquin Somosa," Renie murmured. "Younger still. Elbow surgery. Supposed to be healed by the All-Star break."

"Won't," Judith said, suddenly feeling light-headed. "Dead instead."

"This is scary," Renie declared. "Do you suppose we should ask Dr. Ming and Dr. Alfonso to operate on us in the privacy of our own automobiles?"

Judith started to respond, but just then the back door banged open. Gertrude Grover stood in the hallway, leaning on her walker and wearing a very old and slightly shabby wool coat over her head. Worse yet, Judith saw two of her. Maybe she should have taken only one Percocet.

"Where's my supper?" Gertrude demanded, thumping the walker on the floor for emphasis.

Judith spoke into the phone. "Gotta go. Mother's here." She rang off. "I'm heating the rolls," Judith said with a feeble smile, trying not to slur her words. "Mother, you shouldn't come out in the rain. You'll catch cold."

"And die?" Gertrude's small eyes darted in the direction of Joe's back. "Wouldn't that suit Dumbo here?"

"Mother," Judith said with a frown, accidentally ramming the wheelchair into the stove. "Oops! Course not. You know better." She tried to ignore the puzzled expression on her husband's face. "Hasn't Joe taken good care of you while I've been laid out? I mean, laid up."

"It's part of his plan," Gertrude said, scowling at Joe, who was still turned away from his mother-in-law. "He's waiting until you go into the hospital. Then,

when I'm supposed to be lulled into . . . something or
other, he'll strike!" Gertrude slammed the walker again.
"He knows the ropes, he used to be a cop. They'll never
catch him, and he'll make off with all my candy."

"Mother . . ." Judith wished she didn't feel so muddled. She wished she could walk. She wished her
mother wouldn't insist on wearing a coat that was at
least twenty years old. She wished Gertrude would shut
up. She wished she didn't have two mothers, standing
side by side.

Joe had finally risen from the chair. "I don't eat
candy," he said in his most casual manner. "You got any
jewels stashed out there in the toolshed, Mrs. G.?"

"Ha!" Gertrude exclaimed. "Wouldn't you like to
know?" It was one of those rare occasions when
Gertrude addressed Joe directly. As a rule, she spoke of
him in the third person.

Clumsily, Judith opened the oven. "Here, your dinner's ready. Joe can help dish it up for you, Mother."

"I'm watching his every move," Gertrude said, nar-
rowing her eyes. "He might slip something into my
food. I should have Sweetums eat it first, but that ornery
cat's too finicky."

Joe got the salad out of the refrigerator and removed
the beef noodle bake from the oven. He filled Gertrude's
plate with a flourish, added a roll, and started for the
back door. "At your service," he called over his shoulder. "Let me help you out."

"Out?" Gertrude snapped. "Out where? Out of this
world?"

She was still hurling invective as the two of them
went outside. It was a conflict of long standing, a personal Thirty Years War between Joe Flynn and Gertrude
Grover. When Joe had first courted Judith, Gertrude had
announced that she didn't like him. He was a cop. They
made rotten husbands. He was Irish. They always
drank too much. He had no respect for his elders. He
wouldn't kowtow to Gertrude.

Judith and Joe had gotten engaged anyway. And then disaster struck. Joe had gotten drunk, not because he was Irish, but because he was a cop, and had come upon two teenagers who had overdosed on drugs. Putting a couple of fifteen-year-olds in body bags had sent him off to a bar—and into the arms of the sultry singer at the piano. Vivian, or Herself, as Judith usually called her, had shanghaied the oblivious Joe to Las Vegas and a justice of the peace. The engagement was broken, and so was Judith's heart.

Judith was still dwelling on the past when Joe returned to the kitchen. "She's still alive," he announced, then looked more closely at his wife. "What's wrong? You look sort of sickly."

"Nozzing," Judith replied, trying to smile. "I mean, nothing—except Mudder. Mother. It bothers me when she's so mean to you."

Joe shrugged. "I'm used to it. In fact, I get kind of a kick out of it. Face it, Jude-girl, at her age she doesn't have much pleasure in life. If it amuses her to needle me, so what?"

Judith rested her head against Joe's hip. "You're such a decent person, Joe. I love you."

"The feeling is eternally mutual," he said, hugging her shoulders. "How many pain pills did you take?"

"Umm . . ." Judith considered fibbing. She was very good at it. When she could think straight. "Two."

Joe sighed. "Let's eat. Food might straighten you out a bit."

"Wouldn't you think," Judith said halfway through the meal when she began to feel more lucid, "that when you and I finally got married after your divorce and Dan's death, Mother would have been happy for us?"

Joe shook his head. "Never. You're an only child, and your father died fairly young. You're all your mother has, and she'll never completely let go. The same's true with Renie. Look how your Aunt Deb pulls Renie around like she's on a string."

"True," Judith allowed. "What I meant was that even if Mother resented you at first, after I married Dan on the rebound, and he turned out to be such a . . . flop, you'd figure that Mother would be glad to see me married to somebody with a real job and a sense of responsibility and a girth considerably less than fifty-four inches. Dan's pants looked like the sails on the *Britannia*."

Joe grinned, and the gold flecks danced in his green eyes. "Your mother didn't want a replacement or an improvement. She wanted you, back home, under her wing."

"She got it," Judith said with rueful laugh. "After Dan died, Mike and I couldn't go on living in that awful dump out on Thurlow Street. The rats were so big they were setting traps for us."

The exaggeration wasn't as extreme as it sounded. After losing one house to the IRS for back taxes, defaulting on another, and undergoing two evictions, Judith and Dan had ended up, as Grandpa Grover, would have put it, "in Queer Street." Dan had stopped working altogether by then, and Judith's two jobs barely paid for the basics.

The Thurlow rental was a wreck; the neighborhood, disreputable. After Dan died, Judith and her only son moved back into the family home on Heraldsgate Hill. Her mother had protested at first when Judith came up with her scheme to turn the big house into a B&B. Eventually, Gertrude had given in, if only because she and Judith and Mike had to eat. But when Joe reappeared in Judith's life during the homicide investigation of a guest, the old lady had balked. If Judith married Joe, Gertrude refused to live under the same roof with him. Thus, the toolshed had been converted into a small apartment, and Gertrude took her belongings and her umbrage out to the backyard.

She complained constantly, but refused to budge. Judith pictured her mother in the old brown mohair chair, eating her supper, watching TV, and cursing Joe

Flynn. Gertrude would never change her mind about her son-in-law, not even now in her dotage.

A little after seven, Judith called Renie back to get the details on her cousin's surgery. Neither of them knew exactly what time their operations would be scheduled and wouldn't find out until Friday afternoon. Judith hunkered down and tried to be patient. It wasn't easy: Even in the wheelchair, she experienced a considerable amount of pain and an unexpected apprehension.

Friday morning, Mike called from his current posting as a forest ranger up on the mountain pass that was fortuitously close to the city.

"Guess what," he said in his most cheerful voice.

"What?" Judith asked.

"Guess."

The first thing that came to mind was that Mike had been promoted. Which, she thought with plunging spirits, might mean a transfer to anywhere in the fifty states.

"Don't keep me in suspense," Judith said. "I'm an invalid, remember?"

"Mom . . ." Mike chuckled. "It's only temporary. Which is good, because you're going to have to be up and running by the time your next grandchild gets here around the Fourth of July."

"Oh!" Judith's smile was huge and satisfying. "That's terrific! How is Kristin feeling?"

"Great," Mike replied. "You know my girl, she's a hardy one."

"Hardy" wasn't quite the word Judith would have chosen. "Robust," perhaps, or even "brawny." Kristin McMonigle was a Viking, or maybe a Valkyrie. Mike's wife was big, blond, and beautiful. She was also constrained, conscientious, and capable. Almost too capable, it seemed to Judith. Kristin could repair a transmission, build a cabinet, bake a Viennese torte, shingle a roof, and balance a checkbook to the penny. Indeed, Judith sometimes found her daughter-in-law intimidating.

"I'm so thrilled," Judith enthused. "I can't wait to tell Joe. And Granny."

"That reminds me," Mike said, "could you call Grandma Effie, too? I don't like making out-of-state calls on the phone in the office. I'd call her from the cabin tonight, but I'm putting on a slide show for some zoologists."

"Of course," Judith said with only a slight hesitation. "I'll call right now."

"Thanks, Mom. Got to run. By the way, good luck Monday if I don't talk to you before you go to the hospital."

Judith clicked the phone off and reached for her address book on the kitchen counter. She ought to know Effie McMonigle's number by heart, but she didn't. Ever since Dan's death eleven years earlier, Judith had called his mother once a month. But somehow the number wouldn't stick in her brain. Maybe it was like Gertrude not speaking directly to Joe; maybe Judith hoped that if she kept forgetting Effie's number, her former mother-in-law would go away, too, and take all the unhappy memories of Dan with her.

Effie was home. She usually was. A former nurse, she resided in a retirement community outside Phoenix. In the nineteen years that Judith and Dan had been married, Effie had visited only three times—once for the wedding, once when Mike was born, and once for Dan's funeral. Effie was a sun worshipper. She couldn't stand the Pacific Northwest's gray skies and rainy days. She claimed to become depressed. But Judith felt Effie was always depressed—and depressing. Sunshine didn't seem to improve her pessimistic attitude.

"Another baby?" Effie exclaimed when Judith relayed the news. "So soon? Oh, what bad planning!"

"But Mac will be two in June," Judith put in. "The children will be close enough in age to be playmates and companions."

"They'll fight," Effie declared in her mournful voice. "Especially if it's another boy."

"Siblings always fight," Judith countered. "I guess." She had to admit to herself that she really didn't know. Judith and Renie had both been only children, and while they occasionally quarreled in their youth, they had grown to be as close as, if not closer than, sisters.

"When are they coming to see me?" Effie demanded. "Mike and Kristy have only been here twice since Mac was born."

"It's Kristin," Judith said wearily. "I'm not sure when they'll be able to travel. With the new baby on the way, they'll probably wait."

"Oh, sure." Effie emitted a sour snort. "I haven't had a new picture of Mac in ages. I'm not even sure what he looks like these days."

"I thought Mike and Kristin sent you a picture of the whole family at Christmastime."

"They did?" Effie paused. "Oh, *that* picture. It wasn't very good of any of them. I can't see the slightest resemblance to my darling Dan in either Mike or Mac. If they both didn't have my red hair, I'd have to wonder."

As well you might, Judith thought and was ashamed of the spite she felt inside. "Mac doesn't look like me, either," she said in an attempt to make amends.

"When are you coming down to see me?" Effie queried.

"Not for a while," Judith admitted. Indeed, she was ashamed of herself for not having paid Effie a visit since the year after Dan died. "It's so hard for me to get away with the B&B, and now I'm facing surgery Monday."

"For what?" Effie sounded very cross.

"A hip replacement," Judith said, gritting her teeth. "I told you about it on the phone a couple of weeks ago. I wrote it in my Christmas letter. I think I mentioned it in my Thanksgiving card."

"Oh, *that* hip replacement." Effie sniffed. "I thought you'd already had it. What's taking you so long?"

"It's the surgery scheduling," Judith responded patiently. "They have to book so far ahead. You know how it is. You used to work in a hospital."

"Hunh. It was different then. Doctors didn't try to squeeze in so many procedures or squeeze so much money out of their patients," Effie asserted. "Medical practice today is a scandal. You'll be lucky if you get out alive."

Judith glanced at the morning paper on the kitchen table. It contained a brief item about an autopsy being performed on Joan Fremont. In the sports section, there was a story about possible trades to replace the Seafarers' ace pitcher, Joaquin Somosa. At last, Effie McMonigle had said something that Judith didn't feel like contradicting.

Some people weren't lucky. They didn't get out of the hospital alive.

All Judith could hope was that she and Renie wouldn't be among the unlucky ones.

Murder Is on the Menu
at the Hillside Manor Inn
Bed-and-Breakfast Mysteries by
MARY DAHEIM
featuring Judith McMonigle Flynn